CONTEMPLATION OF A CRIME

CONTEMPLATION OF RACINE

CONTEMPLATION OF A CRIME

A Helen Thorpe Mystery

BOOK 3

SUSAN JUBY

/||MIRA

/||MIRA

ISBN-13: 978-0-7783-8760-2

Contemplation of a Crime

Copyright © 2025 by Susan Juby

Recycling programs for this product may not exist in your area.

Visuddhimagga: The Path of Purification, translated by Bhikkhu Ñāṇamoli. Reprinted with permission from the Buddhist Publication Society, Sri Lanka.

Rick Hanson, "Tranquility: The Fifth Factor of Awakening," https://www.rickhanson.net/meditation-talk-tranquility-the-fifth-factor-of-awakening/.

John O'Donohue, *To Bless the Space Between Us: A Book of Blessings*, from the blessing "May the Light of Your Soul Guide You." Convergent Books and Doubleday, March 4, 2008.

"Daily Chanting," Saraniya Dhamma Meditation Centre, 2019, https://saraniya.com/buddhism/knowledge/buddhist-prayers/.

All rights reserved. No part of this book may be used or reproduced in any manner whatsoever without written permission.

Without limiting the author's and publisher's exclusive rights, any unauthorized use of this publication to train generative artificial intelligence (AI) technologies is expressly prohibited.

This is a work of fiction. Names, characters, places and incidents are either the product of the author's imagination or are used fictitiously. Any resemblance to actual persons, living or dead, businesses, companies, events or locales is entirely coincidental.

For questions and comments about the quality of this book, please contact us at CustomerService@Harlequin.com.

TM is a trademark of Harlequin Enterprises ULC.

MIRA
22 Adelaide St. West, 41st Floor
Toronto, Ontario M5H 4E3, Canada
MIRABooks.com

Printed in U.S.A.

For my niece, Emily, who sees the good in everyone.
Well, almost everyone.

A suitable resting place for one of hating temperament is not too high or too low, provided with shade and water, with well-proportioned walls, posts and steps, with well-prepared frieze work and lattice work, brightened with various kinds of paintings, with an even, smooth, soft floor, adorned with festoons of flowers and a canopy of many-coloured cloth . . . smelling sweetly of flowers, and perfumes and scents set about for homely comfort, which makes one happy and glad at the mere sight of it.

—*Visuddhimagga: The Path of Purification,*
translated by Bhikkhu Ñāṇamoli

CONTEMPLATION OF A CRIME

CONTEMPLATION OF A CRIME

PART I
WHEREVER YOU GO, THERE YOU ARE. UNFORTUNATELY.

PAIN WAINSCOTT III

DAY ONE

Pain Wainscott III, eighteen years old, sat in the hard plastic chair and stared at his counsellor, a man who was too old for the kelly-green Chuck Taylors and orange knit beanie he wore. The guy had to be at least thirty-five. The lawyer stood beside him. She was no longer pretending to like Pain, whose name was pronounced "Pan." He'd been named after bread because when he was born, his mother imagined he was going to "nourish the world." Whatever the fuck that meant. His dad said she'd been way into sourdough at the time, as though that was a good explanation. Instead of nourishing the world, Pain was into taunting it, and worse. He'd ended up being a "right little sadist," according to the testimony in his trial. You can't name a kid Pain and expect good results. He sometimes asked his parents to call him "Big Dough" but they refused.

"This is a good offer," said Fern, his piss-face lawyer. Every time she looked at him, she made a face like she needed to spit a bad taste out of her mouth. "The program is only five days long, and when it's complete, you'll be discharged to your parents. The group"—she looked down at the sheet in her hands—"Close Encounters, is interested in testing how effective the program is for younger participants."

"It sounds cool, dog," said the counsellor.

Dog.

"What would I have to do there?" asked Pain.

"Take part in the workshops. Get some counselling. Nothing new for you," said the counsellor. Was he making a sideways dig about Pain's dad being a psychiatrist? Fair enough. What competent mental health professional would let their wife name their kid Pain because she started making bread?

3

"Individual and group," said Fern, who still wore that shit-on-her-shoe expression. "They will report back on co-operation. This whole invitation is predicated on you . . ."

"On me not being an asshole," said Pain, smiling at her and then at the counsellor. He liked smiling at people because he knew it creeped them out.

There were about twenty other guys here at the centre who would be better candidates for the program than him. Unlike him, they *wanted* to do better. They wanted to *be* better. Everyone at the centre had committed their offence (in his case *offences*) when they were young enough to be deemed salvageable by a judge. Everyone knew that if they went to adult jail, they'd just get more criminal. So they'd been sent to the centre, which was some bleeding heart's idea of a treatment facility-slash-jail. Other than the lack of good snacks, it wasn't too bad in here. And most of the guys were okay. They'd just messed up. Pain was one of the few who was a genuinely awful person. He knew it. His counsellor knew it. His lawyer definitely knew it. But he was the one with an expensive lawyer and rich parents. So he got the chance to go to the Close Encounters program. Real fair. But hey, unfairness was sort of his thing.

He'd been arrested for trying to ruin the career and college prospects of a rising hockey star in the women's league for reasons only he and 4chan understood. During the investigation, the cops uncovered his online harassment of the spokesperson for Tidy Tot Toys and his doxing of the minor Canadian rock musician, one who, in Pain's defence, had later been accused of sexual misconduct and was awaiting trial. Criminal harassment. That's what he'd been convicted of. The charge would have been more serious if the hockey player's suicide attempt hadn't been half-assed at best. People were really too sensitive.

Fern had argued that he had borderline personality disorder, internet addiction, oppositional defiance disorder, and an avoidant attachment style, all of which caused him to behave in an aggressive manner. In response to that outrageous slander, Pain had dug around and found out that Fern had a daughter the age of the hockey girl he'd targeted for abuse. Her daughter was an elite junior curler. He'd thought he might go after her when he got out of treatment. That would teach her mother to treat him like he had some kind of moral leprosy. But here Fern was with a get-out-of-jail-free card. Maybe he'd let her and her daughter off the hook. And maybe he wouldn't.

CONTEMPLATION OF A CRIME

"So what do you think?" said the counsellor, whose name Pain refused to remember.

"Sure. I'll do it."

Fern and the counsellor looked relieved. No one liked having Pain around. Pain didn't even like being around himself.

Oh well. The people at Close Encounters were going to get a lesson in dealing with the dark side.

YANA HEPPLER

As her landlord drove her toward the parking lot where she was supposed to meet the others and catch the small ferry to Side Island, Yana tried not to think about the emissions being spewed by the car. It was a canary-yellow Dodge Challenger and the engine made gurgling noises that reminded her of a pump running dry. Her landlord, Cristopher, lived with his much younger husband in a McMansion in a new development that sat on top of what used to be a wetland in the north end of Nanaimo. Everything about Cristopher's home and the neighbourhood was monstrous to her.

Cristopher was a former professional soccer player from some Latin American country. He had a large, white smile, a full head of dark swoopy hair, and tanned legs the size of tree trunks. His husband, whom she thought of as Mr. Cristopher, was very beautiful and soft-spoken. Both of them were friendly and well-liked and had a dynamic social life filled with friends from all walks of life. Her landlords were also an environmental disaster. Their house in Nanaimo was one of three they owned in different parts of the world. It was five thousand square feet of egregious wastefulness from the old-growth fir floors throughout to the rare tropical hardwoods they'd used in their kitchen. They'd invited her inside once to have coffee and sign the lease, and she'd never set foot inside again. It was too much for her climate-concerned heart to bear.

She lived in their basement suite, which was new, soulless, and in spite of her hatred of new houses and new developments, extremely comfortable.

Yana Heppler was definitely part of the problem, which just made her feel worse and hardened her resolve to do what needed to be done.

Cristopher had seen her trying to start her ancient Prius and asked if she needed a ride, and she'd reluctantly accepted his offer. She didn't want to miss the ferry because she'd been told that there wouldn't be another one. The letter had said something about the dock at Side Island being out of service during

CONTEMPLATION OF A CRIME

their stay, which meant they should all be sure to bring everything they needed because boats would not be able to dock at the island.

Yana had been passed the invitation by someone in her online climate action group who wasn't able to attend, and she still didn't entirely get the point of the workshop. She was going to spend five days with "differently minded people" so they could "find common cause in their shared humanity." She'd looked up Close Encounters for Global Healing (motto: Five Days That Will Change Your World) and found out that it was one of those groups that tried to bring people together from across the various political divides that seemed to widen every year. She'd spent enough time listening to climate deniers and anti-science whack jobs to know that five days of talking wasn't going to fix a damned thing. As far as she was concerned, all anti-climate people should have to do two years of hard labour in a drought-stricken environment, followed by another year of cleaning up after yet-another act-of-god flood, and take intensive science lessons and media literacy reprogramming for four hours each night so they could recover from their addictions to right wing propaganda and organized religion. That was just to start. Yana had many, many ideas what should happen to foes of the climate.

"You are going somewhere nice?" asked Cristopher, his smile bright enough to match the all-leather white interior of the ridiculous car. "Maybe a fun time with the girls?"

Yana faked a smile in return. "Something like that," she said.

"That is good. You maybe need a little break?" he said.

"Sure," she said. They were speeding down Brechin Road toward the BC ferry terminal. "You can go straight. I'm supposed to catch the ferry near the boat launch."

Cristopher drove like a man who was used to everything going his way. He wheeled quickly off Zorkin Road and screeched into the large, pitted parking lot.

"Oh my god," muttered Yana.

"Handles so beautiful, ah?" said Cristopher.

Yana removed her hand from where it was clutching the passenger door.

"Thank you," she said.

"You arrive in great style!" he said.

A small group of people with luggage watched them. Yes, she certainly was arriving in style and it was a style she was going to have to explain. She was vegan, didn't fly, didn't turn on the heat in her unit, didn't have pets because they were bad for the environment, and campaigned ceaselessly to combat climate change. She was also a person who planned to give the people at Close Encounters an encounter they would never forget because she'd given up on creating change through the usual channels. Now was the time for revolutionary action. None of that would be evident after her big entrance with Cristopher.

But at least she wasn't the bozo who'd just pulled up beside them.

WAYNE KRUPKE

Wayne looked at his phone. A message from his sister had come in while he was driving. He hadn't noticed because he was too busy returning some of the raised middle fingers he'd gotten as he drove. Twelve fingers in eight kilometres, which was fewer than usual.

It was his truck. He had a jacked eight-year-old Dodge Ram with four Canadian flags on white plastic poles extending from the cab windows. There was a F$%# THE PRIME MINISTER sticker on the rear window. He was thinking about getting one of those parade-sized Canadian flags mounted against the cab. He didn't want any whiny crybaby liberals confused about who he was and what he believed, even though, if he was being completely honest, his beliefs changed fairly regularly.

His mother had watched him get into the truck. "Are you sure you don't want to take off at least a couple of those flags?"

"No, Ma," he said. "This is who I am."

"Wayne, you are not a cartoon. And only a cartoon has this many flags on his vehicle. Who are you trying to impress?"

"No one, Ma. I'm just exercising my free speech. You should try it sometime."

She sighed and reached for her smokes inside her hoodie. She'd been quit for years, but then he'd gotten into politics and she started up again. He felt bad about that. But then she'd start talking about his flags and his friends, and he remembered that she didn't know anything about anything. His mother had basically lost her mind in the pandemic. It was really too bad.

Now she did whatever the government told her. Never read critically. Just sucked down the mainstream media message like . . . like . . . one of her smokes. They'd argued about it a thousand times, especially after he'd gone to Ottawa.

She didn't see his efforts to make real change as important. She didn't even understand he was fighting for her freedom, too. All she did was focus on what had gone wrong. Instead of following his lead, she took whatever poison they told her to take and had worn her face diaper like a communist, except when she had to pull it down to smoke. He loved his mom, but sometimes he thought she was a lost cause.

"Get back on the vape, okay," he said.

"Get some friends who aren't criminals," she replied and hugged him with the arm not holding her smoke. "Maybe you could call Andrew when you get back."

"Maybe," he said. Andrew had been a buddy before Wayne got politically active. For years, Wayne had helped Andrew compete in the bathtub races. They never talked anymore, but the last thing Wayne wanted to do was discuss his busted friendship with his mother.

He needed to haul ass out of there before their conversation got any more depressing. His mom was all right but she didn't understand him and she definitely didn't know when to shut up. Just like his sister.

He left the truck's engine running while he checked his sister's message. He liked idling because it upset the idiots.

—Please give this a chance.

Christ almighty. The women in his family were driving him nuts. If his old man was still alive, he would understand that Wayne had done what he did for everyone. And because, honestly? It had been pretty fun.

Unlike the course he was going to, which didn't sound fun at all. He looked out the window at the people standing around with their suitcases and backpacks. Hard to tell what they might be like. He guessed he'd find out soon enough.

All he knew about Close Encounters was that he was allowed to have his beliefs. They actually specified that in their welcome letter. If things went well, he'd bring a few people around to his way of seeing things. If not, well, he was getting a five-day stay at a decent resort. He was going to take part in this soft-bellied, brainless program, and when he was done, he would tell everyone about how dumb it was. Or maybe he'd pretend that he'd taken it seriously, and as a reward, his sister would introduce him to some of the girls at the insurance office where she worked. When he'd asked her to set him up before, she'd said his truck was "too embarrassing," meaning that *he* was too embarrassing. Five

CONTEMPLATION OF A CRIME

days at Side Island might change that. Girls loved guys who were into personal growth. If he got a date with one of Chantelle's co-workers, he might even take some flags off his truck, at least for a while. He would tell his date how much he'd learned about himself at Close Encounters with Fucking Dummies, and maybe she'd be so inspired by his raw honesty that they'd bone. It was something to consider for sure.

His phone buzzed. Another message on Signal. He looked nervously out at the parking lot and the group of people waiting around with their thumbs up their asses. They had to be the other participants. There was a sweet Challenger parked off to the side. Maybe there was at least one other person he'd be able to relate to.

Buzz. Another message.

By the terms of his plea agreement, he wasn't allowed any contact with people from the convoy, which was the excuse he'd used for not joining the oldies who stood on the overpass waving their Canadian flags at the people below. Fuck that noise. He'd gone to jail for two weeks and that was enough for him, thank you very much. Even getting interviewed on Rebel News hadn't made up for it. Maybe he should have told his PO or someone else about the messages he was getting or about the package he'd received, but nah. He wasn't going to take orders from anonymous bastards or advice from anyone, really.

Buzz. His palms started to sweat. He put his hand on his dog, Potato, who lay panting on the seat next to him.

He should just delete the app. He couldn't be responsible for messages he hadn't seen. Maybe he should call that lawyer who was handling a lot of the convoy cases. But he didn't trust the guy.

Wayne wiped his fingers against his jeans, and against his better judgment, which even he knew wasn't very good, clicked on the new messages.

—Do not ignore this. If you do, the police are going to get a copy of this audio.

His heart nearly stalled out like an EV without enough charge. He looked at the audio file and knew what exactly it was going to be. He'd done some talking on the channels. May have mentioned storming the Parliament Buildings and doing some, well . . . some things to the prime minister and members of cabinet. Commie sons a' bitches.

Don't freak out, he told himself. No one could prove it had been him saying those things. And anyway, he'd just been talking. All he'd really done in Ottawa was honk, take a filthy hot tub in the middle of the street when he was drunk, talk to about a hundred reporters, including one from *The New York Times*, get yelled at by residents, and try to get over a harsh lingering case of the 'vid.

Wayne shoved his phone into his jacket pocket. Outside, someone in the group was waving at him. He ignored them and took the long step down to the ground, helping Potato get down. She was a little—okay, a lot—overweight and he worried about her legs.

The stuff that had been left in the back of his truck the previous night was hidden in his duffle bag. He hoped like hell there wouldn't be a search when they checked in. Maybe the organizers would be distracted by Potato, who looked mean but had a personality like a freshly poured bowl of Cheerios. When he'd agreed to come but told them he had to bring his dog, they said they'd make an exception to the no-pets rule for him. That was actually sort of nice.

His phone buzzed again, and this time he looked at the message.

—We will provide all the data they need to trace the recordings to you. Do as instructed or we will send it.

Fuuuuck.
Guess he was going to be doing what some asshole told him after all.

HELEN THORPE

Helen sat beside Mr. Levine as he steered the bus-like Toyota Sequoia (Capstone edition) off the ferry. Delight turned him into a small, happy sun. This was an adventure and she was pleased for him, if not for herself.

Her employer, Mr. Benedict Levine, was going undercover as a favour to his son David, who was running a five-day conflict-resolution workshop called Close Encounters for Global Healing. Helen was also going undercover so she could assist Mr. Levine. She was also missing the first week of her first holiday in nearly two years.

She had planned to take her mare, Honey, to a three-day clinic in Langley with a renowned instructor who specializes in helping novices to build bonds with their horses, while developing groundwork, husbandry, and basic equitation skills. After that, Helen was heading for a two-week stay at a luxurious rental home in Comox, on Vancouver Island, where she would be meeting her friends from butler school for a reunion. The Comox house featured a stable, an indoor arena, and access to miles of trails, so Honey was coming with her. When that was done, Helen, who had eight weeks of holidays saved up, planned to spend another ten days with her horse at a combination meditation/riding retreat in Washington State. The retreat was being taught by a top American dressage rider from California who had studied mindfulness under Jack Kornfield, the famous meditation teacher. Helen had been looking forward to every part of her planned holiday and was acutely aware that she wasn't happy about missing the first part.

Clinging. That's what she was doing.

Helen gave her head a little shake to bring herself back to the present moment. *Feel the resistance and let it go. Come back to this moment*, she told herself.

Helen Thorpe was Benedict Levine's butler. She was also a notably even-tempered former monastic. Since switching careers, she'd had two major traumatic experiences. The first took place immediately after she finished butler school. She'd had to go back to the retreat centre where she had worked for years and sort out her former employer's estate. It turned out that her employer had been murdered and Helen had, almost inadvertently, discovered the responsible party.

In the second instance, her employers, Dr. and Mr. Levine, had loaned out Helen's domestic services to a wayward young woman who was part of a content creation collective. In that case, Helen had become enmeshed in another series of crimes and had been assaulted. She hadn't entirely recovered. She still dreamt about her assailant's voice. And his touch. Her body shivered and her mind shrank away from the memory.

Helen needed a period of repair and reflection. She needed quiet and space and time with her horse. She needed every moment of her holiday.

But she also wanted to take care of her employers. After all, they had given her what mostly felt like an ideal life: one of service and grace and right liveli-hood. Delaying a much-anticipated holiday by a week would not hurt her. At least that's what her mind said. Her nervous system seemed to feel otherwise.

Helen had immediately agreed to accompany Mr. Levine on this trip to an island located off the coast of Nanaimo, BC, when he asked. They were going to attend a program Mr. Levine's son David had been recruited to lead. That part was simple enough. What was less simple was the guise under which they were taking part.

David, the Levines' youngest child, was uncomfortable with his extreme privilege. When he'd gone off to college, he'd taken the name Lewiston so he could not be connected to his family name. Only David's closest friends knew who his family was. He gave away almost all the money he received from his trust each year to charitable causes. He was on a one-year leave from his career as an environmental lawyer and professor of law. He was working on a book about legal approaches to the climate crisis and had been asked to take over as lead facilitator for a course called Close Encounters for Global Healing that brought together various competing (and hostile) factions at the far ends of the political and ideological spectrum.

David himself had attended the course two years before and been so in-spired by the deep connections people made and the way closed minds had been opened and changed that he'd joined the board. When the founder, Nelly Bean, decided to get married and go on a honeymoon, she'd asked David to step

CONTEMPLATION OF A CRIME

in and teach the course for her and he'd agreed. That meant he had to run the October session at a lodge on Side Island, near Nanaimo.

What did any of this have to do with Mr. Levine and Helen?

From what Helen understood, the course required a certain set of characters, almost like a board game. For example, there was always a spiritual person, who offered counselling support to participants, and a "person of means," as Mr. Levine put it. Helen didn't know why a wealthy person was required to participate or why they would *agree* to take part. Was it assumed that someone needed to speak up for the trod-upon rights of capitalists? Whatever the reasoning, the token rich person who had been slated to participate had dropped out only four days before the course was due to start and David had asked his father to fill in.

The wrinkle was that there are rich people and then there are vastly, unfathomably rich people, and Mr. Levine was the latter. When Helen thought of her employers' financial situation, she was reminded of an explanation she'd once read about the difference between a million and a billion. A million seconds is eleven days. A billion seconds is thirty-two years. If someone with a million dollars spent one thousand dollars a day, they would run out of money in three years. If someone with a billion dollars spent a thousand dollars a day, they would run out of money in 2,740 years. The Levines were billionaires and they had to be constantly on guard against those who would like to relieve them of their money. Mr. Levine's enormous wealth meant that attending the course as himself was too much of a security risk. So he'd decided to pretend to be someone else for five days. A rich man, but not an ultra-rich one.

As they drove out of the ferry terminal, Helen thought back to four days before, when the Levines had received their son David's request.

She'd been arranging glasses of spring water with sprigs of mint and a squeeze of lemon on the table between the two sensory-deprivation tanks containing Dr. Bunny Levine and Mr. Benedict Levine. The towels were in the warmer, ready to be handed over when Helen's employers emerged. The tanks looked like props from a science fiction movie about interstellar travel.

Dr. and Mr. Levine had rejected the white tank option as looking too much like giant toilets and gone for the silver version. Instead of looking like high-tech toilets, the tanks were like a cross between a tanning bed, a futuristic kitchen appliance, and a Dutch clog. The blue lights inside were said to enhance the benefits of floating in a silent, gravity-less environment that exactly matched the temperature of the human body.

The pods sat in a hushed spa room with low lighting. After the Levines emerged, they liked to spend some time in quiet contemplation before going to bed. That evening, they'd already been for a swim in their indoor/outdoor pool, had a cold plunge, and spent a pleasurable half hour in the Japanese seaweed bath in the garden before wrapping up a full evening of self-care in their tranquility pods. Helen and the Levines' personal spa and gym manager, Kellie, made sure everything was just so. Seeing her employers happy and well-cared-for made Helen feel like *she'd* been to the spa.

"All set," she'd said to Kellie, a trim woman who had been a nurse before branching into home spa and recreation management. She still had something of the efficient medical professional about her.

"All set," confirmed Kellie. She was laser focused on creating an experience of "peak wellness" for clients in highly specialized and health-optimizing environments.

Everything—the cut stone walkways surrounded by expanses of rock-tumbled agates, the glowing Himalayan salt walls in the infrared room, the various handmade tubs in the outdoor soak area with the Japanese privacy walls and carefully curated collection of bonsai—had been chosen to induce relaxation, support immune health, and minimize distractions. That was why Helen and Kellie frowned when Mariska walked silently into the softly lit confines of the float tank room holding out a cellphone. The device was on and emitting the sort of light and energy that was anathema to the spa environment.

"It's David," whispered Mariska. "He says he need to speak to his father. He says emergency. Very important crisis emergency." She glanced at the pair of silver float tanks and then quickly away, as though she'd just found her employers hanging from hooks in matching bondage gear.

Mariska had emigrated from Ukraine, where she'd worked in a deli. Helen imagined that even before the Russian invasion, Mariska's life hadn't been filled with ultra-luxurious home spa experiences and float tanks. Then again, for all Helen knew, Ukrainians might be devoted to spa life. Perhaps living on Russia's border required all of its neighbours to self-soothe with maximum rigour.

Kellie consulted her watch. It was not a smartwatch, because she believed any form of technological connectivity disrupted the deep peace of the personal spa space.

She put up seven fingers to indicate that the Levines were due to float for that many more minutes.

Helen considered and then knocked softly on the lid of Mr. Levine's tank and then on the lid of Dr. Levine's. The couple always put family first.

The lids were pushed open at the same time, revealing two figures bathed in blue lights. They looked like very calm clams. Or alien embryos.

"I am so sorry to interrupt," said Helen. "But David is on the phone. He would like to speak to Mr. Levine. Immediately." She indicated the phone at her side. "When you're ready, sir."

The couple sat up and exchanged looks of concern blunted by extreme tranquility.

"Thank you, Helen," said Dr. Levine. Then she looked at her husband, concerned, as he wrapped himself in a capacious oatmeal-coloured organic cotton towel. Helen passed a matching towel to Dr. Levine and the phone to Mr. Levine, and she, Kellie, and Mariska silently retreated from the room to await instructions.

Fifteen minutes later Benedict and Bunny Levine called Helen into the anteroom outside the home spa. They'd sat side by side on the oatmeal-coloured couch wearing their matching oatmeal-coloured terry bathrobes and slippers. The scene was a veritable sea of calming oatmeal. Benedict stared at the glass of lemon-and-mint water in his hand.

"Benny has something to ask you, Helen," said Dr. Levine.

Mr. Levine told Helen about how David was leading a five-day workshop on an island near Nanaimo and how he wanted his father to replace someone who had dropped out.

"Bunny can't come with me," he said. "And she's not comfortable with me going alone."

"I'll be in Montenegro for my annual get-together with the girls," said Dr. Levine.

"David will be there, my love," said Mr. Levine, in the worshipful tone he reserved for his wife. "I'll be perfectly fine on my own."

"David will be busy running the course," said Dr. Levine. She turned to Helen, who found she was holding her breath.

"Benny doesn't want to travel with security. You know how he is. The thing is, Helen, we know you have a wonderful holiday planned with your little horse and your friends."

Helen nodded. A sinking feeling came over her.

"My heart tells me Benny should go. But my mind tells me that the other people in the course must not know *who* he is."

"David also prefers the participants not know I'm his father," said Mr. Levine. "He thinks it might throw off the dynamics."

"Too many rich people spoil the broth," said Dr. Levine, drily.

"I see," Helen said, though she didn't, not really.

"We've discussed it and I've decided to attend the course under a pseudonym!" Benedict Levine grinned at her.

"He's going to pretend to own Toyota dealerships," said Bunny. "Do not ask me why."

"Toyota is a fascinating company!" said Mr. Levine. "The use of Jidoka and the just-in-time ethos is brilliant. I've always said so."

"This way, David will have his well-off participant, and his father will get to see first-hand what happens at this course David speaks so highly of."

"According to David, they do some groundbreaking stuff in the social enterprise space," said Mr. Levine.

He and his wife stared at each other adoringly, apparently forgetting Helen was there.

"I'm sorry, Helen," said Dr. Levine. "You know how spacey we get after we've been in our tanks. As I was saying, I would really feel more comfortable if you accompanied Benny. David said he'll find something for you to do. He says we mustn't let anyone know that you're Benedict's butler."

"No, indeed," said Mr. Levine. "No one else there is going to have a butler."

Helen felt the anticipated riding clinic and visit with her friends slipping away. She let it go with a pang of regret.

"So I will be there as a . . . ?"

"An attendee. Or maybe staff? Something like that. David says he'll find a role for you. The course is said to be tremendously rewarding," said Mr. Levine.

"We hope it will be a lovely change of pace for you," said Dr. Levine. "A warm-up for your proper holiday. We will absolutely make up the days you need to miss. If you like, we can host the teacher of the horse program here at Paddock House? Would you like that?"

"That won't be necessary," said Helen. "My holiday can begin after the workshop."

"Thank god," said Dr. Levine. "I will feel so much better if you're there, Helen."

"We'll be with David, darling," said Benedict. "It will be fine. David always has things well in hand. It's a bit of luck that his rich person has dropped out."

"Sweetheart, I know he doesn't like to admit it, but David *is* a rich person. Perhaps *he* could fill this role. Do double duty, as it were?"

Benny Levine sighed heavily. "David donates every penny of his trust and is working on ways to divest any forebears of their share."

Bunny pursed her lips. "The degree of privilege it takes to do that is remarkable."

Dr. Bunny Levine did not come from the same level of wealth as Mr. Levine. Her father had been a successful physician from Georgia and her mother was a food scientist from Halifax. Dr. Levine's mother's people had arrived in Nova Scotia after the American Revolution, after fighting on the side of the British. Her father's family had been active in the struggle for civil rights for their whole lives. Bunny had grown up an upper-middle-class person in the South, had gone to a historically black college, and had had a career as a celebrated heart surgeon. She retained an acute sense of the historical wrongs done to Black people in North America and had a fierce pride in her own accomplishments, as well as those of her relatives and her children. Helen had heard Dr. Levine mention several times how bewildering she found the complicated relationship her children had with their family money.

"Wealth has been a burden for David since the day he learned that not everyone has enough to eat," said Mr. Levine.

Bunny nodded slowly, allowing the point. "He has always been our most sensitive child."

Helen was aware that Dr. and Mr. Levine worried about David. He was widely regarded as the smartest one in the entire Levine family, which was saying something, as they were all high achievers. Alongside his overabundance of intellectual power came a great sense of social responsibility. He was the family member who felt things most deeply. He spoke four languages, had gotten his Doctor of Law by the time he was twenty-three, and was vegan, a gifted artist, and a competitive long-distance runner. In addition to being a superstar at his firm and at the law school where he taught, there was a worry, never directly stated but alluded to by his parents, that he was always in danger of being eaten alive by the ugliness of the world. David's experience at Close Encounters had seemed to change that vulnerability. It had restored his optimism and some degree of resilience, which meant everything to his parents.

"Helen, what do you think of this plan?" Mr. Levine asked from his oatmeal-coloured cocoon.

"I think it's a fine idea," she'd said, even though fine was something of an overstatement.

Helen would never let either of her employers go into an unfamiliar or difficult situation unaccompanied. Her entire world revolved around making life pleasant for them. She derived great satisfaction from that. But darn it, she *had* been excited to attend the horse clinic.

Four days later, instead of driving off in the Levines' truck and trailer towing Honey to the equestrian clinic, she and Mr. Levine were in the brand-new Toyota driving the short distance from the Departure Bay ferry terminal to meet the much smaller ferry that would take them to the island, where they would lie about their identities. It seemed like an odd way to begin a program aimed at building genuine connections between people, but it wasn't her decision to make.

Her employers, she reflected as Mr. Levine headed for the boat launch, had a habit of making things too complicated. She could see multiple other ways to have handled this, including hiring a less rich person to take the course. But Mr. Levine wanted the time with David *and* he wanted to check out the course. He also, for some strange reason, seemed to want to pretend to own Toyota dealerships.

Dr. and Mr. Levine were usually driven around by other people, often in one of their fleet of experimental electric vehicles. Mr. Levine's lack of practice led him to drive far below the posted speed limit. But he was picking up the pace as they headed for the parking lot where they were to meet the others.

"Bulky, but handles well," he said of the bus-like Sequoia.

"Yes, sir," said Helen.

CONTEMPLATION OF A CRIME

He looked at her. Mr. Levine was in his sixties, handsome in the way of a happy, well-tended man of good character, who was endlessly pleased by life. He was devoted to his wife and children and did good things in the world. But he had another side, too. He was a celebrated economist and businessperson, a member of one of the wealthiest families in North America, and renowned as a brilliant negotiator. For all his Buddhist practice, he had a hard side and, it appeared, a love of acting.

"Remember to call me Scooter," he said. "God, I love that name. It was brilliant of Bunny to come up with it. Scooter Bruin. Just the sound of it . . ." He breathed deeply to show his appreciation.

David had remarked that the name was too close to that of the music producer and entrepreneur who'd famously had the falling-out with Taylor Swift, but his parent was unmoved. In the four days since he'd agreed to go to the course—and with Helen's assistance, his wife's input, and a hired firm—Mr. Levine had create an entire false online identity as an owner of multiple car dealerships. Mr. Levine seemed eager to be someone new for a week. Perhaps, Helen thought, it was a burden to be the same person for one's whole life, even if that person lived a life of extreme fortune. She recalled the story of Siddhartha, Buddha before enlightenment, who left his father's palace in a chariot and went out into the world where, for the first time, he saw the realities of aging, illness, and death. Perhaps this trip to Close Encounters for Global Healing was Benedict Levine's attempt to reckon with a life beyond immense wealth. Or maybe he just thought it would be cool.

Now here they were, nearing the place where they would pretend to be other people for five entire days.

"You can let me out here," said Helen. They'd just turned at the light before the boat launch. The GPS said they were nearly at their destination.

"Are you sure? I'd hate for you to have to walk all the way over there with your luggage."

"It's fine," said Helen. "We aren't supposed to know each other, so it would look peculiar if we arrived together."

"Right. Of course."

He pulled the vehicle over and looked at her again. "This is going to be really something," he said. "Thank you for coming."

Helen smiled at her employer and got out.

21

She walked along the sidewalk, her suitcase bumping along behind her and the ocean breeze ruffling her hair. According to the Google map, the walk to the boat launch would take two minutes. Two minutes in which she would be blessedly alone. She allowed her steps to slow. Maybe she could draw it out to three minutes.

TOM AUCIELO

om Aucielo got off the bus, bent almost in half under the weight of his giant pack. He was going to miss the boat if he didn't run. But how could he run while carrying such a huge load?

Tom could not afford to miss the ferry. If he didn't get his ass onto that island, pronto, he could be in real trouble. That's what his counsellor and lawyer had told him, anyway.

Most of the key people from CFRP were in prison, in part thanks to information provided by Tom. But CFRP was part of a much larger network. And some of the people in that network wanted him dead. There might even be a bounty.

To the larger world, he was a disgusting racist who'd gotten off on attempted terrorism charges by turning in his fellow bigots. But the actual hardcore racists knew he was just a dummy who made terrible decisions and who had hardly any race pride at all. He'd ended up in the Compound because of Gracie, the daughter of Warren Wiggins, head of Canadians for Race Pride. Tom would have followed Gracie into Satan's lair. In fact, by going into the Compound, he sort of had.

When Tom was a teenager, his unerring instinct for saying the wrong thing had gotten him beaten up multiple times. At the Compound, he'd finally learned to be quiet because everyone there was so terrifying. It was a shame, really, because his voice was the most handsome thing about him. Maybe him turning mute was why Gracie had dumped him and gone to Germany to be with a Nazi she'd met on a racist dating site. God, Tom really, really had the worst judgment in almost every category. That's why he was so proud of his voice. It was all he had.

Tom's voice made him sound bigger and more serious than he was. Unfortunately, everyone eventually figured out that the deep voice was saying stupid words.

Not that Tom himself was stupid, exactly. He had a large vocabulary. He even thought he might be an *autodidact,* a word he loved. He read a lot, including the books he heard about on podcasts and from YouTubers. When he went into the Compound to be with Gracie, he'd read all the books in their tiny library, including *The Turner Diaries,* which was basically a racist bible, *Mein Kampf,* as well as *Anschluss.* The books scared the shit out of him. When the cops raided the Compound and and found those books by Tom's bedside, he'd had a hard time convincing them that he wasn't an actual racist, at least not a proper one. He told them he was just trying to impress his girlfriend's gruesome father, but no one believed him. Worse, Warren turned out not to be the kind of guy impressed by reading of any kind.

As Tom struggled along the broad side street, his legs burning and ferry traffic streaming by on Stewart Avenue, his mind went back to the issue of the bounty on him. Was there a way *he* could claim it? Could he fake his own murder in exchange for the money? In his experience white nationalists were all weirdly cheap, so if there was some kind of bounty, he bet it was embarrassingly low.

Tom had asked his PO if he could get police protection and she'd just laughed at him. Nice.

His whole life was one long run of bad luck. He'd had nothing to do with the plan. He never touched the guns or helped build the bombs. Didn't know the targets. Warren and the others hadn't told him anything because they thought he was useless. When they were doing their serious racism, he was usually washing dishes with the women. White nationalists were seriously sexist and they'd treated him like a female. But in the months he was at the Compound, he'd overheard enough to give information to the cops, which had gotten him a lighter sentence, served in isolation due to the threats from inside the jail. He'd also averted a terrorist attack, but nobody seemed to care about that. He'd tried to protect some of the women in the Compound from their abusive asshole boyfriends and husbands. He did that by directing the men's anger onto him. In a couple of instances, he helped the women leave. But quite a few of the women there were just as bad as the men. It really was a terrible place, and because he'd lived there, everyone thought *he* was a terrible person.

The lawyer and counsellor and cops kept asking about his racial ideas. That was unfair. If they asked any Black dudes or a brown girl or Asian people or one of those complicated gender people, they'd find out that they *all* had ideas, too. But nobody cared about that because it was okay to be prejudiced against

CONTEMPLATION OF A CRIME

straight white guys like him. He'd had this friend in high school, a cool Chinese Canadian girl who cut her hair using garden clippers and wore massive glasses and *exclusively* dated white girls. Wasn't *that* a little racist? But Bernadette, his friend, was obsessed with racism. Everybody was a racist to Bernadette, even her own grandparents and parents. Obviously, he never said anything to her about the hypocrisy of going for girls who were so white they were basically mushrooms. Bernie would have kicked his ass from one end of that school to the other if he had. He knew where she was coming from. He liked those girls, too, even though when he fell hard, it was for Gracie, who was surprisingly dark for the kid of a white nationalist. And if he was being honest? He liked girls of every shade, even though until Gracie, none of them had liked him back, notwithstanding his deep voice.

Maybe if he wasn't so scared of ending up an incel, he wouldn't have ended up in a militia or gone to jail or have to go to an intensive workshop for fuck-ups from all ends of the political spectrum out of concern for his own safety. Participants weren't supposed to say how they ended up in the program, at least not at the beginning. That was one of the first rules. They were only allowed to talk about who they were, not what they believed or how they'd ended up on Conflict Resolution Island. In his case, skipping his pathetic story would be a relief.

By the end of the workshop, he would have his income assistance for the month, plus an emergency grant, and he could be on his way. His social worker was going to have to help him find a place to stay. Foreigners had bought up so many buildings on Vancouver Island that there was nowhere for regular, hard-working people to live anymore. Not that he had ever been hard-working.

Shit, there was the parking lot.

He was huffing and puffing like a bastard. Where was everyone? Tom tried to pick up the pace. He saw a group of people with luggage piling onto a boat that was so small it looked like a toy ferry.

"Hey!" he cried, in his deep, deep voice. "Wait for me."

DAVID LEWISTON

David looked at the offending stew, or rather *stews*. The vegetables were local, organic, and non-GMO. Everyone loved a local vegetable, so that was fine. The stock was organic. But it was from a cow and was therefore not remotely vegetarian, much less vegan.

"Why is there meat stock in the vegetarian stew?" he asked.

"Because," said the cook, a woman who'd told him her last job had been in the Alberta oil patch. "Makes it taste better. There's no *cows* in it."

David sighed.

"Right. Yes. I appreciate that. But we have carnivores, vegetarians, *and* vegans coming. And for the opening night's meal, we want to provide a vegan option."

"They won't know," said Bobbi-Lyn. She stared down at the richly bubbling stew. "'Less they have a cow allergy."

The previous cook at Side Island, a twenty-six-year-old man named Jake who was covered in tattoos and piercings, had been completely up-to-the-minute on the ins and outs of the various food requirements of vegans versus meat-atarians and everything in between, but he had decided to take a paternity leave.

"I'm going to take three years, but dude, I really think it might be permanent," he'd told David a week before. "No way I'm missing my kid's childhood."

David imagined Jake trailing his kid to prom, eyes fixed devotedly on her back.

"Nancy is due in six months, right?" David had said, glad he would have enough time to replace Jake, who was an accomplished performer in the kitchen.

"Yup. But I'm going to shift to home right away. I don't want her doing things for herself."

"Now?" repeated David, too stunned to keep the dismay from his voice.

"Look, I can't just grind my whole life. I'm going to be a father. I got to

teach my kid about right priorities or, as I like to call it, no-work life balance."
He laughed heartily at his own joke.

"I get it," said David, running his hand over his hair. "Don't suppose you have any chef friends who are looking for work? Even just to get us through the upcoming program?"

Jake huffed out a breath, which made his septum piercing fly up. "Nah. Not really. The people I know are mostly opting out, if they can. There was Denise, but she's doing the whole van life thing. There's Selena. She's kind of a workaholic."

At the word *workaholic*, David's hopes rose.

"But she's out there, doing the right thing for Chef José Andrés at World Central Kitchen. Right on the border with Ukraine, man. So cool. Maybe I'll do that when my kid leaves home."

David sincerely hoped that Word Central Kitchen would not still be providing aid to Ukraine in eighteen to twenty-five years but didn't say so. He simply watched Jake pack up his knives and leave. Jake's was the first in a wave of resignations.

After some frantic, last-minute searching, he'd found Bobbi-Lyn, who, he suspected, was not professionally trained. She had an American accent and was unfamiliar with many modern food conventions, such as not putting meat stock in vegan dishes. She did not travel with her own knives but had arrived with an entire shopping bag full of cartons of cigarettes.

On the positive side, her cooking was excellent, even though David, a vegan since age twelve, had, under her regime, eaten the first animal products of his adult life multiple times, thinking she'd finally grasped what constituted an animal product.

"Anchovy paste might not look like fish," he'd explained after eating a delicious bowl of pasta. "But it comes from fish."

She looked doubtful at this news. "Came from a tube."

He was beginning to think Bobbi-Lyn was putting him on.

"Bobbi-Lyn," he said, looking at the stews. "We need something we can feed the vegans and vegetarians. And we're going to need it by seven this evening."

She considered. "I'll have a smoke and think on it," she said.

"Great," he said. "Thank you. We can freeze one of these stews. On that note, do we have a vegan biscuit option?"

Bobbi-Lyn peered at him as though the cigarette dangling from her mouth had already been lit. "They all got butter," she said, with zero regret. "Don't taste a damn without it."

"Right. So we will need biscuits that don't have any butter. Or cream. No dairy whatsoever. Maybe run the ingredients list by me before you start."

Bobbi-Lyn, who had wiry grey hair that she kept in a skinny braid that fell halfway down her back, saluted him. Then she thumped her own chest, which was covered in a threadbare Molly Hatchet T-shirt. "Aye-aye, Captain."

David had never heard of Molly Hatchet and kept meaning to find out whether it was the name of a band or a video game. He prayed it wasn't the name of a hate group. The thought reminded him, unhappily, that a genuine white nationalist would be arriving soon to attend the program. What if Molly Hatchet was a racist band and the white nationalist attendee thought he was going to be supported in his abhorrent beliefs?

No, David reassured himself. The white nationalist, Tom Aucielo, would surely realize that a mixed-race person would not be running a program to support racists. But just in case, he quickly googled Molly Hatchet. A heavy metal band from the eighties. No mention of racism. Thank god.

There had been a Christian nationalist in the Close Encounters group David had attended two years before, but that man had been so focused on creating a Christian state that he hadn't bothered, particularly, about the colour of anyone's skin. In fact, the Christian nationalist had grown quite close to both David and Shannon, who was a Tahltan woman from Telegraph Creek. She was an accomplished hunter and trapper who, for her part, had many long conversations with the young white animal rights activist from Quebec who'd spent six months in jail for his efforts to stop all hunting and trapping by sabotaging traplines and hunting cabins. The Christian nationalist had left Close Encounters as simply a Christian, and he and David kept in regular touch.

Close Encounters for Global Healing brought together people on opposing ends of the hot-button issues of the day so they could find common ground and achieve rapprochement. And when it worked, as it had the year that David attended, it felt miraculous. Revolutionary, even. When it didn't, well, David didn't want to think about what that would be like. Nelly, the founder and usual facilitator who'd asked him to take over so she could get married and go on her honeymoon, had assured him that people would eventually mesh. The participants

CONTEMPLATION OF A CRIME

would connect and their anger would dissipate. David fervently hoped she was right. He didn't want to be the reason that Close Encounters failed for the first time in its history.

It was noble work, but daunting. For one thing, David had not chosen the people taking part in the program. They were referred from various parts of the community. His job was to follow Nelly's curriculum to allow people to find shared values and begin to appreciate each other's humanity.

But still, an actual white nationalist!

David sighed and walked outside to go and meet the ferry. It would be the last ferry for five days because the dock at Side Island was being towed away and repaired after the guests were dropped off. That meant there was no place for even a small pleasure cruiser to dock. Boats could anchor nearby and, depending on whether it was low or high tide, people could wade or swim to shore or take a rowboat over. And of course, canoes and kayaks and paddle boards could reach the rocky shores of Side Island, which was located northwest of Saysutshun marine provincial park. Protection Island lay to the east. Tiny Guide Island was located across the channel from Side Island. There were other smaller islands, whose names David didn't know, dotting the Nanaimo harbour. The dock end of Side Island faced Nanaimo and it was a twenty-minute ferry ride from the dock to the waterfront in Nanaimo. The staff had agreed they could use their personal boats to get back and forth each day while the dock was being repaired, or they could stay on the island.

The waters around Side Island were busy. Seaplanes buzzed past, lifting out of the water like overstuffed birds and landing with a confident splash. The big BC ferries on their way to and from Vancouver surged by the other side of the island like old dowagers. Kayakers paddled around the island. Every conveyance had its own speed, its own style. The traffic made Side Island feel somehow both private and lively, sort of like a quiet bar in a busy neighbourhood.

As David walked along the path, with its thin layer of leaf litter, broken shells, and dirt atop stone, to meet the ferry, he took a deep breath and let his shoulders relax. It was a crisp and seasonally appropriate October day. That alone felt like a victory in an era of intense and unpredictable weather. David was trying to pay special attention to the normal days so he didn't get completely lost in anxiety over the days that felt overwhelmingly strange.

What else is good right now? he asked himself. The query was one he used to help himself relax. Answering was easy. He was looking forward to being near his father for five days, even if they did not plan to reveal their relationship.

David adored his father, a former titan of industry and academia and current devout Buddhist. He admired his father's mostly gentle and endlessly curious approach to life. Even at the peak of his career, his father had been a calming presence, a gifted leader because empathy came so naturally to him. His mother was fiercer, partly because of her training as a surgeon and partly because, as a Black woman, she'd had to outwork everyone around her to achieve her goals. She was kind, but she possessed bright, firm boundaries that she was not shy about defending. Together, David's parents were the kind of couple that other people pointed to as an example of how well-matched two human beings can be. David and his brother and sister had always known that even though their parents loved them, they loved each other even more.

That might be a good thing, but David sometimes felt that his parents' grand and unflagging love for each other was a high bar that he would never be able to attain in his own romantic endeavours. What if he picked the wrong person and it didn't work out? David could hardly bring himself to think of his parents' faces if he had to tell them he was breaking up with someone they liked or, god forbid, if he ever divorced. Maybe something about those dynamics in his family had drawn him to Close Encounters. It seemed easier to help political and ideological opposites find common ground than it was to find a connection as deep as the one his parents shared. In short, he hoped this week together would deepen his relationship with his dad. They'd never spent five days together, with just the two of them. Of course, this wouldn't be just the two of them. They had some other folks to contend with.

He turned to look behind him at the lodge. The lodge at Side Island was the sort of place people visited every year at the same time for decades with a cohort of other regulars. Wood cabins of different sizes were spread out on either side of the lodge, and the lodge contained ten guest rooms upstairs. The lodge was old-fashioned in a way that he quite enjoyed. He associated it with puzzles and comfy armchairs and senior citizens who used to be biologists and professors of music and the like, along with a smattering of younger folks who owned bookstores and were proprietors of boutique ceramic mug companies. There was a concrete saltwater pool at the ocean's edge, and the shift from natural flat rock to poured concrete was almost seamless. In the summer, tables and chairs

CONTEMPLATION OF A CRIME

and slightly faded umbrellas were arranged at the water's edge near a giant inlaid chess board with wooden pieces the size of young children. Guests at Side Island Lodge were served three hearty meals per day and snacks twice a day. Trails criss-crossed the thirty acres of the island, and the resort was fully booked year-round, save for the odd cancellation due to ill health or family emergency. In the late fall the lodge was closed for a month for maintenance and so the owner and staff could take holidays. For the past ten years, Close Encounters had been allowed to use the lodge and cabins for the retreat. There were three other Close Encounters sessions held at centres around Canada, but Side Island was where David had taken the course, and to him, Side Island *was* the program.

He reached the floating dock, where the workers from the dock company were waiting to take it apart and tow it back across the water, where they would do the repairs to the frame and replace the floats in a shop beside the marina. Something about removing the dock felt metaphorically appropriate to David. Pulling up the drawbridge and all that. In reality, of course, anyone could get on and off the island if they were willing to risk getting wet.

The small red ferry approached, piloted by Wesley White, a young Snuney-muxw man who split his time between captaining the Side Island Ferry and designing clothing and jewellery. He was starting to make a name for himself. Nelly said she thought he might soon hang up his captain's hat to work full-time on his fashion line.

Everyone would be sad to see Wesley go. He was twenty-four and extremely popular with the guests. He'd started piloting the ferry when he was just eighteen.

The ferry putted into position and David moved to take the mooring line. As he did so, he reminded himself not to pay special attention to his father. No hugs! It was going to feel very, very strange to see his father outside of his usual environment, which was curated to be as filled with ease and beauty as possible. David was relieved that at least his father would have Helen to smooth the transition into the real world.

David and his siblings were dazzled by the calm hyper-efficient new butler his parents had found to replace their old retainer, who had been with them for twenty years. Their old butler had seemed irreplaceable, but Helen was in a class all her own.

David was looking forward to getting to know Helen better during the five days of the course, not as his parents' butler but as a person. He'd noticed, with a pang, that he sometimes felt alienated by his parents' relationship with Helen in a way that a psychotherapist would probably find fascinating. Helen's commitment to them made him feel left out. He'd long believed that those who are able to take care of themselves should do so. If able-bodied individuals without serious mental or emotional challenges couldn't do for themselves, then they'd made their lives too complicated. "If you had less stuff, you wouldn't need so much help," he remembered saying to his parents, when they informed him they were getting a new butler.

His parents, who'd been understanding when he'd changed his last name before he went to university in Toronto and hadn't complained about his refusal to be publicly identified as their son, were also sanguine about his critiques of their lifestyle, which was lavish but not tastelessly so. Most people at their level of wealth had dozens and sometimes even hundreds of staff.

"Too many dogs to manage for ourselves, sweet boy," his father had said, patting the bony head of one of their elderly rescue greyhounds.

"And horses," his mother added.

Back at the dock he stood up and watched as Wesley helped the guests off the boat. First came a thickset young man in a backwards baseball hat. That would be Wayne Krupke, who had been arrested for his actions during the protests in Ottawa. Wayne carried an old duffle bag and wore a plaid shirt. He was accompanied by an exceptionally rotund tan-coloured dog. Krupke looked strong and capable, although, even from a distance, his energy seemed aggressive.

A grey-haired woman disembarked. She didn't return David's welcoming smile. She would be Yana Heppler, the environmental activist. He felt he had some insight into her condition of hopelessness when it came to protecting the planet. She looked like she was already writing a negative review in her head.

Next up was a thirtyish woman with carefully straightened brown hair. She wore a puffy white jacket, toothpaste-white jeans with lots of holes in them, and spotless white platform runners, and dragged an enormous hard-sided hot-pink Juicy Couture suitcase with a brilliant pattern of red and orange flowers behind her. Ah, this would be Madison Croft. She was here not because of her political beliefs, but presumably because she had none. Madison was a shopper and completely disengaged from all forms of public discourse. David had very little information about the participants, including how they'd been recruited. All he

CONTEMPLATION OF A CRIME

had to go on was their intake forms. He'd noticed on hers that Madison had the handwriting of an eighth grader.

A young man slunk off the boat. That would be Pain Wainscott III, internet provocateur. He was apparently eighteen, but so pallid and small he could have passed for sixteen.

"Welcome," said David, immediately feeling compassion for the teenager who was so much younger than everyone else.

"If you say so," said the boy.

Then came the guest he was most concerned about, and half of his nerves instantly disappeared. Tom Aucielo didn't look any more imposing than the internet kid. He wore the racist's uniform of the neat hair, Dockers, and a polo shirt under a bomber jacket. But he looked more haunted than threatening.

"Hello," said David.

"Hi," said Tom, and David nearly recoiled in surprise at the deep voice that rolled out. How bizarre that such a big voice was housed in that hunch-shouldered, skinny body. Tom stuck out his hand eagerly and David shook it. Interesting.

And here came his father, followed closely by Helen, who watched carefully to make sure his father got off without incident, which of course he did. Benedict Levine was a graceful man. Always had been.

"Hello," said David, and he felt the smile spreading across his face. He couldn't help it.

"Hello," said his father, returning the smile with his own expression of pure delight. "How are you?"

Don't hug him. Don't hug him.

"Fine," said David.

"It is *wonderful* to be here," said his father, gazing around at the small mossy field bisected by the path that led back to the cabins and the lodge.

"I'm glad to meet all of you." David turned to Helen.

"Welcome," he said.

Helen nodded and looked at him with her calm, serious eyes, and all of a sudden, David felt that everything was right with the world or soon would be. What a gift she had. What a gift she *was*.

When the guests and their luggage were assembled and standing some distance away on the path, David thanked Wesley.

"Hey," Wesley said. His voice dropped to a whisper as he looked toward the group standing a short distance away. "You got some live ones this time."

"Oh?"

"I mean, watch yourself," whispered Wesley, who was usually so positive about everyone. "A couple of these ones give me a vibe."

"Okay," said David. "I'll be careful."

"For real, eh," said Wesley. Then he clapped David on the back, stepped back onto the small boat, and motored away from Side Island.

PART II
BE HERE NOW.
I INSIST.

HELEN THORPE

Helen should have requested what was sometimes called "role clarity." They'd covered the topic in some detail at the North American Butler Academy. It was often up to butlers to set boundaries, because if they didn't, they would end up working twenty-four hours a day, seven days a week. Additionally, butlers were in charge of establishing clear expectations for other members of household staff.

No organization could function well if it wasn't clear who was in charge of what. And Helen's sense was that David hadn't thought things through, at least when it came to her role in the Close Encounters workshop.

"Have a seat, everyone," he said. They were gathered in the lodge and had left their luggage outside. David explained that staff from housekeeping would deliver their things to their cabins.

"Why did we have to drag it all the way over here, then?" asked the man who had all the flags on his truck. "Couldn't they have met us at the ferry and then driven our stuff where it needed to go?"

David looked down at his sheet of paper and sighed.

"Yes. That's a good point. I'm not sure why guests have to bring their luggage to the lodge."

"Arbitrary stupid rules. That kind of shit really grinds my gears. Is the government running this thing?"

David nodded. "Let's set that aside for now. First, allow me to introduce myself in more detail."

"I have to piss," said the pale young man who looked as though he might still be in high school. Helen had the distinct impression that he actually just wanted to use the word *piss*. David blinked. Then something in him stiffened.

"Please wait a moment. This won't take long."

The boy snorted but stayed in his seat on the sofa upholstered with a heavy floral pattern.

"My name is David Lewiston. I'll be facilitating our work together for the next five days."

Mr. Levine began to clap enthusiastically and then remembered himself and stopped.

"Thank you, I appreciate that," said David before continuing. "I'm a lawyer and I have training in mediation. Most importantly, I'm also a graduate of this program."

"I'm not only the Hair Club President, I'm also a client," muttered the grey-haired woman dressed head-to-toe in ragged Patagonia. Several people shot her a look and she lapsed back into silence.

"So why aren't you lawyering?" asked the truck guy.

"What kind of law do you practice?" asked the boy who'd said he had to go to the bathroom.

Helen looked out the windows at the ocean, which was being roiled by the rising wind. Small whitecaps scudded across the surface.

The younger woman with the pin-straight brown hair snuck a glance at her phone.

"I'm on leave from my job," said David.

"Must be nice," muttered the truck guy. He kept a hand on his dog's broad skull. "It's like people who work for the government. At least half of them are on stress leave at any given time. It's a fact. Look it up."

David, who'd probably been in the legal practice long enough to be familiar with angry, reactive people, didn't respond. Helen approved.

"You've all read the introduction to the program that was sent to you along with your contracts, but we'll go over everything again in more detail."

"Hope I don't end up pissing on the couch," said the boy. Again, he over-emphasized the word *piss*.

The grey-haired woman finally turned her head to glare at him. "Maybe you should be wearing diapers if you can't hold it," she said.

The boy shut up.

"We will be spending the next five days together. Close Encounters for Global Healing is aimed at working across our differences to find our similarities."

"Kind of like that movie *The Breakfast Club*," said a narrow man with very short hair and an excess of nervous energy. He wore a white polo shirt and khakis and seemed like he was on the verge of jumping out of his own skin. "That's one of John Hughes's most successful films."

The others looked at him with disdain, except for Mr. Levine, who beamed. "I like that," he said. "What a great comparison."

"Well," said David, who seemed to relax at his father's encouragement. "I hope that taking part in our encounter will be nothing like going to detention, but coming together the way the characters do in that film is the ultimate goal. This is an intensive workshop for personal discovery and community building."

"Blah, blah, blah," muttered the boy.

David glanced at his smartwatch and frowned at what he saw there. He returned to his introduction.

"Our days will be organized around a series of activities designed to help us get to know each other. Not our belief systems, but our inner selves."

"My name is Wayne and my inner self wants to fuck up the status quo," said the guy with all the truck flags, sounding extremely pleased with himself, even though he pronounced quo "kwaa."

"Thanks, Wayne. For the initial part of the course, we will not be discussing anything that could be considered political. Just names, ages, and interests that have no political angle."

"All of my interests have a political angle," said the grey-haired woman. "Because I'm fighting to help us all stay alive."

"If you say so, Greta," said the boy.

Helen saw David release a long, soft breath. "We will allow you to get settled in your cabins and then meet back here for introductions and an icebreaker."

"Icebreakers," said the boy. "Kill me now."

"Bro, why did you agree to come to this thing if you don't want to be here?" asked the truck guy.

"Do *you* want to be here?" asked the boy.

"Shit no. But I said I'd do it. So I'm not going to bitch about it the whole time. Take some personal responsibility, man."

The others nodded.

"Great attitude," said Mr. Levine. "Love it."

Everyone shot him an irritated look, except the woman with the brown hair who wore very white clothes that were a touch too tight. What was the expression on her face? Helen wasn't sure, but there was something like avidity in the woman's eyes when she looked at Mr. Levine and it made Helen uncomfortable. She noted her feeling of not liking and let it go. Helen had spent years paying attention to her reactions, large and small, and her attunement to the present moment came as naturally to her as deep sighs came to other people.

David began to hand out sheets of paper. "I've got a map of the grounds here for each of you and I'm going to call out the cabin assignments. Yana, you will be in Brightside."

"You really need to give us paper copies?" said the grey-haired woman. "Maybe you could have sent this digitally?"

"We will be shutting off our phones soon," said David, evenly, as though he'd been expecting her objection.

"Tom, you're in Farside, which is the furthest cabin over toward the ferry. Madison, you'll be in Rockside. The rest of you are in cabins on this side of the lodge." He pointed in the opposite direction from the ferry. "Mr. Bruin, you're in Hearthside, and uh, Hetty, you're in the cabin next door."

"Let me guess. She's in the supply side?" interrupted Yana, the grey-haired woman.

"Amazing joke," said the boy, poisonously, though not inaccurately.

David smiled at her. "Eastside Cottage." He turned to the boy. "Pain, you're in Beachside, and Wayne, you're in Treeside."

"Lot of sides to this place," said Mr. Levine, enjoying a moment of dad humour. No one laughed but Helen smiled, appreciating him and his boundless good nature.

Holding their maps, the guests filed back out of the lodge to find their accommodations.

"May I have a brief word?" David asked Helen as she started to follow her employer out of the lodge.

She nodded and stood off to the side of the entryway until everyone was gone and the heavy wooden door had swung closed.

David indicated that Helen should follow him. They left the cozy foyer with the wood stove and he led Helen into what turned out to be an office and

CONTEMPLATION OF A CRIME

reception area for the lodge. There was a half door and a shelf that functioned as a narrow reception desk. He lifted it and lowered it after them. When Helen was seated, David closed the top door to the office to give them privacy. Through the slatted window blinds and rising above the window ledge, she could see the cradle of smooth rock in which the lodge was nestled.

He sat at a desk.

"I'm glad you're here, Helen. You and my dad."

Helen nodded.

"It was generous of you both to come at such short notice."

"I know your father was happy to do it. And I'm glad to be of service."

"You're missing part of your holiday to be here. I know that and I appreciate it."

"Of course," said Helen.

David cleared his throat and ran a hand along the side of his head. He was a handsome young man with high cheekbones and gentle eyes. She knew that his temperament matched his appearance. He cared about others, and because of that, he sometimes suffered. It was hard for sensitive people to cope with the ugliness that could easily overwhelm the beauty of life on earth. But David seemed to have found his way.

"I just received a message," he said. "From Sophie. She's an Anglican minister and psychotherapist. She was going to join us tomorrow to support the guests, but she's got the flu."

Helen waited. Noted the light dread that washed over her.

"Sophie acts as a spiritual advisor for anyone who wants to talk. Not exactly counselling, but spiritual and psychological assistance."

Silence filled the little office.

"We hadn't yet come up with a role for you. As you know, Dad is using a sort of . . . a pseudonym. He's meant to be well-off, but not 'having a butler' well-off, if you know what I mean. Would you be willing to take over for Sophie?"

Helen realized that she'd been quite attached to the idea that even though she was missing part of her holiday, at least she wouldn't be responsible for anything other than her own behaviour during the encounter. Now was her turn to let out a long, low breath.

"We usually have three people on staff for the course. Plus Nelly. But two housekeepers sent me messages today saying they can't attend. Yesterday the third housekeeper informed me she's decided to move to Tofino with her boyfriend. So we're in a bit of a situation here, staff-wise."

At that bit of news, Helen felt her disappointment lift and her resistance fall away.

"Yes, I will act as a spiritual advisor for the course. And will you allow me to make a phone call? I may have an idea that will help with . . . everything."

HELEN THORPE

They waded to shore as elegantly as herons. Well, two of them did. The third slipped and fell as he got out of the rowboat. He briefly plunged under the surface, even though the water was only a foot and a half deep. He came up gasping and dripping.

"Save the pekes!" he cried.

The other two stood watching him. The ocean came only halfway up their tall Swedish rubber boots. They each held two leopard-print, soft-sided bags, each bag containing a dog. A Pekingese dog, to be exact.

The two dry people were fully certified butlers whom Helen had met at butler college. The one struggling out of the water as though he'd just swum the English Channel was a butler-in-training.

They were all there to help.

That was the butler way. They were like a manners-oriented Navy SEAL unit. When they were needed, they appeared. For each other and for their clients.

The situation reminded Helen of her first job after butler school. She'd had to go to her old retreat centre to help settle her late boss's affairs and Gavin and Murray had come along to assist her. She'd hired Nigel at that time and they were all now good friends as well as superb butlers.

Gavin and Murray stepped out of the water and hugged Helen, who gratefully hugged them back. Then she said hello to the dogs inside the bags. Hannibal, Clarice, Miggs, and Jack, the Pekingese, belonged to Nigel's employer, Ms. Cartier Hightower, who was attending some sort of post–Burning Man retreat at which dogs were not welcome.

"I brought you a blanket," said Helen, who'd suspected that the journey to shore would be a difficult one for Nigel, who tended to be ungainly.

"You are so next level," he said, as she put the blanket around his shoulders.

Gavin Vimukthi, as attractive a man as had ever lived, put down the bags of dogs and pulled the rope to drag the rental rowboat onto shore, and Murray helped to retrieve their tidy collection of luggage.

Helen hitched the rowboat to an arbutus tree a few feet from the high-tide line. Then the four of them looked at each other and exchanged smiles. Helen's relief and happiness at seeing her friends was beyond measure. Buddha had called having good companions the whole of the holy life and she thought he'd been right about that.

Nigel, who was beginning to shiver, broke the companionable silence. "It's really cool to be here. But I might need to get changed before I, like, expire."

Murray, an Irishwoman who'd moved to Virginia as a teen and then to Canada after butler school, laughed. "Of course. Maybe you'll get in on the cold-dipping craze while we're here. You'll be plunging into the ocean each morning before dawn." Her faint Irish accent gave her voice a lovely lilt.

Gavin, who was tall and had the posture and grace of a dancer, carried his leather bag in one hand and had Nigel's larger backpack slung over his other shoulder. With his free hand he gently patted Nigel's hunched and blanketed back. Helen and Murray bent over to let the dogs out of their cases.

"I am fascinated to hear more about our assignment," said Murray. "Gav tells me you've assured him there will be no murders this time."

Nigel gave a bleak bark of laughter. "I hope not. I have done more homicide detection than Miss Marple since I met you guys."

"I'm certain this week will be murder free," she said. "Certain-ish, anyway."

Helen led her friends to the largest cabin. Poolside Cottage was located next to the lodge and directly behind the inground pool.

The four of them climbed the stairs to the first deck and the front door.

"This is one of the newest cabins on the island," said Helen, opening the door and inviting them inside. "There are six bedrooms, four bathrooms, a kitchenette. Hot tub on the main deck."

"Ah, it's lovely, Helen," said Murray.

"Perfection," said Gavin.

"Can we turn up the heat?" asked Nigel. They looked at him, and he muttered "Never mind" and went to take a shower.

CONTEMPLATION OF A CRIME

While Nigel showered, Gavin and Murray chose a bedroom. They'd been a couple since soon after they helped Helen with her first assignment, which had taken place days after they all graduated from butler school.

"I am so glad the timing worked out," said Gavin, after they all settled around the kitchen table. "This way we get to spend more time with you before our vacation begins." Gavin and Murray were taking three months to travel before they decided what their next position would be.

"It's because Helen's a Buddhist. She's got that whole karma thing going."

Helen wondered what it said about her karma that she'd been involved in two murder cases in the first few years of her career as a butler. Then she let the thought go. Karma was one of those concepts best left for others to consider.

"I hope you don't mind helping out here."

"Not at all," said Murray. "We were staying with my sister and her wife in their condo in Vancouver. I think we were all ready for a break."

"They work out," said Gavin. "Both of them."

Murray nodded. "From morning until night. Biking, running, swimming, weightlifting, Pilates, barre. But mostly weightlifting."

"Oh," said Helen, who thought that it all sounded very Vancouver.

"They were never home," said Murray. "Which was a relief because of how they made me feel like a lump of suet."

Gavin turned an affectionate gaze on her. "You are magnificent."

"I do not have any muscle definition in my biceps and no sign of a six-pack. My sister and her wife pointed that out. More than once. All the Irishness seems to have been dieted out of them."

She patted her flat stomach. "They're training for one of those things where people show off their bodies. A muscle show, I think it's called," she said, unknowledgeably.

"Your sister called it a natural body-building competition," said Gavin.

"Did she? I tuned her out after the first hour of talking about protein. All they do is eat chicken breasts and broccoli and exercise. My sister has always been an obsessive. Anyway, it is a relief to be here and we are so happy to be of assistance. You always have the most fascinating assignments."

Gavin nodded. "We'll have fun."

Nigel returned from the shower wearing one of his brilliantly coloured track suits. As he'd continued training to be a high-level domestic, he'd slowly weaned himself off the clown-like outfits he preferred. Helen was glad to see this return to form.

Gavin got up and prepared a large Moka pot of coffee. Murray put out small cups and Gavin poured a hot coffee for Nigel, who accepted it with a deep sigh of satisfaction. This was how things were when the four of them were together. Pleasant things appeared; unpleasant things disappeared. Life got easier, more gracious.

Helen took another moment to appreciate her friends again before explaining the situation.

"We need help with housekeeping, but we only have six guests, seven if you include me, and I don't need any assistance. Then there's David, Mr. Levine's youngest son. He's facilitating the workshop. There is a chef on staff who will be handling the basic meals and snacks. No one needs daily housekeeping services, and meals are served buffet-style."

"No problem," said Gavin and Murray, and Nigel nodded. Even the Pekingese, who'd sniffed around and then settled in various comfortable poses near Nigel, seemed to nod.

Helen knew her friends could take care of fifty guests and make it look effortless.

"I predict a lot of time in the hot tub," sighed Nigel. He had a bag of treats on the table and was feeding them to the Pekingese, who lay like hairy little lumps at his feet.

"I must warn you that the atmosphere right now is somewhat fraught," said Helen. "The person who was going to act as spiritual support for participants just dropped out. David asked me to take over that role."

"Condolences," said Murray.

"Do not worry for one second," said Gavin. "We can handle anything that comes up. Remember, we've been working at your Yatra Institute for the past several years. We know about retreat centres. Your guests will be so well cared for that they'll forget to dislike each other."

Helen grimaced. "I hope so."

Nigel got to his feet and cleared the small coffee cups.

CONTEMPLATION OF A CRIME

"Take us to your leader," said Murray. "We are ready to be of service."

Helen could have kissed them. Instead, she just hugged each of them again in turn. Three butlers and one butler trainee were, she felt, the best preparation anyone could possibly have. So why did she feel a strong current of unease running through her as she contemplated the days ahead?

CLOSE ENCOUNTERS FOR GLOBAL HEALING
DAY-ONE SCHEDULE

1:00 p.m.	Arrive, get settled
2:00 p.m.	Introductions
3:00 p.m.	Icebreakers
4:00 p.m.	Afternoon walk
5:00 p.m.	Personal time
6:00 p.m.	Dinner
7:00 p.m.	Evening walk
7:30 p.m.	Games
9:00 p.m.	Rest

PAIN WAINSCOTT III

So far, the course was every bit as pointless as he expected. More, even. The other people were all older and stupid. Pain nearly died of boredom during the round of introductions. The organizer guy, David, wouldn't let them say anything offensive or what he called "positional." David really liked that word. *Positional.* He used it multiple times.

Literally no one seemed interesting. Then again, Pain was not a big fan of other people in person or online. The other people in the course were zeros. Sub-zeros, even. And not the cool kind.

There was the old environmentalist. He wouldn't mess with her. His time on the internet had taught him not to bother with the climate people. They were not having it. The good ones, like scientists, just patiently explained the science, which was dull and had too many charts. And the activists were almost impossible to draw into arguments because they were too tired out by the conspiracy theorists who genuinely believed there was nothing wrong with the weather. Both sides of that debate made him laugh. You'd have to be pretty crazy not to notice the forty-degree heat domes, whole provinces and countries on fire, floods, all of it. The people who didn't believe in climate change were almost as pathetic as the climate activists, who thought posting all-caps information online was going to fix anything. Human beings were not worth saving and, as far as Pain was concerned, everyone should stop trying.

The convoy guy was totally predictable. In some ways, he reminded Pain of the climate freaks. He seriously believed he was making a difference with his flags and his F$%# the PM stickers. Sure, buddy. It reminded Pain of something he'd seen in someone's yard last Christmas. A giant inflatable Santa "peeing" yellow lights onto a neon sign that spelled out the prime minister's last name. Pain had laughed out loud every time he saw it. Someone had paid good money for that display. Hilarious. He imagined all the parents trying to explain it to their kids: "Well, Santa hates the prime minister. And then Christ was born and he probably hated him, too."

Then there was the guy in the bomber jacket who was as nervous as an alligator in a boot factory. He was dressed like a Charlottesville Nazi, but maybe that was a coincidence? Pain would go online and try to find out. They had all promised to give up their phones and laptops before bed. Ha. Not a goddamned chance he was doing that.

The religious lady had missed most of the afternoon activities. Maybe she was praying or something? He'd met her type before. They were the people who came to the detention centre and tried to "connect with the kids." The most damaged kids clung onto those do-gooders like the parents they never had. Made no difference. Those kids were still just as fucked in the head. They needed a hug *and* to be kept away from matches.

Pain had to admit that the obviously rich guy was a bit cool. He was all smiley and did not GAF, like, at all. He was just happy, probably because he was so rich. If Pain ever got a lot of cash, he was probably going to be the other kind of wealthy person. The rich asshole.

Finally, there was the cougar. What was her name? Madison? Something like that. Pain couldn't figure out why she was there. She also didn't GAF, but in a different way than the wealthy guy. She was about thirty and hardcore addicted to her phone. She couldn't even turn it off when David, the organizer, asked her to. She just put it in her purse and looked at it in there.

So far the introductions had been bad. The icebreakers went nowhere. But the worst part was all the walking. If there was one thing Pain hated, it was going for walks, and these people were obsessed with it. He'd hated walking when he was in the juvenile detention centre and he hated it here. No one had told him that this program was basically just going for walks. They were long-ass trudge-fests, too. He was going to have to come up with an excuse to get out of them. It would be one thing if they were allowed to fight about their beliefs while they walked, but they were supposed to stick to neutral topics. Grass and trees and shit.

Whatever.

His plan for the week was to slowly stop co-operating. He'd participate at the beginning, then start missing events. You had to work up to being a total asshole. He was good at that. Once people got tired of dealing with him,

CONTEMPLATION OF A CRIME

they'd stop pressuring him to take part. If he was difficult enough, they'd be happy when he didn't show up. He could stay in his cabin and mess with people online using the tablet no one knew he had.

But at dinner, the whole feel of the place had shifted. At first, he didn't realize what was happening.

When he walked into the lodge after personal time, which had been irritating because he could hardly get on the internet, he noticed that the cozy factor had been dialled up to an eleven. The lights were turned low, but not too low. There were candles all around and soft music playing. And there was some kind of a smell. Fragrance might be a better word. Apple spice? Pumpkin spice? Whatever it was, it made his whole body relax. It reminded him of when his mother was getting ready to entertain the other wine moms and pulled out all the stops to show off her self-care skills.

Everyone was already there, waiting for dinner, and they had these dopey expressions on their faces, like they were really enjoying themselves.

The big buffet table had been decorated with little bundles of green leafy stuff and branches. And there were new helpers.

A woman who was maybe thirty was arranging bread baskets at the end of the table. When they first got to the island, he'd seen a teenaged housekeeper driving the golf cart. But this helper was way more . . . serious. She had perfect skin and long, braided black hair and an in-charge vibe, like she knew what she was doing and like she knew what everyone else should be doing, too. Like you could ask her how to build an Ikea kitchen and she'd do it for you in about an hour.

Pain saw another new guy in the dining room and his mouth practically fell open. Had they decided to hire only models? The guy was tall and movie star handsome. Dark hair, dark skin, and graceful. The new man looked like he had it all under control, like nothing would ever dare get out of control around him.

Pain prided himself on being aggressively asexual. Not because he was asexual, exactly, but because he hated everyone so equally that he didn't want to get attracted to anyone, ever. But these two might change that.

The model theory disappeared when a tubby guy brought chafing dishes out of the kitchen and set them on the warmers. The guy had a round face and wore a denim chore coat, and looked like someone who'd never gone past a

McDonald's without stopping in for McNuggets. But he also gave off a happy vibe, like he'd be fun at a party or on a road trip. Not that Pain went on road trips or to social events of any kind, if he could help it.

Pain stood to the side and watched the three new people speak to each other briefly. Then they spread out and started moving around the room. To his shock, the handsome guy came straight for him. Looking at him, smiling. Holy shit. The guy's teeth were . . . great. Just really great. For the first time, Pain wished he'd done what his parents wanted and gotten his teeth straightened.

"Sir," said the man, who had what sounded like a British accent.

Pain nodded, feeling ugly.

"Dinner is ready. Please help yourself at your convenience. A table has been set for you in the dining room."

Pain looked around the guy and into the big, empty dining room.

"Sure," he said.

He didn't move. The man didn't move.

"Do you, uh, work here?" asked Pain. The question was so stupid Pain wanted to die. Of course the guy fucking worked here. He'd just set the table and invited Pain to eat.

"I do. My name is Gavin. I'll be at your service during your time here on Side Island."

"Oh," said Pain. "Okay."

Then, on numb legs, he went to serve himself.

How was he supposed to troll the hell out of everyone for the next five days if he was struck dumb by the waiter?

HELEN THORPE

After dinner, which was simple but excellent, Helen stood with the others, listening to David. He was saying that they were going for a walk and then would play some games that had been specially designed for the course.

The feel of the group had shifted, and Helen knew it was because Murray, Gavin, and Nigel had brought that special butler sparkle to the proceedings. The three butlers had attended to the guests like they were all VIPs. They'd magicked the dinner dishes away, offered everyone dessert, and without letting on that they were doing it, ushered everyone into the front foyer at the appointed hour.

It was all done so graciously that even the grumpiest guests forgot to complain. Helen loved what exceptional service could do for a gathering. Even a tricky situation could be made enjoyable when people were attended to with care and intuition.

She was reminded of a talk she'd listened to by Rick Hanson, the neuropsychologist and author. He'd said that in order for people to feel cared about, they needed five things: to feel included, seen and understood, appreciated, genuinely liked, and loved. Her teachers at the North American Butler Academy, all accomplished butlers of long service, had taught something along the same lines. Butlers might not show clients love, exactly, but they made people feel cared about and important.

Helen suspected that having the butlers present would make all the difference here. Even the young man whom David had described as an internet troll seemed softer, somehow. He kept staring from Gavin to Murray as though he couldn't decide which one he liked best.

That was a typical response to the pair, who were truly a joy to behold.

"As you can see, it's dark outside, so I have headlamps here for each of you. If you prefer, you can use a flashlight," said David.

SUSAN JUBY

The assembled group wore their various forms of outerwear. Pain, the boy, came out of his Gavin-and-Murray-induced reverie. "Dude, we just had a walk," he complained. "I'm full from dinner. I'd rather just stay in here."

"I hear you," said David. "But this is the schedule that has been laid out."

"So we're all just supposed to follow orders?" said Wayne. "Where have we heard that before?"

At this, some of the others recoiled.

"No offence," said Wayne. "But there's a lot of people who just follow orders and it's always bullshit. Vaccines. Lockdowns. Loss of personal liberties."

"Give it a rest already," said Yana Heppler.

The meanly satisfied look was back on Pain's face as he listened to the exchange.

"You shouldn't just do what people tell you," continued Wayne. "Learn to think for yourselves."

"Don't forget to do your own research," muttered Yana.

"The moon is nearly full," said Mr. Levine. "It should be beautiful tonight."

"Thanks, Mister Rogers," said Wayne.

Mr. Levine looked down at himself. He was, in fact, wearing a cardigan, like Mister Rogers. Only his was a hand-knit linen blend Ralph Lauren cardigan that had cost over two thousand dollars. It was perfect lodge wear. Helen knew the make and cost because she'd removed the tag before she packed it for him.

"You're welcome," he said, cheerfully. Then he pulled his own headlamp out of his jacket pocket. He was just like Mister Rogers if Mister Rogers wore a forty-five-hundred-dollar raincoat by the Loro Piana brothers for his evening constitutional. His daughter had bought the coat for him, explaining that it was "total gorpcore." Helen didn't know what that meant and she suspected her boss didn't, either, but his daughter bought Mr. Levine many of his clothes and he wore them all with pride.

His good humour seemed to settle everyone else and they accepted their headlamps and headed out for their second walk.

"Walking after dinner helps keep the weight off," said Madison. "But it's going to be hell on my Uggs."

CONTEMPLATION OF A CRIME

David led and the others followed. Helen drew up the rear. The sight of the bobbing lights moving through the dark reminded her of coal miners heading to and from work. Helen had read a bit about the area and learned that Nanaimo and the surrounding islands were dotted with decommissioned coal mines. Saysutshun Island, the marine park that was part of the traditional territory of the Snuneymuxw people, which lay between Side Island and the Nanaimo Harbour, had been, among other things, the site of a coal mine. Protection Island had been mined for "black gold" and so had tiny Guide Island, which lay across from Side Island. The area directly under Nanaimo was said to be honeycombed with mine shafts, some of them two stories deep.

Helen had been struck by the image of all those humans burrowing into the earth. Heading to their shifts in the pre-dawn dark, working underground, and perhaps coming home in the dark. It must have been a hard life.

As the group walked, aided by their modern headlamps, the darkness seemed to ease and Helen began to notice all the lights on the water and across the way: lights dotted the decks of the freighters anchored in the Georgia Strait, the houses on Protection Island, and the hillsides of the area south of Nanaimo twinkled.

Her breath sounded in her ears and she was glad to be walking. Glad to be breathing.

One of the walkers ahead stopped and waited for her.

Mr. Levine.

"Sir," she said, before catching herself. "I mean, Mr. Bruin."

His smile flashed in the dark.

"How are we doing?" he asked.

"We're doing well, sir."

He fell into step beside her.

"Do you need anything?" she asked, when she was sure no one was close enough to hear them.

"Absolutely not. I'm just grateful you're here. And I see that we've been joined by some of your colleagues."

"That's right, sir. I went to butler college with Gavin and Murray. You may recall Nigel from the time I spent working for the Hightowers."

"Of course. How wonderful they could come to help out. I can tell David appreciates it. He looks more relaxed already. Don't you think?"

"Yes," she agreed. David certainly looked more confident now that he was not facing the prospect of running the course with almost no staff.

"I'm sorry you've been put to work," said Mr. Levine.

"Happy to help, sir."

"Quite a group, aren't we?"

"Yes, sir," she said.

"I really think important connections can be made here. Unusual alliances. That sort of thing. Tremendous opportunities for personal growth."

"Yes," she said. She thought of her unfathomably wealthy boss unprotected on this island full of people who disliked each other. People riven with resentments and obsessed with grievances. During her time working for the Levines, she'd observed that ultra-high-net-worth people generally insulated themselves from regular people, as well as from the everyday annoyances that regular people had to contend with, such as waiting and hearing the opinions of others. Some of them avoided almost all public settings, and they certainly didn't go on retreat with people from the general public, at least not without some sort of security present. All Mr. Levine/Scooter Bruin had to shield him from the resentment of the lower classes was Helen. Former nun, current butler. And a person with very little security training.

"Are you quite comfortable?" she asked, hoping that he would pick up her meaning.

"Helen, I am finding this experience liberating. I believe I have lost sight of how sheltered our existence has become. I know Bunny would feel the same way. We may need to begin going around in disguise. We will be like Siddhartha leaving his father's compound."

Ah, so he *did* see the similarity. It was exposure to the realities of age, infirmity, poverty, and monasticism that had set Buddha on the path to enlightenment. Perhaps being exposed to the fractured nature of contemporary society would do the same for Mr. Levine. And perhaps not. Probably not, if she was being entirely honest.

"Would it be strange if I sang?" asked Mr. Levine. "Perhaps a little something from *La Traviata*? 'Sempre Libera' would be perfect."

CONTEMPLATION OF A CRIME

Helen knew that Mr. Levine, a soprano, had classical voice training. She had no idea how the others would react, but she thought it would wake everyone up and add a certain flair to the walk.

And so, bringing up the rear of the group, he began to sing in a soaring voice. Every single headlamp swung toward him. Helen thought she had never loved her employer quite so much as she did in that moment. Her earlier, unsettled feeling was gone. Almost.

MADISON CROFT

So far, Close Encounters for Global Healing had been a trip, in the hallucinogenic sense. The trip reached its peak when the car dealer guy started screeching opera on the night walk. Maybe screeching was the wrong word. His singing was loud but impressive. Madison didn't have the words to describe how it made her feel. He'd sung at the top of his voice for a long time, and once she got over the shock and really listened, she thought that his song had done something to her. Opened her up. Made her feel things she hadn't felt in a long time or maybe ever.

Madison had graduated from high school with a C average and gone straight into retail. Sometimes she felt bad that she wasn't better educated. Maybe she should ask the AI app she'd installed on her phone to tell her some facts about opera. She could ask the guy what song he'd been singing. Show an interest in something other than shopping and celebrities and gossip about her friends.

Madison knew she'd been invited to Close Encounters because of her lack of education and interest in, like, world events. She was famous for being shallow. But so what? Her friends were the same. What did getting bent out of shape about things you couldn't control get you? Stress, that's what.

She'd rather be shallow than live like the other people at the retreat. Most of them looked like they gargled with vinegar every morning. But she could tell something was happening for them, too, even though they had only been on Side Island for a few hours.

Everyone seemed to be in a good mood when they returned from the walk, what with the moon and the opera singing and the dark and the trees. The staff, who were incredible, gave everyone tea and warm milk and handed out fresh-baked cookies.

The facilitator, David, was explaining the game they were supposed to play.

"You have each been given a notebook. I'm going to ask you to write down one thing you appreciate or admire about each participant."

The opera singer put up his hand. "Shall we include you, David?"

David smiled. He was nice-looking, but not Madison's type. Not enough tattoos.

"If you like, Mr. Bruin."

The pinch-faced internet kid put up his hand. "What if I don't like anything about anyone?"

"If you think hard, I'm sure you'll find there is something to appreciate about everyone," said David.

"Except maybe Pain," said the grey-haired woman, who seemed almost as bitter as the kid. She pronounced his name like the windowpane. Like it hurt.

"It's pronounced *Pan*," corrected David. Madison thought it was nuts that they'd invited someone whose name was spelled "Pain" even if it wasn't pronounced that way.

David continued. "You don't need to go into detail. Maybe you like someone's . . ." His eyes flicked over to the opera guy. "Sweater. Or the way they wear their hair."

There were a lot of sighs, but nobody got too nasty because they were so relaxed from eating cookies near the fireplace. If Madison had known the encounter was going to be this nice, she wouldn't have initially turned down the invitation, which had come from her sister, a counsellor who worried that Madison was "wasting her talents."

Madison didn't have any talents. At least, not important ones. And that was fine with her. Madison didn't want to stand out, she didn't want to take the lead, she didn't want to be in charge. She just wanted to live her life as comfortably as possible. Like a pet.

She could tell that a bunch of these people were the opposite. They were practically dying to tell other people things they didn't want to hear. No thanks.

David stood in front of them. "All I ask is that you keep polarizing material out of your description."

He used the word *polarizing* a lot, along with *positional*. Madison supposed it would be polarizing to mention that Tom Aucielo, the short guy in Dockers and polo shirt, looked exactly like one of those guys who went around chanting "Jews will not replace us." Ugh.

Maybe she just thought that because the angry kid, Pain, had gone around earlier and whispered to everyone that Tom was a white nationalist. Madison wasn't sure what a white nationalist was. She thought it was like being a Nazi. She could tell from the way everyone else kept their distance from him that it must be pretty bad.

It would be positional to mention that "Pain, pronounced Pan" was obviously a total incel who was probably going to spend his whole life in a basement. He'd told everyone in a super-positional way that his mother was a "dumb bitch" for naming him after bread. Madison wasn't judging anyone, at least not much, but she sort of agreed with the kid about his mother's judgment.

The less said about the anti-government convoy guy the better. He seemed angry and also like he wanted everyone to like him. He reminded her of a nice dog that someone has almost ruined by chaining it in the yard, or something. His name was Wayne Krupke, and when she looked over at his paper, he had the handwriting of a grade-schooler. So did she, for that matter.

Yana Heppler, the climate change activist, was one of those people who you just know owns a kayak, a Tilley hat, and will criticize every little thing you do, like stepping on some moss, or whatever. She had that up-yours grey hair with no style and pants with no shape and looked like she hadn't smiled since she was born, which was probably sometime around 1907. Madison planned to give her a lot of space. Every time David left the room, Yana and Wayne got into it about freedom and trucks and climate change and other things that Madison didn't care about.

Opera man was obviously rich. He seemed much more confident than everyone else, and not just because he sang opera without being asked. Maybe it was because he was the only one who seemed to be having fun. He was pretty old and not handsome in a normal way, but he had this energy and a shine to him that Madison liked. She bet he'd be fun in the sack. Hooking up with him would be something to do. Also, on the first walk, he'd mentioned to the possible Nazi that he owned a few Toyota dealerships. That caught her attention. Toyotas were good cars, and she was tired of driving junk heaps because she spent all her money on clothes. His name was Scooter Bruin, which was another mark in his favour, as far as she was concerned. It would be cool to go back and tell her girlfriends that she pulled a rich dude named Scooter at the Global Healing workshop. Ha!

Tom Aucielo, the alleged racist, had this habit of using his own name all the time, like he was worried people would forget it. She wanted to tell him that's

CONTEMPLATION OF A CRIME

not how it was done. The idea was to say other people's names a bunch of times, so they would think you cared about them. That was the first rule of customer service.

"If any of you need someone to speak to, please just ask," said Hetty, the lady who was there to support them "emotionally and spiritually."

"I'm here for anyone who would like to talk."

"Exactly," said David.

"I have a question," asked the rich opera singer. "Do we have any didgeridoos? Or singing bowls?"

"Afraid not," said David.

"Too bad. I love a didgeridoo in the morning."

He was weirdly hot for an old guy, but he was also just plain weird.

Using the least possible effort, Madison wrote down a nice thing or two about everyone. The Nazi, Tom, had a "tidy haircut" (true!), Pain had an "interesting name," Yana cared a lot (ha!), Wayne looked strong, Hetty seemed calm, Scooter Bruin had a good singing voice (and was rich and could get her a deal on a Toyota! Yes!!).

Then she went back to thinking. About herself.

What were *her* qualities? She was easy to get along with. She knew about pop culture, or at least some parts of it. She wasn't a crazed fan of any fantasy novels or video games, but she knew which reality stars were dating each other, what pop stars were actually singing about addiction and their exes, and who all the biggest creators on TikTok and YouTube were.

She looked over at Hetty, the religious lady, who was probably writing down incredibly thoughtful and, like, perceptive things about other people. Hetty looked like she cared about and was invested in everyone and everything, and yet she also seemed very chill. It was a wild combination. Whenever Hetty looked at Madison, Madison felt seen, somehow. Like slightly more alive or colourful or something. Hetty was a true leader. You could just tell.

Madison was basically the opposite because she didn't like making the "hard call," as her old manager at The Sharpest Knife in the Drawer used to say. Madison had worked at the knife and scissor specialty store at the mall for years. At one point, Head Office had tried to promote her. They'd sent in the regional manager to give her an interview to see if she was "management material" because her store manager was leaving. The two managers had taken her to the food court for her interview and given her a long list of truly dumb questions. There was the ever-popular What are your strengths? followed by What are your weaknesses? She'd given the standard answers: I am hard-working and organized and good with people. My weakness is that I try too hard and care too much (Ha!).

She did not add that she was practically psychic when it came to knowing who was about to steal something. She didn't mention that she was so massively in debt from her shopping habit that she would never turn down a shift and would work any and all hours they gave her. She also didn't mention that she didn't care about knives, scissors, customers, or the store. At all.

Then her store manager, Jimmy, a friendly but no-nonsense and clearheaded twenty-two-year-old, threw her a curveball.

"Can you make the hard call, Madison?" he asked.

The regional manager, a hard-bodied, sun-damaged woman who looked like she ate knives for breakfast, scissors for lunch, and Apache helicopters for dinner, stared at him, because the question wasn't on the approved list from Corporate.

"We can't ask that," she'd hissed. "All candidates need to be asked the same questions. It has to be fair. HR rules."

Madison ignored her and answered the question. "No," she said. "I can't." The real answer was that she *wouldn't*, but her answer was close enough.

Jimmy had nodded. "I know," he said. "It's okay. If you *could* make the hard call, you'd end up being a manager like me, and you do not want that. More hours. More responsibility. Same shitty money."

Now the blade-faced regional manager was gaping at him.

"Working retail is bad, Madison. You know that as well as I do. But being a manager in retail is much, much worse."

Then Jimmy, who had a friendly, freckled face, unpinned his name tag and left it on the pink table in the food court of the mall where the interview was being conducted.

Madison never saw him again. She heard that he'd applied to university. She only stayed at Sharpest Knife for another few weeks. In that time, no one mentioned management track to her again. They brought some unsuspecting nineteen-year-old to take Jimmy's place.

She was glad Jimmy had asked her that question. Once a person knows that they can't make hard calls, everything gets easier somehow.

CONTEMPLATION OF A CRIME

But when Madison looked at Hetty, she wondered if maybe she was wrong about what she could and couldn't do. Maybe she *could* do hard things, like the influencers preached. She decided to watch Hetty like she would watch one of the shoplifters at work. She wanted to see what made her tick, even if she had no plans to change herself.

With that decided, Madison got up to go to the bathroom so she could look at her phone in peace. She couldn't believe David was going to collect all of their devices before bed so they could all be "fully present." Ugh. Nightmare. While she was in the bathroom, she was going to look up Scooter Bruin. Get a little background under her belt for when it was time to put on her charm offensive. Too bad she didn't know Hetty's last name or she would look her up, too.

Hmmm. Maybe her AI could help if she took a photo. Surreptitiously, Madison used her phone to take a picture of Scooter and then of Hetty. No one noticed. Madison hadn't spent her entire career watching (but not doing anything about) shoplifters for nothing.

She saw that David was putting up what looked like a big poster with a bunch of human figures on it. He was writing down their names under each silhouette. Oh god. That must be the game.

Maybe if she stayed in the bathroom long enough, she could miss it.

CLOSE ENCOUNTERS FOR GLOBAL HEALING
DAY-TWO SCHEDULE

6:00 a.m.	Rise and personal contemplation
6:45 a.m.	Morning walk
7:30 a.m.	Breakfast
8:30 a.m.	Lodge for activities (sharing special skill)
10:30 a.m.	Break for personal time
11:30 a.m.	Late-morning walk
12:30 p.m.	Picnic lunch
1:30 p.m.	Free time
3:00 p.m.	Group exercises
6:00 p.m.	Dinner
7:00 p.m.	Evening walk
7:30 p.m.	Chanting and drumming
9:00 p.m.	Rest

WAYNE KRUPKE

DAY TWO

Wayne was not naturally an early riser. Nor was he naturally sneaky. Those things made his 5:00 a.m. mission extra shitty.

He tried to tiptoe as he walked down the carpeted stairs and into the foyer of the lodge. If David, the workshop leader, who was the only person staying in the lodge, found him wandering around in the semi-dark, Wayne planned to say he liked to get up early. If David asked why he wasn't doing "personal contemplation" in his room, he would explain that he'd come in looking for coffee.

Wayne had placed a recording device just outside David's room, where it would be completely useless. Wayne wasn't a goddamned cat burglar from *Ocean's Eleven*, so he wasn't going to creep into David's room while he was sleeping to plant a bug. David was obviously a pacifist, but even he might get a little rancid if he found Wayne in his room.

When he reached the foyer he took a breath. There was no sign of staff. The night before there had been helpers everywhere. The people working at Side Island Lodge seemed like pros. Like they saw everything and were everywhere at all times. He'd been freaked out when the tall, good-looking guy asked him if he wanted a cup of coffee about one second after the thought entered his brain that he could go for a cup of coffee. The staff at Side Island might seem like ninjas, but at least they didn't start work before dawn.

The great room and the kitchen were still dark, which was a relief. He placed the recording devices all around the room, sticking them under the furniture. Then he put bugs under the main tables in the dining room.

Wayne had no idea what the people who told him to bug the place were trying to find out. It wasn't like Close Encounters for Global Healing kept their mission on the down-low. The organizers couldn't shut up about how they wanted to bring people together. The "encounter" was supposed to help people with what his lawyer had referred to as "problematic world views" move past "entrenched belief systems" and "leave anger behind in the search for greater understanding." In other words, it was the usual fuzzy-headed lib bullshit.

The only thing the recordings were going to reveal was that no one here liked each other. Whoever was listening in would mostly get an earful of people bitching about having to go for multiple walks a day.

Was it illegal to plant listening devices? Probably. That would be just his luck.

On the website and their social media, Close Encounters really pushed their success stories. There were video testimonials from loony lefties who said they'd learned to appreciate the "old school" values of hardcore conservatives. Dudes who hated gay people started liking them and even getting a bit in touch with their inner gayness. Women who hated men learned to like at least one man, and so on. In one video, a lesbo and a massive MMA fighter talked about how they became best buddies after he discovered he was dealing with "complex trauma." Whatever that was. Basically, the whole program was five days of putting cats and dogs together to see what happened and hoping for some heartwarming stuff. It was probably just a scam to get donations.

Relieved of the recording devices, Wayne silently let himself out of the lodge and started walking back to his cabin. He felt about a hundred pounds lighter now that the job was done. He wasn't a guy who hung on to tension the way some people did.

David, the retreat leader, for example, seemed like a person who took things to heart. That made sense. He was probably worried that someone would go apeshit on someone else during the encounter and there would be a murder and everyone would say *I told you that people can't get along*. David was nice enough and Wayne felt a little bad for him. In Wayne's experience, crybaby commie-types acted terrible online, but a lot of them were basically okay in person.

Potato was waiting for him at his cabin. She must have been worried be-

CONTEMPLATION OF A CRIME

cause she'd chewed off one of the chair legs and ripped apart a pillow. Damn. He'd have to pay for that.

Without turning on any lights, he got right back into bed, Potato beside him. Personal contemplation could take a hike. So could the morning walk they were supposed to do at 6:45.

HELEN THORPE

elen had moved from her assigned cabin into the Poolside Cottage so she could spend more time with the butlers. When she headed for the lodge at 5:40 a.m., the others were also up. Gavin was doing his complicated stretching routine and Murray had prepared coffee. Nigel was outside with all four dogs on their rhinestone leashes. They weren't allowed off the leash unless they were in a fenced area because their owner, Ms. Cartier Hightower, had not bothered to train them. They were sweetly silly and reminded Helen of hairy goldfish with legs.

When she reached the lodge, she thought she saw someone disappearing around the corner, heading away from her.

Maybe one of the participants had gone looking for coffee, not realizing that each cabin had a machine and ground coffee to make their own?

She stepped inside, where everything was silent and dark, except for soft lights that illuminated the foyer so any guests who wandered downstairs wouldn't trip over anything.

Helen peeked into the dining room and toward the kitchen, which was also dark.

She made her way into the great room and turned on a few of the lamps. Should she start a fire? No. That wasn't her job. It was tempting to fall back into tidying and organizing, which she'd always found soothing. But she was going to be on holiday soon and she needed to get used to doing less.

She settled for straightening some magazines on the coffee tables.

What she really wanted to do was check whether her employer needed anything. She couldn't be seen going to his cabin, but it wouldn't hurt for her to walk *past* his cabin. Just in case.

Helen left the lodge and turned right toward Hearthside Cabin. The faint dawn light revealed overcast skies and concrete-coloured ocean to her right. Fine mist seemed to come from all directions. Helen, snug in her waterproof coat,

CONTEMPLATION OF A CRIME

reflected that she loved traditional West Coast weather. After a drought that had persisted through the summer and into the fall, they needed at least a week of steady rain. Failing that, mist and drizzle would have to do. She imagined the rigid green leaves of the arbutus trees and the mosses and grasses all breathing in the moisture.

When Helen was nearly at Mr. Levine's cabin, she turned to stare out at the water. Seagulls called and wheeled around the hovering sky. A bald eagle flapped once and then soared over the treetops.

For the first time in a while, her battered equilibrium felt intact.

Since her time with the influencers many months before, her sense of internal balance had become much more precarious. She'd tried meditating for longer and more often, but Helen had a demanding job. A two- or three-month retreat, which was what she was fairly sure she needed, was out of the question. Perhaps next year. In the meantime, she tried to be aware of anicca, anatta, and dukkha, or impermanence, no-self, and suffering or dissatisfaction. The trio were known as the three markers of existence and were tricky but fundamental concepts in Buddhism. Paying attention to them was said to be a path to enlightenment.

Helen was wryly aware that she used elements of her job as a butler to shield herself from the three markers. She organized everything carefully so life would feel ordered and calm and stable. She worked tirelessly and enjoyed making her employers and those around her happy and comfortable. She sometimes avoided the more difficult parts of life and clung to the more pleasant parts. But try as she might, nothing stayed organized, no one stayed happy, events unfolded in ways that felt personal. Dissatisfaction and suffering arose despite her best efforts. Avoiding the awareness of anicca, anatta, and dukkha is what humans do. It was sometimes disappointing to find that she was so much like other people.

Make friends with the discomfort, she told herself, as she looked at Hearthside Cabin, where Mr. Levine was probably meditating or doing Tai Chi. Imagining him doing that made her feel happy, and she turned and headed back toward the lodge, having reassured herself that all was well with her boss, at least for now.

The rain grew heavier and she pulled on her hood. She didn't hear the person who appeared behind her until he spoke and made her jump.

"Sorry," said David. "I didn't mean to startle you."

He was dressed in a sopping wet T-shirt and wore shorts over running tights. His Hokas were muddy and a headlamp dangled from his hand.

"Good run?" she asked, feeling happy and strangely comforted to see him. He ran every day when he visited his parents' house. Sometimes twice a day.

"Oh yeah. Great trails here." He pulled the sopping T-shirt away from his lean body. "I should have started getting ready for the day earlier, but—" He stopped and looked around to make sure they were alone. "I wanted to go and see my dad first. Make sure this is all going okay for him. I was just at his cabin."

"Oh good," said Helen. "I was just out for a walk. I think I'll turn around now."

They began walking back to the lodge together.

"He said he's 'having a gas.'" David shook his head. "A gas. Classic my dad." Helen was pleased though not surprised to hear it.

"I'm not so sure about the other participants. Things seem a little more, uh, tense at this point than when I took the course. Maybe I'm just feeling sensitive because I'm in charge and I want it to go well. There's just this feeling . . ."

He was right. There *was* a strange energy to the group. Helen hoped that having the butlers join would even things out. Make everyone feel more supported. Maybe everyone simply needed more time together so the course could work its magic.

Still, she couldn't help but wonder why they hadn't chosen participants who were a little less *extreme*. Wouldn't choosing people from Canada's main political parties have presented enough ideological divides to bridge?

"I think today's activities are going to help people get to know one another better," David said. "We all need to see each other as fellow humans who just want to be safe and happy."

"Get everyone to let go of the stories they tell about each other," said Helen. "See who they are beyond those superficial narratives."

"Exactly. I don't suppose you have any Buddhist advice to give me?" he asked.

Helen considered for a moment. "Have your parents ever spoken to you about the concept of anatta?" she asked.

"No. Should they?"

"I was just thinking about it. It's the idea that there is no permanent self. We

CONTEMPLATION OF A CRIME

are all products of our experiences and our circumstances. The practice teaches that the self is always in flux. Trying to protect and build a solid, unchangeable sense of self leads to suffering. Having very strong and inflexible beliefs is a form of self-protection."

David looked at her. "That's interesting," he said. "I think I get the connection."

"Nothing stays the same. Not people and not the world," she said. "Nothing."

They had reached the front door of the lodge.

"I don't know how to feel about that," he said.

"Almost no one does."

"On that note," David said, "I'm heading in for a dip. You and your friends are welcome to join me anytime. I go in every morning between six and six fifteen. I stay in for twenty minutes or so."

"I appreciate the invitation," said Helen.

"One more thing," he said, as she turned toward the heavy front door.

"Yes?"

"I'm wondering whether we could deploy your spiritual skills today?"

Helen didn't know what that meant. She'd already agreed to act as a spiritual support for anyone who needed it.

"What I mean is that I'd like you to help me facilitate a couple of the exercises. Don't worry. It will be quite straightforward. I'm thinking you could just sort of . . . guide people. Or manage them, I guess I mean."

"Oh?" she said.

"You seem to have a gift for helping people to not hate each other. Don't worry. I'll give you all the information you'll need. I think these exercises will come very naturally to you. I mean, you taught at the Yatra Institute for years. Those courses must have gotten quite intense sometimes."

The only classes Helen ever taught at the retreat centre where she worked before becoming a butler were meditation classes. Participants often had strong feelings about themselves or others, but they'd all wanted to be there. They'd all been spiritually seeking. And most importantly, they'd all taken vows of silence that they mostly maintained when they weren't having interviews with Helen.

This group of people was anything but silent.

"Don't worry," said David. "I'll make sure you can still keep an eye on Dad."

"Thank you," said Helen. But she didn't really mean it. Dukkha. Dissatisfaction. That's what she was experiencing. The feeling only increased when she walked into the great room and found Tom Aucielo standing near the coffee bar with orange juice running down his face and onto the floor while Madison Croft glared at him.

Then Madison burst into tears and rushed past Helen and out of the lodge.

It was barely six in the morning and there had already been an assault.

Cloudy with an eighty percent chance of dukkha.

YANA HEPPLER

Yana stared at the sky, then at the trees, and finally into the middle distance. She was outside her cabin, which was old and modest enough that it didn't offend her sensibilities. On Side Island—an oasis of intact old-growth forest among the endlessly logged landscapes of Vancouver Island and the Gulf and Discovery Islands—it was easy to forget the dire state of the world. But she couldn't allow herself to do that. The planet was counting on her.

Yana was only sixty-two, but in the time she'd been alive, it felt as though everything had changed. Where the forests were once cacophonous with birdsong and the buzzing of insects, there was now silence. At least, mostly silence. Sure, the sun still rose and set each day, but the shifting seasons seemed to be operated by a glitchy gearshift. One minute spring was softly emerging from winter, and then, in a matter of hours, it felt like full summer, two months ahead of schedule. Rainstorms, snowstorms, droughts. Cold snaps and heat waves, and atmospheric rivers. Weather systems that came out of nowhere and then just stayed, freezing everything, frying everything, drowning everything. End-of-time winds, act-of-god hail. Anything was possible now. Anything. How she hated it.

She'd promised herself at least a thousand times that she would stop grieving over the loss of stable and predictable weather patterns. Those were gone forever. It made no sense to be so consumed by sadness over what was gone that she couldn't enjoy what was left, including those increasingly rare occasions when the weather was seasonally appropriate, as it was today. But she couldn't seem to stop. She didn't want to stop. To do so would feel irresponsible. A cataclysm was upon them all and she wouldn't look away.

Yana's therapist had suggested that right below the surface of Yana's increasingly dire depression was a raging inferno of fury at every person who had allowed greed and short-term thinking to ruin the entire planet.

Well, duh, thought Yana. She was no longer the optimistic, energetic hippy girl who wanted to save the planet. She wasn't a girl, she wasn't eager, and she definitely wasn't optimistic. She was sick to death of everyone and everything. And, if she was being perfectly honest, she'd always been a little melancholic.

Only one other person in her online climate grief group knew what she was going to do. The two of them had come up with a plan that scared her and excited her in equal measure. It was a plan that would stop her from ever having to attend another meeting with officials who would lie to her face about their commitment to addressing the climate crisis. It was a plan that would bring attention to the crisis and show everyone just how she felt about their apathy.

She would be on the razor's edge for the next four days about whether to execute or not. What a word! *Execute*. It gave her shivers. Would the course help her find a way to cope without taking drastic action? Or would the wrong person say the wrong damn thing and she'd go for it? Yana was too depressed to know which outcome was most likely, and she almost didn't care.

If she "executed," the world would *have* to pay attention, at least for a news cycle or two.

MADISON CROFT

After Madison threw her juice at Tom, the religious lady asked her to come outside to speak with her while the rest of them went on the first morning walk. They sat side by side in Adirondack chairs on the flat sandstone expanse in front of the lodge.

"Do you want to talk about what happened?" asked Hetty. Madison didn't usually appreciate plain, unstylish people, but there was something about this woman that fascinated her, so much so that she had worn all navy today because that's what Hetty had worn the day before and Madison thought it looked sharp.

"Do I have to?" asked Madison. "It's so early. And it's kind of freezing out here." Why had she agreed to take part in this stupid workshop? She wasn't political. She wasn't anything.

"No," said Hetty. "Of course not. I'm Hetty, by the way." Apparently she thought Madison might have missed or forgotten her name. Hardly. When David informed the group the night before that Hetty would be supporting them if they needed to talk, Madison had felt instant relief, though she didn't know why. Also, a career in retail had made Madison very good at remembering names.

"I'm Madison." She wiped at her tears and hoped her makeup was still okay. She'd have to go to the bathroom and check. Must be nice to be like Hetty and not wear any. Not that Hetty seemed like someone who cried very often.

"I don't usually cry," said Madison. "So this is embarrassing."

"It's physically uncomfortable to cry when you're not used to it," said Hetty. "At least, in my experience."

"Have you got a lot of experience? With crying, I mean?"

"When I first began my practice, there were many tears. An ocean of tears."

"What kind of practice?"

"My faith practice."

Madison didn't ask what the faith practice was because she was worried that Hetty would tell her.

"Did it bother people? You crying so much, I mean?"

"No. Not at all. I eventually got interested in why I was crying and why I found it so unpleasant."

"I hate that it wrecks my makeup and makes me look like crap."

Hetty, who'd been staring out at the ocean, turned her head and smiled. "Maybe it just makes you look like someone who has been crying."

For some reason, that made Madison want to start weeping all over again.

"I'm probably going to get kicked out of this course," she said. "For throwing my juice on that Tom guy. I think there's a rule about getting physical. Or being abusive."

Hetty didn't answer.

"I don't know why I went off like that. It's not like what he said to me was all that bad. He just caught me at a bad moment or something."

Again, the woman sitting beside her just waited. Listened.

"You know how when you aren't expecting someone to . . . come at you, it's worse? When you're not prepared for incoming fire and someone gets you right where it hurts? That's what happened."

As she spoke, Madison realized that she was being more honest and open with this stranger than she'd been with anyone in a very long time. Madison was a laugher. A shopper. A gossiper. She didn't talk about things that mattered because . . . she didn't want to.

"I came in to have a coffee and a juice before the walk, and I was looking good, you know? I got up at like the Pleistocene era to get ready. Hair, makeup, the whole deal. I was kind of looking forward to the day. I even did the personal contemplation, or at least tried to." Madison didn't mention that that part of her morning had taken all of about one minute because she was trying to get her flat iron to work properly.

Hetty nodded, like she'd gone through the exact same thing many times, even though Madison was sure the woman beside her had never once gotten up early to do her makeup. Hetty had very nice skin, unlike Madison, who thought she looked like an old rice noodle when she skipped the foundation, contouring, and bronzer.

CONTEMPLATION OF A CRIME

"So I'm just at the coffee station, minding my business before the walk. Feeling good, like I said. Getting a juice and a coffee. Then Captain Racism comes up to me and says, 'You ever think you're trying too hard?'" Madison felt her lips tremble as she repeated Tom's words.

"Out of nowhere, he said that to me. Before I even had my coffee! And then he said, 'Have you tried just being yourself?'" Outrage at the injustice of it made Madison's nose begin to run again. At the same time, speaking the words out loud made her wonder why she'd gotten so upset. Why *had* his comments felt like getting punched in the throat?

"I didn't even think about it. I just threw my orange juice in his face." She snuck a look at Hetty, who was watching her with an expression Madison couldn't read. Was it pity? She did *not* want to be pitied.

"Don't look at me like I'm so pathetic."

"I don't think you're pathetic. It's clear that those words were extremely hurtful to you."

Tears were now running freely down Madison's face again and she couldn't stop them. Goddamn. Her makeup was definitely going to be ruined. And her face would be puffy all day, no matter how many walks she went on. *Nice work, asshole.*

"But why?" she said. "I don't understand why what that little nothing said to me was so upsetting. It's not like he matters."

"Everyone matters," said Hetty, which was so true it made Madison cry even harder. When she slowed down, the religious lady spoke again. "May I suggest something?"

"No," said Madison, realizing that she sounded like she was thirteen. "Okay, fine."

"Close your eyes," said Hetty. "If you feel comfortable."

"Is this some religious thing?" said Madison, but she closed her eyes.

"Take a few slow breaths."

Madison did as she was told.

"Now tell me what you feel," said Hetty.

"I feel terrible. And stupid," said Madison. "It was dumb to put on makeup and do my hair to go for a walk on a rainy island first thing in the morning."

"That's what you're *thinking*. I want to know how your body feels."

"Awful," said Madison.

"Okay. But *where* does it feel bad? What is the sensation? *Where* is the sensation?"

"My face hurts," said Madison, just realizing it was true.

"Is the feeling hot or cold? Is there pressure? Is the sensation moving around or is it steady?" asked Hetty.

Madison, eyes still squeezed shut, paid attention to her body for what felt like the first time. She realized it wasn't just a single feeling. There were many sensations and they were happening from her head to her toes.

She'd never really realized what it actually felt like to be upset.

"It's hot. And tight. A black pressure in the back of my neck. Like someone is pushing on it." Madison held a hand up as though to check for injuries.

"What else do you feel?"

"Are you hypnotizing me or something?" asked Madison, cracking one eye open.

Hetty laughed softly. Kindly. "No."

"There's a lump in my stomach. It's grey. The burning in my face has moved to the top of my shoulder. It's like orangey-red."

As Hetty asked questions, Madison realized that the experiences in her body were coming and going. What she thought was a burning sensation in her face was in fact a feeling of cold. The pit in her stomach was there for only a second or two. Whole parts of her body felt completely fine. And as she tracked the sensations and reported them to Hetty, Madison grew calmer. Her breath settled and her chest expanded.

"I think I'm okay," she said, finally, and opened her eyes. The morning, still so early, seemed brighter. And she *was* fine. Absolutely and completely fine. "What kind of crazy voodoo was *that*?" she asked, staring at Hetty. Why did her entire body and mind feel so different?

"You just did a body scan. It's a Vipassana technique."

"Vi-what?"

"It's a meditation practice that focuses on tracking what's happening. Not thoughts, but sensations."

"Crazy," said Madison. She let out a long breath. "I have a strong sensation that my ass is wet. I better dry off before the walk."

Madison got up and wiped her hands on her rear end. Her jeans were soaked through. Normally, she would hate that. But she felt empty in a good way, like absolutely everything was fine.

"I still don't understand why I freaked out in there and I also don't understand what just happened. Is that normal?"

"Yes," said Hetty, who was still sitting and seemed completely unperturbed by her own wet seat or about Madison acting like a mental case. Because obviously Madison was unstable if she was crying and throwing orange juice and losing it because some weird little racist guy with an abnormally deep voice said she tried too hard and then she paid attention to her body for a minute or two and felt as calm as a blank wall.

Then again, maybe it made sense to lose it when someone as terrible as Tom saw something real about you. That thought landed deep inside Madison. Instead of going off like a bomb, it sat there like the truth. She felt badly for herself, but not *about* herself.

As she walked into the lodge, one of the staff members, the tall, handsome guy with the fantastic hair and perfect features, silently handed over a towel.

"Thank you," she said, feeling the warmth of the terry cloth and taking in the warm, rich scent of the lodge.

"Coffee? Cream and sugar?" he said, and handed her the hot mug.

She stared at it in wonder, then at him. He was gorgeous. He was helpful. He remembered what she took in her coffee.

What the hell was going on at this lodge? Whatever it was, Madison loved it. Maybe when the course was over, she'd refuse to leave.

With that happy thought in her head, she walked back to her cabin to redo her hair and makeup before the walk. She was a woman who tried too hard and nobody could make her stop.

DAVID LEWISTON

He was torn between annoyance and gratitude when Nelly made her first call of the day. He had many things he wanted to ask her but he wished she would wait until she was in a quiet place before calling. With the hubbub of the wedding all around her, it was hard to have a proper conversation.

"David?" she said when he picked up. Nelly Bean, the founder of Close Encounters, had a distinctive voice that was both gravelly and nasal. It reminded him of a duck's quack and he found it quite charming. In the background, David could hear people laughing and talking. It sounded like the wedding party was out for an early breakfast. Nelly's wedding seemed to be one of those that was going to take place over many days. He was happy for her. David thought she was someone whose happiness was well worth celebrating.

She had a tendency to talk on the phone in public. It was a habit he found in poor taste, which in turn made him feel badly about his own elitism toward people who'd had fewer opportunities than he had.

"There you are," she said. "Give me a second." There was a rustling noise and then she came back. Now he heard traffic in the background. "Sorry. It was really noisy in there. How's it going this morning?"

"One of the guests has already thrown something at another guest."

"Something heavy?" she asked. "Any injuries?"

"No. Just an orange juice. But we haven't even started doing the more sensitive work. It worries me that it's not even eight in the morning and there has already been an assault."

"Did you debrief with the people involved?" she asked.

"Hetty spoke to one of them. I'm going to speak to the other when he finishes breakfast."

"Remind me who Hetty is?"

"She's filling in for Sophie, who had to cancel. Hetty came with the guest who is filling in for Morgan Bailey." Morgan was the wealthy guest who'd cancelled at

CONTEMPLATION OF A CRIME

the last minute. "It was just our good luck that Hetty has this background in, uh, spiritual practice and counselling."

A siren sounded behind Nelly.

"Oh, wow. That is fortunate."

"I mentioned it last night."

"Right. Sorry. We have a lot going on here. I didn't realize a wedding with only fifty people could get this complicated. It's my fault for planning so many activities. Thank you again for filling in for me."

"Of course," he said. "It's an honour to do this work." Then he hesitated. "So, they're kind of a tough group."

"That's how they ended up at Close Encounters," said Nelly, breezily.

"I don't remember my group being as—"

"Oh, but you were. I mean, not *you* specifically. You're a pacifist. Very easy to deal with. But when you attended Close Encounters, there were certainly issues between the participants."

"I don't remember any drinks being thrown. Or people sniping at each other this much."

"Not every issue or incident gets discussed with the whole group. Look, when I met Fields, she hated me. She thought I was a . . . what was it she called me? A medical fascist." Nelly laughed softly. She didn't smoke, but she had the laugh of someone who smoked three packs a day. "And now look at us. Getting hitched."

Someone spoke to Nelly, but David couldn't make out what the person said.

"Okay. I'll be done in a minute," Nelly said.

"Is that Fields?" he asked.

"No. She's inside. It was my mom telling me that it's rude to spend the breakfast party my aunt arranged for us standing on the sidewalk and talking on the phone."

"Your mom's not wrong. Don't worry about us. Just focus on your wedding," he said. "We'll be fine." His lack of confidence must have been evident in his voice.

"It always seems impossible in the beginning. By the end of today you'll see real change. Genuine connections," said Nelly.

"I hope so," said David. "We've got a long ways to go."

81

"It's important, world-changing work. I told you that Praxis wants to expand the program. To take Close Encounters into the US and maybe into Europe and beyond. They're talking about offering it to every community that wants it. Isn't that amazing?"

"It is," he said, and he meant it. After all, he could attest to the power of the program. It had renewed his faith in people and the possibility of peace and change.

"The Praxis people are going to do a detailed analysis after the course is over. To make sure the program is as effective as we say it is. If there are no major problems, we'll be fine. The growth plan they have proposed is predicated on the idea that there have been no scandals. No serious incidents between participants. Orange juice *doesn't* count. It's so exciting that Praxis thinks my little program could be useful in some of the most challenging social and political situations in the world."

On the street another siren sounded, grew almost unbearably loud, and then faded again.

"I'm coming," Nelly said to someone. "I've got to go. Thank you again, David. I know you have this handled. This encounter will be amazing. Increase the peace, my friend."

"I will. We will," he said. "And best wishes to you both."

"You too."

Then she was gone.

David looked out the office window at the soft grey sky, the expanse of ocean, the rust-coloured freighter in the distance. He would not be the reason Close Encounters failed to meet its potential. He would not be the reason the program wasn't expanded around the world. This group of people who didn't care for each other were going to find common cause if it killed him.

David reached for an antacid. His mother, a doctor, would be worried if she knew his stomach was giving him trouble again. He hoped he wasn't getting another ulcer. He'd gotten them off and on since law school.

"Baby, you take everything straight to your gut," his mother often said. When he was in university, she made him go to a gastroenterologist to make sure he didn't have IBD or Crohn's. The gastro had found nothing wrong with him, and his mother and his therapist had prescribed meditation and yoga. Those things had helped, when he did them. But in times of stress, he often

CONTEMPLATION OF A CRIME

stopped doing the things that helped him cope. In law school, he'd developed ulcers and had not told his parents about it.

He felt now the way he had back then. As though his guts were on fire. Tums were not going to cut it.

As soon as he finished facilitating the encounter, he planned to take a break. Really do some solid self-care to deal with the stress.

Meanwhile, he'd take Nelly's assurances to heart. He'd deliver the course material and trust in the process. Helping people connect on a personal level was slow, frustrating work, but he believed in the mission. The world could not afford to stay as divided as it was right now.

He took a deep breath and felt glad again that his father was here. He'd gotten lucky in the parent department.

David got up, stretched, and made sure the grimace was gone from his face. Then he walked out of the office and straight into another scene of assault.

Tom Aucielo was bent over, holding his stomach near the open space at the entrance to the great room.

David stopped dead.

"You hit me! Right in the stomach! Are you some kind of psycho?" Tom was half yelling at David's father, who stared aghast at the wan, younger man.

"I—" his father said.

David stopped the word *Dad* before it could come out of his mouth.

DAVID LEWISTON

"**W**hat's ha—" David began.

"He hit me," interrupted Tom Aucielo, who still had his hands on his knees. "He freaking hit me!"

"I didn't mean to," said Benedict, who, to David's knowledge, had never in his life hit anyone before. He was a lover, not a fighter, as David's mother said more often than her children would have liked. Plus, he was a Buddhist.

"Looked like you meant to," said Pain, who stood watching. Wayne was on one side of the young internet troll and Yana was on the other.

"I was showing a move," said Benedict.

"A move?" said David, who suspected what was coming.

"The tinikling and wing chun hybrid I've been learning. It's called tinikling-chun."

"What kind of bullshit foreign-ass nonsense is that?" demanded Tom, through gasps.

"There it is," said Yana, who was watching. "Never lose an opportunity to be a racist a-hole."

"It wasn't *that* racist," said Pain.

"Pretty rude, though," said Wayne, who David suspected knew a thing or two about the subject of being rude.

"Tinikling is Philippine bamboo-stick dancing." David's father looked down at his feet, where there was a noticeable absence of sticks. "Wing chun is a close-quarters form of kung fu. It uses the immovable elbow theory. Focuses on the centre line. Very powerful stuff. Tremendous fun, when combined with stick dancing. Said to be ideal for staving off dementia. A German came up with the idea of combining the two."

"Yeah, those Germans had some great ideas," said Pain. "Right, Tom?"

"Oh good! We have *two* bigots here," muttered Yana. "Lucky, lucky us."

"Anyone ever tell you that you're a real ray of sunshine?" said Wayne to Yana.

CONTEMPLATION OF A CRIME

"As I was demonstrating a move, an unexpected sideways feint unfortunately caught Mr. Aucielo in the stomach."

"Tom is always slinking around," said Yana. "Same with Convoy Ken over here." She jerked a thumb at Wayne, who looked surprised at being called out. "They both deserve to get an elbow from someone doing . . . whatever that was."

"Tiniklingchun," said David's father, patiently. To emphasize, he jigged back and forth with his feet, his elbows up and at the ready before one of his arms shot out sideways in a powerful strike that explained why Tom had yet to entirely recover his breath.

Oh, Dad, thought David. His father never let a new health or mind–body technique pass him by. And come to think of it, the strangest ones had all been created by Germans.

"Sounds like an accident," he said. He felt sorry for Tom. Being a white nationalist must be miserable. Always so angry and unhappy. Tom had taken an orange juice to the face and an unexpected blow to the stomach, and there were hours to go before noon.

"Are there any bamboo poles on-site?" asked Benedict. "It might be fun as a group exercise."

"No forms of fighting are permitted in the course," said David, allowing a slight smile onto his face.

"We don't need to do the wing chun. We can stick, if you'll excuse the pun, with the tinikling! It's named after the way tikling birds avoid rice traps. Quite delightful. Athletic and very peaceful."

Tom had finally straightened up. "Bullshit it's peaceful. You're lucky I didn't react. Because I could have."

"Really?" drawled Yana. "How terrifying."

Madison came out of the washroom and joined the group. She hid a smile at Yana's words.

"Ha," said Pain. "This whole course is improving. There should be boxing next. Get some real global healing happening."

David felt another bolt of pain in his stomach. And a piercing pain in his head. He wanted to tell them all to be quiet. Tell his father to cool it. But that wouldn't help create any personal, never mind global, healing. And he loved that his father was such an enthusiastic person. Mostly.

At this rate they were never going to get to the exercises so the healing connections could be formed.

"Let's sit down to start our work," he said.

Tom limped off to slump onto a couch, hands held theatrically to his stomach. Yana stomped after him, glaring at the back of Tom's head. Wayne trudged, and Pain seemed to slither. Madison drifted to her seat and stared moodily out at the ocean. Something seemed different about her.

Benedict snuck a wink at David and then followed after the others, walking with his distinctively jaunty toe-to-heel stride.

That left Helen, who'd appeared in the doorway. Behind her were the butler friends who'd come to help out. They looked so orderly. So calm. Like none of them had ever encountered a situation they couldn't make better. One of *them* should be facilitating this course.

Helen stepped forward. "Can I help with anything?"

"Can we meet after this session?" he said. "In my office."

"Of course," she said.

Somehow, those two words made him feel calmer than he had all day. If Helen was here, things would be okay.

TOM AUCIELO

The encounter wasn't going well, which wasn't a big surprise. Nothing ever went well for Tom. He sat as far away as he could from Madison the Drink Thrower and Scooter the Sucker Puncher. His motto, well, one of his mottos, was that you could assault him once but never twice. He did a little quick math. That left quite a few people here who could take a shot at him.

He snuck a look at Madison. Why had he said what he had to her? Why make a comment about her makeup and her try-hard vibe? He knew better than to say something like that to any woman.

He'd just noticed her full face of makeup and the too-tight clothes and hair all perfect and thought it was probably a lot of work looking like that all the time. He figured that if he was going to take a break from being hunted while he was at the course, maybe she would want to take a break from looking perfect.

She caught him looking at her and glared, and he couldn't help noticing that she was already looking a little less put together. She had her hair tied back. Less makeup.

She was actually a good-looking girl. Not that he'd say that to her and risk getting a karate chop to the nuts. She was clearly super sensitive and couldn't take any advice or a compliment or a joke or anything.

After he'd given her the feedback (wasn't that why they were here?), she'd thrown her juice at him and burst into tears while everyone watched.

He'd said sorry, but she was already gone.

Fucking embarrassing and not his fault. How were they all going to bond if they couldn't say honest things to each other?

Oh well. He could give a shit about the bonding, although it bothered him that everyone seemed to think he was a huge racist, even though he wasn't, not really.

He probably *could* have done a better job of washing the juice off his face. He hadn't wanted to go back to his cabin in case he missed out on breakfast.

Now he felt like a piece of flypaper. Every speck of dust in the place was landing on him and sticking.

They were sitting in the comfortable furniture in a semicircle around David, who was writing on his rolling whiteboard.

Something made Tom look toward the kitchen. An older woman he hadn't seen before stood in the doorway. She had long grey hair and she was staring straight at him.

She was different from the other helpers, who all seemed a little too . . . fancy for the job. Too confident. Too polished. Even the pudgy guy was too . . . something. Most of the staff here reminded Tom, who had lived in the Compound long enough to become highly attuned to power dynamics and hierarchies, of a pride of lions looking after a bunch of house cats. Not threatening, exactly, but there was something out of whack about them versus the participants.

This grey-haired lady didn't look too classy for the place. The opposite, actually. Worse, he thought he might have seen her before. His heart started jackhammering. Was she a wife or girlfriend of one of the other guys from the Compound? The ones who hadn't been in abusive relationships with awful dickheads had been some hard-faced, stone-hearted bitches. Was she one of those? Here to take him out for the reward? Naw. He was being paranoid.

He nodded at her. Maybe if she moved or waved or something, he'd remember where he'd seen her before.

But she didn't nod. She just watched him in a way that made his skin crawl.

He felt an overpowering urge to run. But they'd taken the goddamned dock away! How was he supposed to get off the island?

"Okay," said David, from the front of the room. "Let's talk about what we're good at."

Tom decided that the best defence was to stay in the middle of the action. The scary kitchen lady wasn't about to eliminate him while he was participating in the workshop.

"Like our jobs?" he said, keeping one eye on the grey-haired lady, who was still glaring at him from the doorway. Then one of the other helpers, the dark-haired woman, asked her something and the lady finally went back into the kitchen.

CONTEMPLATION OF A CRIME

"Not necessarily," said David. "What activities do you enjoy and feel competent at?"

Yana leaned her head back to look at the dark beams overhead. "God spare us," she said.

"What makes you say that?" asked David.

Yana gave a big, dramatic sigh. "These activities feel like they were engineered by a corporate consultant somewhere. When are we going to get real with each other?"

Wayne muttered something and Yana turned to him. "What did you just say, chickpea? You have a comment? Why don't you share it with the group?"

Wayne stared right back. "You sure complain a lot."

"I complain?" said Yana, her voice rising. "*I* complain? You have done nothing but complain since we got here."

"He really doesn't," said Madison. "He mostly just complains when we have to walk."

"Hey, thanks," said Wayne to Madison.

"I hate it, too," said Pain. "Walking is an old person activity."

"There is definitely too much walking," said Wayne. "It's brutal." He looked at Yana again. "And you can stop calling me chickpea. I don't call you names."

"Miss your truck and its horn?" said Yana. "Wish you could drive it around here? Ruin the landscape with your noise and your pollution?"

"I'll start," said the rich guy, smiling as though the squabbling wasn't happening. Maybe there was a lot of bickering at Toyota dealerships.

"We know, man," said Tom. "You're good at the weird stick dance where you do the little punches." Tom's hand went to the place on his torso where the old guy had hit him.

"I enjoy my work as a business owner. I like working with Toyota, the company, and I feel great about our product lineup. Our dealerships have phenomenal staff. And I love my role in giving our customers a quality experience," said Scooter Bruin.

"Save it for the infomercial," said Pain.

Tom had to agree. He couldn't even afford bus fare so he didn't like the rich guy rubbing it in about how he was a successful business owner.

"But that's not the skill I wanted to talk about," said the guy.

89

"Okay," said David. "Go ahead."

"I'm objectively excellent at choosing colours."

"What do you mean?" asked Madison, starting to pay attention. "Like, what kind of colours?"

"Any kind. On ties. Shirts. Walls. Furniture. You name it. I know what colours look good on people. What colours go well together."

"Really?" said Madison. "Now that you mention it, you do look pretty well put together."

The Toyota dealer beamed. "It's my colour choices. Makes a huge difference."

"Did you take a course to learn that?" asked Yana, who also seemed interested, in spite of her hatred for all things that were not climate change mitigation.

"Nope. I think it's hereditary. My dad was the same. Good colour sense runs in our family. Through the male line, mostly." He looked at David and smiled.

"I thought you just looked good because you're rich and you have nice shit," said Wayne.

"That helps. But even without that, I still know how to use colours."

"You can come shopping with me anytime," said Madison. "I've got a bold colour sense, but I overshoot the mark sometimes. And I get stuck on some combinations. They're just slightly off. Drives me crazy."

As they all talked to Scooter about his unexpected skill, Tom understood the point of the exercise. It felt good to see people being proud of themselves. It felt good to see them shine. Even he felt it.

"That's cool," said Wayne. "If I ever get married, maybe you could help me out with my suit."

"Be happy to," said Scooter.

"Pain?" asked David, moving on. "What are you good at?"

"I'm pretty good in GTA."

"Is that a video game?" asked Yana.

Tom and Wayne nodded. "Yeah," said Tom.

"I'm the shits," said Wayne. "And I play all the time."

"And I can make almost anyone mad," said Pain.

"No kidding," said Wayne. And then he did an amazing thing. He ruffled Pain's greasy hair. And Pain just smirked, but with less malice than usual. The friendliness of the gesture floored Tom. When was the last time anyone had touched *him* like he wasn't radioactive?

CONTEMPLATION OF A CRIME

"Anything else?" asked David. "Something you were born with other than the ability to play video games and make people mad?"

Pain lifted and lowered his shoulders, like he was warming up for a fight. "I can draw pigs."

"Pardon?" said David.

"Pigs!" said Scooter, understanding right away. "I love pigs. Someone get him a piece of paper."

Tom found himself cringing internally, worried that the kid would draw a portrait of someone in the group.

But after David handed over a piece of blank paper and a Sharpie, they all watched as Pain quickly sketched out a pig and held up the drawing for everyone to see.

"Damn," said Wayne. "Some pig." That made everyone look at him in surprise.

"What? I watched *Babe*. I know about *Charlotte's Web*. Anyway, that's fuckin' good, man."

"It has a lot of personality," said Madison.

Yana nodded.

"Can you draw chickens?" asked Tom, suddenly very curious.

"Yeah. I can do a few farm animals." Pain, the meanest troll on the internet, got busy and drew a cow, a chicken, and a sheep. None were as good as his pig, but they were all competent, at least to Tom's inexpert eye.

"I would not have guessed that for you," said Madison.

The exercise continued and everybody got more encouraging about each other's small skills. It was nice, although Tom was worried about what he'd do when it was his turn. Having a deep voice didn't seem like a skill, exactly.

Madison said she was good at remembering the common names of plants and their Latin names. "Can you do the daisy," said Scooter, leaning forward.

"Kingdom: *Plantae*, Phylum: *Magnoliophyta*, Class: *Magnoliopsida*, Subclass: *Asteridae*, Order: *Asterales*, Family: *Asteraceae*, Genus: *Bellis*, Subject: *Bellis perennis L.* Common names: English daisy, European daisy, lawn daisy. There are many, many, many kinds of daisies."

"Wonderful," said Scooter. "That is remarkable."

"I know," said Madison, simply. "It really is. And I'm not even a good gardener."

"How can you do that?" asked Wayne. He also seemed genuinely interested.

"I have no idea. I took a horticulture class after high school, before I realized that I was too lazy to be a landscaper. Turns out I have a freakish memory for plant names."

"Can you remember everything like that?" asked Wayne.

"I have a good memory, but it's the plant names that really stick."

"Maybe you're an auti," said Pain.

"A what?"

"Auti," he muttered. "On the internet, it's what people with autism call themselves."

"Is it an insult?" asked Wayne.

"No. It's what they call themselves," said Pain. "It's not a bad thing there."

"I don't think I'm on the spectrum," said Madison. "I just have this one thing. And I can sing 'Mull of Kintyre.'"

"What's that?" asked Wayne.

"A song," said Yana. "By Paul McCartney and Wings." She asked Madison to sing it, which she did, looking shy and pleased.

Tom thought it sounded nice, but he'd been listening to drunk racists singing songs about a white motherland and blaring racist hardcore music for a year and a half, so his musical standards had been destroyed.

"Can you sing other stuff?" asked Pain.

"Nope. Just that one song."

Wayne said he was very good at backing up in complicated situations and at parallel parking. "I can get in there if there's only a few inches to spare. Even without a backup camera."

"I've always admired people who can do that," said Scooter.

"I need at least five car lengths before I will attempt parallel parking," said Madison.

"My dad drove a transport truck. Food. He had to manoeuvre the trailer in these tight parking lots and back it into loading bays. I must have picked it up from him."

"I bet you're popular when you go camping. A lot of couples can't get their trailers backed into the campsite without getting into a screaming match," said Madison.

Wayne grinned.

CONTEMPLATION OF A CRIME

"Yana," said David. "What's your special skill?"

They all waited. The energy had changed. No one made a nasty comment to fill the quiet.

"It's pointless," she said.

"All our skills are pointless. Well, not Wayne's," said Tom, who couldn't quite believe how much he was enjoying this. He'd even forgotten that all the dust in the lodge was sticking to him and his stomach was sore.

"Mine's also pointless since almost everyone has a backup camera now. Side sensors, too."

"I'm strong," Yana said, finally.

"Emotionally? Physically?" asked Scooter, leaning forward.

"Definitely not emotionally," said Yana. "Strong arms and strong legs. Strong back."

"I would not have guessed that," said Pain.

It was true. Yana didn't look powerful. She had to be way over fifty. Maybe she was over sixty.

"Can you give us a demo? Like, pick up something heavy?" asked Pain.

Yana looked around and her gaze settled on a boulder that lay just outside the window on the expanse of sandstone that ran down to the sea.

"No way," said Wayne. "That's gotta be two hundred pounds."

"I don't want you to hurt yourself," said David.

"I can move it," said Yana.

And with that, she marched out the double doors at the front of the great room and everyone else followed her.

"I don't think—" said David again as Yana approached the rock.

"Don't worry," she said. "I'll put it back when I'm done." She squatted and gripped the rock where a natural edge offered a purchase.

"Use your knees!" called Tom, who identified as not strong.

With a low grunt of effort, Yana moved the rock a couple of inches to the side.

"The fuck, dude," said Wayne, sounding awed. "That's crazy."

"Could you do that?" Pain asked Wayne.

"I'll put it back," said Yana. Then she went to the other side and moved the boulder back into place. It looked like she was wrestling the rock, and winning.

"It must be lighter than it looks. Let me try," said Wayne. He bent down and pushed. The rock didn't budge. Nor did it move when Tom and Scooter tried to move it. By the time they were finished, Yana was beaming.

"How old are you?" asked Wayne, whose admiration seemed total.

"Sixty-two," said Yana.

"What do you weigh?"

"One forty-five."

"What do you eat?"

She laughed. "I'm vegan. I eat a lot of nuts and beans."

"That's *rad*," said Wayne.

They went back into the lodge. This was by far the best exercise they'd done. But he was worried that he'd ruin it, so he turned his attention to Hetty, who had that calm way about her he'd seen in other spiritual people.

"Let me guess," he said. "You can run a mile in under a minute?"

Hetty laughed. "No. Afraid not."

"So what's your special skill?" asked Madison.

"You seem like you might have a lot of cool skills," said Wayne, and Tom thought that was probably right.

"I'm profoundly average."

"No," said Yana. "Definitely not."

"You're really good to talk to," said Madison.

"You make me feel like things are, I don't know, okay, I guess," said Wayne.

"I think you seem fair," Tom found himself saying. "You don't judge."

Pain was staring hard at Hetty. "You're one of the few people I've met who is not completely full of shit."

"So true!" said Scooter. "Here's to Hetty being not full of shit."

Everyone joined in. "Hetty! Not full of shit!"

Finally, David looked at Tom.

"And you, Tom? What is your special skill?"

Tom wished the ground would open up.

"I, uh . . ." he said.

"Dude, it's your voice," said Wayne.

Then David, who of all of them probably had the biggest reason to hate him, added, "It's a great voice. Reminds me of Barry White. Or Patrick Stewart."

"Morgan Freeman!" said Pain.

CONTEMPLATION OF A CRIME

Were they messing with him because they thought he wouldn't want his voice compared to a Black man's voice?

Before he could think it through, he started telling them all about Gracie and how he'd entered the Compound. How he wasn't actually a hardcore racist.

"You were living with white nationalists who were planning a racially motivated terrorist attack," said Yana. "How can you justify that?"

Tom bobbed his head, nervously. "I know. I mean, I don't know. It just . . . got away from me." Christ, that sounded inadequate. Because it was inadequate. He chanced a look at David. And then he went for it, even though he was afraid. "I'm sorry," he said. "I really am."

David looked taken aback. Not angry, but like he wasn't sure he wanted Tom's apology, which made Tom feel even worse. Damn. Now he was sort of crying. He really couldn't get anything right today.

"Oh man," said Wayne. Tom, who had his eyes closed, felt Wayne's hand pat his shoulder. Which made him cry harder. Silent, furious crying. Why did Wayne have to keep patting everyone?

"Let him have his feelings," said someone. Yana?

The group sat quietly while Tom, who was more surprised than any of them at his breakdown, sat on the couch and wept into his hands.

Another hand patted his other shoulder, and he realized it was Scooter Bruin, who had a real fatherly vibe to him, unlike Tom's own father, whose vibe was more "guy in search of the nearest punching bag."

"Let him have his feelings," repeated Scooter. "Very important."

And so they did. They sat with him while he cried like a goddamned baby who probably didn't deserve their sympathy, a fact that just made him cry harder.

When he was finished, they were all still there waiting for him. Waiting with him.

"My skill," he said, after he rubbed his arm over his face, "is that I never show how I feel. I'm basically a black box, emotionally speaking."

At that, they all cracked up and Tom felt better than he had since he could remember.

HELEN THORPE

David and the four butlers gathered in the office after the guests went back to their cabins for personal time.

"That was a bit wild," he said. "I don't even know what to say."

The butlers, including Helen, nodded. But they were butlers, so they didn't make a big deal about the events of the morning.

"Do you feel like everything is on track? You've taken the course before," asked Helen.

David sighed. "The year I took part, it felt as though the participants were more on board, if you know what I mean. They had major differences, but they were committed to being here together. Bridging their differences. This group seems less motivated. I mean, things are happening for them. Between them. But I don't entirely understand what's going on. I wonder why some of them are here, in spite of the breakthrough that just happened."

"Who chooses the participants?" asked Helen.

David opened a folder in front of him. "The applications are all in here. I've read them. There's nothing about who nominated each person. I assume that Close Encounters has a network of referrers. But that's all I know. I took over after this year's guests had been chosen. There's been so much upheaval with so many staff leaving and participant cancellations that I haven't had a chance to consider that."

A buzzing noise sounded. Nigel looked down at his watch and smiled. A Pekingese was asleep on his lap, another on Murray's lap, and a third underneath Gavin's chair. Helen held Hannibal in her arms. He was snoring softly.

The butlers were too polite to ask who he was texting, but Nigel volunteered when he realized they were all looking at him. "It's Cartier. I just sent her a few pictures of the lambs."

"You're very friendly with your employer," said Murray.

CONTEMPLATION OF A CRIME

Nigel cleared his throat. "I've been working with her since before butler school."

"Right," said Gavin. His eyes were searching and Nigel was not one to prevaricate.

"I'm . . . I mean, we're . . . uh . . ."

"You're what?" said Gavin.

"We're friends."

Helen wondered if that's all Nigel and his employer were to each other but it wasn't her place to ask. Cartier Hightower had been a lonely young woman when Helen had worked for her. Helen didn't begrudge her any happiness.

"Are you dating your employer, Nigel?" asked Murray, shock making her Irish accent more pronounced.

Nigel blushed bright pink. "A gentleman never says."

"Is she going to hire another butler?" asked Gavin, reasonably.

Nigel nodded, still blushing like a new rose. "I don't know. We haven't discussed that."

Murray patted his arm. "Best of luck," she said. "In your latest assignment."

"We didn't mean for it to happen. We haven't told Mr. Hightower."

Small wonder, thought Helen, remembering Cartier's permanently outraged father.

"He's been so sick."

Mr. Hightower was a shipping magnate. Finding out that his daughter was in a relationship with her butler would not likely improve his temperament.

"Well," said David. "I'm pleased for you, Nigel. But I hope you don't mind if we continue discussing the course." He pointed to the small pile of cellphones on the table. "We've made some progress. All of the devices have been collected. So now it's just us and the clients. The program has been laid out carefully, but I'll warn you that the exercises can get quite intense from this point on. Helen, do you feel prepared for what might come up?"

Helen did not feel prepared. All she could do was stay present for what unfolded. Try to support the participants. Try to facilitate understanding. She was a butler. A former nun. But she was not a trained counsellor or, as seemed to be needed here, a psychiatric nurse.

"I will do my best to help."

"At least without the ferry, people can't leave every time they get upset," said Nigel, stroking the ears of the Peke on his lap.

"That's either a good thing or another ingredient in the pressure cooker," said David. He looked at Helen again.

"Thank you again for bringing your friends to help. I know you are all meant to be on holiday together. I am so grateful to all of you. My dad is, too."

"Of course," said Helen.

"Do you think he's doing okay?" asked David.

"I think he's enjoying himself," she said. "He's very proud of you for doing this important work."

The worried expression left David's face. "Thanks, Helen. I am starting to understand why my folks think you hang the moon." He looked from Murray to Gavin to Nigel. "If I didn't give away most of my trust fund every year, I would probably hire a butler, too. You folks are very pleasant to have around."

The four butlers nodded while the Pekingese snored.

Everything was going to be fine.

CLOSE ENCOUNTERS FOR GLOBAL HEALING
DAY-THREE SCHEDULE

6:00 a.m.	Rise and personal contemplation
6:45 a.m.	Morning walk
7:30 a.m.	Breakfast
8:30 a.m.	Trust-building activities
10:30 a.m.	Break for personal time
11:30 a.m.	Late-morning walk
12:30 p.m.	Picnic lunch on beach
1:30 p.m.	Free time
3:00 p.m.	Group exercises
6:00 p.m.	Dinner
7:00 p.m.	Evening walk
7:30 p.m.	Chanting and drumming
9:00 p.m.	Rest

HELEN THORPE

DAY THREE

On the third day, Helen woke early, even by the standards of a former monastic. She meditated in her room for forty-five minutes, put on her rain jacket, and let herself out of the cottage just after five. No one else was up. The plan was to stop in and check to see if Mr. Levine needed anything, then go back to have coffee with the butlers before the day began.

Outside, the dark settled around her like black silk, but she didn't turn on her headlamp. The lack of light seemed to deepen the quiet.

No light leaked around the blinds in Mr. Levine's cabin, which was a surprise. Normally, he would have been up doing his Tai Chi at this hour. He and Dr. Levine maintained a disciplined morning schedule of exercise and spiritual pursuits. Unless they were sick, they were always up by 5:00 a.m. It was now 5:10.

Helen climbed the stairs to the front door of the cabin after making sure no one was around to see her. She knocked quietly.

No answer.

She knocked again. Still no answer. The silent pre-dawn dark no longer felt so comforting.

Mr. Levine must have gone on a walk or a run with David. They were probably out on the trails with their headlamps. That must be it. But some alarm system in Helen had begun to ring.

She climbed down the stairs, and after hesitating, headed for the lodge.

Helen began to hurry and then reminded herself to slow down. She took a deep breath of salt air. Heard the waves slap against the shore. The lodge came into view, illuminated by small exterior spotlights.

Helen climbed the heavy wood stairs up one of the back entrances of the lodge, and she let herself into the quiet hallway on the fourth floor. She was

CONTEMPLATION OF A CRIME

on the side of the building farthest from the front entrance. The hallway was carpeted and well lit, but utterly still and quiet. David was staying in the Observatory, which was a small suite with a living room and a desk.

Helen knocked on his door.

No answering noises inside.

She knocked again.

Nothing.

No problem. David and his father were out for a run. Of course they were. She checked her watch—five thirty in the morning.

She stared at the door for a long moment and felt the wrongness of the moment. She couldn't describe or quantify what she sensed, but that didn't make the feeling any less real.

David and his father were pretending not to know each other during the course. Why would they risk being seen together?

Answer: they wouldn't.

Helen slowed her breath. She felt the same way she had when she'd received the call letting her know that her mother was ill and the same way she had when she learned that her former employer and benefactor, Edna Todd, had died suddenly. Loss. She felt it in her body.

Don't panic. Check downstairs. They might be having coffee together.

Eliminate the most obvious explanations before leaping to conclusions.

Helen made her way down the short hallway and the two flights of stairs until she reached the entryway and the main floor, where the lights were turned low.

Helen poked her head into the great room. The only illumination came from a lamp on the empty coffee station. The walls of windows showed that it was still pitch-black outside.

Helen closed her eyes.

She should check the kitchen.

She went to the nearest set of swinging doors that led into the kitchen, knocked, and then pushed through.

The kitchen was empty and the only illumination came from a small light over the stove.

Where *were* they?

Finally Helen remembered her cellphone, which she had not handed over. She texted David first.

—Hello David. I hope you had a good sleep. Please let me know if I can be
of assistance to you or your father this morning.

David was a millennial, and for all his sensitivity, he kept his cellphone close
and didn't miss messages.

There was no reply. The message sat there, not showing as delivered or read.

He must be out of range. This explanation rose like a bubble in her mind,
just like the others she'd come up with since she'd discovered Mr. Levine wasn't
in his cabin. She decided to try texting him next.

—Hello sir,
Do you need anything this morning?

She was his butler, so she kept things formal, even though he tended to
speak to her as though she were a member of the family.

His message didn't show as delivered or read either. Had it gone through?
Her phone said it had been sent.

Where on earth *were* they? Why did they feel so alarmingly *absent*?

Helen, heart thudding unpleasantly, went back out to the great room. She
stood by the large windows that looked out in the direction of Mr. Levine's
cabin. She imagined seeing two bobbing headlamps coming toward the lodge
through the darkness and the relief that would flood her body. But there were
no headlamps visible. All she could see was her own image reflected back from
the black windows.

Stillness came naturally to Helen, but in this moment, it brought her no
peace. Instead, she felt perched at the edge of a void, barely maintaining her
balance.

When her phone vibrated in her hand, she nearly dropped it. She'd been
clutching it so hard her hand hurt.

Finally!

She tapped the screen and saw a message notification from WhatsApp.
Why were they responding on the encrypted program?

Maybe it was a wrong number? People had sent her WhatsApp messages by
mistake before.

But maybe . . .

CONTEMPLATION OF A CRIME

Her phone vibrated again, and she saw that there were multiple messages from Mr. Levine's number.

She clicked on the first one.

—Helen, I don't want to alarm you, but it appears that we have been kidnapped.

Helen's stomach seemed to cave in on itself and she nearly dropped her phone. Next message:

—Dad, we have definitely been kidnapped. Please just give Helen the instructions.

—Yes, dear one. That seems to be the case.

They were clearly dictating their messages into a voice-activated recorder. Some of the messages made no sense and they arrived in a tumble.

Helen struggled to compute what she was reading.

—Okay okay Helen, it's Benedict. Please be calm. Oh, what am I saying of course you'll be calm it's who you

—Hurry up. Get to the point

—Helen. It's David. The kidnapper is in a hurry. They have some requests.

Helen waited. The message bubbles kept arriving. One after another. Her phone was on vibrate and it was beginning to feel like she was holding on to one of those personal head massagers.

She looked away from her phone screen and stared wildly around. Was this real?

Helen felt her feet on the floor, her breath moving in and out. It was real. This was happening.

—We can't talk they know who we are and they want ten million dollars.

—It reminds me of the apple tree

Helen blinked. Apple tree? What on earth did that mean?

103

—Get a move on you two or I'm taking over.

—Being kidnapped is like being trapped in traffic. Isn't all of life that way?

What was he talking about?

Thoughts roiled through her brain. Was this an elaborate scam? She needed to tell Dr. Levine right away. The thought made her feel sick. Dr. Levine would move heaven and earth if she thought her husband and child were at risk. She would be so disappointed that Helen had let this happen. Because Helen *had* let this happen.

No, she corrected. *That is unfair. Calm down.*

—Are you okay? she typed.

—You will get instructions. They will let us go after they receive the money. We are safe.

—When will they send me the instructions? she typed. Her fingers were still steady. That was somehow reassuring.

—You have to deliver the workshop as planned. This is important. Do NOT call the police or notify anyone else. No one can know this has happened or

The message ended abruptly.

—Or? she typed.

Then came the words that definitely did not belong to Benedict Levine or his son.

—Or they will both be killed

—It's a real situation in the kitchen

PART III

WHEN THINGS FALL APART. THEN GET EVEN WORSE.

DAVID LEWISTON

For once David felt calm. He and his father had been kidnapped in the dead of night, hooded, taken by boat to . . . somewhere. And now they were chained up in what he thought was a large army-style tent on a concrete pad.

He and his father had each been given a camping chair, a foam mattress pad, and a thick fleece blanket and pillow. There was a large bucket with a lid within reach of each of them. They'd been left with a few bottles of water as well as organic buckwheat crackers, spreadable vegan cheese, bananas, and toilet paper.

Not luxury accommodations, but not terrible either, as kidnappings go.

The watery light provided by the portable LED lamp in the corner of the tent did not illuminate the entire space but allowed David and his father to see each other. They were eight feet apart, chained by their waists and their ankles. The chains were bolted into the concrete pad.

None of this was good. But now that several of David's worst fears had come to pass all at once, he felt that a lifetime of worrying had finally paid off. Something terrible had happened, and he found himself not only unsurprised but ready.

"Son?" said his father.

"Yes?"

"How are you doing?"

"Not bad, all things considered," said David.

His father nodded. They were both in their pyjamas. His father's were, of course, exquisite. Johnstons of Elgin from Scotland. Black cashmere pants and long-sleeve top, soft as clouds. David had been given his own set of matching pyjamas the previous Christmas but rarely wore them because it embarrassed him to wear two-thousand-dollar loungewear.

He wore a T-shirt from the BMO Vancouver Marathon, underpants, and socks with plastic sandals. It was not an ideal outfit for the situation. He kept trying to get the blanket around himself completely, but the chains made it difficult and some part of his skin was always exposed.

"Don't worry," said his father, who looked remarkably composed for someone chained in a lawn chair.

"Oh no?"

"No," said his father. But instead of saying more, he lifted a hand and moved a finger from his ear to his mouth and slightly shook his head.

David understood. They were being watched. Listened to. They could not speak freely.

They hadn't been in the tent for long. Maybe half an hour? David sometimes thought he could hear the kidnappers whispering outside, but it might have been the wind.

The initial capture was taking on the unreal quality of a nightmare. He'd been taken at gunpoint from his room by someone dressed like a commando. Their voice was computer generated and came out of a device. The voice belonged to Clint Eastwood and the effect was terrifying.

David had been asleep when Clint Eastwood's voice had whispered "Get up, asshole" in his ear.

He'd shot up in bed so fast his nose collided with the kidnapper's gun. Blood had poured down his face in a hot gush.

The kidnapper hadn't said anything. Maybe the kidnapper was relieved that the gun hadn't gone off in his face.

David's instinct was to stop the blood from getting all over the bed so he swung his legs over the edge and leaned his head forward. The sudden movement made the downpour from his nose increase in intensity.

The kidnapper had stepped back. They were silhouetted by moonlight outside the window. They waved the gun at him, gesturing toward the door. He rose to his feet, hands up, a position so many young Black men had been forced to take and one that he'd somehow avoided, thanks to a life spent mostly in exceptionally privileged and protected spaces. And still this was happening to him. Goddammit.

He'd slid his feet into his Hoka slides and walked ahead of the kidnapper.

The sense of inevitability was eerie, as though he'd been waiting for something like this to happen for his whole life. His efforts and his parents' efforts to avoid it had been pointless. All the name changes in the world couldn't protect

CONTEMPLATION OF A CRIME

him from what he saw as the mixed blessing of being born into a legacy of historical trauma on both sides of his family *and* unfathomable financial privilege. It had always been deeply weird. David had studied issues of race and inequality at university. Was fluent in all the lingo. Understood the history, the theories, and the structural dynamics at play. Was exhausted by all of it and also felt compelled to do something useful. To *be* someone useful. But then he was marched out of a room in his nightclothes by someone using Clint Eastwood's voice. His parents, as Buddhists, probably would call it karma. David called it bullshit.

He'd once dated a woman who was into astral projection and fortune-telling. He'd met her at a weekend-long music festival in Europe. She was Swedish, quite beautiful, and slightly dopey, thanks to a steady diet of edibles, but also smart about people, in the way some New Age people can be. She'd told him that he was going to "go through something." She'd told him that the thing he went through would be "very hard" and he would have to "change everything or all would be lost," but that he could not waver or let go or he would "go under." She told him that the experience would be necessary for what she called his "integration and rebirth." Sitting with her outside her purple caravan, he hadn't appreciated her prediction. But she was no more solid than afternoon smoke from the campfire. Being angry with her would have been pointless.

They'd travelled together around Europe for an entire summer, enjoying a fantastic, if somewhat theory-heavy, sex life thanks to some of her more esoteric trainings in Tantric practices.

He and Agneta tried to make it work long distance but eventually broke up after she developed a bad case of playa foot at Burning Man and decided to move to Bali to heal for what to him seemed to be a very arbitrary one and a half years. Despite her passion for astral projection, she hadn't liked being so far apart.

He frequently missed Agneta. She was so very odd but loving. This memory and many more flitted through his mind as the kidnapper led him outside.

The gun barrel stayed jammed into his side as the person who'd taken him from his room slid a heavy hood over his head.

That scared him even worse than the gun. But he said nothing as it was fastened around his neck and the kidnapper spun him around several times before making him walk.

David tried to determine which way they were going. Were they moving away from the ferry? Or toward the missing dock? David tried to keep his bearings but was too disoriented. The barrel of the gun stayed in his side, and a hand on his arm directed him onto a rocky footing and then over a log.

Should he have tried to get away? Punched his kidnapper?

Probably.

But he really, really hadn't wanted to get shot.

"Get in," said another voice. A man with an accent, located in front of him. Also famous. Australian. Was it . . . Mel Gibson? Why was *Mel Gibson* telling him what to do? The whole thing was so bizarre he almost laughed.

He stumbled forward and nearly fell before his foot hit the water.

"Come on," said Mel Gibson. Hands shoved him and he was in water up to his shins. He reached out his hands, then banged into something and felt the cold wet sides of . . . At first he couldn't figure out what it was. Rounded edges and firm surface. It was a boat. One of those inflatable Zodiacs, he thought.

David was so twisted around he couldn't figure out how to get in without falling all the way into the water. He started to climb in, trying to keep his sandals on his feet. He got over the side and landed heavily on the bottom of the boat on his hands and knees.

He was feeling around for a bench seat when a voice he recognized instantly as his father's said, "Son? Is that you?"

A delay, then Clint Eastwood's voice said, "Shut up."

So David and his father, who sounded like he was sitting right behind him, shut up.

Once the kidnapper who'd been guiding him clambered into the boat and pushed off into deeper water, they started the engine, which was noisy enough that David hoped someone on the island could hear. The trip was short but also seemed to take forever.

The boat slowed and then one of the kidnappers cut the engine and they drifted into shore. Were they on one of the small, uninhabited islands nearby? He doubted it. Those were largely exposed and certainly had no place to hide two kidnap victims.

He didn't think they'd travelled far enough to have reached the Nanaimo harbour. Maybe they were on Saysutshun or Protection Island? They didn't disembark at a dock. Instead, they had gotten out into the water and waded to shore. David fell in and got completely soaked. The shore, when they reached

CONTEMPLATION OF A CRIME

it, was rocky and steep, and they'd had to climb over a jumble of logs, which would have felt challenging enough during the day and was terrifying while wearing a hood at night. They walked a short distance on a dirt path before they slowed and his feet touched smooth, flat concrete underfoot. The sound of a zipper being pulled open. His feet in the plastic slides were blocks of ice. But the wind had stopped and gone quiet, and he could tell they were inside. The kidnappers pushed them toward the chairs, chained them up, shoved them, and then took off the hoods. When David's eyes adjusted, he saw that their assailants were both wearing full-face masks—one black, one purple. They left without speaking.

Now, some unknown time later, David was just about to ask his father how he was feeling when the kidnappers pushed through into the tent. The brief glimpse before the tent flaps closed showed that it was still dark outside.

The two masked figures stepped into the middle of the room, well out of range of their captives. One wore a black gimp mask, which David was able to identify thanks to Quentin Tarantino movies, and spoke with the voice of Mel Gibson. The one who spoke with the rock-gargling voice of Clint Eastwood wore a purple gas mask and goggles. Rather than making the kidnappers look frightening, the masks made them look deranged. David wondered why they'd chosen those voices. Couldn't they have picked actors he found somewhat less personally objectionable? But that was kidnappers for you. They never respected a person's needs and wishes.

"I've got your phone," said the one in the black mask to David's father. "You need to contact your assistant." The kidnapper thrust the phone at David's father, who looked unperturbed.

"And what shall I say to her?"

"Tell her that you've been taken. Give her the instructions. Let her know that everything needs to proceed as normal. No one can learn about this."

"I'm running the course," said David. "People will notice that I'm gone."

The person in the purple mask furiously typed into a device. Then Clint Eastwood's voice said, "Tell her to run the program as scheduled. She can make something up about where you are."

"Helen doesn't like to lie."

"Dad," said David, giving his head a small shake.

His father settled back with an expression David had seen many times. His father was a generous, peaceful man, a devoted Buddhist, but he was also skilled at getting his way. He hadn't doubled the family fortune without uncanny powers of negotiation and a remarkable degree of stubbornness.

The thought that the kidnappers had no idea who they were dealing with flashed through his mind, followed by the recognition that he and his father were the ones chained up in lawn chairs listening to people speaking with the computer-generated voices of elderly celebrities. Best not to get too cocky.

"Tell her you're safe," said Mel Gibson's voice from under the gimp mask. "This will all be over soon."

David found himself staring at the kidnappers. The one with the black mask and Mel Gibson's voice was a good six inches shorter than the other. Their body types were hard to discern under the bulky layers of black clothes. Combat pants, sweaters, vests with a lot of pockets.

"We want ten million dollars," said Clint Eastwood.

"Would you like it in bitcoin?" asked David's father, as though he were discussing how to pay for his portion of a holiday. The suggestion surprised David. His father was nearly as hostile to cryptocurrency as Warren Buffett.

The black-masked kidnapper typed furiously and then Mel Gibson said, "Do you know how much damage bitcoin mining—"

The tall kidnapper put a hand on the short one's arm and the voice abruptly stopped.

"We have funds available for this eventuality," said David's father. "We can transfer the money wherever you'd like in whatever form you'd like."

The kidnappers exchanged a look.

"With the exception of cash. We cannot pay cash unless you want to involve multiple other people, including my wife, who is out of communication for a week."

One of the kidnappers nodded. "We know where your wife is. We have set up an untraceable transfer route."

David's father clapped his hands together in apparent satisfaction. "That's it, then. I'll have Helen transfer the funds to wherever you'd like."

"*You*," said Clint Eastwood's voice. "You will make the transfer."

"I'm afraid I can't."

As they all waited for him to continue, David realized he wasn't breathing. His father had always kept his business dealings out of the house. None of his

CONTEMPLATION OF A CRIME

children had followed him into the business, and so David had never seen his father negotiate something important before. He seemed perfectly relaxed, as though he were kidnapped, taken away by boat, and chained up in a lawn chair on a near-monthly basis.

"For an amount of this size, Helen needs to be involved because she's been given a code that I don't have. And she cannot initiate the transfer until the branch opens. It's in Switzerland."

David felt his own blood pressure rise. What was his father talking about? What kind of computer transfer depended on time of day?

"What the hell?" said Clint Eastwood, echoing David's dismay.

"It's something the security firm set up. It's sort of like two-factor authentication, only it involves two people. I have my account numbers. She has separate numbers that need to be entered. The kidnapping-and-recovery specialists said it's a safeguard measure. I don't entirely understand it myself."

The kidnappers were staring at David's father, heads cocked in dismay. Then they looked at each other and seemed to confer silently. The one in the gimp mask typed the response. "It's got to be now."

"I'm sorry," said David's father. "The security company was adamant about the two-person authentication part of it. If both numbers aren't entered, then any large transfer will raise flags at the bank." He shrugged and sounded genuinely sorry.

It sounded like BS to David but he tried not to let his doubt show on his face.

One of the kidnappers held up a finger to the other one, and they left the tent, presumably to discuss.

David stared at his father, who smiled back, the way a shark might smile before eating a seal pup.

A few minutes later, their captors were back. The one in the purple gas mask held up Mr. Levine's phone. "Contact Helen and tell her that you will both be released unharmed as soon as we have received the money."

"Sounds great," said David's father.

"Give me your passwords," said the kidnapper.

David's father did so.

The kidnapper unlocked the phone and then held the receiver up to David's father. "Speak into the microphone."

"Voice to text?" said David's father.

The kidnapper made a hurry up gesture.

David's father spoke in a clear, ringing voice.

—Helen, I don't want to alarm you, but it appears that we have been kidnapped.

David couldn't help himself from interrupting. His father's words lacked a certain urgency. He sounded borderline British.

—Dad, we have definitely been kidnapped. Please just give Helen the instructions.

—Yes, dear one. That seems to be the case.

His father kept talking, at points going way off topic. He said something about an apple tree. Something about how being kidnapped wasn't so different from being stuck in traffic, and wasn't life just like being stuck in traffic?

What the hell was he talking about?

One of the kidnappers interrupted and told his father to hurry up and get to the point.

David realized that he'd instantly fallen into the pattern of doing exactly what the kidnappers wanted, but his father hadn't. Not at all.

A reply came in, indicated by a beep. Then the generic audio voice read out Helen's reply.

—Are you okay? The knowledge that they'd made contact with Helen was reassuring. Of course Helen wouldn't panic.

His father recited the information. They were going to need ten million dollars. She would be told when it was time to transfer the funds. He reiterated that she should operate the workshop as planned. No one could know what was happening.

Then Clint Eastwood, who seemed to be the nastier of their two captors, interrupted with the coup de grace:

—Or they will both be killed.

CONTEMPLATION OF A CRIME

Only at first, the microphone couldn't pick up the deep, gravelly voice of the fake Clint Eastwood, so the kidnapper had to say it two more times before it was sent, which really drove home the point.

David's father spoke up again:

—It's a real situation in the kitchen.

The kidnapper turned off the phone and stared at his father. "Talk any more nonsense like that and you won't be running any more marathons."

David cocked his head. What did that mean? Do *what* again? Talk about situations in the kitchen? His father jogged but he didn't run marathons.

It dawned on David that the kidnappers were using a combination of typing and pre-programmed statements chosen from a menu. They'd written a response that threatened his ability to run marathons and accidentally used it on his father.

Who *were* these people?

"Understood," said his father. "Let us know how we can help in the meantime."

Typing. "You can help by shutting up."

"Of course. A perfectly reasonable request. If you'll excuse me, I'm going to drop in and do some meditation."

Meditation? Come on, Dad, thought David. He wished his father would stay in the real world, where they were chained up and being threatened with death. Maybe they should both be paying attention to what was happening around them?

But David didn't speak. The fact that his father could slip into meditation, eyes closed, face serene, while being held for ransom was impressive and even a bit soothing. It made the situation feel oddly manageable.

It seemed to have the opposite effect on their captors, who were rougher than necessary when putting the hoods back on their captives. "There," said the kidnapper using Clint Eastwood's voice. "That should help you focus."

HELEN THORPE

Helen stared at the screen, willing more messages to appear. Willing the kidnappers to send confirmation that David and Mr. Levine were safe. Willing someone, anyone, to give her clear instructions on how to proceed.

There actually had been a course at the North American Butler Academy that covered what to do in the event of a kidnapping, but it was an elective and she hadn't taken it, assuming it was designed for those who planned to work in kidnapping-prone regions. Helen had avoided all the electives that focused on crime. She preferred to focus on food, lifestyle, and organization, as well as choosing lighting to illuminate various kinds of artwork, caring for priceless furnishings, specialized watch repair, and curating extensive personal libraries of rare books, as well as the care and keeping of the clients. She'd assumed that, if necessary, she would hire security consultants to take care of the more dangerous elements of the job. Human resource management was a core part of the curriculum and she'd passed with perfect grades. In fact, she'd aced every part of her butler studies, which was why she'd been recruited by the Levines before she'd even finished school. She'd replaced their old retainer, who retired after decades of service.

Now she was deeply sorry that she hadn't taken the kidnapping class, and she racked her brain to remember what to do. She needed to hire a freelance security company. But that would count as telling someone what had happened.

Helen's mind was usually a clear, bright place. When she was filled with equanimity, she could easily recall information. At the moment, however, she was woefully short on both equanimity and clarity. She was in the midst of a new crisis for which she felt unprepared.

But Helen had not forgotten her mindfulness training. She noted herself seeing. Tuned in to the sounds that met her ears. Felt subtle air currents against her skin.

CONTEMPLATION OF A CRIME

After a few seconds she was back in the present. Her heart rate had resumed a more normal pace.

She hadn't taken the kidnapping course, but Gavin had. He'd planned to work for international clients, possibly on board yachts, which were sometimes targeted by pirates and other criminals. Murray and Nigel might also have taken the training.

Helen left the lodge and headed for Poolside Cottage.

As expected, the lights were on inside. It was a quarter to six in the morning.

She knocked and Murray opened the door as though she'd been waiting for Helen.

"Good morning," said the Irish butler. Then she took a closer look. "Helen?"

Helen took a moment to collect herself while she observed the scene. Nigel lay on the living room floor. He was being treated like an obstacle course by the four Pekingese.

"Helen!" cried Nigel. "The dogs and I are just working out."

Gavin was pouring coffee into small cups. Her friends had been waiting for her, and that gave her a warm feeling in the midst of all the stress.

"Hush, everyone," said Murray.

At her words, even the dogs stopped fooling around and dropped the small tug toys they'd been battling over. Nigel sat up.

Helen's friends waited for her to speak the way only trained butlers can: with patient, full attention.

Helen cleared her throat. It felt important to get this right. She was speaking a new, deeply unpleasant reality into being.

"Mr. Levine and David have been taken," she said, simply. She was still standing in the doorway.

Another audience might have peppered her with questions immediately. Asked for more information, for clarification. Another group might have insisted that she call the police. But the butlers . . .

Murray put a hand on Helen's shoulder and gave it a reassuring squeeze.

She explained that she'd stopped to check in on Mr. Levine. "I thought perhaps Mr. Levine and David had gone for a run. But it was so dark. I left them both messages. They're early risers." Helen looked at her watch. "I got the call about ten minutes ago. A WhatsApp message. From the kidnappers."

Gavin took in every detail. His concentration was absolute. But he didn't interrupt.

She told them about the messages. She repeated the death threat that had ended the communication.

"Come sit down," said Murray and she led Helen to a couch.

There was a long silence while everyone processed the information.

"Should I call the police?" asked Helen. "I didn't take the kidnapping course at school. I'm afraid that I don't know what to do." Saying that felt horrible. And Helen was attached to knowing what needed to be done in almost every situation. She wanted to add that she felt responsible for what had happened. It was her job to take care of her clients and she'd lost them. Instead, she said, "I just want to pay, get Mr. Levine and David back, and then get them both off this island."

Gavin set the cups of coffee in front of everyone. "I took the class, and while it wasn't particularly in depth, I think you have the right idea. If memory serves, the key is to stay calm—"

"Helen's superpower!" said Nigel.

"Keep the lines of communication open with the kidnappers, be honest with them, and establish a rapport. Hang on to all of your messages in case you need them later. And it's important to establish throughout that the people being held are safe."

"There was one other thing," said Helen. "Mr. Levine kept saying strange things. For instance, he said it reminded him of the 'apple tree.'"

"Apple tree?" said Murray. "Was he giving you a clue? Are they being held in an apple orchard?"

"I don't know. It was difficult to tell who each message was from because it sounded like multiple people were speaking into the same phone. He said something about something reminding him of an apple tree, and how it was like being stuck in traffic and wasn't life like being stuck in traffic."

"Interesting. Let's write that down," said Gavin. He produced a soft-sided notebook and made a notation in his elegant hand. "David or Mr. Levine may be trying to communicate in code, and it will be up to us to figure it out."

Helen's nervous system rose up in revolt. She felt like she was trapped in one of those drawing room mystery games while a real-world crime was happening just outside the door.

CONTEMPLATION OF A CRIME

Gavin stared at her. "Helen," he said. "This is not your fault. You were not hired as a security consultant. This entire situation is very . . ."

"Unfortunate," finished Murray.

"Your employer and his son are generous people and possessed of a community spirit. In this instance, those finer instincts have exposed them to danger. We will do everything in our power to get them back safely."

Helen felt a rush of gratitude at his words.

"Right now, I think you should do as they've asked. We don't know who we're dealing with. We don't know how serious they are about their threats. And we have no way to know what they know."

Whoever had taken Mr. Levine and David had known that they were on the island, which accommodation they were in, and who they were. They knew about the course and that Helen worked for Mr. Levine.

That must narrow the list somewhat.

"Do you think one of the guests is responsible?" asked Murray, quietly.

"Maybe. Maybe more than one. But we are, for lack of a better word, undercover. Mr. Levine is here under a false name, filling in at the last minute for the person who dropped out. David doesn't use his real last name and hasn't in years. No one here should know that they're related. No one other than David and Mr. Levine knows who *I* really am. We only received the invitation a few days ago. David organized all of it," said Helen.

"Interesting," said Gavin. "That's an angle worth pursuing. The kidnappers are very unlikely to hurt anyone unless they have no other way to get the money. They don't sound like a Mexican cartel, for instance. This took careful planning, but something about it feels . . . custom, if you follow my meaning."

"They didn't take just anyone." Nigel glanced at Helen. "I mean, obviously, there's no such thing as *just anyone*. But maybe they'd been trying to get to Mr. Levine for a long time and this was their opportunity? Or they figured out who David is? Probably a lot of people know that."

Helen took a moment to consider who was most often targeted by kidnappers. Young people. Vulnerable people who find themselves at the mercy of gangs and criminals. People are kidnapped during wars. And sometimes kidnappers succeed in taking very high-value targets. She was terribly worried about Mr. Levine and David, but they were people of immense privilege. She hoped

119

that would protect them. The other privileges Mr. Levine and his son had were intelligence, confidence, and a familiarity with human nature.

"Something tells me the kidnappers are not . . ." Helen shook her head and tried to sort out her thoughts. Something about the interaction on WhatsApp had suggested to her that the kidnappers were not immediately dangerous. The messages that she was sure had come from Mr. Levine had an almost chatty tone. He understood risk. He'd never have been as successful in business as he was without that. She'd seen him being grave. She'd heard him when things were dire. His voice had not sounded like that. If he thought he, or more importantly, David, was in imminent danger, he'd have found a way to let her know.

"Dr. Levine should be told," she said.

"Where is she?" asked Gavin.

"She's with her friends. In Montenegro," said Helen.

"Montenegro is nine hours ahead," said Gavin. "The fastest direct private flight here would be ten to twelve hours. If we're lucky, this will be over by then."

"She and her girlfriends are at a retreat centre. I believe they are completely out of communication. I would have to find a way to contact the centre, and then she would have to get back to the plane and make her way here."

"The kidnappers instructed you not to tell anyone," said Gavin. "I think we should do as they say. If necessary, I know some security specialists who could come in to help, but again, we'd be violating the kidnappers' requests. My advice is to run the course as scheduled and await further instruction."

"I think that's what David and Mr. Levine want," said Helen.

The butlers nodded.

Helen pushed the coffee away, with some reluctance. "I'm going back to the lodge to wait for news and to set up for the day."

"No caffeine to help you get through?" asked Nigel.

"I don't think my nervous system needs any more activation," said Helen.

"Going to skip your morning meth, then?"

Helen laughed. "I think so. Mint tea until this situation is resolved."

WAYNE KRUPKE

He got to the lodge at 6:18 a.m. and went upstairs. He wished he didn't have to do this. He'd sort of been enjoying himself. Oh well. He had his orders.

He stopped outside the Observatory and listened. Heard nothing. No lights from under the door.

He knocked. He'd heard David say he usually went for a run around six each morning and then he went in the ocean to freeze his nuts off. That's not exactly how he put it, but that's what you were doing if you went in the Pacific Ocean on anything other than the hottest days of the year.

Wayne hoped the guy would stick to his routine today. If David was inside and answered the door, Wayne wondered if he could get himself invited in and then distract David while he hid the microphone? Or he could send a delivery of . . . something with the microphone hidden inside. Flowers? Naw. That would confuse him. Candies? No. Wayne had no candies and David didn't look like he ate junk food. He'd probably throw them out, the mic along with them. Right now, there was the microphone he'd left behind the painting right outside David's room, but they'd been specific that he needed to put a device *inside*. David didn't want whoever was blackmailing him to release the audio to the cops, so he decided to chance it.

He knocked again and no one answered.

Wayne hated this bullshit. He would rather be elsewhere. Doing other things. He was definitely not cut out for this spy vs. spy bullshit. For a split second, he even missed marine engine repair, which had sucked balls so bad he'd gotten into drywalling, which was even worse, but at least it paid good.

He leaned forward and slowly, quietly, turned the doorknob.

Holy crap if it didn't turn all the way. The door swung open, noiselessly. Wayne glanced behind him. Nobody in the hallway. All the doors up and down the hallway were closed.

He slipped inside.

"Hello?" he said. "Uh, David?" Wayne kept his voice low. The door to the bathroom was open and it was dim inside. The room looked neat, kind of like David, who was one of those people who made Wayne feel like a slob, partly because he *was* kind of a slob. Although David's bed wasn't made, which surprised him.

"I just wanted to ask you a few questions about what we'll be doing today," he continued in a voice just above a whisper. "I hope you don't mind me coming in."

Damn this was shady.

At least no one could say that he'd broken in. The door had been open, just like all the other doors at this lodge. He'd knocked and everything.

"Yeah, so I'm feeling pretty good. Like connected and whatever. To the other participants, I mean. Just wanted you to know that."

As he talked nonsense, he scanned the room for the best place to put the last microphone. The desk. Underneath and off to the side. That way it would pick up anything David said when he was sitting there. An orderly stack of papers, a couple of folders. Two books. Everything lined up perfectly. The guy really was a perfectionist, which must be tiring. Wayne felt good about himself for having the thought.

"I like your desk," he said as he took the microphone from his pocket and put the tiny microphone under the piece of furniture.

"Looks high quality," he said. "We can talk about that when you've got more time."

He'd done it! He'd gotten into David's room and planted a recording device. He was probably going to end up working for . . . he didn't know who. Did Canada even have a spy service? If so, he wanted no part of it until there was a new government that respected people's basic rights and freedoms!

It was time to get out. He didn't want David coming back from his healthy twenty-plus-mile run and finding Wayne in his room. Things were going smooth and he wanted to keep it that way.

But instead of leaving, something made him walk across the room to the window. He looked out to the ocean. The sky was a little lighter, maybe, and he thought he could make out the horizon. When he turned to leave, he looked down and noticed the dark spot on the carpet. A dark spot the size of two hands. Maybe bigger. Four or five hands.

CONTEMPLATION OF A CRIME

Had David spilled a coffee? A guy that tense probably shouldn't drink coffee. Wayne pulled his phone from his pocket and turned on the flashlight. He shone it at the dark splotch. It wasn't coffee unless coffee was dark red. He moved the beam over to the bed. Red stained the white sheets.

Panic shot through him at the realization that he was looking at blood. He'd just broken into this room. Put his hand on the doorknob. His fingerprints were on the desk from where he'd felt around for a good place to put the microphone. A microphone! What if the cops got involved and found a microphone, also covered in his fingerprints! And DNA! He was probably shedding DNA like a bastard all over the room that he had no business being in.

He told himself to calm the fuck down. David probably just dropped a glass of some kind of healthy, healing red liquid. What was it the health nuts were always swilling? Kombucha? That was red sometimes, wasn't it? Or maybe David was a secret alcoholic, and he'd gotten into the sauce last night and dropped half a bottle of wine on the floor. It was possible. If Wayne had to do David's job, he'd definitely be a secret drinker.

"Fuck," he muttered, and then he backed away from the stains and used the bottom of his T-shirt to wipe off the edge and top of the desk.

He put the T-shirt over his hand and wiped off the inside doorknob, stepped outside, and wiped off the outside.

It wasn't wine in there. Or tea. Or kombucha. It was blood. And even before he'd seen it, he could tell something fucked-up had happened in that room. He was sure of it but didn't know how he knew.

And he had a strong suspicion that those bugs he'd put all over the place had something to do with it.

Wayne almost ran downstairs and only slowed when he reached the big living room. Still mostly dark. Good. Nobody was up yet. He was heading for a chair to sit in so he could calm the hell down when someone cleared their throat. He let out a high-pitched scream and jumped halfway out of his skin.

"Jesus Christ," he said, when he spotted the religious lady sitting in the dim corner, watching him. "You scared me. Sorry, uh, sister."

"I'm not a sister. But thank you, Wayne."

He felt like he was going to have a jammer right there. He tried to let out a breath so she wouldn't see that he was hyperventilating. *Come on, man,* he told himself. *Pull it together.*

"You're up early, eh?" he said. His voice still sounded half strangled.

She nodded.

There was something going on with her. She wasn't as jacked as he was, but she didn't seem entirely mellow, either. She usually had this calm force field around her. But sitting alone in the dark living room, she reminded him of a fox at the edge of a field. Waiting. But was she waiting to hunt or was she being hunted?

Get a grip, he told himself.

He was being paranoid. She had no idea that he'd bugged the place. She was one of those people who give everyone else the benefit of the doubt. Hetty. She was the coolest person here. A super-nice lady.

"Thought I'd grab an early coffee but it looks like it's not out yet," he said, trying to make his voice sound calm.

Hetty smiled. "The coffee should be along soon."

"Right on. Well—" He pretended to yawn, which sounded fake as shit, and to make it even worse, he did a fake stretch. Strictly eighth-grade-quality theatre work, not that he'd been into that. "Guess I'll go use the, uh, bathroom." He didn't want to say the word *john* around her. She was such a nice lady.

He had an overpowering urge to tell her about the stain in David's room. But he couldn't say anything about that or he'd have to explain why he'd been in there. Maybe he could leave her a note? She seemed like someone who would know what to do.

Maybe what she would do was call the cops on him for spying.

He shook his head. There was no law against bugging a place. Was there? Goddammit, there probably was.

Sweating profusely, he turned and left the room, and when he reached the foyer, he nearly screamed again when he came face-to-face with the heavyset young guy who served food standing in the dark. He was also staring at him.

What the fuck was going on here?

Wayne wanted off this island.

PAIN WAINSCOTT III

Though it almost killed him to admit it, even to himself, he was having a pretty good time. If he'd known the workshop was going to be people hating each other and trying to pretend they didn't . . . well, actually, that sounded like a normal day with his parents. But the people at Close Encounters for Global Healing took it to a whole other level. It was like Twitter after Elon bought it. People were being their very worst selves. He'd been worried when they did the talent exercise and everyone showed off their stupid, pointless things and said encouraging things to each other that people would go soft. Since that, everyone had acted more sincere, but he hoped it wouldn't last. And apparently, it hadn't.

He should have been a narc or something. It wasn't too late. He had just turned eighteen. Maybe his talent for shitposting would be an asset in the narcing field.

When Wayne, the guy who had about forty-two flags on his shitty truck to show how much he hated the government, had gone creeping into the lodge and then upstairs into David's room, Pain had followed him. When Wayne let himself into David's room, Pain snuck into the room directly across the hall and watched through the peephole. Nothing was locked in this place.

Convoy Wayne was up to no good and Pain approved.

Pain was a mostly terrible person, but he was good at noticing things, in addition to drawing pigs. Like the fact that when Wayne let himself out of the room a few minutes after he went in, his face was white as a blank document.

Pain waited until Wayne was gone and then he let himself into David's room. He wondered if he was going to find a body in there. That would be cool.

He should probably be scared, but he wasn't. He was almost never scared. One of his friends online had described him as "lizardy." Fair enough.

He looked around. The bed wasn't made, but everything else looked fine. At least David didn't leave his stuff all over the place like Pain did.

Pain walked farther into the room, then went to the window. He immediately noticed the big bloodstain on the carpet. What was this now?

Pain had spent some time on true crime fan sites and he'd seen plenty of gruesome crime scene photos. True crime nuts couldn't get enough of the gore. The more disgusting, the better for those freaks. A few times he'd pretended to be a relative of a victim or a serial killer. He'd offer them information no one else had and then jerk them around. He'd done it until he'd crime-phished a cop and nearly gotten caught promising to pass along details of a mass murder that only the criminal could know.

That had been a close call.

His friends on the internet didn't just call him lizardy. Quite a few of them said he was a psycho, and they weren't wrong.

The stain on the carpet in David's room looked like a murder blotch. Pain's heart rate sped up a bit. Man, he sure was glad to be here. The goal of the troll is always to make things worse. And Pain thought it would be easy to do that here.

HELEN THORPE

Helen looked at the participants slumped in chairs arrayed around the room. It was 6:40 a.m. Nigel, Gavin, and Murray stood behind the guests, hands crossed. The sight of the butlers reassured her.

"I'm afraid that Mr. Bruin and David are not feeling well," she said. Lying did not come naturally and she hoped it wouldn't get any easier because of all the practice she was getting. "They are self-isolating. Mr. Bruin is in his cabin. David has moved into another cabin. They don't want any of you to catch whatever they have."

"Have they got the flu?" asked Wayne.

"They're not feeling well and don't want to spread their germs," she said, avoiding the question.

"Is it covid?" said Yana. "I don't want to catch that again."

"Oh boo-hoo, we might all get a sniffle. Better get ten more vaccines so you can get tracked by the government. Maybe get a little heart failure thrown in for free. They've already proven that the whole thing was a hoax by the vaccine companies and the government," said Wayne.

"Dude, you forgot to mention Fauci, Dr. Bonnie, the Great Reset, China, Plandemic, and child-sex rings. I expected more from you," said Pain.

"Shut up, kid," said Wayne. "You've got a big mouth."

Then he and Yana started bickering in earnest.

Safe to say the good feeling of the evening had evaporated. Now Helen felt like she was drowning in conflict while she tried to resolve a kidnapping.

She waited until they'd finished needling each other.

"David has asked me to deliver the course until he's feeling better," she said, hoping she sounded more confident than she felt.

"I have an autoimmune disorder," said Yana. "I really, really can't afford to catch covid again. Could we all start wearing masks?"

"Fuck no," said Wayne. "I won't do it and you can't make me."

Helen was at a loss for how to head off this next battle. Then Murray came over to her and whispered something in her ear. Helen nodded.

"It seems that they have both tested negative for covid. So at this time, masks are not mandatory."

"Sometimes it takes a while for the tests to turn up positive," said Yana.

"God, you people just can't get enough of the face diapers, eh?" said Wayne.

"Let's get on with our day. If anyone would like a mask, we can provide you with an N-95."

Only Yana put up her hand and Nigel handed her a white mask.

"We have a full schedule to get through today, but I would like to start us off in the right way," said Helen. Her phone buzzed in her left hand and she nearly dropped it.

"Please excuse me," she said. "I need to take this."

She glanced at her phone. There was a notification. She clicked it open, feeling incredibly rude doing this in front of a group. The email was from Insight Meditation Society with a list of upcoming programs. She swallowed and closed her email.

"*We're* not allowed to use our phones," said Pain. "But you can?"

"She's teaching the course," said Madison. "It's different."

Helen, who was having trouble maintaining her focus, took a closer look at Madison. There was something about her. She was dressed entirely in navy. Her hair was no longer straight-ironed within an inch of its life but was tied back in a low ponytail. She wore less makeup. She looked . . . sort of like Helen.

Helen thought her scattered attention was causing her to see things.

Here now, she told herself. *Accept what is. Keep breathing. Be gentle with yourself.*

She continued. "I'd like to start with a blessing by John O'Donohue," she said:

"May the sacredness of your work bring healing, light and renewal to those who work with you and to those who see and receive your work."

Helen was a Buddhist and O'Donohue had been a Catholic, but his words never failed to stir her. She continued:

CONTEMPLATION OF A CRIME

"May your work never weary you.
May it release within you wellsprings of refreshment, inspiration,
*   and excitement.*
May you be present in what you do.
May you never become lost in the bland absences."

She looked up from the sheet of paper and saw that everyone seemed captivated.

She read out the rest of the blessing and waited while people took in the words. Then Pain put up his hand.

"So is the course going to turn religious now? Because you're running it?"

"No," said Helen. "The poem is a blessing for our work together. But the course will remain secular."

"It's nice," said Tom. "I liked it. The poem, I mean."

Madison nodded and once again Helen was struck by the odd change in her style.

"Okay, so we're going to start with—" Helen began but was interrupted by buzzing from her phone.

"Excuse me," she said, staring down at her phone as she hurried out of the room.

"Not fair that she gets to have her phone," griped Pain.

MADISON CROFT

Madison was borderline devastated when Hetty announced that David and Scooter Bruin were out with some kind of illness. (She also wondered for like the tenth time what it meant that Scooter's name was so close to the name of Taylor Swift's former manager.) She was especially upset because she thought she'd been getting somewhere with the Toyota dealer. He was hot, for an older dude. Those teeth! And those shoes that he'd worn on the walk! She'd looked them up before she gave up her phone and discovered that they were worth almost two thousand dollars. That's what she wanted. An older man with some taste and some style. Who cares if he was older than her father?

When Hetty left the room to answer her phone, Wayne started up again.

"It's such bullshit that we're still living with this hoax," he said. "People get sick. Get over it."

"Over fifteen million people have died of that *hoax*," said Yana, turning on him.

"Yeah, just like the flu every single year," said Wayne. "Also, that number is a massive exaggeration."

"Oh god," said Yana. "Here we go. Let me guess. Climate change is all made up, too?"

"I'm just saying it's all a very convenient way to distract people who will believe anything the government tells them."

Tom watched them arguing. He'd been quiet all morning. He'd been quiet since he'd broken down the day before, like he had a lot on his mind. Or maybe, like Madison, he was missing his TV shows. Did people in racist militias watch TV or were there too many actors of colour for them to do that?

"Have you checked out this season of *Alone*?" she whispered to Tom. "It was filmed in Saskatchewan."

He looked at her like she'd just said the dumbest thing ever, so she stopped talking.

CONTEMPLATION OF A CRIME

While they waited for Hetty to come back and tell them what they would be doing for the day, Madison reflected that there was something different about the religious lady this morning. She was dressed in her usual plain clothes, which Madison had tried to mimic in her own outfit this morning. It was hard to do because Madison liked to dress with style and Hetty had no style whatsoever. Plain navy trousers, plain navy sweater with a button-down shirt. Hetty looked like a . . .

Madison stared into the middle distance and tried to decide what Hetty reminded her of. Someone who worked on a cruise ship, maybe? Or maybe a flight attendant on a very boring airline? But she was a decently attractive woman. She could have used a set of eyelashes. Some help with her eyebrows. A swipe of a nice lipstick. Maybe a scarf. Madison was getting distracted again. Hetty was dressed the same this morning, but she also looked tense in a way that she hadn't before.

This morning she looked drawn, like she hadn't slept much. She'd kept glancing around, and she was hanging on to her phone like a tween hoping to get invited to a party. When Pain dropped a book on the floor, she'd startled visibly.

Maybe Hetty was nervous about having to step in for David. Fair enough. Madison wouldn't have wanted to do that, either.

Madison liked watching people and she was good at picking up on small signals. For instance, in her job, she could tell right away who was going to buy something. Who had money. Who didn't have money but wanted to act like they did. Who was going to be a nightmare to deal with. Who wasn't going to be able to make a decision. She was also very good at predicting who was going to try to steal or cause a distraction while someone else stole.

Religious Hetty had turned from the chillest, non-consumingest person into one who was about to yell fire in a crowded Winners.

Interesting.

Oh, here she came. She had a bunch of papers in her hand.

"Here is today's schedule," she said. "We'll be doing some trust-building exercises."

"Wouldn't that require us to trust each other?" said Yana. Everyone ignored her.

"We will start with a walk again this morning before breakfast."

"Seriously?" said Wayne. "You know, there's such a thing as too much walking."

"I'll pass," said Pain. "I have reached the end of my step allowance for the week."

"I'm afraid it's mandatory," said Hetty, which for her was super-harsh.

Madison made a note of the exact mix of polite and direct in Hetty's words. "It's mandatory," she whispered to herself. She liked the way that sounded. Madison knew she was doing it again: mimicking another person. Taking on their look, their mannerisms. Madison hoped that she didn't do it in a creepy way but rather in a student-of-humanity way. Or a fashion way. If you saw something you appreciated, you used it. You *became* it, at least for a while.

So far, it was fun dressing like Hetty because Hetty, stressed or calm, seemed like someone who could make a hard decision. Maybe after Madison had been dressing like Hetty for a few days, she would be able to do that, too.

HELEN THORPE

When Helen went into the office to check the message, she found a video recording. First it showed someone's smartwatch displaying the date and time. 6:35 a.m. Was it David's watch? Then the video turned to show a dark space. It took a moment for her to understand what she was seeing. And then she got it. A hooded figure, sitting in a chair.

Helen felt her breath catch.

A hand pulled off the hood. There was Mr. Levine, blinking and shaking his white head.

He started speaking when he looked toward the video camera. She couldn't quite make out what he was saying. It sounded like "trouble in the kitchen" and . . . what was that? "Wouldn't even kick a flea." He'd also said the thing about the kitchen in the previous message.

His words rang a bell.

He looked uninjured and not even terribly dazed for someone who had been kidnapped and hooded, and was being held in the dark. He smiled and seemed oddly cheerful, but not in his usual way. Even from the small screen and the dim video, there was an edge to his smile.

Helen understood then. Her boss was angry.

The camera panned over to another hooded figure. Hands pulled off that person's hood and there was David, who, like his father, looked better than expected, but there was some blood on his chin. He looked toward the camera and waved. Did he say something? She couldn't make it out, but it looked like, "We're okay."

The video went dark. Helen saw that there was a text message below asking her to join Signal.

By this time, Gavin and Nigel had joined her. Murray stayed in the great room to keep an eye on the participants.

"It's David and Mr. Levine. The video was taken at . . ." She looked at her watch. "Ten minutes ago." And then she snapped her mouth closed and put her hand over her mouth. What if they were under surveillance? What if the room was bugged? She was probably being paranoid, but this seemed like a time when paranoia was appropriate.

Gavin understood immediately. He stood and looked around. Then he gestured for the others to follow him. They walked out of the office and up the stairs to the second floor. They walked to the end of the hallway and let themselves onto the outside landing staircase at the back of the lodge. There was a couch on one side of the landing surrounded by a railing that looked over at the parking lot on one side and a rack of kayaks on the ground floor below.

"We can't come out here every time Helen gets a message," said Nigel.

"We'll figure something out. In the meantime, we can pretend Helen was just speaking out loud to herself. A stress reaction," said Gavin.

Helen nodded. She certainly was having a stress reaction.

"The message," said Gavin. "It's proof of life. That's good. That's very good."

"They want me to join Signal. I don't even know what that is."

"It's an encrypted messaging app."

"I thought that's what WhatsApp is."

"Signal has more privacy features. It's open source. Collects less information about its users. Protects metadata," said Gavin. "Journalists use it, government employees use it."

"And criminals," said Nigel.

Gavin nodded. "Them too."

"I'm not good at this sort of thing," said Helen, looking anxiously toward the door, hoping none of the participants would come out here and find them all huddling outside, looking suspicious.

"We'll do this together," said Gavin. "Nigel, can you please install Signal on Helen's phone. Helen can go back to the guests. If necessary, we can take turns running the workshop components, as needed, while we deal with this."

Helen put a grateful hand on his arm. "Thank you," she said.

Nigel had taken a seat on the sofa and was already busy installing the program on her phone.

Helen took a deep breath and was about to go back into the lodge when Nigel spoke up.

"One thing," he said, looking up at them. "We know it isn't any of the

CONTEMPLATION OF A CRIME

guests if this video was taken a few minutes ago. They've all been in the lodge for at least ten minutes now."

They looked at each other.

"We know none of them is *with* David and Mr. Levine right now. We don't know that none of them is involved," said Gavin.

Nigel nodded. "Odds are that at least one of them is in on this."

Helen felt sick at the thought. So much for Global Healing.

TOM AUCIELO

Tom Aucielo had spent a year and a half in a white nationalist militia compound in British Columbia's northern interior. He knew what it felt like when shady things were happening in the background. It felt like poison gas seeping into every room. Side Island Lodge wasn't taking unusually large deliveries of fertilizer and other bomb-making precursors. There weren't groups of camo-wearing angry white men taking secret meetings constantly and shutting up whenever he came to the dinner table to drop off food.

That's right. When Tom was in the Compound, the men ate first. After the Neanderthals had their fill, Tom and the women and children got what was left.

Maybe him eating with the women and kids was what had caused Gracie to go off him and go looking for someone new? Ah, hell. She'd never been that into him. It was time he learned to deal with that fact. She hadn't wanted to be with one of her dad's men because they were, in her words, "old, stinky assholes," but he was just a placeholder until she found that German skinhead on the racist dating app. Tom had seen a picture. The guy was bald, had a chiselled jaw and tattoos everywhere, was in a band, AND he was a hardcore Nazi. A real dreamboat. Plus, he was taller than Tom, at least judging from the photos Tom had seen.

Tom was getting distracted again. Heartbreak was like that.

But his attention came back into focus when, right before they went for their eight-millionth walk, the kid put up his hand and told Hetty that he hoped "nothing bad" had happened to David and the Toyota dealer guy and she looked upset. The tall guy who helped in the dining room appeared from basically nowhere and stood beside her.

"What makes you say that?" asked the man, who was very handsome, for a person of colour. That was the term Tom was trying to remember to use inside his mind, which had been filled with much worse words during his time in the

CONTEMPLATION OF A CRIME

Compound. He kept telling people he wasn't a racist, but he was realizing that he probably was, especially now that he'd been semi-indoctrinated. Not in his heart, but in his mind. In his vocabulary.

Had he always been racist? He didn't even know anymore. It was all just categories, right? Did noticing differences make him a bigot? His counsellor told him the problem was the *way* he noticed differences. She'd have probably said that his surprise that the tall, dark guy was good-looking was an issue. She was right. He had to learn to *interrogate* his assumptions. That's what she'd told him. And damn it, she was absolutely right.

Tom didn't dislike anyone. But he also didn't think people were all the same. He'd once tried to explain some of Warren Wiggins's racial theories to his counsellor. The look she'd given him! It made him lose whatever small amount of self-esteem he had left. He hadn't even been saying that one kind of person was better than another kind. Or maybe he had.

Talking about anything racial made him sound like a bigot, and so he stopped saying honest things in his sessions. But he was trying.

Anyway, the tall, handsome guy seemed very smart, which was *not* a surprise to Tom, who thought the guy was probably from one of those very intelligent groups. Not like the Compound racists, who were the opposite of an intelligent group. Tom was no genius, other than his vocabulary, but even he had been shook up by how catastrophically stupid most of them were. Quite a few of their wives, too. Even their kids had seemed a little dull-witted, but maybe that was just the kind of home-schooling they got. Tom didn't like to admit it, but Gracie wasn't about to get early admittance to Stanford, either. It had been impossible to find someone to have a good conversation with at the Compound, especially about books. Maybe some of the women who were with the abusive guys were decently intelligent, but they hardly ever spoke, so who knew?

He tuned back in and heard the kid, Pain, say he was just making a comment. "Has anybody checked David's room?" he asked.

Wayne, the convoy fan, whipped around to look at him.

Hetty, who was normally peaceful-seeming, like someone who spent a lot of time on a beach thinking about the tides and the moon as well as driftwood and smooth rocks, put a hand to her heart, as though she needed to stop it jumping out of her chest. The waiter, if that's what he was, stepped forward.

"We're taking care of Mr. Lewiston. I'm sure he'll let us know if he needs anything from his room." The way he said it made it clear that no one else should say anything about the matter; even though he was a server and they were the guests, no one else did. Tom respected that. Sometimes people who did service jobs had impressive *gravitas*. He'd tried to develop some gravitas—a word he loved—during the brief period when he worked at Shoppers Drug Mart, but no one took him seriously after they realized he had about as much authority as a one-dollar bath sponge.

"Okay, everyone. Let's get ready for our walk. We're only a little behind schedule."

Everyone bitched lightly, but they did what the handsome guy said. When Tom got up and turned around, he saw a bunch of staff standing in the doorway of the kitchen. There was a heavy guy with all the little red dogs and the pretty girl with dark hair. They were watching . . . who? Pain? Wayne? All of them? And just behind them was the chef, with her old concert T-shirt and that skinny grey braid. She stared only at him.

Tom shivered and ignored her. Ignored all of them. If he wasn't afraid of being kidnapped or worse by racists for being an informer, he'd have quit the course right then. Only: no ferry and no money to hire a boat. No money to eat. Nowhere to stay.

So much for leaving.

But damn, he wished that cook would stop giving him the death stare. Maybe he'd speak to the tall waiter guy about it. People with gravitas were often good at problem-solving.

HELEN THORPE

Helen had just opened the front door to take the group on their next walk when her phone buzzed yet again. She stopped in her tracks, and Madison, who was walking close behind her, bumped into her back.

"Excuse me," said Helen.

Gavin, who had agreed to join them so he could help keep an eye on everyone and act as backup, nodded his understanding.

"Gavin will accompany you while I take care of this."

The participants gave each other quizzical looks. Madison's expression was disappointment. Helen had no time to consider why. She needed to focus on taking the message.

"I have some questions for us to consider on this walk," Helen heard Gavin say as he headed off down the path. "I hope you're all in the mood for more icebreakers."

Helen didn't know whether they kept going in that vein because she turned back to the lodge and headed to the second-floor landing. It was just after seven o'clock in the morning.

As she walked, she looked at her phone screen. Where was the message? She didn't know what to press. She held it up to Nigel, who'd followed her. He took it from her and began moving through screens.

Meanwhile, Murray stood out in the hallway to make sure the chef didn't appear and ask what was going on.

Nigel, who had quickly found the right screen, held the phone up to Helen. She looked at the message, which was not a text but rather a squiggly line.

"It's an audio recording," said Nigel. He'd brought the dogs with him, and he picked up one of the Pekes and held it under one arm as he reached over and pressed play with the other.

"You have not held your end of the bargain," said a deep, accented voice. Helen hit pause as her heart hit the ground. That voice!

SUSAN JUBY

"Mel *Gibson* kidnapped them?" said Nigel, mouth ajar.

Helen closed her eyes. This was happening. No sense rejecting reality. Feel it and move on. Move *through*! She hit play again.

"You have told other people," said the voice of Mel Gibson. "You are forcing us to use violence."

Helen felt her vision blur. Then she steadied herself. She was a rock in a river. Unmoving in the maelstrom. Let it all rush past.

Should she admit to the kidnappers that she'd told Gavin and Nigel and Murray?

No. She should not. The Buddhist prohibition against lying did not apply here. She was dealing with criminals and trying to save her boss's life and the life of his son. She had to do what it took to get them back. Didn't she?

Helen glanced at the thick stand of fir trees on the other side of the landing, and then she caught sight of the line of people walking down the path before they disappeared around a corner.

—I did not, she typed.

—We heard you. The text response came an instant later.

So they *were* bugging the office. Were they also filming? She thought not.

—I speak to myself when I'm stressed. No one overheard me.

She winced internally as she tapped out each lie.

—If we find out you are not telling the truth we will cut his Achilles heel and send you the video.

They didn't know the difference between an Achilles heel and an Achilles tendon. Maybe that was useful information and maybe it wasn't. It was a relief to be communicating via typed message rather than listening to the weird audio recordings of Mel Gibson's voice.

—I am telling the truth.

—The instructions will be sent this afternoon. Stay by your phone. Tell no one.

140

CONTEMPLATION OF A CRIME

Then there were no more dots indicating that the person was typing. Helen watched, fascinated and appalled, as the previous messages disappeared one at a time from her phone screen.

"Where did the messages go?" she asked and showed the phone to Nigel. "They just evaporated."

She scrolled. "The message with the audio clip is gone, too."

"They disappear," he said. "It's a Signal feature."

"It's very disorienting," she said.

"Take a screenshot of every message you get right away. Download any audio clips. Gavin said to keep track of all communications. Just in case. Here." He showed her how to take a screenshot and how to download audio files.

He brought Clarice, the smallest Pekingese, closer to his body, and Helen reached down to pat the other three, who lay at his feet.

"Did they believe you?" he said.

She nodded. "I think so. But I really need a minute to think. Something about this doesn't feel . . ."

"Right? Good? Well, no. Your boss and his son are kidnapped. That's not going to feel great."

"That's not the part that feels wrong. I'm going to stay out here for a moment and think."

She took a seat on the sofa, which was comfortable, if slightly damp.

"I'll take the dogs back to the cabin. Let me know if you need anything." Nigel began to make his way down the wide stairs, followed by the small pack of Pekingese dogs, who took the stairs with ungainly hops. Helen closed her eyes. She was missing something. Several somethings, she thought. And it would take some calm and concentration to figure out what those things were.

DAVID LEWISTON

How long had they been chained up in the tent? It felt like a long time. Years, even though it had probably only been four or five hours. One of them had taken his father's phone and the other took David's Garmin watch. His father didn't wear a watch because he felt it interfered with his ability to stay in the present. At least they hadn't put the hoods back on.

Before the kidnappers left, they recorded David's father reading out the instructions and codes for transferring the ransom. David was aware that his father had a phenomenal memory for numbers, but he still felt impressed listening to him recite the numbers and letters for the branch and account and transfer information without having to look them up.

"You're sure this is all correct?" said the one wearing the gimp mask and using Mel Gibson's voice.

"Oh yes. Absolutely. Transfers from that account won't trigger an alert, even if I take out more than a million dollars," said his father, pleasantly. "Helen knows all about it."

The kidnappers exchanged a glance but said nothing. They seemed to have grown tired of having to type in responses to his father's statements, very few of which could be easily replied to with the pre-programmed menu of responses.

Then one of them hit a button, and Clint Eastwood said, "If anything goes wrong, you'll be sorry."

David's father laughed, a startling sound in the gloomy confines of the dark tent. "Do I feel lucky?"

The kidnappers' eyes darted back and forth between David and his father, and he thought they probably didn't get the reference, which meant they hadn't chosen the audio voices because they were big fans of Eastwood and Gibson. A small point in their favour, at least.

"I just need to add one thing," said David's father.

CONTEMPLATION OF A CRIME

The one in the purple mask hit a button and tilted the phone toward David's father again.

"Helen, make sure to enter the codes exactly as I've read them out, and remember, you won't be able to do this until the branch is open. That's one of the wrinkles with this account. Transfers can only take place during their local business hours. And you'll need to enter your own code at the end to finalize the transfer. Don't contact anyone, no matter what. Just run the course. Trust the process. Invest in the higher good. Give my love to—"

The kidnapper snatched the phone away and then typed furiously into their device.

"What the hell was that?" asked Mel Gibson.

"Instructions," said Mr. Levine.

More typing. Then Clint Eastwood's voice said, "Are you playing games?"

David's father looked at the kidnappers, suddenly serious. "I think it's important to keep Helen calm and reassure her that this will be over soon. She will do exactly as I've asked."

David thought he saw the kidnappers' shoulders drop slightly. They were both probably as keyed up as he and his father. It occurred to David that these people weren't professionals, even if they had managed to get David and his father off Side Island in the dead of night and were using AI voice technology. It remained to be seen whether their amateur status was a good thing or a very bad thing.

Professionals might execute them because it would be easier. Amateurs might kill them because they panic. Either way, they'd be dead.

Calm, thought David. His father was right. The key here was to keep everyone calm. David had been told as much when he'd been given security and kidnap-awareness training, as a kid and again as a young adult before he went to university and reinvented himself as David Lewiston so he could live a more normal life among his peers. He'd forgotten almost everything the security people had told him, but he still paid attention to people and vehicles more than most probably did. He always crossed the street rather than walk past an open van of any description.

The kidnappers filed out of the tent in silence.

After about an hour, David's father spoke up.

143

"You okay, son?" he said. "I think they're gone for a while."

"Shhhh," said David. "Remember that we aren't supposed to talk."

"I think we're okay."

"Why?"

"I saw one of them collecting something that looked like recording devices while the other one was talking to us."

"Why would they do that?" asked David, incredulous.

"Because if someone finds us here and discovers those bugs and can trace them to the kidnappers, that's about as damning a piece of evidence as they could get. But if someone comes upon us and no devices are broadcasting to them, no one can tie them to the crime. That's my initial theory, anyway."

David felt it was a somewhat less than rock-solid conclusion. Surely the kidnappers had left more evidence of themselves than two men in nightclothes chained up in a tent? The tent, for instance. Who had put it up? He tried to work through the line of reasoning but his brain was too muddled by stress, so he just let it go. Through a gap at the bottom edges and the door of the tent, he could see that it was now light outside. The thought was cheering. Maybe someone would find them. That was more likely to happen during the day.

"Dad, what are you up to?" They both knew he was referring to the preposterous idea that the transfer couldn't happen until the Swiss bank opened, hours later.

"I'm giving Helen and the gang time to find us."

"The gang?" said David. "Who is the gang?"

"The Close Encounters group. I think of them as a gang."

"But Dad, I think it's very likely that at least one and maybe more of them is involved in this."

"Why?" asked his father.

"Because we met them on an island and we got kidnapped less than a day and a half later."

"That's not conclusive. I think they're a troubled bunch, but I don't think any of them would do this."

It was David's turn to ask why not.

"I'm not sure," said his father. "But Helen will certainly find out if one of them is implicated."

David wanted to know how she was going to do that while getting them

CONTEMPLATION OF A CRIME

released and running the course. Poor Helen. David was starting to get a sense of how much responsibility people put on her.

"You know, Dad, she's great. Very smart and competent. But maybe this is asking too much of her. She's not a security specialist or a psychic. She's a butler who meditates."

His father smiled at him. "Oh, I think she's more than that. You'll see."

David wanted to ask his father if he was out of his mind, but he didn't. He loved his father and respected him even though sometimes he wondered about both of his parents and their . . . what was it? Not silliness, exactly. But sometimes they both seemed a bit unworldly. It was strange, given that his parents were both brilliant and high-powered in competitive fields. They'd been excellent parents, involved, loving, with clear boundaries. But since they'd retired and taken up Buddhism with such abandon, they seemed to have gone soft. And their reliance on their butler was bizarre. David realized that if *he* thought a person was getting soft, it was reason to be concerned, because David was one of the softest men around. He was gentle and sensitive and always had been. Still, he liked to think he lived in reality. And right now he wasn't so sure his father did.

"Don't worry, son. Helen and her butler friends will handle this, with a bit of help from us. They're tremendously competent people. That combination— Helen, her butlers, the guests—that's a *dynamite* group of people, don't you think?"

David wondered if he might die of incredulity right there in his lawn chair. Had his father not *met* the guests for this season's Close Encounter?

"Dad, there's a *Nazi* in the mix. A kid who shows every sign of being a sociopath, if not an actual psychopath. Yana Heppler is as depressed a person as I've ever seen. Madison Croft is . . . well, I don't know what she could do unless we need some light shopping done. Wayne Krupke is . . . nice enough but not one of life's great . . . Let's just say that I'm not getting problem-solver from him."

"Oh David," said his father. "I'm surprised at you. You've taken the course. You know it's all about getting past first impressions into hidden depths in order to see the person's true nature. And I don't believe for a minute that Pain is a sociopath."

"Seriously?" asked David, hearing his voice rise. "What makes you think he's not? And Tom Aucielo. The man was in a *racist* militia. One that was planning a terrorist attack."

As he spoke, David realized he sounded like the last person who should be leading Close Encounters for Global Healing. He sounded like the kind of person who wrote off other people based on incomplete information. What had happened to his optimism? His faith in the human spirit? Well, for one thing, he'd been kidnapped in the dead of night. And it was likely that one of the guests had something to do with it. Also, this group of guests felt far more challenging than the people with whom he'd attended Close Encounters.

"It's natural that you'd be feeling a bit defended, son. I agree that Tom has some work to do on himself. But I don't think he's hardcore. I think he's lost and he's afraid. Like so many young people." David's father sounded completely at peace.

"Dad. I know you are . . . gentle. You believe in people. But you're not Gandhi. And the particular group we've got at Side Island this session seems *off*. At least compared to the group I was in."

"Do you think these kidnappers will hurt us?" asked his father, changing the subject without warning.

"Yes. My god, yes! Of course I do. They've threatened my tendons!" David shifted in the lawn chair, which was no longer comfortable. He was tired of trying to see in the low light in the tent. Of having to keep shifting to cover up the parts of his body that the blanket left exposed.

"David, they left us buckwheat biscuits. Vegan spread. They're *not* going to kill us. I don't think they'll hurt us in any way. I bet you anything that when they come back from wherever they've gone to hide out for the day, they'll bring more blankets. More snacks. I think we might even be dealing with pacifists here."

David gawped at his dad.

"You know I love your Buddhism. Your faith in inner true nature and all that. I admire the practice that you and Mom have developed. But these people don't deserve your . . . whatever this is."

David got to his feet. He might not be able to pace around in his agitation, but he couldn't sit in the chair any longer. He awkwardly moved the blanket so it was draped around his shoulders.

His father also got to his feet. He smiled.

CONTEMPLATION OF A CRIME

"I agree that these people deserve nothing," said his father. "And that's exactly what they're getting from me." He began to stretch his limbs as far as the chains would allow.

"I'm sorry, what?" said David, not sure he'd heard his father correctly. His pulse shot up again.

"I'm not paying them."

"But, but . . . how are we going to get out?"

His father shrugged. "Helen and the gang will find us. The kidnappers will be arrested and prosecuted to the fullest extent of the law. And we can go back to doing the good work before us."

David didn't know what to say, so he just bent over and put his hands on his knees, which made his chains rattle. CHAINS! He was in CHAINS!

"Don't worry, son. I've dealt with people like this. A thousand times worse. We are strong, we are smart, we are resilient. And we are not giving these people five cents."

In that moment, David regretted every penny of the annual installment of his trust that he'd given away, leaving him with what? Maybe two hundred thousand in liquid assets? A fortune for most people. But nowhere near the required ten million, which was a rounding error for his father.

"Shall we try some limited-motion Tai Chi?" asked his dad.

HELEN THORPE

On the landing Helen did what she'd been trained to do for most of her adult life. She sat and paid careful attention to the moment, which was not static but a flickering, sparking river of experience flowing by too quickly to capture. She noted sensations coming and going in her body. The activity in her mind. She felt the impermanence of the situation. The sensation of discomfort and the wish to avoid that discomfort.

She dropped into awareness and found the situation was no longer overwhelming or even hers, particularly. She felt both in the moment and out of it. Without conscious effort, strange bits of information that she'd received coalesced into understanding. As she sat in silence, a certain spaciousness opened in her heart centre and she knew what she had to do.

The insights might have felt random but she trusted them. First, pretending to be a minister named Hetty at a conflict-resolution workshop was causing a considerable amount of anguish. She'd come to this island as part of an effort to help build trust between people. And so she would try to do that.

Helen got to her feet, feeling more centred than she had since she and Mr. Levine had arrived at Side Island. She was aware of the great irony in the fact that the concept of non-self or of not taking things personally created room for people to be more free in themselves and their actions. It was a near impossible thing to describe, but it was true.

She went downstairs to find that the group had returned from their walk and were eating breakfast. Gavin, Murray, and Nigel followed her to the landing and she told them her plan.

"Are you sure?" said Murray, her dark eyes concerned.

"I know we aren't following the kidnappers' guidelines," said Helen. "But when they said not to tell anyone, they meant the authorities. We are all part of this group. And the participants deserve to know. And I think Mr. Levine has been sending me clues. I hope I'm right about that."

CONTEMPLATION OF A CRIME

Murray nodded and then so did Nigel.

No one argued and she appreciated their confidence, even if she wasn't sure it was warranted.

When they went back downstairs, Helen went to the office and pulled the files for each participant. She reviewed the paperwork. There was no way to tell who had referred each person, which seemed like an oversight. It reaffirmed for her that the only way to get to know them was to spend time with them. If one of them was responsible for the kidnapping, she trusted that they would reveal themselves as guilty.

She put the files away and went out to the dining room. When the participants were finished eating, she made her announcement.

"Please listen, everyone," she said, nervous about defying the instructions she'd been given. "It's time to go for another walk."

"But we just did one!" said Wayne.

"The schedule says we don't have to walk again until eleven thirty," said Pain.

"We will go now," said Helen.

Something about the way she spoke prevented the usual complaining. Everyone rose to their feet and went to the foyer to get their coats. Nigel, Gavin, and Murray followed, as did all five of the dogs.

When they got outside, Helen led the group away from the lodge and past the cabins. Then she led them off the road and onto a section of white sand beach. When they stood in an irregular circle, she held up her hand for silence, which wasn't necessary since no one was speaking.

This gamble would pay off or it wouldn't. And if it didn't, Mr. Levine and David might not survive. Helen swallowed.

"I have something to tell you," she said. "My name is not Hetty and I am not a minister."

"I knew it!" said Pain. "You're a shrink, aren't you?"

Tom looked alarmed at the news that she might be a psychiatrist.

"The fuck?" said Wayne.

"My name is Helen and I am a butler."

As one, the participants of the workshop tilted their heads to the right and made the same face. She'd seen that exact expression from many people over the years.

"A butler?" said Yana, finally.

149

"Why?" said Tom, sounding panicky. "Why would a *butler* be here?"

"People who are rich enough to have butlers are what's wrong with this world," said Yana, automatically.

"Oh, be quiet," said Madison, who was staring at Helen like she was made of chocolate mousse.

"Well, shit," said Wayne. "That's crazy, man."

"I work for the man you know as Scooter Bruin. Only that isn't his real name."

At this news, their mouths fell even farther open. They were approaching baby bird territory.

"Is this an RCMP undercover op?" demanded Wayne. "Because I didn't do *shit,* man."

Helen refused to allow her confession to be derailed by the bickering.

"The man you've been calling Scooter is actually David's father. He is not a car dealer."

A look of disappointment came over Madison's made-up face. "What is he, then?" she asked.

"He's a very wealthy person."

"We *know* that," said Yana. "The man reeks of capitalism run amok."

"He came to support David. It's a bit tricky to explain. They always try to have a well-off person take part in the program, and this year, David's father has been serving in that role."

"Why?" said several of them together.

If she was going to be honest, she needed to be completely honest.

"Probably because a lot of people resent wealthy people. And wealthy people sometimes lose sight of what it is to be . . . less wealthy."

"You mean poor," said Tom.

"Yes. David agreed to facilitate the course, and then the person of means who was scheduled to take part dropped out at the last minute. So Mr., ah, David's father stepped in. We came together. I am here to support him."

"So David's rich, too?" said Tom.

"David comes from a very well-off family, but he is not personally rich." Helen didn't try to explain that David spent significant amounts of time and effort giving away the money that flowed over him with the regularity of tides pulled by the moon.

CONTEMPLATION OF A CRIME

"So you're David's butler? Or like, his dad's butler?" said Pain.

"His father's butler. That's correct."

"And why did you two lie about who you are?" asked Yana.

"Because we didn't think it was safe for him to be in a place like this."

"He's at *that* level?" said Pain. "Cool."

"This is a really nice place," said Tom. "He must be crazy rich if he can't even come to a fancy place like this."

"Super-wealthy people usually have security," said Yana, confidently. "We've targeted a few of them for protests and it's basically impossible to get close. They have layers of security. Basically, rich people live in a bubble. Or a fortress."

That, thought Helen, was accurate, although the Levines were far less guarded than many in their income bracket.

"So he's even richer than a person who owns multiple Toyota dealerships?" asked Madison, obviously trying to get her head around the magnitude of the concept.

"I bet he's rich like the *president* of Toyota," said Wayne. "Does Toyota have a president? Or do they have a prime minister? Like a country?"

Helen didn't answer. She was preparing herself to tell them the rest of it. She exchanged a look with her friends, who watched and waited reassuringly.

"So who are *they*?" said Pain, hiking his head at the butlers.

"My friends," said Helen.

"They aren't just regular helpers, are they?" said Tom in his deep baritone. "They're special."

"What do you mean?" asked Wayne. "Special?"

"They're way too . . . *elite* for here," said Tom. "Haven't you noticed?"

Now the guests were all staring at the butlers. They were even staring at Nigel, who was not particularly elite or fancy.

"These are my friends." Pause. "Who also happen to be butlers."

The group reacted like mimes feigning shock. Staggered backwards. Threw hands up to their foreheads. Cries of "What the hell?" and "How is that even possible?" rang out.

Yana collected herself first. "Are you saying your boss is so rich he needs FOUR butlers when he travels? Is he Saudi royalty or something?"

"No. The other butlers are friends from butler school."

"Butler school!" repeated Madison in a reverent voice. "Cool."

"And they just thought they'd all come here and work the buffet table for us?" said Pain. "That's a likely story."

This was taking too long. Helen had wanted to clear up the lies and then ask them to help her. She was taking a gamble and felt impatient to find out if it was going to pay off.

"We were supposed to be going on a holiday together," she started.

"You and all these other butlers?" said Madison.

"That's right. But Mr. . . . my boss asked me to accompany him here. When we got here, David said some staff had left unexpectedly and he needed more help in the lodge and with the program. So my friends agreed to come."

Gavin held up a hand and gave a gracious nod. "I'm Gavin," he said.

Murray nodded her dark head. "I'm Murray."

Nigel grinned awkwardly. He held the smallest Pekingese in his arms. "I'm Nigel. These are . . ." He looked down at the dogs. "Never mind. These dogs belong to *my* employer."

"Who is your employer?" asked Pain. "Jeff Bezos or something?"

"Definitely not," said Nigel.

"Wow. This is all so crazy," said Wayne, sounding quite delighted. He took his ball cap off, rubbed his forehead, and then put it back on backwards and gave it a pat.

"Why are you telling us this now?" said Pain.

"Where are David and his father?" asked Yana.

"They're not really sick, are they?" said Tom.

Helen took a deep breath. Felt the sand shift beneath her feet. She glanced back toward the path to make sure the cook hadn't somehow joined the assembled group. "They aren't sick," she said. "At least, I hope they aren't. And I don't know where they are."

"Did they take off? Call their private helicopter and blow the joint?" asked Wayne.

"No," said Helen. "They disappeared last night. This morning I received word that they have been kidnapped."

At this, the Close Encounters for Global Healing participants finally had nothing to say. They stared at Helen, who briefly closed her eyes. It was done. What happened next would be critical.

CONTEMPLATION OF A CRIME

"By telling you this, I'm betting that none of you is responsible." Her earlier certainty about her plan wavered but she held on to the strange inspiration and forged ahead.

"Together, we are going to do our best to find and save them," finished Helen. "That will be today's activity."

More silence among the odd assembly of people while the ocean lapped at the white shell beach and the seabirds called.

"Well," said Pain, finally. "At least it's better than going for another walk."

153

NELLY BEAN

Nelly Bean was not used to having irrational urges, and she wondered when she'd become so emotionally incontinent.

She was an organized person. A genuine optimist. Her brother called her the "Git 'er Done Queen" and she took it as a compliment, even though she knew he didn't entirely mean it that way.

No one but Nelly Bean could have come up with a concept like Close Encounters and kept it afloat for as long as she had. Nelly had persistence and powers of persuasion, and she absolutely refused to let negativity win.

And here she was, practically drowning in negativity. Feeling defeated. Overwhelmed.

She looked at Fields, who was lying on the small curved sofa, painting her toenails. That was a change. Nelly's fiancée was not one to do for herself what other people could do for her, but she had agreed to take care of her own aesthetic needs during this critical time. For someone so proud of her ability to do her own research, Fields was surprisingly un-self-sufficient. She did not take care of her own skincare, nails, and hair, nor her Pilates and aerial yoga routines. Fields believed her body was her temple and she usually had staff maintain that temple. What she didn't have at the moment was money to pay that staff.

Which was where Nelly came in. Or should have.

Nelly was the CEO of a high-profile charity. An innovator in the social justice space. She should have been making great money. She deserved to earn large. That's what Fields said and Nelly agreed with her.

But Nelly earned a pittance. She'd won major awards, including one for her early advocacy against bitcoin mining. She'd received a large trophy and some media coverage. No money.

"Those who do good works should get paid, babe," Fields had said, many times.

Nelly had tried. She really had. But right now, they had seven hundred and

CONTEMPLATION OF A CRIME

fifty dollars between them and maybe another five hundred in available credit. They were currently staying on a 2015 Campion pleasure cruiser. It was called *A Slice of the Pie* because the boat's owners used to operate a food truck specializing in pie. The owners had retired the truck after inheriting several low-income apartment buildings in Kelowna, but retained many fond memories of the pie business and a persistent delusion that they were self-made entrepreneurs. *A Slice of the Pie* was tied up at one of the mooring buoys near Saysutshun while its owners were on a wine tasting tour in California. Nelly and Fields were staying on the boat, which was for sale. Nelly frequently house- and boat-sat for them and they thought she walked on water.

They were not so fond of Fields. In fact, few people understood why Nelly and Fields were together. Sometimes, Nelly wondered if those people had eyes.

Fields was gorgeous. A tall, natural-seeming beauty with perfect skin, long limbs, and sun-kissed hair that literally cascaded. Nelly, who was not tall, was cute. Cute-ish, anyway.

Nelly was approachable.

Fields was not.

Nelly was idealistic and kind.

Fields talked about positivity on her Instagram, but she was notably mean.

Nelly couldn't get enough of her.

And that was how she found herself in this situation.

They were moored in front of Saysutshun, just out of sight of Side Island. They'd been on *A Slice of the Pie* when they got the idea, the year before. Or rather, when *Fields* had come up with the idea.

Fields was good at coming up with plans, and Nelly only registered them as crazy once she was in too far to back out.

This was by far the worst plan Fields had come up with, and Nelly was trying to convince herself that she'd been right to go along with it. She wasn't normally a pushover. But maybe her resentment at having to struggle when people who did nothing worthwhile with their lives had caused her to snap?

Nelly considered her fiancée, who had this way of lounging around that made it seem tacky to be busy. In other words, she made Nelly, who never stopped moving, feel terminally uncool.

They could do this. It was fine. It was one, admittedly massive, lapse in her moral and ethical framework that would be over in a matter of hours. When everything was resolved, she could go back to doing good works and she could do so from a position of financial stability.

The boat's owners had an inflatable dinghy attached to *A Slice of the Pie,* and that's what Fields and Nelly had been using to get around. They tried not to take the dinghy out during the day if they could help it. The channel was busy with float planes and ferries and boats. Every time they got in the Zodiac, Nelly felt her shoulders tense up and her head pound.

Fields, on the other hand, well, she seemed quite comfortable with "criming," as she put it. When Nelly expressed reservations, Fields pointed out that they weren't stealing from anyone who couldn't afford it. "If you really think about it, we aren't stealing at all," she'd said. After all, where had Benedict Levine gotten his billions of dollars? From capitalist rapaciousness, that's where! From unbridled greed! Fields made these arguments because she knew that Nelly wasn't a fan of late-stage capitalism. And Fields always ended by saying that they weren't going to hurt anyone.

Nelly wasn't, but she was starting to wonder about her wife-to-be. There was something about the way Fields had acted around their . . . guests that had made Nelly nervous. Fields had been a little too eager to shove them. A little too unconcerned about what would happen if one of them fell out of the boat or had a panic attack while wearing the hood. And those messages she'd sent to Mr. Levine's assistant! Fields had threatened their guests with bodily harm. With murder! Nelly thought they'd agreed that no one would be hurt. She'd never have gone along with the plan if she thought there would be so much lateral violence in the form of threats. (Of course, kidnapping and confinement was also a form of violence, but at least they'd left their guests snacks and warm blankets and good chairs. That should make up for some of it.)

Nelly hated to admit it, but Fields was starting to scare her.

She'd always thought that her fiancée was sort of like tofu. She took on the taste of whatever and whoever was around her. And right now, she was taking on the taste of the cold and remorseless kidnapper she was pretending to be.

Since they'd gotten together a few years before, Fields had talked a good game about her interest in social justice. She discussed her passion for building bridges and overcoming divisions, even though during the pandemic, she'd been one of the most divisive voices of all. She'd kept her small vegetarian restaurant open in spite of health orders and had gotten internet famous for her impassioned tele-

CONTEMPLATION OF A CRIME

vision interviews about "freedom" and the "plight of the small business owner." Which, fair enough. Nelly didn't disagree with her. At that time, however, Fields was entirely bankrolled by her parents. Their support ended when she was sued because several patrons had contracted food poisoning at her restaurant during an unsanctioned, non–socially distanced protest opening. When the lawyers figured out she had no money of her own, they'd gone after her parents.

Fields said it was all horribly unfair. She'd been so busy promoting the rights of small business owners that she'd forgotten to follow food safety standards.

Who among us? thought Nelly, disloyally, after she heard the story for the fortieth time and then the four hundredth time. She'd seen Fields's food handling techniques and thought perhaps her beloved could use a bit more science in her life. For someone who was passionate about natural health and wellness and wouldn't allow her body to be tainted with dangerous vaccines (but was happy to use copious quantities of Botox and, increasingly, fillers), Fields was quite relaxed about germs on food and viruses in her immune system.

Only days after the food poisoning incident and right before the lawsuit hit, Fields had brought a virulent case of covid home to Nelly and her own parents. Fields's father had ended up in the hospital. Her small restaurant closed two months later under an avalanche of orders from the health department and unpaid bills. Fields blamed the prime minister and all levels of government.

None of Fields's inconsistencies bothered Nelly. She liked her wife-to-be's fierceness. She found her capriciousness charming. Whimsical, even!

During her years of running the Close Encounters groups, Nelly had met and grown to appreciate many highly opinionated, ideologically driven people: anti-vaxxers, anti-capitalists, flat-earthers, communists, libertarians, the dogmatically religious, conspiracists, fanatics, kooks, and even a cult member or two. Underneath, they were all the same, mostly. They wanted to be heard. They wanted their fears and dreams to be validated. They wanted to feel seen and to be important. And they deserved that. Everyone did. And that was the fundamental insight of Close Encounters, the organization Nelly had founded and that she believed had the potential to heal the world. Nelly was a genuinely non-judgmental person, but she was also unrelenting in her advocacy for her program. She was a person who could see the good in everyone.

So Fields's peculiarities didn't bother Nelly. Fields had other qualities that more than made up for her tendency to be careless. Not only was she incredibly sexy, but she was also something of a self-trained tech savant who should have been doing that instead of trying to be a restaurateur. Fields had begun to play around with AI as soon as it became available to the public and had focused on its audio capabilities. At first, Fields used AI to make fake recordings of the prime minister saying things that he most definitely had not said. She played these on her podcast that no one listened to. She'd messed around with every possible recording device, the latest tiny speakers and text-to-voice translators that could read out text and change audio to make it sound like any number of famous people's voices. Nelly had thought it was just an interesting, but mostly useless, hobby. But then they'd gotten The Idea. Well, Fields had gotten it.

It had started two years before while David was attending his five-day session. A man had called to leave him a message because David's phone was off. Nelly had taken the call from a Ben Levine who said he was David's father. Nelly got curious about the difference in their last names. She'd casually googled Ben Levine and realized that he might be *the Benedict Levine*, husband of Dr. Bunny Levine. They were one of the wealthiest families in Canada. Worth billions!

Well, well, well.

Their son David, whom Nelly liked very much, had a different last name, but he was clearly heir to those billions of dollars. Maybe he already had billions of his own.

Nelly didn't let on that she knew who he was. She didn't treat him any differently. She didn't immediately ask him to take over the role of token rich person at the next session. But she made sure to send him personal fundraising letters and appeals and she checked in on him personally. Talked about how important he'd been to the breakthroughs that had happened in the session he attended. It was true. He was a genuinely decent, open, and compassionate person who seemed able to relate to people he'd have been justified in disliking automatically. David was kind to everyone and everyone liked him. He made the program better.

When she sent fundraising appeals, he gave, but modestly. He explained that most of his charitable giving was already committed.

The small size of his donations irritated her. Didn't he think the work done by Close Encounters was important?

At some point, her irritation turned into resentment.

Nelly didn't usually talk about participants, but she finally told Fields about

CONTEMPLATION OF A CRIME

her wealthiest-ever participant and shared her dismay that he didn't give more generously to the program.

At first, Fields just listened. Then, slowly, she emphasized just how unfair it was that David was not more helpful. It was terribly unfair. Nelly agreed. So slowly that Nelly was barely even aware that it was happening, Fields convinced Nelly that if David wouldn't give willingly, they should get money from him another way. After all, Close Encounters did important work. And Nelly deserved to make a decent living!

Over the course of a year, they came up with a plan. Nelly reluctantly, Fields enthusiastically. They would get David back to Side Island again, confine him briefly (neither of them ever used the world *kidnap*), convince him to give them enough money to change their lives, and then let him go. He wouldn't remain in captivity for longer than a few hours. He'd be back in time to finish running the course. Why wouldn't he cancel the course? Because he'd want to protect it, of course. He wouldn't want to be the reason Close Encounters was shut down.

That part of the plan felt a little shaky to Nelly. She thought that even if his confinement only lasted a few hours, he was likely to go to the police, but Fields assured her it wouldn't happen, and if it did, they wouldn't get caught. They'd already checked into a hotel in Vancouver. No one would know that they'd taken *A Slice of Pie* from Vancouver and Nanaimo to give themselves a home base while they completed their . . . initiative.

They'd settled on five million as a good number to ask for. No one could do much with a million dollars these days and five million was not a ridiculous amount to give for someone who probably had a billion dollars at his disposal.

David wouldn't even miss the money! They definitely wouldn't hurt him or even injure him. Fields and Nelly were pacifists. Fields reassured Nelly that they wouldn't scare him too badly and would keep their identities secret by using masks and voice changers. He'd never know who was responsible for his extremely brief confinement. The key, Nelly realized, was to take advantage of his overweening sense of social responsibility, which was extreme, even by Nelly's high standards. He hid his wealth and his identity as a rich person. Everything he did was aimed at improving the world. He wouldn't want to be the sort of rich person who got kidnapped and ruined an important program.

At first, everything went smoothly. David readily agreed to take over running the workshop while they were in Vancouver to get married. Then Fields

159

got the idea to cancel the rich guy who was meant to attend in hopes that David would invite his father, who, by all accounts, was a devoted parent, as well as richer than god herself.

Nelly had sent a note from the general email account, cancelling the scheduled wealthy participant. And sure enough, David had asked his father to join him so the course would have a token rich person for the other participants to envy and resent. His father had arrived and given an alias. He had an assistant in tow, who took over the role of spiritual advisor after Nelly cancelled the usual person who took that role. Perfect. It had been a powerful unfolding of events that had convinced Nelly that the plan was not only sound, it was blessed by fortune.

Once David's father agreed to come, it made sense to take both men. And to raise the price from five to ten million. After all, they had two people to look after now. Two people who would need vegan crackers.

Nelly and Fields took *A Slice of the Pie* to the mooring buoys at Saysutshun and then, under the cover of dark, took the Zodiac over to Side Island. Luckily, the engine didn't wake anyone up. They'd snuck onto the island and removed David and his father easily enough, getting them to the beach and into the boat before the tide made it tricky for them to leave. They'd transported them to the site they'd prepared. It had been nerve-racking to operate the Zodiac in the dark with the lights off. If another boat had spotted them, they'd have been caught. If they'd hit a log, they might have capsized or sunk. It was illegal to navigate without operating lights. There would be no way to explain why they had two hooded men with tied hands in the boat. They could have been run over by another larger boat. But they'd made it.

Nelly felt like she hadn't drawn a full breath for the entire time they were in transit with the guests, which is what she insisted they call David and his father. Even after they left them in the tent and had motored back to *A Slice of the Pie*, she'd felt a wreck. She'd be very glad when this was all over, and David and his father were free and she and Fields were on their way to Cuba for their honeymoon. The fact that the transfer couldn't take place immediately and would take hours was a deeply disturbing wrinkle, not least because they actually were slated to get married the following day. They had planned a party for after the small ceremony with themselves and a justice of the peace.

The delay in getting the money was throwing a severe wrench in their plans. There was nothing to do but trust. The money would come through as

CONTEMPLATION OF A CRIME

soon as the Swiss bank opened. Then they would throw the keys to the guests, run for the Zodiac, get to the boat, and head back to Vancouver. They'd left two paddleboards on the beach so David and his father could get back to Side Island.

Meanwhile, Nelly and Fields would be back in plenty of time for the pre-wedding brunch and all the rest of the festivities with their friends. No one would ever know what they'd done. The tent, which had been used for Girl Guide camping trips and left, would reveal nothing. They hadn't touched anything with their bare hands and had bought all the supplies in other towns.

It was all going to work out. But right now, Fields was quietly furious at Nelly for sticking to her guns about not accepting bitcoin for the payment. Nelly had tried and tried to explain that she was an innovator in the anti-crypto-mining space. That she had to respect her own ethos. That she had *won an award* for her anti-crypto activism when she was still in university! It had been a sticking point in their planning process, and finally Fields had agreed to find a way to ask for money that couldn't be traced.

Now they were stuck with this delay and Fields was once again furious. So was Nelly. Presumably, so were the guests. Oh well, it would all be resolved soon.

They'd sent the assistant the instructions to transfer the money at the appointed hour. Nelly hoped that Fields was right that the account they'd set up to receive the money was totally secure and untraceable. Fields had said something about how the money would be moving from account to account at lightning speed, switching countries each time, until it arrived at its final destination. The entire process was supposed to take only a few minutes.

Until then, Nelly busied herself with wondering how the course was going. Yes, they'd taken the organizer and one of the participants, but that didn't mean she didn't care.

She knew she'd made a bit of a nuisance of herself calling David repeatedly before and after the course started. But she wanted things to go well.

She should probably call the lodge again. Just to show some consistency.

"Hey?" said Fields, who'd finished her nails and was staring at something on her computer.

"Yes?"

"What's the name of David's father's assistant?"

"She said her name was Hetty something. Thicke? Thorpe? Something like that."

"Hmmm," said Fields. Post-polish nail care had been forgotten as she scrolled down the page. "I just found some stuff on her. Someone obviously tried to scrub it. But some of it is still findable if you're looking."

Nelly's stomach cramped and she felt like her optimism was about to be taken out back and shot. Seriously.

"Turns out that the assistant is actually a butler named Helen Thorpe and she has caught not one but *two* murderers."

Boom. Optimism down.

"She's a . . . butler?" said Nelly, as though that was the relevant detail, not the fact that she was a murder-solving crime fighter. What would be next? Did Benedict Levine have his own personal Navy SEAL protective detail who would be arriving soon?

"That's not all. This butler person is a former Buddhist nun. Who, again, just happens to have caught two separate murderers."

"What?" wailed Nelly. Something about the idea of Helen being a former Buddhist nun terrified her. "When is she doing all of that? Why isn't she busy buttling or whatever it's called?"

Fields shrugged. "Maybe in addition to being a Buddhist and a butler, she's some kind of security expert?" She cocked her head and looked at her screen, and then angled it so Nelly could see. "This is the only picture of her online."

The photo was taken from the side and the butler's face was mostly turned away. But she certainly didn't look like any sort of murder-solving security expert.

"Her?" said Nelly. "She just looks like . . . a regular woman."

"I know," said Fields. "Exactly. I mean, she's attractive enough."

Nelly shot her a look. Fields had begun noting the attractiveness of other women out loud more frequently lately and Nelly didn't appreciate it.

"Will she call the cops, do you think?" asked Nelly. "Even though she was told not to?"

Fields puffed out a dismissive breath. "Nah. I think she's like you. Hyper-responsible. Totally committed to doing the right thing." Fields spoke as though those were bad qualities.

Maybe they were. It occurred to Nelly that maybe *she* was the tofu in this relationship. How had someone committed to global peace efforts and person-to-person healing journeys ended up with someone who threatened other people's Achilles heels?

CONTEMPLATION OF A CRIME

She pushed the thought away. Never mind. They were doing this for the greater good. "Greater" as in she and Fields really needed the money. And they would be able to do great things with that ten million untraceable dollars. At minimum, they'd be able to leave the country and live well somewhere else after Praxis took over the program and cut her out of her life's work.

"She's not going to catch us. She's a Buddhist. She's going to do the right thing and keep her word. That's how Buddhists are. I think there's even a sutra about it," said Nelly.

"There is a sutra for everything," said Fields. "I dated a girl who practised Zen for a while. She had a short answer for everything."

Nelly didn't know what that meant but didn't ask any questions lest she get more of Fields's thoughts.

"And anyway, we aren't murderers. We're . . . entrepreneurs! It will be fine."

"Maybe we should hurt one of them. At least a little?" said Fields. "To make sure no one talks?"

"Absolutely not. They're co-operating. I'm already worried that they're going to be cold in that tent."

"We'll bring them extra blankets when we go back," said Fields in an irritated voice.

"Remember, we're not going to hurt anyone. We will stay calm. And the butler is definitely going to stay calm. Buddhists are known for being very mellow. Even if the worst happens and someone finds them, no one can trace them to us." Nelly pointed to the small assortment of listening devices on the counter.

"I really don't know if removing those things from the tent was a good idea," said Fields. "We should be listening in on them."

"If they get found, these things could lead them straight to you."

"I think you mean *us*," said Fields.

Nelly looked at her watch. It was only ten o'clock in the morning. It was going to be a long, long several hours to wait until the butler transferred the funds.

163

MADISON CROFT

f you had asked Madison before she attended Close Encounters for Global Healing, she'd have said she preferred her drama to happen on-screen and during nights at the bar with her friends. But when Helen inquired whether anyone wanted to leave the retreat, Madison found herself on the "hell no" side of that equation. In fact, everyone wanted to stay. It turned out that Madison enjoyed being in the middle of a kidnapping drama with a bunch of people she didn't know or trust. Also, she liked being a part of something, and she liked being needed and trusted, by Helen, at least.

Helen told them about herself and about her boss and said her boss had given her clues that made her think that he and David were being held nearby. She said she knew that none of the guests were likely to be involved because she had their cellphones and because she'd been getting messages from the kidnappers while Yana, Pain, Tom, Madison, and Wayne were within sight.

Pain had pointed out that they could still be involved somehow and Helen had agreed with him. She wasn't defensive at all. She said she'd decided to trust them, which Madison thought was badass of her.

Helen had been instructed by her boss and the kidnappers not to tell anyone, which meant that they were all now part of the inner circle, a place Madison had always wanted to be, especially since some of the people in that inner circle were so filthy rich that they needed butlers. Heck yeah.

She wondered if she and the search team she'd been assigned to would get a huge cash bonus if they found the kidnapping victims. Madison thought they probably would. Maybe she would spend part of her reward money paying for butler school. She was seriously into Helen and the other butlers. Like really, *really* into them. They were so . . . she didn't even know how to describe it. Like upper management, only well-dressed and not assholes. Maybe if she was a butler, she'd get a sense of purpose in her life.

Plus, she still thought Helen's boss, whose real name Helen hadn't given them, was a smoke show for an older man.

Helen had organized everyone into search teams, each of which included at least one butler. Madison's group had gotten the least attractive butler, but that was fine. They were assigned an area to search and told that if they found anything, they should let Helen know immediately. Helen said the kidnapping victims might be in a cave or an outbuilding. They probably weren't on the island at all, but the possibility needed to be eliminated.

Nigel, the youngest butler, was not like the others, from a hotness perspective, but he was funny and kind of . . . charming. That was the word. He didn't seem to care what people thought of him and all those hairy little dogs on long patent-leather leashes that kept getting tangled up. Thanks to his dogs and Wayne's overweight tan-coloured pit bull that was like a water balloon on legs, their search group looked like a dog-walking service.

Of course Yana couldn't shut up about the dogs. She'd been complaining about Potato since Wayne brought her onto the ferry the day they all arrived.

Yana was against literally everything. She had let them know in the first fifteen minutes of searching that she didn't approve of using water or electricity, having children, driving, flying, and eating meat, dairy, fish, seafood, or sugar. And don't even get her started on Amazon: the company or the rainforest! She was severely bent about both.

Finally Wayne, who was not an earth-first guy, had said, "I hope you aren't in charge of recruiting people to save the climate or we're all going to burn." Which was like, fair enough. Yana was a next-level downer.

Yana didn't even respond, which told Madison that she *knew* how she sounded.

But Yana was extra hung up on the dogs, for some reason, even though Potato was very cute in a "know the dangers of overfeeding" sort of way and the other ones were adorable.

"Dogs are awful for the ecosystem," said Yana, for about the eighth time, as they poked around in an old woodshed in a small mossy clearing that was empty of kidnapping victims.

"Maybe I should talk to my boss about getting carbon offsets for them," said Nigel, the butler. His face was a little red from all the walking and searching, but he stayed cheerful. "Come here, Hannibal." One of the little dogs ambled closer to him and he removed some tiny sticks and brambles from its coat. "Okay. You can sniff around," said Nigel. But the dog just sat at his feet, staring up at him like he was made of meatballs.

Madison was curious about Nigel's boss and about butlering, but she also felt that she should show some, like, decorum and proper respect while they looked for the kidnapping victims, which was obviously a serious thing. Who was Nigel's boss? *Where* was Nigel's boss?

Madison considered herself a student of celebrities and the super-rich. She read all the magazines and the gossip sites about wealthy people. She even read *The New York Times* sometimes, which had a lot of articles about "ultra-high-net-worth individuals," a term journalists use when they don't want to keep having to write the word *rich* over and over.

The members of the search team were walking four abreast, except when Nigel fell behind so he could get the dogs untangled. They poked the ground ahead of them with sticks because Nigel said he'd seen searchers do that on TV.

"They're still alive, I think," Wayne had said. "So we don't need to look for their bodies."

"We need to put these sticks back where we found them," said Yana.

"So is your boss travelling?" Madison asked Nigel, hoping the question came across as casual.

Everyone looked at her.

"She's at a debrief session," said Nigel. "Sort of a post-mortem for DJs after Burning Man."

Madison sucked in a breath. She'd always wanted to go to Burning Man. To be precise, she'd always wanted to say she'd *been* to Burning Man. She didn't want the hassle of actually going. And his boss was a *DJ*? Was his boss Paris Hilton? Madison would straight-up die if she was.

"Wow," she said. "Did you go there with her? To Burning Man, I mean?"

"No. I stayed back with the dogs. I've only been out of butler school since June and I'm getting her new household set up."

"Really." Madison sighed, feeling almost faint from the glamour of it. "I bet her house is incredible."

"It's pretty nice," said Nigel.

He didn't offer any details and Madison didn't ask. He was being discreet.

166

CONTEMPLATION OF A CRIME

He probably had an NDA. After all, it seemed like you wouldn't want people to know too much about your clients or they might get kidnapped, like Helen's boss and David. But Burning Man! DJs!

The day was, as West Coast fall days went, perfect. It had rained recently, erasing the most obvious signs of the summer's long dry spell. The sky had cleared, other than a few round, white clouds that moved overhead like gauzy blimps.

They'd been assigned what Madison thought of as the right-hand side of the island, which was on the same side as Protection Island and Guide Island, as well as the cabins and the lodge. Madison wasn't good at identifying north, south, west, or east. When she was in Nanaimo, she oriented herself using stores and restaurants as landmarks.

So far they had found a lot of trees, grass, moss, trees covered in moss, mushrooms, dirt, rocks, and some outbuildings, also covered in dirt and moss. But mostly trees and rocks. They'd searched six cabins, including cupboards and bathrooms, and found no kidnap victims or anything suspicious. They were heading onto a narrow path above the steep cliffs at the far end of the island. If the kidnappers had stashed David and his father at the base of those cliffs, they'd have already drowned.

They walked in silence for a while, and Madison discovered that she didn't like being alone with her thoughts. She usually listened to music or a podcast or talked on the phone with a friend. She was finding the experience of not talking or listening tiring. It wasn't just that it was a lot of work to try to look for clues, it was the way her mind jumped around. Every so often, her thoughts went back to David and his father. What were they doing? How were they feeling? She hoped they weren't cold and uncomfortable. Or, god forbid, injured. How awful would it be to be injured *and* kidnapped?

The thought was intolerable. Then her mind would skip like a record onto something better or at least less important. Things she'd like to buy and eat and have. She'd never before in her life noticed what her mind did.

She'd fallen behind the others, who were walking slowly through and over fallen branches and salal and Oregon grape bushes beside the trail. Wayne had gone ahead and was out of sight. Nigel and the dogs were about ten feet ahead of her on the left. Yana was between her and Nigel. Seeing Yana's sturdy figure in the faded Patagonia jacket reminded Madison of how strong the woman was for her age. Hell, Yana was strong for a person of any age. Maybe that's how you needed to be if you were going to pay attention to all the things that were wrong with the world. And even with all her strength, the heaviness of knowing so many bad things seemed to be crushing Yana. Madison gave her head a shake as a wave of something came over her. Caring? Was that it? Was she caring about Yana, who only moments ago she'd thought was as human version of a wet, mouldy blanket? If so, she wished it would stop.

What was happening to her? She needed to do some online shopping, stat. Get her head right.

Madison was so lost in her thoughts and feelings that she didn't notice she'd fallen even farther behind the others, who'd rejoined the main trail after their detour along the cliff's edge. She wandered over toward a small pond to the left of the trail. There were two people ahead of her on the other side of the small body of water. They were partly hidden by some fallen trees and undergrowth. They faced each other.

Madison found herself stepping softly so she wouldn't make any noise as she got closer. She wanted to know who was there and what they were saying. She sidled as near as she could get until she was stopped by Wayne's dog, Potato, who was not on a leash. She wagged her skinny tail and came over and leaned against Madison's legs. Madison bent and gave the dog a scratch.

The words from the pair ahead floated to her ears.

"I saw you," said one. It was the mean kid. Pain. He was talking to Wayne.

"Saw what?" said Wayne.

Madison stayed bent over in the hip-high undergrowth of ferns and bushes so they wouldn't see her.

"Coming out of David's room."

Wayne seemed to mutter something that Madison couldn't hear. Then, ". . . just checking." She couldn't hear the rest of the sentence.

"In his room? Were you checking that you kidnapped him properly?"

"Shut up. I had nothing to do with that."

"You didn't say anything to anyone about the blood in his room, did you?" said Pain.

Madison felt her whole body tighten, and suddenly she didn't want to hear this. And she definitely didn't want Wayne or that scary dead-eyed kid to know she'd overheard them. If they did, the next blood they found might be hers.

CONTEMPLATION OF A CRIME

Potato leaned harder into her legs and Madison got ready to back away. She had to be silent.

"Why were *you* in his room?" asked Wayne, in an accusing voice.

"Following you," said Pain's voice. He sounded both sour and happy. How had the kid gotten so nasty?

"Helen probably already knows about the blood. I don't need to say anything. I had nothing to do with it."

"What do you think she'd say if she found out you snuck into his room at the ass crack of dawn?"

Another muttered word Madison couldn't make out. Her back was starting to ache from being bent in half.

"I bugged his room."

"Holy shit. So you're the kidnapper!"

"No. I just—"

But before Wayne could finish, he was interrupted. And to Madison's deep shock, she was the one doing the interrupting.

"Oh my god. How could you?" she blurted, after shooting up out of the underbrush like a startled pheasant. A second later, she lost her balance and fell over into a patch of dying ferns and was immediately subjected to a kiss attack from Potato.

169

HELEN THORPE

Back at the lodge, Helen tried to maintain a semblance of normalcy with the only person who didn't know what had happened. Or rather, what *was* happening.

She walked into the kitchen, her phone with the ringer on clutched in her hand, to check on lunch preparations.

Bobbi-Lyn was using an oversized spoon to stir an enormous, dented pot on the massive stove. Something about the scene reminded Helen of a witch in a fairy tale. A witch wearing an old Whitesnake T-shirt featuring a slightly blurry-looking snake with dripping fangs over the words written in cursive: *Slide it in*.

Eeew, thought Helen, imagining a chef wearing a shirt like that in the Levines' large and elegant kitchen.

It was too late to ask Bobbi-Lyn to wear proper kitchen attire and it wasn't Helen's place to do so. But seeing the cook standing with a hand in one back pocket of her heavily stitched jeans and the other moving the food around restlessly made Helen feel slightly twitchy.

"Hello," she said. "I just wanted to see how things are going for you today."

"Fine," said Bobbi-Lyn in her smoker's voice. "We're going to have sandwiches for lunch. Pasta for dinner."

"Wonderful," said Helen, who under normal circumstances would know to the last ingredient what the guests would be served. "Do you need anything?"

"I need people to be on time for meals," she said. "You were late for breakfast and food tastes like shit when it gets cold."

Helen blinked. She really had gotten a bit soft during her time with the Levines. No staff members there swore around her, probably because she was essentially in charge of all of them and because her overall mien discouraged foul language.

Helen knew some people found her too proper. She did not want that properness to slide into being judgmental or easily offended.

CONTEMPLATION OF A CRIME

"Of course," she said. "I understand."

"So David and the older guest are sick?"

Helen nodded and automatically looked at her phone. No message.

"Do you want me to make up a couple of plates and deliver them?"

Right. Bobbi-Lyn was a little rough around the edges, but she *was* in the business of feeding people, and so far she seemed to be good at it.

"No, thank you," said Helen. "You're busy in here. I'll ask Nigel or Gavin or Murray to deliver the food."

"I don't mind," said Bobbi-Lyn. She'd stopped stirring the pot. The spoon was now suspended in the air and she'd fixed Helen with a surprisingly sharp gaze. Her eyes were dark and small.

"That's not necessary," said Helen, firmly.

"Where is everyone? David said you were going to be working in the lodge during the day."

"I have added a few other exercises to the program. Time spent outdoors is very, uh . . ."

Bobbi-Lyn waited.

"Therapeutic," said Helen.

"If you say so. Are the rest of them friends of yours going to be back here to help set the table and serve soon?"

Helen glanced at her phone again. No message.

"Yes. I'll make sure they are."

Bobbi-Lyn turned back to the pot. "Good. I'd hate to see anyone else disappear," she said with her back to Helen, who stood in the doorway with her mouth slightly ajar.

Helen's phone rang and she quickly held it to her face and saw an unknown number.

Maybe they didn't want to use Signal anymore. She decided to answer.

Helen left the kitchen and answered the call when she reached the foyer.

"Hello? Is this, uh, Hetty? I hope you don't mind me calling. I got your number from David when you took over as the spiritual support person. He told me you wouldn't mind me checking in."

Helen wasn't sure who was speaking. The woman had a distinctive voice but Helen couldn't place it.

"Oh, sorry. It's Nelly Bean. I'm the founder. The one who calls David every five minutes. Well, not really. But I like to keep in touch about how things are going since I can't be there myself. I haven't been able to get in touch with David today, and I thought you might be able to pass along a message and give me an update."

Oh no. Helen didn't want to be questioned by the founder of Close Encounters for Global Healing right now. She had no good answers. She took a deep breath and then asked Nelly Bean to hold while she walked upstairs and went outside onto the landing.

After she gave Nelly Bean an inaccurate account of how things were going, lying that David was ill in bed, probably asleep, and reassuring her that all was well, she ended the call. Nelly seemed satisfied with Helen's explanation, thank goodness. After that, Helen went back inside and into the office and, as silently as possible, picked up a file folder with the bios of the participants, a pad of lined white paper, and an old-style Rolodex of contacts.

She took those items out to the landing and found herself thinking about the conversation with the cook. She didn't need to overthink Bobbi-Lyn's words. The cook had simply been referring to the fact that David and Mr. Levine had abruptly retreated from the workshop. The woman had no idea they'd been taken.

At least, Helen hoped that was the case. Bobbi-Lyn gave off a strange, unsettled energy that put Helen on edge.

Helen, usually in tune with such things, noticed her own reaction, but she didn't take it too seriously. Bobbi-Lyn was a hard-edged person who wore unattractive concert T-shirts by bands Helen had never heard of. That part was not a surprise. Helen hadn't heard of most bands. Spending the majority of one's early adulthood in a monastery and then at a spiritual retreat centre meant missing a lot of popular culture, particularly heavy metal acts. If Bobbi-Lyn had a T-shirt for a well-known hand-drummer, Helen might have had a chance since the retreat centre she'd worked at hosted many of the best.

Everyone deserved the benefit of the doubt. Everyone.

She took a seat on the damp couch. Then she glanced at her phone again. No message on Signal or any of her other apps.

She looked at the notes she'd written on the pad of paper after the message from Mr. Levine.

"It reminds me of an apple tree," was one. Mr. Levine had used those words

CONTEMPLATION OF A CRIME

in the initial voice-to-text message when he informed her that he and David had been kidnapped. "It's a real situation in the kitchen" was another. Then, in the video that served as proof of life, he'd spoken the words "wouldn't even kick a flea."

These non sequiturs were, Helen was sure, clues. She just needed to interpret them correctly.

In her time as the Levines' butler, Helen had learned to pick up on Dr. and Mr. Levine's silent cues. Sometimes one of them would nod almost imperceptibly at a guest, and Helen knew to pay more attention to that person. Maybe they needed something or they needed monitoring because they were drinking too much or becoming argumentative. Maybe the guest had even pocketed something they shouldn't have. That happened more than Helen would have imagined possible. Rich people stole things with alarming frequency.

The method for handling the issue depended on the situation. If a drunk socialite needed to be cut off, Helen would do it in such a way that the woman in question wouldn't even realize it had happened. Instead she would feel like it had been her decision to have a coffee and perhaps take a tour of the Levines' garden.

But Mr. Levine's words weren't suggestions. Or were they? She didn't think so. She was almost sure he'd been quoting dialogue from memorable social occasions that he knew she would be likely to remember.

"It reminds me of an apple tree."

She remembered those words because they'd been spoken by the leader of a ferociously effective reproductive rights advocate from Alabama. The woman, who'd had a head of tremendous blond hair, had a delightful if somewhat portentous way of saying things that made it sound like she was giving a benediction. Helen had escorted her and Mr. and Dr. Levine out to the enormous event tent where the Levines were hosting a dinner to honour the good works and activism of nearly a hundred people from around the world and where they would be announcing millions of dollars in new charitable contributions.

The woman, Chiffon von Sutton, had walked over to the main centre pole of the tent, which was disguised to look like a tree and hung with twinkling illuminated balls. "My word, my word, it reminds me of an apple tree designed by an angel," she'd said.

Was Mr. Levine quoting Chiffon von Sutton? If so, why? Was it because he and David had been kidnapped by a southerner? A woman? An activist?

No, she thought. Did it have something to do with *where* they were being held? Maybe they were in an orchard? Or a tent? Or perhaps it was some combination of those things.

His line "It's a real situation in the kitchen" was a variation on words Dr. and Mr. Levine often used to indicate that they wanted to get away from a social obligation in order to supposedly check on something in the kitchen. When they were in the kitchen, they usually just sat around chatting with the chef and other household staff while Helen continued to take care of the guests. What did it mean in this context? Maybe that he and David wanted to or planned to get away? Or did he want Helen to take care of everything while he and David conferred with each other?

Again, she wasn't sure. But her employers only used the "situation in the kitchen" excuse when the situation was manageable. They'd never disappeared into the kitchen and left Helen to deal with anything she couldn't handle.

Had Mr. Levine simply been suggesting that the situation was going to get worked out by Helen in her role and by him in his role? Could it be that simple?

And finally the "wouldn't even kick a flea" quote. It came from a Fortune 500 Silicon Valley company CEO who had talked in less than flattering terms about his son, who, the CEO said, lacked the requisite killer instinct to succeed in business. "My son wouldn't even kick a flea," he'd said in a voice filled with disappointment.

"How awful for you," Dr. Levine had said and winked at her husband, who grinned.

In that instance, Helen was sure that Mr. Levine was trying to tell her that the kidnappers were not dangerous, or at least not immediately dangerous, and she trusted his ability to read people.

Of course, she could be misinterpreting all of these clues, and either way she would receive no confirmation until Mr. Levine and David had been released. If they were released.

Helen turned her attention to the Rolodex and the file folder containing the registration information. She flipped through the list of participants. There were names, addresses, and intake forms that each had filled out. She stopped at the unfamiliar name: Morgan Bailey. Sixty-three years old. Entrepreneur. This must be the wealthy person who'd dropped out. She found his contact information and, before she could second-guess herself, dialled the number.

CONTEMPLATION OF A CRIME

"Bailey and Associates," said a professional-sounding woman's voice.

"Hello. My name is Helen Thorpe. I was hoping to speak to Mr. Bailey."

"May I tell him what the call is about?" asked the woman.

"I wanted to speak to him about his participation in the Close Encounters workshop," said Helen.

"Oh, yes. I think he'll want to speak to you."

Helen was placed on hold and then a booming voice came on the line. "Morgan here."

"Mr. Bailey," said Helen. "My name is Helen and I'm calling from Side Island. I'm assisting with this year's Close Encounters for Global Healing program and I have a question for you."

He laughed. "Not as many questions as I have for you."

Helen's attention brightened and she felt her whole being home in on the voice on the other line. "Ah, I see. Perhaps you should go first."

"Well, Helen, first off, why was I cut from the team? Have you got a whole list of rich folks who want to get guilt-tripped by the less fortunate for a week? A whack of high-net-worth masochists who want to wade in a sea of low-income resentment?"

For a moment, Helen didn't respond.

"We're very sorry not to have you here," she said, finally, with some sincerity at the understatement of it. "May I ask who let you know that you were not—"

"Invited to the party?" said Morgan Bailey, who, judging from his voice, was heartiness and good cheer personified. "Hmmm. Let me think. I believe I got an email. Not from Nelly. Let me have my secretary find the message."

There was a moment and some muffled conversation before Mr. Bailey came back on the line. "Someone named David Lewiston. He was polite enough about it. He sent the email a few days before I was due to show up. I'll be honest with you, Helen. I was initially offended. I mean, yes, the five days is an unholy bummer, especially at the beginning. But my counsellor seems to think it would be good for me. So does my pastor."

Helen thought he might be one of the many wealthy individuals who struggled with a sense of guilt, similar to David. "Yes," she said. "I am sure attending the course helps to put your position in perspective."

Morgan Bailey laughed. "I don't know about that. I'll tell you, Helen, I don't like whiners. I don't like people who don't work hard. I've busted my you-know-what for everything I've got. I had eight McDonald's at one point. Sold 'em all. And now I'm worth a small fortune. I started from nothing. That's what I tell the people in that workshop. Stop whining. Start grinding. You know?"

"Yes," said Helen.

"And I guess the other people help me understand that not everyone has my drive. My business sense. My vigour and business acumen. And my luck, if I'm being perfectly honest. Some of us are blessed, while some of us have it rough."

"Agreed," said Helen.

"I've attended the workshop several times now. Only missed for a medical reason one year and when the course didn't run due to covid. I always got something out of it. I'll be honest, I was even sort of disappointed when I got that email saying my attendance was no longer required. Bizarre, right? Now my pastor and counsellor have me serving food down at the food bank. Between you and me, I'd rather be at the lodge."

"Well, thank you for speaking with me," said Helen, who felt her mind wanting to leave the conversation to begin pondering the information she'd just been given.

"No problem. Hope you get some nice breakthroughs this year. Common humanity and all that," he said. "Tell Nelly or David or whoever that I'll come back next year if they need me. It's my penance for living the good life. I should have been a born again. They never worry about being rich." He chuckled at his own joke.

Helen paused. "Mr. Bailey? Would you be able to send me a copy of the email you received? I'm trying to sort out a few things and it would be helpful to have the correspondence trail."

"Am I going to get someone in trouble? Normally, I wouldn't mind that, especially if someone did me a dirty. But the whole point of Close Encounters is to bring people closer together."

"No," said Helen. "No one is getting in trouble. I'm just trying to sort out a few issues as we move forward." She was pleased with her use of vague corporate language that provided no real information.

Morgan Bailey was apparently fluent in that same language. "Sure. I'll have Rene forward it to you. Can I help you with anything else? I've got a tee time in a few minutes."

CONTEMPLATION OF A CRIME

"No, sir," said Helen. "Thank you so much."

With that, the retired fast-food magnate transferred Helen back to his secretary, who, like any good admin assistant, was highly efficient. The email from David arrived in Helen's personal in-box a minute later.

She looked at it. It was perfectly polite and very clear. Mr. Morgan Bailey's participation was no longer needed. There were apologies for the last-minute cancellation and expressions of gratitude for his participation. No explanation was given.

The letter had an email signature from David.

How strange. Helen was sure that David said it had been this man's decision to drop out at the last minute.

Then Helen checked which address the email had been sent from. It was from the general email address for Close Encounters. Office-closeencountersforgh@gmail.com.

Helen looked at an email she'd received from David about what his father would need for his trip. That one had come from David.lewiston-closeencountersforgh@gmail.com.

Of course, David probably had the ability to send email from any of the Close Encounters email accounts. But she knew enough about David to know that he wouldn't lie to his father. Someone had told Morgan Bailey not to come so that David would invite his father. But no one knew who his father was.

Who was in a position to arrange something like that?

Helen's recent experiences with the internet and the ways in which it could be manipulated came to her mind. She'd learned during her work for Nigel's boss, Ms. Cartier Hightower, that there was almost no such thing as fully effective online security. That truism applied to social media and internet commerce. It seemed very likely that it applied to emails and internal computer systems.

In spite of her best efforts to resist judging the participants, she thought about which of them would be capable of hacking into Close Encounters email accounts. Pain could do it. Maybe one or more of the others could, too.

Helen heaved a sigh. The email account could have been compromised by anyone, really. It would not do to point the blame at anyone right away.

GAVIN VIMUKTHI

Gavin Vimukthi watched Murray talking to Tom Aucielo. Murray kept her hands either behind her back or at her sides, and she allowed her steps to match Tom's and her gaze to sweep side to side as they searched for signs of the kidnapped pair. Gavin admired her willingness to engage with Tom, who had a personal history Gavin found repellent. Gavin's distaste for the man was not much mitigated by Tom's emotional and, it seemed, somewhat self-pitying outburst earlier in the course. Was Tom really sorry he'd joined a white nationalist terrorist organization bent on hurting others? Or was he sorry he got caught and punished and now had a target on his back for informing on the other troglodytes? Gavin figured it was fifty-fifty either way.

Gavin had spent his early life in Sri Lanka before his family moved to England, where his mother taught at an international school for the children of the super-rich and his father helped to run a small airport for private aircraft located just outside of London.

His parents were naturally elegant, well-educated people, and they'd passed their considerable social graces on to their children. Gavin had two sisters. One had an advanced degree in political science and was on her way to becoming a diplomat. The other was a doctor with Médecins Sans Frontières.

Gavin sometimes worried he was a disappointment to his parents. He'd taken a degree in the humanities in the UK, and then his father's connections had led to him taking a job as a flight attendant on private aircrafts. Before he went to butler school, his parents had hinted that he should consider becoming a pilot.

"My Gavin," his mother would say. "You are wasted handing out packages of peanuts on those planes."

But he'd liked being a flight attendant. He enjoyed the travel, and he was interested in the people he flew with. He'd taken care of luminaries from

CONTEMPLATION OF A CRIME

all over the world: businesspeople, actors and musicians, royals from many nations.

Some of them travelled with personal assistants and some with butlers who had told him about their jobs and their training. Butlering, he'd learned, was a growth industry. As the ranks of the super-rich grew, so did the demand for qualified butlers. "You would be perfect," one butler had told him, while lightly hitting on him. "You're gorgeous *and* you're competent."

So Gavin had saved his money and enrolled in the North American Butler Academy, where he'd met Helen and Murray. He and Murray had gone to help Helen at the Yatra Institute right after graduation. That's where Helen had solved the murder of her former employer and where Gavin and Murray had fallen in love. Gavin and Murray had been helping to run the Yatra Institute ever since. But they were both feeling somewhat underutilized, especially Gavin, who was metaphorically and literally a bit of a high flyer.

They would not be going back to Sutil Island and the Yatra Institute after their holiday. After this brief stint at Side Island and their later, proper holiday with Helen and Nigel, they planned to find a position together. They could go anywhere in the world. Work for any number of people or organizations that required high-end service.

But as Gavin wandered through the woods on Side Island looking for kidnap victims, he realized that he really enjoyed a bit of excitement with his butlering. He enjoyed being in the midst of a mystery. Stressful as it was, helping Helen solve the murder of her former employer had been one of the most invigorating experiences of his life. Later, he'd been almost jealous when Helen became embroiled in another mystery involving an influencer she'd been asked to look after.

Gavin, it turned out, liked danger. He wanted to rescue people *and* to make sure they were living their best lives.

He wondered if Murray felt the same. She'd had an unfortunate experience during the internship that was part of her butler training and it had nearly ended her career before it started. Perhaps that, and the fact that she'd been attacked when they were investigating the death of Helen's employer on Sutil Island, had put her off. He would do anything to keep Murray and Helen and Nigel safe. But by god, it really felt meaningful to be helping with more than just the table settings.

SUSAN JUBY

Gavin doubted Helen's employer and his son were still on Side Island. He thought they would be nearby, but not that close.

He'd once flown with a kidnapping specialist who worked for a phenomenally well-off family from Pakistan. The family kept the specialist on retainer because members of their staff kept getting kidnapped. That man, an ex-soldier from Poland, had been a fascinating combination of tough and savvy. He'd told Gavin about getting a different family released by a drug cartel, negotiating to get a journalist out of captivity in Kazakhstan, and an aid worker freed from a militia in Somalia.

The man was infinitely rougher than Gavin. No one would have hired him to greet guests and arrange formal dinners, but he was doing something important.

Maybe, Gavin thought, it was time to get in touch with that kidnapping specialist to ask for his advice about security training. Maybe being a butler *and* a security expert would be an ideal combination?

They were making their way down the wood-chip-covered path back toward the lodge. They'd searched the section of the island that faced Saysutshun and Nanaimo and found nothing. There were very few spots where anyone could land even a small watercraft on the island. There was the length of beach where the ferry dock was usually located, but most of the island rose steeply from the water. He'd noticed on the marine maps in the dining room that the area around Side Island was full of hazards in the form of large rocks and other obstacles that could be very challenging for a boat that wanted to approach, especially in low visibility. If the kidnappers had taken them off the island, and he was sure they had, he wondered where they launched from and what sort of vessel they'd used. It couldn't have been very big, since there was no dock.

Had the kidnappers put them in a kayak or some other smaller, more manoeuvrable vessel with no motor? That would have been an incredibly dangerous thing to do. If David or his father had put up a struggle, they could have capsized. Gavin was not a sailor and he knew almost nothing about the channels and waters around Side Island, but he decided to do some research. David Lewiston and his father had been taken at night by boat. The kind of boat seemed relevant.

CONTEMPLATION OF A CRIME

In the meantime, he let Murray continue talking to Tom. Gavin had met and worked for plenty of racists before, but he tried to keep his distance from them when possible.

Their conversation seemed to deepen, and Gavin grew curious. He allowed himself to draw closer.

"Did I mention she met someone else?" Tom was saying.

"Oh?" said Murray.

Gavin loved her soft accent. He had one of those untraceable accents common to people who speak multiple languages and who were carefully educated at English public schools. He and Murray had been told more than once that they should narrate audiobooks.

Murray had noticed Gavin coming up behind them and reached back to briefly touch his hand.

"I bet Gracie's new boyfriend is terrible. She's used to brutal guys. Her father is a total pig. The whole Compound was full of abusive assholes. I'm not exaggerating, either."

"Ah," said Murray.

"Those guys were racist first, misogynist second, and sometimes the other way around."

"I believe you."

"I mean, in some ways, the whole scene was like my family all over again."

Tom glanced at Murray, and Gavin felt a flash of unexpected sympathy for the deep-voiced guy who seemed so uncertain about who he was. Then he reminded himself that Tom Aucielo was a racist who might be involved in the kidnapping. Any of the guests might be.

"That must have been hard," said Murray, leaving it open whether she was talking about Tom's time in the Compound or his upbringing.

She walked steadily on. There was something about her neatness and self-possession, her occasional fierceness and frequent wit that made Gavin feel thrilled and comforted by her presence.

"Yeah. I mean, I wasn't really part of what went on there, but we all had to go to the lectures. Watch the videos. Like I mentioned, I stayed mostly with the women. I even helped a few of them get out," he said.

Gavin saw Murray flash a sidelong glance at the small man beside her.

"Really?" she said.

"Yeah. It's the only thing about that time that I feel okay about."

Tom seemed to have become aware that Gavin was right behind them and that Gavin, a person of colour, might be offended by him. He looked back at him. "Sorry, man."

Gavin nodded. What could he say?

182

HELEN THORPE

elen was keeping one eye on the lunch table, where Nigel and Gavin were arranging the plates and dishes, and another eye on the guests, who were making themselves sandwiches to take outside for a picnic.

The two search parties had returned. They hadn't located Mr. Levine or David, but they seemed to have found some sort of connection with one another and they were all brimming with things to tell her.

Helen thought they could talk outside while they ate. That way, Bobbi-Lyn would not overhear them. It felt very strange and possibly nonsensical to maintain the pretense that everything was normal in order to prevent the cook from finding out they were in the midst of a crisis. Exclusionary, really. But Bobbi-Lyn wasn't involved in this and Helen wanted to keep it that way.

Bobbi-Lyn, who was apparently finding her groove in the kitchen, had put together an impressive selection of salads: butter lettuce with a light cream and dill dressing; massaged kale with chopped broccoli, shredded Brussels sprouts, and dried fruit; black bean and spelt with strips of tortillas. She'd also laid out three kinds of fresh bread, a variety of cheeses and spreads, and lettuce and tomato.

Helen hoped they'd all eat heartily. Who knew what the next hours would bring?

As revved up as they were, Madison, Tom, Pain, Wayne, and Yana all filled up their oversized melamine plates. As they made their way through the front doors of the great room and headed for the outdoor table that Nigel had set up on the deck at the ocean's edge, Helen's phone buzzed in her pocket and she quickly turned away from the dining room and went into the office.

It was another message on Signal.

—It's time.
—Please log into this account and enter these transfer numbers when prompted.

Helen felt her breath grow shallow. This was it. She would transfer the funds, they would release Mr. Levine and David, and this ordeal would be over.

—At the end you need to enter your security code.

Wait. What? Her code? What code? She had no code!

—We will confirm when the funds arrive.

Helen, still reeling from the idea that she was supposed to have a security code, made herself keep typing. She could not let on that she didn't have a security code. Or maybe she had one and she didn't know it? Maybe she would be prompted to put in her own bank code? She prayed that there would be more information forthcoming. Mr. Levine would never ask her to do something that she couldn't possibly do.

She kept typing.

—When will Mr. Levine and David be released?
—When we have the funds we will wait three hours and then tell you where to find them. They will be fine.

Helen didn't want to wait five more seconds for her employer and his son to be released, but she would just have to be patient. She did not like what was happening. Not one bit. She had no code! And her body was reacting, which meant that her mind was closing and getting narrower.

Breathe, she told herself. *This is what is happening, like it or not.*

The dark clutch of fear around her heart released and her chest seemed to soften again.

—Okay. I will do it now.

Before she could click on the link they'd sent, there was a knock at the office door. Helen looked up to see Pain and Wayne standing there, Madison right behind them. They carried plates of food.

Helen felt frustration exacerbated by stress rising up, and she wanted to

CONTEMPLATION OF A CRIME

snap at them and tell them to leave her alone. She had reached her limit and couldn't cope with any more requests, complications, or bad news. In spite of her exasperation, she did and said nothing. Her teachers had always emphasized the importance of what they called "the sacred pause." It was the practice of taking a moment between having a feeling and reacting to it. The idea was to check one's intentions before acting. Helen thought it was one of the most useful things she'd ever learned. It had helped her avoid any number of unskilful responses to difficult situations. Telling three of the guests to please get lost already would be highly unskilful.

"Hello? Anyone in there?" said Pain in his reedy voice.

Helen let the sacred pause go on a little longer, just to be safe.

When she opened her eyes, all the guests were gathered around, staring at her. Nigel and Murray and Gavin behind them. The whole group was waiting for her to stop sacred pausing.

The realization nearly made her laugh out loud.

"I'll join you outside in a few minutes," she said.

"What's going on?" asked Madison, who was not one for pauses of any kind between the impulse and the reaction.

"Please. Let's give Helen a little time," said Murray. Then she made big eyes at everyone else to remind them that the office was bugged.

Madison winced and mouthed sorry.

Like a single malformed organism, the group backed away from the office and presumably went outside to eat. Helen wrote down the account numbers and double-checked them to make sure she was transcribing them correctly. Then she clicked the link.

She still didn't understand why she had been asked to make the transfer. Wouldn't it be better for Mr. Levine to do it? She had to trust that there was a reason it was being done this way. When the situation was resolved and everyone was safe, she knew Mr. Levine would have a good explanation.

The link in the message took her to a sleek, understated website with a dark green background and a small gold logo at the top showing three rectangles resting on top of each other. Stonehenge? Gold bars?

She entered the codes as prompted until she hit a transfer screen. There was no place for her to enter her own code and she breathed a sigh of relief. She didn't understand, but things seemed to be proceeding properly. Then she typed ten million dollars into the amount field. That made her heart flutter. It seemed like such a lot of money, but to Mr. Levine, it was an interest payment.

She hit send. The screen went blank for a second and then a message appeared.

ACCOUNT SUSPENDED.

Helen's breath stopped. She leaned forward and stared in disbelief and horror at the screen.

Account suspended? What on earth? What did that even mean? Had she typed in a number incorrectly? She'd been so careful! Or had she missed the place where she was to put in a code that she didn't even have?

She checked the numbers she'd written down against the Signal message she'd received, but of course the original message was now gone and she hadn't taken a screenshot. She was certain she'd written down and then entered all the numbers correctly. After all, she'd been able to log in and get to the transfer screen. But maybe in her stress, she'd made a mistake? A deadly one.

Once again the frantic buzzing of her nervous system threatened to overwhelm her.

Account suspended.

She had no idea what to do. She had no codes other than the ones Mr. Levine had given her. She didn't even know which bank she'd just logged in to or where it was based. The only identifying information had been the link and that gold logo. She couldn't exactly start calling banks and explaining that her attempt to transfer millions of dollars to kidnappers who were holding her employer and his son hostage hadn't worked, and could they please put her in touch with their IT department?

She let out a long breath and sent a little wave of compassion to herself. *You're doing fine, sweetheart*, she said, using the sweetheart practice she'd learned from a wonderful Buddhist therapist she'd once seen.

The other non sequitur from one of Mr. Levine's messages moved through her mind like a banner pulled behind a plane.

"It's a little like being stuck in traffic. And wasn't life itself a little like being stuck in traffic?"

Mr. Levine was fond of talking about traffic, even though when time was

CONTEMPLATION OF A CRIME

tight, he always had the option of taking a helicopter or private plane. He liked the idea that even if one had a personal driver, one would still occasionally experience traffic.

"I'm not a head of state," he'd said once, humbly, when he and Dr. Levine and Helen were stuck on the Seven Mile Bridge on their way to Key West to visit their daughter, who was staying there for the season. They could have flown over, but Dr. and Mr. Levine had wanted to experience the bridge crossing by car. They'd spent three hours in traffic, and both of her employers had taken it with good grace. Several times Mr. Levine happily compared the experience to life itself.

Then there was the time a famous artist had come to the Levines' house in West Van to supervise the installation of four oil paintings they'd purchased from her. The paintings had been shipped from the artist's studio in Berlin and the painter had arrived with no fewer than three assistants in tow to make sure the art was displayed "in the correct way," as she put it. The painter was famously volatile and had been known to take back paintings she felt were not handled and shown with appropriate appreciation. She would not accept payment or sign sales contracts until the work had been hung to her satisfaction.

Those paintings, each the size of a standard sheet of copy paper, depicted Siddhartha, or the Buddha before he was the Buddha, as a sheltered young man seeing four things that set him on the path to enlightenment. One showed him seeing an old person, the second depicted his first glimpse of a sick person, the third showed him reacting to the sight of his first corpse, and the fourth was him seeing a monk in meditation. But the Buddha, in the famous artist's rendering, was a genderless figure who looked a little bit like k.d. lang and a little bit like an otter, which Helen found baffling. The scenes were full of characters reminiscent of pop culture figures combined with animals. For example, the aged person spied by the k.d. lang figure who would go on to become the Buddha looked like Iris Apfel, the centenarian socialite known for her exuberant sense of fashion, combined with a tarsier monkey wearing enormous round glasses.

The paintings "took some looking" as Dr. Levine said. Combined, they were worth two million dollars.

Needless to say, the Levines didn't want the artist to take the strange new artwork away in a fit of pique. When the artist and her entourage arrived, Helen had ushered them into the room where the paintings were to be displayed by themselves on a wall that had been specially prepared for the purpose.

"Good," said the artist, an unsmiling woman with a severe profile and obedient hair, as she looked around. "This is good."

She was staring at the wall, which had been painted the exact shade of green she'd specified.

"Where is the stuff to hang the pictures?" she asked in her heavy accent as she waved her hand imperiously, waiting for her assistants, who were dressed identically to her in blue denim jumpsuits. They also had long hair tied back severely. Each held a small case. They looked like they'd walked off the set of an eighties new wave music video.

"Ah," said Mr. Levine, who had slipped in behind them, unnoticed. "A few of the materials we need have just arrived at the airport. Now they are stuck in traffic, unfortunately."

"I do not like traffic," said the artist. "It is hateful and inconvenient."

Mr. Levine nodded. "It is," he said. "In that way, it reminds me of life."

It was a funny thing to say, as his life was one of the most blessed Helen had ever come across.

They were joined by Dr. Levine, and together the couple coaxed the artist and her entourage into the salon for refreshments and took them all on a tour of the rest of the art collection. Meanwhile, Helen kept calling to make sure the hand-crafted brass rod, brass chains, and clips the artist had requested to hang the paintings were on their way, being driven at top speed from the airport by Terry, one of the Levines' most trusted employees.

As soon as the breathless Terry arrived and got the materials into the gallery space, the artist and her assistants were invited back into the room, where they got to work. The assistants hung the paintings with the skill and precision of a team of neurosurgeons, directed by the artist.

When it was over, the Levines stood in front of the paintings. Both had tears in their eyes.

"So profound," said Dr. Levine.

"Yes," said the artist. "I am." She seemed mollified in spite of the delay. After all, who can blame delays caused by traffic?

Which sense of "stuck in traffic" had Mr. Levine been using when he said those words? The idea that delay was part of life? Or the sense that being stuck

CONTEMPLATION OF A CRIME

in traffic was a very useful excuse in times of high tension and an excuse to put people off? Helen wasn't sure, but she thought it was the latter.

He was telling her to delay. At least, that was her best guess.

But how? The kidnappers would realize something was wrong when the money didn't arrive. Would they hurt David and Mr. Levine? Helen couldn't tell them that the funds were stuck in traffic somewhere on the internet.

She would have to figure out what to say. In the meantime, she decided it was best not to tell them that the account had been suspended.

HELEN THORPE

Helen went outside and found everyone sitting in chairs around a long table near the outdoor pool. There was something different about the guests and maybe even the butlers. She thought, with some hope, that she detected a bit of cohesion in the way they interacted with each other.

After Helen took her seat, the others turned to Wayne, who had the uncomfortable posture of someone sitting on a chair made entirely of splinters. He kept a hand on his spaghetti-squash of a dog, who panted fatly at his side. He hadn't finished his sandwich or touched any of the salads he'd taken.

"Potato has harsh separation anxiety," he explained. "I don't want to leave her alone too much. In case she gets destructive."

"Stop stalling," said Yana. "Tell her."

Pain nodded.

Wayne cleared his throat. "Yeah, so I, uh . . ."

Helen waited. The others leaned forward. Fascinating that they all seemed to be in on this confession of his.

When Wayne started speaking, he looked over Helen's shoulder, as though he were talking to someone behind her. Helen waited.

"Spit it out," said Pain.

"You know how the, ah, kidnappers know, um—"

"Jesus," said Pain. "This is painful." Only he pronounced it *pan*-ful, which only he found funny.

"You know how it seems like they're listening in?" said Wayne. "In the lodge?"

Helen nodded. Suddenly everyone went very still in their seats, even as the wind gusted, stealing the heat from their bodies and threatening to send heavy cloth napkins sailing. The sky was clear now, though the low dark mountains in the distance were surrounded by oily clouds.

"I put some, you know, bugs. Around."

"Bugs," said Helen.

CONTEMPLATION OF A CRIME

"Listening devices," said Madison.

"Recorders," said Yana.

"I put one in your office. A few around the lodge. And, uh, this morning, I stuck one in David's room."

Helen was oddly relieved. Finally, they were getting somewhere. It wasn't ideal that Wayne was in league with the kidnappers and it was hard to see him as a villain, probably because his fat little pit bull seemed too cheerful to be a criminal associate. The dog was one of the more pleasant animals Helen had ever encountered. Not even the four Pekingese exuded as much goodwill as Potato.

Wayne struck her as a man who had layered a lot of external hostility onto a personality that was essentially good-natured, sort of like his dog. She had little evidence for this assessment, but he had none of the barbed wire of anger that ran through Pain, for instance, or the overwhelmed bitterness so present in Yana. Wayne wasn't electric with nerves like Tom or profoundly distracted like Madison. Wayne Krupke struck her as a guy who kept forgetting what he was supposed to be mad about. In other words, he seemed like a young man who needed a different algorithm, a break from politics and misogynist podcasters, a job he liked, and maybe a romantic partner and a healthy hobby. With those things, Helen would bet he'd be one of those guys who gets along with almost everyone. How exactly, she wondered, had he ended up with so many flags on his truck?

"I put the bugs around because they told me to. But I swear to god I had nothing to do with the rest of it. The kidnapping. I don't know who took your boss and David. All I did was plant the bugs. Like they instructed."

"Who is *they*?" she asked.

"That's just it. I don't know."

The tension in the group went up a notch, except for the five dogs, who blithely enjoyed being near their people and smelling the sea air.

"Right after I agreed to come here, I started getting these anonymous messages. And instructions."

"Tell her everything," said Madison.

Wayne finally met Helen's gaze. He had nice eyes. Brown and plain.

"I don't want to bore you. Or waste anyone's time. But when we went to Ottawa for the convoy, we weren't there to do *crimes*. We just wanted someone to listen to us. Stop treating us like . . . we were diseased. I couldn't even go into the *community centre* to use the john without showing a vaccine card. You have no idea how that feels. And those vaccines! They're totally experimental. A shitload of people died from taking them."

"Oh, for god's sake," said Yana, rolling her eyes.

"You'll find out," said Wayne, "when you're dead in two years from some super-cancer or a heart attack."

"I should get so lucky," said Yana.

In spite of the unfolding chaos, Helen thought she really needed to check in with Yana and see how she was doing.

As for Wayne, Helen would not argue with him about the vaccines. She'd seen too many relationships fall apart over the issue. She was fully vaccinated and so were her employers. But she knew many people, including some she loved, who had only gotten one shot. Or no shots. She also knew people who had died during the pandemic, vaccinated and unvaccinated.

The height of the pandemic had been a time of evolving understanding and overwhelming fear, and she had not been immune from the tumult, even cocooned as she'd been in the Levines' bubble. She'd had to lay off some employees during the pandemic and had found the experience excruciating.

She thought of the young woman who'd worked with the retired racehorses on the estate. The girl had chosen not to get vaccinated and, when the Levine household, which was technically a business, adopted the provincial vaccine mandate for all staff, they had to let the girl go from the job she loved and had been good at. She was given a generous severance package and told she could come back when things changed or after she got vaccinated, but that hadn't softened the blow, which Helen had been required to deliver.

"But I'm not even *inside* with you guys," said the girl, on the verge of tears. "I can't give the horses covid!"

The memory of standing in the wide breezeway of the barn wearing her N-95, facing the girl who wore her cloth mask under her nose, was seared in Helen's memory. She would never forget the hurt and anger in that young woman's eyes.

Many people still seemed not to have recovered from the experience of the pandemic, at least psychologically. Many had not recovered physically.

CONTEMPLATION OF A CRIME

Everyone was still coping, or not coping, with the losses, even while it seemed like the whole world was trying to forget all the people who had died and been permanently injured.

As Wayne talked, Helen reminded herself that trying to argue a person out of a set of beliefs, especially about an issue as tortuous as how the pandemic had played out, was like trying to argue them out of their shame or anger. It couldn't be done. People had to heal in their own way and in their own time.

When the restrictions had been lifted and life began to return to normal, Helen got the Levines' permission to contact the former employee and invite her back to work, but the girl had moved to Florida, where, according to her curt email turning down the offer to return to work, "they still believe in freedom."

Helen watched Wayne carefully as he continued talking. And talking.

"The virus wasn't even dangerous for people my age. Or most people, even. It's like the big reset, right?"

"Bad news. Joe Rogan doesn't care about you," said Pain. "And isn't Jordan Peterson basically a douche who spends part of each year in a coma in Russia?"

Wayne ignored him and kept talking as though reciting a speech he had to give all the way to the end. Finally, Madison touched his shoulder and he wound down.

Helen had only a vague sense of what he was talking about. Wayne lived in a different fact universe than she did. But the truth of a person's heart was deeper than anything one could find online. That's where Helen tried to understand people. That's where Side Island and the program asked them to connect.

She tried to listen deeply to Wayne and his complicated explanation for why he'd bugged the lodge, but she was distracted by what might happen to David and Mr. Levine when the kidnappers didn't get their money.

"I just need people to know that I went to Ottawa because they were taking our freedom. You all get that, right?"

Helen chose her words with care. After all, she was speaking to someone who was willing to drive around with at least four flags on his truck. "It was a hard time for everyone," she said.

"Fuckin' right it was. Sorry."

"That's fine."

"Just tell her what happened," said Tom.

193

Helen wondered how the pandemic had been for Tom, living with white nationalists who thought he was useless and with a girlfriend who didn't love him. What sort of wounds did Tom carry that had led him to such a dark place?

"Right, so back to why I bugged this place. When me and Potato got to Ottawa, we met a bunch of people. Some really cool guys. From Quebec, Alberta, even the States. We set up our own little camp-type area. We honked some, but we never used airhorns. Still, Potato hated it. I had to put earmuffs on her and a puffy coat because it was so cold."

Helen thought of the images she'd seen of protestors milling around the frozen Ottawa streets, the videos that captured the incessant, unrelenting, violent honking. The televised arrests of people near the border, some with ties to militant groups in the US, who were discovered to be hoarding weapons. She remembered reading about the convoy's demands for the prime minister to meet with them and for the government to step aside. Then she thought of Wayne and his dog wearing earmuffs in the middle of all of that and thought that it had probably been a pretty good time. An anti-public-health fan's version of Burning Man.

Burning Barrel.

"Anyway, me and those guys, we hung out a lot. We talked to the organizers. We were on Zello with everyone. It was cool. Had a real community feel. We did some livestreams. Like we were really doing something, you know?"

"I see," said Helen.

"So it was exciting. I might have got a little . . . too excited. A lot of people supported us. I'm not used to that. No one supports straight white guys anymore."

"Hear! Hear!" said Tom.

"Oh my god," said Yana. "Please read a book, you two ignoramuses."

Helen had heard statements like Wayne's before and understood that the people who said it believed it. She wondered how supported Wayne felt in his everyday life. Not very, she thought. Then again, many people felt unsupported in their lives now.

"People donated eight and a half million bucks to us. Holy shit, right? That tells me people are sick of being told what to do. They just want their lives back. It's in the constitution. Free assembly."

CONTEMPLATION OF A CRIME

Yana sighed and rolled her eyes. "If only you people had one-tenth of that energy to put toward the climate crisis."

Wayne ignored her. "Yeah, so me and those guys were talking on this private audio channel pretty constantly. Sort of like Zello, but a different one. We were keeping in touch. Making plans and that. We also did livestreams on Facebook. We wore bandanas." He gave her a slightly shamefaced grin. "We looked badass."

"I'm sure you did." She wondered if he recognized the irony, considering how much he hated masks.

"Over the course of some of those, uh, communications, I said some stuff I maybe shouldn't have said." He scratched at his neck. "About the prime minister. About some of the worst of the public health Nazis. I was just talking out my ass because I was mad. I didn't really mean most of what I said."

"Okay," said Helen.

"Quite a few guys talked like that. Women, too. Some of them got arrested for making threats. But I didn't get caught right away. Maybe because we were using a different program to communicate. I wasn't really serious, anyway. I was just getting people hyped up. Motivated."

The small group of people faced each other across the table, quiet while Wayne finished his story.

"I left after the cops shut us down. After I got home, I stayed in touch with the convoy people for a while. Then we all sort of drifted back into doing our own thing. Some locals wanted me to stand on the overpass waving a flag on the Old Island Highway. That was a big nope for me. They're mostly retired, have a lot of fucking time on their hands. I was in school for drywall. And then I was doing my apprenticeship. The mandates were gone. Plus, I got covid for like the second or third time, which sucked. I keep my flags up because I'm still mad. But not mad enough to hang around on an overpass getting the finger from all the Prius drivers. You feel me?"

"Sure," said Helen, who was not aware of the flag and overpass situation he referenced.

"I thought I was going to get away with it, but about six weeks after I got home, the police made me come in. They were going to charge me with creating a public disturbance or something. It was kind of ironic because, at that point, I was thinking about taking the flags off. My sister says they're a boner killer for girls. It turned out the cops only knew about the livestreams and my interviews with Rebel News, where I didn't really say anything too bad. I said way more on the audio-only channels, which were totally anonymous."

He sighed and rubbed his hands on his knees. "Anyway, I got put in a diversion program. Had to talk to a counsellor and a conflict resolution dude. I had to stay away from other convoy people for, like, two years or something. Then my counsellor asked me if I wanted to go to Close Encounters so I could get done with my restrictions early. I agreed to come here and be brainwashed and pretend not to be so angry. Which, fine. But about a week before I came, I was contacted by someone. And like I already said, I don't know who they are."

Helen watched him. He looked both very young and too old for his age. He scuffed his Timberland boots under the chair, and Potato got up and then lay down on his toes. "They said they had recordings of me saying some, uh, stuff."

"They sent him a recording of himself saying that someone should cut off the prime minister's head," said Pain. "Can you believe that shit? Guess I'm not the only psycho here."

"I was in the moment, bro," said Wayne. "I got carried away. Anyway, the cops don't like that kind of thing."

"The anonymous person blackmailed him," interrupted Madison. The two exchanged a glance that stopped Helen briefly. Were Madison and Wayne developing a personal connection?

Hmmm. Perhaps. At least, Helen thought, that might make Madison a little less focused on Mr. Levine. Then she remembered that her employer was currently missing and a cold wave of anxiety washed over her.

"Yeah. They said I need to help them or they'd send the recordings and the evidence that it was me talking. They told me that I had to hide the bugs around the lodge and the office and David's room."

"Wait a minute," said Gavin. "Did they use David's name? Did they tell you where he would be sleeping?"

Wayne scratched his head under his ball cap, thinking.

"I think so. The messages disappeared so I have no record. But I'm pretty sure they said his name. They told me which room he'd be in."

Gavin nodded.

"They left a box of recording devices in the back of my truck the night before I came here. Which means they know where I live. And they definitely

CONTEMPLATION OF A CRIME

have audio of me saying stupid shit." Wayne looked from face to face. Potato got to her feet and leaned against his legs. He kept his hand on her back, for reassurance.

"Did you see anything when you were placing the devices?" asked Helen. "Did you see David or his father? Anyone else?"

"No. I put most of the bugs out yesterday morning. I didn't put the one in David's room until this morning. When I went in to do it, he wasn't there."

"Tell her about the blood, yo," said Pain.

Helen froze. "What?" she said.

"In David's room. There's a big bloodstain in there."

Helen felt her skin go icy and then hot. Somehow, she'd convinced herself that though this terrible situation was stressful, it would not get overtly violent.

She'd seen the proof of life video only a few hours before and both David and Mr. Levine had looked uninjured, in spite of the threats levelled by the kidnappers.

"It wasn't me," said Wayne. "I would never hurt anyone. Like I said, David was gone when I went in his room. I thought he was going to be out running and then going into the ocean to freeze his ass off. I knocked, even though his door was open. He wasn't in there."

"The bloodstain is big, but not bled-out-and-died big," said Pain. "Unless he had hardly any blood in him. He's pretty skinny so . . ." Pain, who himself was very skinny, shrugged his pointy shoulders.

"I'm really sorry. I don't want to be a part of whatever is going on here. And I hope I haven't messed everything up by bugging the place," said Wayne.

"You did the right thing by telling us," said Helen. "The more information we have, the better."

She noted that Madison reached over and lightly touched Wayne's hand and he gave her a grateful look.

"Maybe we should call the police now?" said Yana.

"My employer asked me not to," said Helen, though she wondered if Yana was right.

"Maybe the kidnappers made him say that?" said Madison. "Maybe he actually wants the cops involved but he can't say so."

"If you call the cops, they're going to think I was involved," said Wayne. "I'll end up in jail."

SUSAN JUBY

"We are going to try and handle this ourselves," said Helen. She wondered when the kidnappers would be in touch to say they hadn't received the money. Any moment now, she expected.

"My employer is good at communicating his needs, indirectly if need be. I think I'll know if he wants us to involve the authorities. My gut tells me he and David are safe. At least, right now."

"I wish I had a butler who knew how I really feel," muttered Pain.

It was getting cold out on the deck. The day was still clear but the wind had once again picked up. There were whitecaps out on the water and the clouds moved in, filling the sky.

"Should we get rid of the bugs?" asked Wayne. "I can show you where they are."

Helen looked to Gavin and Murray. "What do you think?" she asked.

Gavin shook his head. "That would tip off whoever is behind it. They'd know that Wayne has spoken to us. Or at least that we've found the devices."

"Who could know what Wayne did in Ottawa?" asked Nigel.

"And who was in a position to get those recordings?" added Murray.

They were essential questions.

"Wayne," said Helen. "Did you place bugs in any of the cabins?"

Wayne shook his head. "No. Definitely not."

"Okay. Good. Has anyone else been asked to do anything suspicious while you're here?" Helen asked the group. "Now is the time to get it all out in the open."

The guests exchanged looks.

"Well," said Yana, after no one else spoke up. "I don't think it's related, but I might have something."

NELLY BEAN

How long do you think it will take?" asked Fields, for the eighth or ninth time.

Nelly tried to keep her tone neutral. Her wife-to-be was very good with computers and audio equipment, as well as CrossFit and hot yoga. She was less good at tolerating uncertainty and frustration.

"I'm not sure," said Nelly. "When you researched this method of transferring money so it couldn't be traced, was there any information about how long it would take until the funds showed up in the final account?"

Fields gave her a sharp look. "Is that some kind of comment on my plan?"

The sleek living quarters of the boat would have been very comfortable for one person or for two people who were getting along. It was not at all comfortable for two people who were heartily sick of one another and stressed out from trying to execute a major criminal conspiracy. They'd kidnapped two wealthy, high-profile people and left them chained up in a tent. Yes, they'd provided them with food and bathroom buckets, but kidnapped was kidnapped. And everyone knew that law enforcement cared more about rich people than everyone else.

"No. I'm just saying that I don't know exactly how long it will take the money to show up. I'm not even sure how the transfers are supposed to work."

Nelly gaped at her. She didn't know exactly how the transfers were supposed to *work*? Wasn't that the most important thing?

Here again, Fields had not done her homework properly. Now they were stuck with the captives until the money showed up. All Nelly wanted to do was let them go and end this nightmare before they got caught.

What if this was one of those "five business days to get your funds" deals?

"If we asked for the payment in bitcoin, we'd be on our way to Costa Rica already," said Fields.

"I refuse to discuss that any further. You have your moral standards. I have mine. I refuse to contribute to the climate crisis," said Nelly. She said this even though she was beginning to think her fiancée had no moral standards of any kind.

"If we get arrested and have to spend the rest of our broke-ass lives rotting away in prison, that's not going to help the climate."

"Well, we won't use as many resources if we're living communally and we won't require transportation anymore," said Nelly, being intentionally obstinate. "So perhaps we will be even more sustainable if we get caught."

Fields made a face at her, and Nelly could see another angry outburst taking shape. Time to defuse the bomb that was her partner's temper.

"Look, sweetheart, we're not going to get arrested. It's only been an hour or so since we gave Helen the information. Why don't you check to see if we can hear what's going on at the lodge. Maybe we'll overhear Helen confirming the transfer? If necessary, I'll call her again."

Fields unfurled herself from the semicircular banquette where she'd been lying like an exhausted Hollywood diva, her feet in bright blue feathered slippers hanging off the end of the sofa. She sat up and put on a pair of Bose headphones and clicked away on her laptop for a few minutes, listening. "Nothing," she said. "It sounds like the lodge and office are empty. Obviously, David's room is unoccupied. Maybe they're all out on another walk? That woman who is running the program, the butler? She obviously has no idea what she's doing. She keeps making them go on walks instead of following the program. If the program wasn't free, these participants would probably be asking for their money back."

"I imagine she's very stressed," said Nelly, who was so tense she couldn't even sit down for more than a minute. The unsettled rocking of the boat didn't help. "Can you check the bank account again?"

Fields did so. "Nothing yet."

Supposedly the funds were going to be transferred from Mr. Levine's account in a Swiss bank to a numbered account in the Bahamas that Fields had set up. Then it was being routed through several other countries that did not have information-sharing agreements with Canada or the US. The money was supposed to land in a bank account in Nevis. Nelly had never even heard of Nevis until now. She'd looked it up and learned that there was a volcano there, as well as a deeply shady banking system.

"Is there someone we can call?" she asked. "To see where the money is?"

CONTEMPLATION OF A CRIME

Fields had fallen back against the cushions and was staring moodily at her phone. She didn't look up. "No. Well, I guess we can talk to our guy."

"Our guy?" said Nelly.

"The man we're *hosting*? Make sure he didn't screw us around? Let him know there will be consequences if we don't get the money soon?"

Nelly hesitated. This was the kind of talk from Fields that was starting to scare her. "Maybe the problem is with the transfer route you set up?"

Fields glared at her. "Don't blame *me* for this."

"I'm not. I'm just . . . I guess I don't understand how it all works."

"It's fine. I did my research and this is the best way to transfer funds so that they can't be traced."

"Okay, okay," said Nelly.

Fields lifted one of her feet and dangled the feathered mule slipper from her toes. It looked as though she'd just kicked some unlucky tropical bird to death. "Do you think the butler screwed it up? Also, have you ever considered that the program might involve too many walks? They're never going to overcome their differences if they don't face them head-on," said Fields, as though she, not Nelly, was the founder and facilitator of Close Encounters. "You can't outwalk conflict."

Nelly found this deeply irritating, seeing as how Fields always had an assortment of reasons why she couldn't join them on most of the walks the year she'd attended the encounter.

"Maybe I should message her," said Nelly. "Just to see how she sounds. I could ask how David is feeling."

"Not yet," said Fields. "You're supposed to be in the middle of wedding prep. They'll get suspicious if you keep calling. And I think you should avoid talking to that butler. She's good at sniffing out lies."

"Fine," said Nelly, and she went back to pacing the few steps available in the tiny quarters of the boat. She was not a religious person, but she found herself praying that the money would arrive soon and not just because she wanted to be rich. She also didn't want to see what her fiancée was capable of if she felt thwarted.

YANA HEPPLER

They all went into Poolside Cottage, and there Yana told them what she'd been encouraged to do. It felt good to get it off her chest, and when she saw Helen and the other butlers exchange glances, it occurred to her how extreme the plan was. Had been.

Somehow, in her hollowed-out state, she hadn't registered it.

"Wow," said Madison. "That's crazy dark."

"You would really do that?" said Wayne. "Do things really feel that bad for you?"

"I get it," said Tom.

Wayne's pit bull seemed to be picking up her energy, and the dog waddled over to Yana and sat down on her feet. Hesitantly, Yana reached down and petted the animal's broad back. She'd always wanted a dog and would have had one if they weren't so environmentally unsound and resource intensive.

To hell with it. Maybe she'd get one when she got home. A small one. Could dogs live on a vegan diet?

"Someone in your online climate grief group suggested this plan?" said Helen.

"Yes. As a way of bringing attention to the cause."

"And you were supposed to do this during your time here? Did they say when?"

"They said I should do it on the third night. Tonight. They said I should take out a boat or a kayak or something. From the boathouse. And that before I went, I should alert the press and the police. They even mailed me some drugs so I wouldn't feel anything."

Yana had been sent a package of what she assumed was fentanyl that she was told would kill her almost instantly. Her online contact had told her how to set the boat on fire so it wouldn't reach her gas-soaked body until she had passed out. A Viking funeral. A sacrifice to call attention to the lack of action on climate change. A spectacular statement through self-immolation. No more talking. Action.

"But you're so strong," said Pain, surprising her. "If I could move rocks like you, I'd stick around. I can barely pick up toast, bro."

Yana laughed, surprising herself. She thought she'd lost the ability to do anything other than emit bleak, angry laughs. But here she was, feeling lighter after telling them her plan to kill herself and then light her own body on fire in the harbour.

"You're not still going to do it, are you?" asked Wayne. "Like, kill yourself after this is done? I really don't think you should. I mean, I get that the weather's pretty fucked up or whatever. I know you think we're all going to end up in refugee camps. But dude, you got to have hope. Keep eating your beans and hating trucks and voting for weirdo commies."

Pain was nodding. "You can't give up, man."

"I have never voted," said Madison. "Not once. If you agree to not hurt yourself, I promise to start voting. But you will need to tell me who to vote for because I have no idea and I'm not really into learning."

She was sitting beside Wayne, who nudged her in the side. "Oh, I'll tell you who to vote for," he said.

"No," said Yana. "I will."

Then they all laughed.

The living room, with its assortment of matching couches and sectionals and chairs, had that "aftermath of confession" quiet to it. Like the walls were absorbing Yana's words.

"Thank you for telling us," said Helen, finally. "I'm sorry that you are in so much pain."

She said it so simply that Yana nearly lost it. Yana didn't want to burn. She didn't want to die to bring attention to the movement. She was glad she'd confessed the plan, which had felt like a dream but also strangely inevitable.

"What do you think?" Helen asked her butler friends, who were very quiet and good at blending into the background.

"I think Ms. Heppler was very brave to tell us this," said Murray, the dark-haired butler.

"And that we might be able to use the information," said Gavin.

"Should we have snacks?" said Nigel, the chubby butler.

Yana, whose appetite was often supressed by her dire mood, agreed. She was ravenous after what she now felt was a near-death experience, even though they'd just had lunch.

Moments later the butlers were bustling around in the small kitchen, helped by Tom, who seemed interested in what they were doing. They laid out olives and cheeses and fancy crackers and dips.

"Is any of that vegan?" asked Yana.

"This platter is entirely vegan," said Murray as she organized carrots into a pleasing pattern on another wooden board.

"Good. Because I'm starving."

HELEN THORPE

When they'd laid out the snacks and small plates and napkins, Helen sat again.

"We need to go over what we know," she said. "Gavin?"

"Ready," he said.

He and Murray had carried the rolling whiteboard over to Poolside Cottage from the great room in the lodge, to the confusion of Bobbi-Lyn, who'd come out of the kitchen and asked why they weren't meeting in the lodge. Gavin said he'd given her an excuse.

"Should we do a timeline?" asked Pain.

"Yes," said Madison. "That's what they do on crime shows."

"Do we have any red string and some tacks?" said Wayne.

"A timeline is a good idea," agreed Helen. "But we'll have to draw the lines showing connections."

"In the future we'll have holograms for this kind of stuff," said Pain.

"Or we'll be using sharp rocks and dirt," said Yana.

"Dude, you need to change your meds," said Pain. Then he remembered what Yana had been planning and apologized.

"It's okay," she said. "You're probably right."

They started calling out clues and points of information.

"They got kidnapped last night sometime," said Madison.

"Before six," said Wayne and Helen nodded.

"So like really early," said Tom, helpfully.

"Sometime between eleven p.m. and five a.m. I bet it was around three in the morning," said Nigel, staring at the board.

"Why do you say that?" asked Helen.

"Because everyone would have been asleep and because they would have wanted to get them far away from here before it got light," said Tom.

Everyone nodded.

Gavin made another column and wrote down the interaction that Wayne had with his online blackmailer and the mystery person who'd encouraged Yana to take her own life in spectacular fashion.

"When did these interactions start?" asked Helen.

"Maybe August?" said Wayne. "Right after I got the invitation and agreed to come."

Yana was nodding, her ruddy face serious. "I started talking to my contact around then also. I'd just agreed to take part in the course."

"And where did your invitations come from?" asked Helen.

The participants all held up their hands.

They'd been invited by counsellors and lawyers and probation officers who themselves had received invitations from someone else.

"Did those invitations from the third party suggest that your direct contact should invite you specifically? Or were they general invitations and your contacts decided who might fit the bill?" asked Helen.

None of them knew.

"Once they got the list of suggested people, they could have researched us," said Tom.

"*They* meaning the organizers?" said Nigel.

"Or David? I don't know at what point and how he was involved. He was asked to facilitate months ago," said Helen.

"Is there any way to find out who chose us?" asked Pain.

"You tell us," said Tom, giving him a searching look.

"What does that mean?" asked Pain.

"You're the internet guy. Aren't you like some super-hacker?"

Pain made a noise like a broken whoopee cushion. "No," he said. "I'm a troll. A provocateur. I mess with people, but I'm not exactly hacking into the Pentagon."

"You can get into people's phones, right? And their email?"

"I guess." Pain shrugged. "But mostly people leave their shit all over the internet. You don't need to be a computer genius to invade their privacy, because they have none."

This was interesting.

"I think we can be confident that David isn't responsible for his own kidnapping," said Helen.

CONTEMPLATION OF A CRIME

"What about whoever usually runs this thing?"

"I don't know," said Helen. "But she's definitely getting married right now. So if she's involved, she's involved from afar." She remembered David's comments about Nelly Bean to his father. "David admires her very much. He says she's a force for good."

"She has an excellent reputation in the environmental community," said Yana.

"Okay, so she seems unlikely," said Gavin. "Let's not narrow our suspects down too much right now."

Tom put up a hand. "Do you suspect any of us?" he asked.

The participants all looked at Helen.

"Do you suspect each other?" she asked.

"I think this is the opposite of community building," said Wayne. "This is making us turn on each other."

The others nodded.

"How can we trust each other?" asked Helen.

"If we see anything shady, say something?" said Pain.

There was a long silence.

"What about you guys?" said Tom. "What if one of the butlers did it?"

"Would make sense," said Wayne. "Butlers are always responsible."

"How are we supposed to trust each other?" said Yana.

The silence continued. Then Madison put up her hand uncertainly.

"There's no guarantee. We decided to work together and we're just going to have to hope. What do you call that? When you give someone the . . . ?"

"Benefit of the doubt," said Wayne, promptly.

"Yeah. We're going to have to treat each other like we trust each other. Treating each other like suspects is not going to work."

Helen was nodding.

"I think you're exactly right. Now let's talk about what comes next."

WAYNE KRUPKE

Wayne had always prided himself on being a useful guy. He knew how to do things. He could change a tire, build a set of stairs, do basic plumbing. Like that.

Back in his bathtub-racing days, his skill was appreciated. His buddy, Andrew, had relied on him for construction and engine repair on the tubs. Goddamn, they'd had the greatest time on some of those weekends. Party hard and win. That was the whole goal.

Wayne thought about those days as he stared out the window of Poolside Cottage while the others pretended to be detectives on *Law & Order*.

One of these days, Wayne thought, Andrew was going to win the Nanaimo Bathtub Races, and he, Wayne, was sorry he wouldn't be a part of it. He was sorry that they'd stopped speaking because of political differences.

He snuck a quick look at Madison, beside him. She'd touched his hand twice now and they'd smiled at each other three times.

He didn't want to misinterpret, but he thought she might be feeling him. Like, not literally, but emotionally. He'd been pretty persuasive when he was talking about the convoy. She probably sympathized. He wondered if she was vaccinated. The days of straight up asking people were over, but he did want to know. There were all those fertility problems to think about.

His mom and sister said he had the wrong end of the stick about vaccine side effects, but he wasn't so sure.

"So we've established that they are not on the island," said the good-looking butler guy. Gavin.

"Where's the next logical place they might be?" asked Helen.

Before he even meant to, Wayne spoke up. "If I had to guess, I'd say they were right across from here. On either Protection or Guide Island."

Everyone turned to him.

CONTEMPLATION OF A CRIME

"Not Saysutshun?" said Yana, who also seemed familiar with the Nanaimo harbour. "Or Nanaimo itself?"

Wayne bumped his fists lightly on his knees. "I wonder if they got a watchman on Saysutshun? There might still be people camping there, at this time of year. Plus, they probably have cameras at the dock."

"Maybe it's a watch*woman*," said Yana.

"Whatever. All I'm saying is that if I was going to kidnap someone, I wouldn't go to Saysutshun. Or Nanaimo. Way too many condos and boats to do much criming around there. You'd get caught."

Helen was nodding. "Okay."

"Protection Island is a maybe, but there's at least three hundred and fifty people there. I guess if you had a house there, you could stash some people, but if I was going to hide people, I'd put them on Guide Island."

Everyone was listening intently to him, which he enjoyed.

He sure enjoyed being useful.

"So we should start our search there," said Helen.

"I would," said Wayne.

"All of us?" asked Pain, sounding doubtful.

"And how are we supposed to get over there?" asked Tom.

Wayne sat up straight. "I have an idea," he said.

"So do I," said Nigel, unexpectedly.

"Do we have the same idea?" asked Wayne, who wondered if the butler had also gone into the boathouse, which Wayne had checked out when they were searching for the kidnap victims.

"Is your idea about giving the kidnappers something to listen to?" asked Nigel.

"Definitely not," said Wayne.

Before they could discuss any further, Helen's phone buzzed and every head in the room snapped toward it.

She looked at the screen. "It's them," she said and stood up to check the latest Signal message.

NELLY BEAN

Nelly let Fields send the Signal asking about the transfer funds. She immediately wished she hadn't, especially after Fields refused to tell her what she'd said in her message.

"So you just enquired whether the transfer went through, right?" said Nelly, feeling the pit in her stomach grow.

"Something like that," said Fields as she stared stone-faced at her phone screen. A long chartreuse nail tapped at the back of the phone.

"Did you ask her if she has a confirmation number? So we can follow up?" asked Nelly.

"Sure," said Fields. She fixed her eyes on Nelly. Fields had the most beautiful eyes Nelly had ever seen: large and startlingly light green, with hints of silver in the irises, surrounded by long, dark lashes that Nelly would have thought were natural if she didn't know better. But she was starting to think there was something missing behind that glorious gaze.

Nelly stopped talking. Of course they couldn't follow up. They couldn't call up the bank and ask where the kidnapping funds they'd requested had gone, especially since according to Fields's plan, the money was being routed through multiple countries.

She found herself holding her breath.

What would the butler say?

The wait for her response seemed interminable, but it was only a few minutes.

The notification sounded and Nelly found herself wanting to snatch the phone.

Fields sat up and read the message. Pursed her lips.

"She says she sent it. She can't give us the confirmation number because she forgot to write it down. She wants to know if we received the money."

CONTEMPLATION OF A CRIME

"Tell her no," said Nelly. "Tell her to send it again. Can you find an easier way to route it somewhere that it can't be traced to us?"

Fields let out a long sigh. "No. I can't find an easier way. And I don't want to get her to send it again until I'm sure she has the right information. Maybe he gave us the wrong numbers. It's time to have a talk with our guests. We may need a new plan."

All Nelly wanted was to get out of this situation. And to get out of the wedding, which they now needed to go through with for their alibi, which was going to be pretty shaky to begin with, since they weren't going to be able to get to Vancouver until they'd freed the guests. She wasn't about to say that while Fields was teetering on the knife's edge between good and evil.

Nelly sucked in a breath. "Look," she said. "Let's cut our losses. Let David and his father go. Get to Vancouver, have the celebration. I'll get another job. You'll start another restaurant. We can live without this money."

Fields smiled and Nelly's deep unease turned into fear. "Don't worry, babe," she said. "We'll get paid. I have a plan."

Oh Christ, thought Nelly. *Not another one.*

DAVID LEWISTON

"**D**ad," said David.

"Yes, son?"

"Do you ever wonder why some people have so much and some people have so little?"

During their hours in captivity, David and his father had napped, and they'd discussed, in a non-gossipy way, each member of the family. They'd reminisced about old family stories. Talked sports, which didn't take long because neither of them was particularly interested. And now they were onto the Big Questions.

His father was quiet for a long moment. "I think it might be a matter of karma."

"Don't you find that as unsatisfying as when people try to say that tragedies are God's will?" said David.

He knew he sounded like a first-year university student who was taking Intro to Philosophy and had just smoked a fattie.

"Don't Buddhists think everything is karma?" he continued. "Like, we're chained up here because of karma? Slavery happened because of karma? Climate change and war? It's all karma." All of a sudden, David felt the lethargy brought on by fear and boredom fall away. Now he was angry.

His father sighed. "I'm not a Buddhist scholar. I get the sense that Buddhist teachers think that the working out of karma happens over countless generations and many lifetimes."

"How can there be any justice when kids are starving and people are being bombed and it can be written off as karma?"

"There can't be any justice," said his father, simply. "The world is filled with terrible things. The practice involves finding peace in yourself and sharing that with the world. Causing no more strife. Being aware of intention. Stopping the cycle of harm with yourself. At least, that's the goal as I understand it."

"Sounds pretty defeatist. I'm surprised you and Mom are on board with

CONTEMPLATION OF A CRIME

such a passive philosophy." David knew he sounded petulant, but his words were coming out faster than his ability to moderate them.

"There's a lot of discussion in the Buddhist world about how to be engaged in helping the world while not getting caught up in the conflicts," said his father, unruffled by David's growing anger. "Buddhists aren't immune from doing harm. Look at Burma and the Democratic Karen Buddhist Army."

"There's an army of Buddhists called the Karens?" said David, incredulous.

"I don't know much about them, but no organization made up of flawed humans, religious or otherwise, is going to be perfect. Every one of us is capable of doing harm."

"Maybe it would have been better if you and Mom were Quakers," said David.

"Maybe," said his father, peaceably. Then, "How is your stomach?"

Surprisingly, David's stomach was fine.

"Do you think I'll ever meet someone I will love as much as you love Mom?" asked David, switching topics without warning.

The air in the tent seemed to shift. They were no longer just chatting and burning time while they waited to be freed or for whatever would come next.

"You and your brother and sister all wonder about that, don't you?" said his father.

"Hard not to. You two are so . . . perfect."

His father nodded his head slowly. "We aren't perfect, but we're deeply fortunate to have found each other. And we are grateful every day for our children. We are so proud of you all."

David's eyes burned and he felt something open in the middle of his chest. Was this some sort of stress reaction?

"Mom won't be able to handle it if something happens to us," said David, when he felt more collected. "Maybe you should just pay the ransom."

"Your mother will turn into a death-dealing Karen Buddhist if anything happens to us," said his father. "Mel Gibson and Clint Eastwood will be sorry they ever left Hollywood."

At that they both laughed.

When they heard the footsteps approaching, they stopped laughing as though a switch had been turned.

"Ready?" whispered his father.

"Yes," said David.

"Trust me?"

David didn't answer. He leaned back in his chair and waited to see who was coming for them. He really hoped their generational karma didn't involve getting killed by kidnappers.

Seconds later the kidnappers pushed open the flaps of the tent. They wore the same masks, the same black combat fatigues. They both held phones, and one of them had a black bag slung over one shoulder. The short one hit a button and Mel Gibson's voice came out. "Where is our money?"

David chanced a glance at his father, who sat as still as any statue of Buddha. "I don't know," said his father.

"Don't play games with us, Mr. Levine. Your butler says she transferred the money. Why haven't we gotten it yet?"

Ever so slowly, David's father tilted back his head. "I wonder if I misremembered one of the numbers?"

His nonchalance was not missed by the kidnappers.

The short one said "Are you ser—" before being elbowed in the side by the tall one wearing the purple ventilator.

Then the taller kidnapper typed into the phone and Clint Eastwood's voice said, "What Stan is trying to say is that we need the money and we need it right now."

But it was too late. The shorter kidnapper in the black mask had spoken in a woman's voice, simultaneously raspy and high. *Are you ser—*

Only two complete words and David knew the voice. He made sure not to let anything show on his face.

The shorter kidnapper sounded like Nelly Bean. In his gut, he knew it was her. He and his father had been kidnapped by the founder of Close Encounters for Global Healing, one the most optimistic and idealistic people he'd ever met. Presumably the other kidnapper was Nelly's partner, Fields.

The enormity of the betrayal was too large to take in all at once and David didn't try. There would be time to reckon with it later. *Close Encounters my ass*, he thought. *Close Encounters for Global Stealing*, he thought. But he said nothing. A slightly hysterical laugh formed in his throat and David made sure it died there.

Nelly Bean. What did he know about her?

Two minutes before, he would have said she was brave, funny, and kind.

CONTEMPLATION OF A CRIME

That she lived her values and did good things in the world. That she was empathetic and patient and profoundly compassionate. Open-minded.

And yet here she was, a masked assailant who'd kidnapped David and his father in the middle of the night and was threatening them for money. *For goddamned money.*

David chanced a glance at his father, who gave a barely perceptible nod and cut his own gaze away.

There was no way his father knew who Nelly was. He'd never met her, as far as David knew. Had never spoken to her. But his father now knew that they'd been kidnapped by a woman, and that she'd let her voice be heard. What would she do now?

The two women hadn't hurt them yet, but David thought they very well might if they knew their identities had been discovered.

"I'll give you another set of numbers," said David's father. "My wife has her own emergency account and I have those numbers. Helen can attempt the transfer again."

"I'm going to give you this phone and you are going to make this transfer yourself," said the kidnapper using Clint Eastwood's voice. "I don't care what account it comes from."

"I'm afraid I can't. As I said before, Helen has to enter her code to complete the transfer. That's how the security people set up the protocol. It's supposed to ensure our safety. I'm telling you the truth."

The shorter kidnapper who was almost certainly Nelly put her fists up to the sides of her head as though gripped by a sudden headache. The tall one nudged her again to remind her to remain calm.

Then the taller kidnapper typed into the phone. And typed some more.

Then Clint Eastwood's voice said: "If we don't have the money by nine o'clock tonight, we're going to take you both out in a boat with your hands and feet tied and drop you overboard."

At that, the short kidnapper stomped out of the tent.

The taller kidnapper typed into the device. "Give the butler the correct numbers this time. From your wife's account. From your account. From your maid's account. I don't care, but I want my money and I want it now. Tell her that time is running out."

David's father shrugged. "I will. But I'm under a lot of stress here. I hope

I don't make a mistake." His words were undercut by the fact that he looked as untroubled as if he were sitting in a hot tub.

Oh, Dad, thought David. *What are you doing?*

The taller kidnapper stared down at the device, furiously thumb-typing. "I think I have a way to help you remember."

"I'm sure fear of death by drowning will be sufficient," said David's father.

Instead of replying, the kidnapper put the phone near David's father and had him recite the numbers into the recorder again.

David's father kept speaking after he finished the list of numbers. "If they don't get the money, they say they will take us out and—"

Before he could finish, the kidnapper stopped recording. Then she hit him in the side of the face with the phone. Hard.

The kidnapper hit David's beloved father again and again, on the top of his head, on the side of his face, using the phone in a clenched fist.

David was too shocked to do anything right away, but when he got to his feet, the kidnapper had already stepped away from his father and held up a finger to tell them both to be quiet before bending over to look for the phone, which had been dropped during the assault. She pressed a button. "Don't try anything," said Clint Eastwood's voice.

On the way out of the tent, the kidnapper kicked a reusable Thrifty bag into the centre of the tent floor so it was just barely in reach.

When they were alone, David finally spoke. "Dad? Are you okay?"

His father held a hand up to his mouth. It came away bloody. "Just a cut lip. And my ear is ringing. But I think I'm basically unharmed. Thank goodness the new generation cellphones are so small."

"Did you give them the right code?"

"No," said his father.

"It seems to me like they *are* willing to hurt us," said David. "I mean, look at you."

"Just a flesh wound," said his father and he laughed softly.

David had no idea how far the kidnappers would go when Helen didn't transfer the money because she couldn't. Would Nelly and her girlfriend really dump him and his father into the ocean?

Twenty minutes before, he would have said there was no way Nelly Bean

CONTEMPLATION OF A CRIME

would do violence to another being. But it turned out he didn't know Nelly Bean at all.

When David was finally sure the kidnappers weren't coming back right away, he spoke up again.

"I think I know who has us," he said.

"Oh?"

David felt sick having to say it out loud. "I think the short one in the black mask is Nelly Bean. The founder of Close Encounters. She has this very unusual voice. I think she and her fiancée have us. I'm so sorry, Dad. I thought . . . I thought Nelly was a good person. An honourable person."

His father, whose left eye had begun to swell shut, smiled. "I know you did. I know you admired the work being done through the program. And maybe sometimes your friend Nelly really is good." He put the back of his hand to his split lip again. "But she's not being her highest self right now."

The understatement to end all understatements.

His father continued. "What do you know about Nelly and her fiancée? I mean, other than the fact that her fiancée is very strong and knows how to wield a cellphone."

David felt the way he had when he was a kid and his father had taken control of some situation. A little bit embarrassed and a lot relieved. It was the feeling of being parented. He shook his head. "I thought she was caring. Committed. Fierce on behalf of achieving peace. I thought she was funny and nice." He grabbed his blanket so it wouldn't completely fall on the cold cement pad that served as a floor. He held it to his body while he got to his feet and dragged the new bag of supplies over.

"It's important to give people the benefit of the doubt," said his father. "Better that than being suspicious of everyone."

"But not ideal if it gets you kidnapped. I trusted her and now we're here. I'm sorry." He considered for a moment.

"Dad, why don't we just have Helen transfer the funds and then tell the police who took us when we get released? She and Fields aren't going to be able to get very far."

"That's true. Unfortunately, I think it might be too late."

"What? Why?"

"Because the numbers I gave the first time locked Helen out of the account permanently. I can't transfer ten million dollars out of my account without contacting our bankers first. Our captors won't take bitcoin, and in any event, I don't keep cryptocurrency in my holdings. We have no way to contact this Nelly person and tell her any of this or offer other solutions. Right now we have no way to tell anyone anything. I'm still holding out hope Helen and the gang will rescue us. I have tried to give them some hints as to our location. At least, what I think is our location."

David let his eyes close. Oh god.

"I don't know Nelly or her partner, but something tells me that they may have crossed some kind of a line already."

David waited for his father to explain.

"I've seen it before in business. People start negotiating and things get hard and something inside them fails. They go too far. Start making things up. Start losing sight of proportion. Decency. It comes from desperation and fear and greed, and it's always dangerous."

"Great," said David.

"Don't worry," said his father, who in spite of his phone-battered face, looked composed in his magnificent black pyjamas.

David, for perhaps the millionth time in his life, wished he had one-tenth of his father's confidence.

GAVIN VIMUKTHI

Wayne led them to a stuffed chair at the far end of the great room while Nigel went into the kitchen to distract the cook. This was Nigel's idea and Gavin was once again impressed by the savviness from the younger man. When he'd first met Nigel after Helen hired him at the Yatra Institute, Gavin had thought Nigel a bit of a clown. That was partly due to the fact that he dressed like a clown, complete with colourful suspenders and checked trousers two sizes too small. But he seemed as unassuming and naive as a sea cucumber.

But Nigel was in fact an astute young man and had gotten more so after Murray and Gavin trained him in the finer points of domestic service. He'd only gotten sharper since butler school. Gavin thought that Nigel's romantic involvement with his employer, a vastly wealthy youngish internet influencer, was a poor idea, but he had a sneaking suspicion that it would work out all right. Perhaps Nigel would end up needing a butler rather than being one.

At any rate, it had been Nigel's idea to throw off the kidnappers by giving them something to listen to on their listening devices.

"If we're going hunting for them, we don't want them to know. They may be armed and dangerous," he'd said by the pool, while untangling his boss's Pekingese. The dogs had been wrestling over some lengths of rope from the boathouse and gotten themselves tangled up. "Oh, you guys," said Nigel, as he extracted one of the dogs. "Now I'm going to have to redo your ponytails."

He wasn't joking. The dogs had been wearing ponytails since arriving at Side Island. Nigel said it made them look "more outdoorsy," which it absolutely did not.

As he extracted the dogs, who trusted him as fully as stuffed animals might, he gave the group some suggestions.

"Say something that makes it clear that the course is going fine, but we're going to be somewhere else tonight. They expect us to spend time in the great room doing the program tonight, and they're going to get suspicious if it's radio silence in there. We have to make sure they don't figure out that we know what's going on or that we are looking for David and his father."

So together, the group came up with some dialogue.

Now that they were faced with delivering it, Gavin had his doubts that they were going to be believed.

"I am so tired," said Yana in a stagy voice. "Really, really tired."

"Uh, me too," said Tom. Then he cleared his throat.

Wayne glared at them.

Yana glared back.

"Hey?" said Madison, who was the only one who sounded even vaguely natural.

"Yes?" said Gavin and Nigel at the same time.

"Would it be okay if we did tonight's activities in the basement? And can we incorporate darts?"

"If you think it's safe," said Yana, again in the voice of one of the world's least convincing actors.

"And ping-pong!" said Pain. "I hate sports but I like the sound of ping-pong."

"Helen said we can veer off the program. And my knee is killing me from so much walking," said Madison.

"Sounds fine," said Gavin. "I'll check with Helen but I'm sure she'll agree. We'll go back to the usual program tomorrow. We can have a rest now, then dinner, and then we'll go into the basement to do some recreational bonding time after that."

Then they all muttered a few things and trooped back out of the great room and out of the lodge.

They stopped halfway back to the Poolside Cottage.

"Okay?" said Wayne. "I didn't put any bugs downstairs in the games room."

"Perfect," said Gavin, though he thought the plan they'd come up with to search for Mr. Levine and David was shaky at best.

Nigel came out of the lodge. "Does the cook suspect anything yet?" asked Murray.

"I don't know. She seems fairly suspicious in general. But I tried to reassure

CONTEMPLATION OF A CRIME

her. She wanted to know what we were doing, and I told her we were facilitating a game before dinner."

"Okay. Let's go back and see how Helen's conversation with Nelly went. Maybe she has new information," said Gavin.

And the group of unlikely allies walked down the path to the large ocean-facing cottage.

HELEN THORPE

While the others were in the lodge, planting false information about their activities for the evening, Helen sat in one of the upstairs bedrooms of Poolside Cottage, staring at the binder that contained all the information required to run the workshop. There, on the first page, was a list of Close Encounters principals: board members, organizers, contacts in the community, and the founder, Nelly Bean.

She dialled Nelly's number and waited for three rings.

"Nelly here." The woman had a rusty-sounding, breathless voice, like she'd just finished a laughing fit. There was a lot of background noise. People talking, music.

"Hello. It's Hetty Thorpe. Do you have a moment to speak with me?"

There was a slight hesitation. Helen felt guilty as she could sense the woman's reluctance. It was uncomfortable to go back to lying about her name and to interrupt someone who was getting married very soon. Helen hadn't been to many weddings, but she knew they were intense for the main participants. The noise behind the woman seemed to intensify. There was a lot of laughing and clinking. Maybe the wedding party was having a high-spirited late lunch before the ceremony? Voices rang out in the background. Something about them caught Helen's attention, but the noise faded as Nelly moved somewhere quieter.

"I'm sorry to disturb you so close to your wedding," said Helen.

"No problem. The ceremony isn't until tomorrow. Everything is going well there, I hope? How is David feeling?"

"Still in bed, I'm afraid. But we hope he'll be back in action tomorrow."

"Poor guy!" said Nelly. "I wish I could help."

"It's absolutely fine. I'm accustomed to facilitating groups. I worked at a retreat centre for many years."

"Well, thank god for that," said Nelly. "Anyway, how can I help you?" The sound of other people in the background had almost entirely disappeared and

CONTEMPLATION OF A CRIME

now there was a rushing noise in the receiver. "Sorry. It's really windy out here," she said.

Helen glanced out the window. She wondered where Nelly was getting married. It was increasingly windy on the island, too.

"First, I wondered if you had any more information available about the participants."

"Why?" Nelly's voice had sharpened.

"So I have better insight into where they're coming from." And in case any of them was involved with the kidnapping of Mr. Levine and David.

"I'm afraid not. Only the material on the intake forms. We try to focus on what happens while they are attending. Who they are off paper and in person, if you understand."

"Okay," said Helen. It was as she'd suspected. "And one other thing. A couple of the participants had some questions about their privacy. It came up in one of our trust-building exercises."

"Oh?"

"Have you had any problems with your email system?" said Helen. "I mean, security-wise?"

Now there was a pause, broken only by the sound of the wind and some other noise Helen couldn't quite make out.

Finally, Nelly Bean spoke again. "Not that I'm aware of," she said. "We use Gmail. Everything is password protected. I don't think anyone has tampered with our system. We get some spam, of course. Phishing emails. The usual stuff. Why are you asking?"

"Oh, a couple of the guests mentioned that they'd received strange messages."

"What does that have to do with our program? What sort of messages?"

"Nothing serious. Just the usual thing where spammers sometimes use words from emails to try to get you to respond. I just wanted to reassure everyone that we aren't being . . . that they can trust the process. Their privacy, I mean."

"Of course they can," said Nelly. "Absolutely. We destroy all personal information about participants. We shred it, except for their contact information, when the course is over."

"Well, that's good. The nervous ones will be glad to hear that."

"They don't still have access to their phones, do they?" said Nelly. "Because that will make it hard for them to stay present. When did they get these emails?"

"We've collected all the phones," said Helen. "But a couple of them got emails shortly after they arrived that they thought were suspicious."

"It sounds like they're feeling a little vulnerable. Sometimes at this stage of the program, a certain paranoia can sneak in."

"Right," said Helen. "That makes sense."

Nelly's voice had grown less friendly. She was probably eager to get back to whatever she was doing. And maybe she thought Helen was second-guessing her and the course.

"Please let the participants know that we get very little information about them, other than what they choose to share on their intake forms. We try to bring in a diversity of opinions and voices. And literal diversity, of course, in terms of race, religion, gender identities."

Helen thought of the participants, who were not notably diverse. In fact, they were all white, seemed to be straight, and, with the exception of Mr. Levine, working- or lower-middle class. None appeared particularly religious. David was the only person of colour. David and Mr. Levine might be the only people of Jewish descent.

"I know this year's group is a little . . . homogenous," said Nelly, as though she could hear Helen's thoughts. "We had a Black woman from Toronto who was going to come. She's amazing. She works to promote call-in culture. But she decided she wasn't up for it. Which I think we can all understand. It's a lot of emotional labour for not much reward. We had a woman from the Squamish Nation who was going to join us, but she also had to bow out, which broke my heart. A Two-Spirit woman. A poet. Phenomenal energy. *Amazing*. We hope both of them will attend next year. Maybe after Praxis takes over."

Helen wondered how the two women Nelly had just described would enjoy being in a group with a white nationalist, an internet troll, a convoy fan, a white lady consumer, and a depressed environmentalist. She didn't blame the two women for finding other places to be.

"I see. Well, thanks very much. I will pass that along."

"Remember to have David call me," said Nelly. "As soon as he feels better."

They hung up and Helen stared out the window at the trees shivering in the wind.

NELLY BEAN

Nelly went back into the cabin of the boat.

"She knows something," she said.

Fields, wearing her Bose headphones, held up a finger.

Nelly felt like she'd been clapped on the side of the head with a frying pan. She was having an out-of-body experience. It was all going wrong. They were going to get caught.

When Fields had finished listening, she slid one of the headphones back. "What?" she asked.

Nelly tried to control her voice. She needed to right the ship. Stabilize everything. She was good at that.

"The butler called. And I think she knows. Or she suspects."

Fields narrowed her eyes, which, in the dim light of the cabin, looked less green and more like black holes. She held up a hand and Nelly noticed that one of the long, fake fingernails was missing. When had *that* happened?

"Knows what?" said Fields. "Obviously, she knows that David and her boss are missing. She's trying to get them back."

"I think she suspects we're involved, or rather, that *I'm* involved. She's asking questions. About how people are chosen for the program. About email security."

"So," said Fields. A statement, not a question.

"So she's investigating. And she said she wouldn't."

"You told me that everyone always wants to know why they got chosen for the program. They start to feel self-conscious. Or they want to feel special."

She was right. Her volatile wife-to-be was absolutely right. This was no time to panic.

"She said she wanted to know more about the participants so she could do a better job of facilitating."

"Normal," said Fields.

"But the email. She said a couple of the participants were worried because they'd been getting strange messages. Do you think she means . . ."

"Of course not. First, I didn't send any emails. And second, they wouldn't tell her. I just listened to them argue about what kind of cheese is smelliest for ten minutes. All that walking they've been doing hasn't healed their divides yet. They're hardly going to start confessing to some strange woman who is taking over the course for a day."

Fields's finely shaped lips curled into a satisfied smile. She was *glad* the course wasn't working. Anger ignited in Nelly's belly. She never used to get angry. Since Fields had convinced her to do this thing, she was either angry or afraid. All the time.

"Anyway, they convinced the butler to let them play games downstairs tonight instead of doing the regular course work. Darts and ping-pong, if you can believe it." Fields laughed. A spiteful sound.

They didn't speak again until Fields held up the hand with the broken nail. "So you really think she's investigating? Trying to find out who took them?"

Nelly wished she hadn't said anything. "Maybe. I don't know. That was just my first impression. I was probably wrong."

"Send her the new numbers again and ask her to resend the money. If it doesn't arrive in half an hour, I have an idea what to do about it."

HELEN THORPE

Helen went downstairs in Poolside Cottage to find the others settling in. A few were staring at the whiteboard, as though it would reveal some secret clue about where David and Mr. Levine were being held. Wayne and Gavin were reviewing the harbour map, which they'd discreetly removed from the office.

Madison was looking bored and Pain was on his laptop, which he'd been given so he could start researching the board members, previous participants, cancelled participants, and anyone else who might be in a position to kidnap David and his father.

Something about the phone call with Nelly Bean was bothering Helen, but she couldn't figure out what it was. She let her senses soften and her attention move lightly over the memory.

"Hey, did you know there's only one picture of you on the internet?" said Pain.

"More like thousands," said Madison. "I'm very active on the socials."

"Not you. Helen. Smart move, really, since facial recognition software is out of control."

"The government is going to control everything we do," said Wayne. "It's only a matter of time until we're living in a totalitarian state."

"And it's only half your face," Pain said. "But the good programs can ID people from just their noses or eyes."

"Imagine if those developers took some of that brain power and used it to fix the climate crisis," said Yana. "Instead of stealing our identities and ruining our lives and the lives of all the beings on earth."

"Imagine if we had to go back to two channels on TV," said Madison. "Like it was before there were a lot of channels. My parents told me about it."

At this, even Wayne gave her a skeptical look. She went back to staring out the window.

Some understanding flitted at the edge of Helen's consciousness. Like a leaf about to land.

"Hey," said Pain again, a few minutes later. "The lady who runs this program usually? The one you said is getting married?"

"Yes?"

"Her wife is hot," said Pain. "Like *really* hot. Have you ever met her?"

"No," said Helen. "I haven't met either of them. I've only spoken to Nelly on the phone."

Again, her attention moved to the leaf of awareness floating in her mind. Something about the phone call with Nelly Bean. Helen looked outside to see what Madison was gazing at. The afternoon outside seemed normal, if windy.

"She's kind of a trip," said Pain.

"Who is?" asked Helen.

"This Fields babe. The founder's wife. She's all over the web. She kept her restaurant open during the pandemic. Got sued."

"Good for her," said Wayne, tuning in. "It's called having balls. Or ovaries or whatever the feminists say."

"Oh god," said Yana.

"According to Reddit, she's some kind of audio pioneer."

"A what?" asked Helen.

"She's really good at audio stuff. She even tried to launch her own private audio platform with private, password-protected channels. She was one of the first to start doing cool things with text-to-speech voice imitators. Like where you type stuff in and a famous person's voice reads it out. She's definitely good at piggybacking on other people's programming work. Kind of impressive, since it looks like she's totally self-taught. Especially surprising since she's a massive anti-vaxxer."

"Do I need to come over there and fix your attitude?" asked Wayne, but he didn't seem mad. In fact, he was smiling. Then he abruptly stopped smiling. "What was the name of her platform?"

"Don't Listen."

"Huh?" said Yana. "If you'd stop talking to us, we'd stop listening."

"No. I mean her platform was called Don't Listen. It got crushed by the bigger platforms. But for a while there, it was looking like it would turn into something."

CONTEMPLATION OF A CRIME

"Don't Listen?" said Wayne. "That's the program we used in Ottawa. The one I used to say some . . . stuff on. Stuff I shouldn't have said."

"Weird," said Tom.

Helen thought it was more than just weird.

Her phone buzzed. Another message.

"Please excuse me," she said and took the phone back upstairs.

HELEN THORPE

She opened Signal and looked at the message. It was just three sets of numbers, a link, and a single word.

—Resend

When the kidnappers sent their last message asking whether Helen had a confirmation number for the transfer, she'd known that it was dawning on them that the money wasn't coming. This new message made it clear that they knew the first transfer hadn't worked. They wanted Helen to try again. At least they didn't know that the account had been suspended.

This time Helen took a screenshot of the message with the new numbers before it disappeared. She checked them against the ones she'd written down the first time. They were all different.

Should she even *try* to transfer the funds again?

It couldn't hurt. Or maybe doing so would trigger some kind of alarm. She couldn't get locked out harder than she already was, could she?

She shook her head. She didn't know what to do.

"How's it going?" Gavin stood in the doorway of the guest bedroom. In his plaid shirt, he looked and sounded like James Bond on a rustic holiday.

Helen let out the breath she'd been holding. "They want me to attempt another transfer."

She was once again sitting on the neatly made bed. There was no desk or chair in the room, which was very small.

"Can you do that?" he asked. "Did the last message say for how long you'd be locked out? Maybe you are only locked out for an hour or two before you can try again?"

"I have no idea. It said the account was suspended."

CONTEMPLATION OF A CRIME

"Ah, that does sound rather long-term," said Gavin. "Do you *want* to try again?"

She looked into Gavin's steady, thoughtful eyes. "I'm afraid to make a mistake," she said. "I really don't want to mess this up."

"If anything goes wrong, it won't be because of you."

Helen looked at the screen of her phone. The message from the kidnapper had disappeared.

"Presumably they got this new transfer information from Mr. Levine?" said Gavin.

Helen nodded.

"And every other message you've gotten from him had some sort of code in it?"

"His spoken messages. Yes, I think so. But this one is just numbers."

"I wonder," said Gavin, "if there might be some message hidden in the numbers?"

He was right. She hadn't even thought to check and see if there was any significance to the numbers she'd been given.

Helen looked at the numbers from the screenshot and wrote them down in her notebook.

277–96
4775263X9074

"Can I sit down?" asked Gavin.

"Of course."

"Can I see?" said Nigel, who'd taken Gavin's place in the doorway.

When she nodded, he sat on her other side.

"They look like bank transfer codes," said Helen. She held up the notebook so they could all look at the numbers.

"Do any of these numbers look familiar? Or suggest anything to you?"

Helen shook her head. They were just numbers.

"Well," said Nigel slowly, staring at the digits. "Isn't the address of Paddock House 276 River Way?" Paddock House was the name of the Levines' estate in Vancouver.

"Yes," said Helen, too stressed to catch his meaning. Then she looked at the second number in the list.

"And 97 is the number of their home in the South of France? I remember because I sent a present to you there," said Nigel.

"And the others?" said Gavin.

Helen searched her memory for the addresses of the Levines' various properties.

"4774 is the number of the building in New York where they have a penthouse apartment. And 262 is the address of their property outside of Calgary."

"So all of these numbers are the same as their house numbers, but off by one?" said Gavin.

"9073 is the number of their home in Santa Fe."

Gavin and Nigel waited while she thought.

"Is he trying to tell us that they're being held at one of those properties?" asked Nigel.

Helen remembered the sound of wind in the receiver and the trees bending over outside the window. She shook her head. "I think he's telling us that they're nearby."

Helen let her mind relax. She tried to open her awareness. Then it hit her. "These numbers all belong to the properties directly across from theirs."

"So he's saying that they're right across from us. Or close, anyway?" said Gavin.

"What's directly across from us here?" said Nigel, sounding excited.

"Saysutshun is behind us. Protection Island is across from Saysutshun. May I?" Gavin asked, and Helen handed him the notebook. He sketched out the relative positions of the islands and the channel that ran in front of the Nanaimo Harbour and between Protection and Saysutshun.

"Which one is this?" asked Nigel, pointing.

"Guide Island," said Helen. "Almost directly across from us."

"And that's exactly where we thought we should start to search," said Gavin. "Let's take this as further confirmation that we're on the right track."

"Can you give me a minute?" said Helen.

"Of course." Gavin and Nigel got to their feet.

"I need a moment to think," said Helen.

HELEN THORPE

H elen sat in silence for another several minutes, taking note of the sound of the wind outside, the feel of small air currents shifting around the room.

An awareness moved in her mind, subtle but compelling. In the midst of all the stress, she'd had a hard time focusing on her senses in the past hours. But she'd always been sensitive to sounds, and when she'd been on the phone with Nelly Bean, the founder of Close Encounters for Global Healing, there had initially been a lot of background noise, including voices she couldn't make out clearly. But some of the voices had come through. Something about them had seemed odd. Helen realized what it was. All of the words she'd been able to hear had been spoken in strong Scottish accents.

Maybe Nelly or her fiancée had a lot of Scottish people in their family? But it had sounded as though *every* voice in the background was Scottish. What sort of restaurant would they be at in Vancouver that was entirely populated by Scots? It had sounded like they were in a Scottish pub.

The other thing that trembled at the edge of her consciousness had to do with the wind. She'd been able to hear the wind in the receiver as she spoke to Nelly. And every time the wind had kicked up enough that she couldn't hear what the other woman said, the wind outside Poolside Cottage had picked up, too. She'd looked outside and seen the trees bent sideways, their leaves fluttering wildly with the strength of it. When the sound in the receiver eased, the trees outside Helen's window had returned to their upright positions and the leaves had settled back into place.

It was almost as if . . .

No. It wasn't *almost* as if. The wind buffeting Side Island was also hitting Nelly Bean wherever she was. Nelly was supposed to be getting married in Vancouver, which was nearly sixty kilometres away. Vancouver definitely wasn't experiencing the exact same gusts of wind at the same time unless those gusts travelled at supersonic speed across the Strait of Georgia.

The evidence was not definitive, but Helen felt in her bones she was right. Nelly Bean was not getting married. Or if she was, she was doing it so close to Side Island that she might as well have been *on* the island.

If Helen had to guess, the background noise with all the Scottish people was a recording. It had a tinny quality. A fake quality. Fields, Nelly's fiancée, was an expert at faking audio. This whole situation was shot through with strange audio connections: listening devices, private recordings, voice memos, faked celebrity voices.

Where was Nelly Bean? Could she have any reasonable explanation for why she was making up a story about being in Vancouver when she wasn't?

No. There was no innocent explanation. Helen knew in her bones that Nelly Bean, the founder of Close Encounters for Global Healing, had kidnapped Mr. Levine and David. That was why she'd asked David to take over the course. It all fit.

The group was confident about where they needed to look for David and his father. But they needed to be sure that they wouldn't tip off Nelly and her fiancée, who'd been very clear that they would hurt them if they suspected Helen was looking for outside help. Was this the time to bring in the police? Mr. Levine had said not to. Plus, with Fields's skills, Helen's phone might be bugged.

They were going to have to do this by themselves.

BIG DOUGH, FORMERLY PAIN WAINSCOTT III

When Helen came downstairs and told them her big insight, Pain knew it was time. He was ready to make his move. To change. Not his personality, which was a lost cause. But his name. His parents wouldn't call him Big Dough, but he thought these people probably would. After all, they needed something from him.

"I'll find out what you want to know about them if you start calling me Big Dough," he said.

Everyone stared at him. But no one laughed.

The Irish butler cleared her throat. "And how is that spelled?" she asked.

"Like when bread is raw."

"Ah," she said. "Fine then, Mr. Dough."

Pain nodded and went back to work, satisfied.

Big Dough was an asshole, and he liked to upset people. But he wasn't Pain Wainscott III, psycho.

Pain had been sent to the Close Encounters for Global Healing—tag line: Five Days That Will Change Your World—to help him develop empathy. Hadn't happened. He'd been sent to multiple places that were supposed to make him a more compassionate person. None of them had worked, either. Pain still saw people through a filter that did not admit emotional connection. He knew he was probably a sociopath. Apparently, that was fairly common. But he wasn't the kind of sociopath that killed people. He wasn't even the kind that was going to rise up in business due to his lack of care for other people, because that would require too much work. His parents had a decent amount of money and plenty of guilt about the kind of kid they'd produced, and they would definitely finance his life until they died and left him everything. That thought was a pleasant one. Not the dead parents part. He didn't have much of a preference, one way or another. But the knowledge that he was always going to be cared for made him feel content.

Pain had once gone to a wilderness camp for screwed-up kids. One of those deals where the campers had to hike and paddle canoes and make fires and learn to be self-sufficient. Mostly what he did was watch the addicted kids go through withdrawal. The ones hooked on antidepressants, which they were allowed to keep taking, couldn't keep up on the hikes because they were used to sleeping all day. The ADHD kids abused their meds and, in some cases, sold their Ritalin to the addicts. Zero kids had breakthroughs and one nearly drowned when he took too much lithium and fell out of his canoe.

Pain didn't take meds, though his dad had tried him on all of them. He didn't need pills. He wasn't unhappy or depressed or hyper. He was just mean and a little numb. But since the butler told them that there had been a kidnapping and asked them all to work together to solve it, Pain felt alive for the first time in his whole life. And he could tell he wasn't the only one who felt that way. He'd turned into Big Dough, Investigator.

Pain, or rather BD (cool initials!), had made it his mission in life to not use his skills for good. When his parents couldn't deal with their computers or figure out some simple issue with their phones, he always told them to call the Geek Squad.

Between gaming and trolling, he spent between twelve and sixteen hours a day online. He could build a computer from scratch. He could hack a network and write malware. It didn't feel like work to him. It was play.

He was never going to do tech support for people who needed to learn to read a help menu, but this wasn't that. He was loving this.

Snooping around everyone's online life had been interesting, but now that he knew Nelly Bean and her wife were the kidnappers, he was in seventh heaven. So much to discover! He learned that the program started out as a research project Nelly Bean had done for her master's degree in social work and community planning. It began as a course offered once a week for four weeks. Then it turned into the five-day retreat.

The more divided the world became, the more attention the course got. Big D found dozens of articles about Close Encounters and Nelly Bean, including a recent one about how a major social enterprise organization called Praxis was probably going to take it over.

Nelly Bean had been interviewed for that article. She liked talking to the press. "Our hope is that expanding the program will help create the conditions for global peace."

Seemed unlikely, as least from his experience so far.

When the interviewer from the *Nanaimo News Daily* asked what her role would be in the program after Praxis took it over, she said she wasn't sure, which Big D took to mean that she thought she was going to get shit-canned.

All the information was available from a simple Google search. Nelly Bean had created a program that got a lot of attention and had attracted a big buyer. With a bit more digging, Big D learned that she hadn't figured out how to get paid for her work. Like at all.

"She was broke," he said to Helen, when she checked in to see how the search was going. "Her and her hot girlfriend. There are people in bankruptcy proceedings right now who have better credit scores than those two idiots. They even got turned down for a car loan last year."

"I didn't think that was possible," said Nigel, who was fixing them pre-dinner snacks. For Big D's money, Nigel was the best of the three butlers because he was all about the food.

Big D kept working, and every so often, he spoke up to tell the rest of the group what he was finding. They were all super into it. Considering Fields was savvy about the internet, she was a dummy about online privacy. It was incredible. He checked records and socials and discovered that Nelly and Fields were basically homeless. They posted pictures of their house-sitting gigs, where they stayed for weeks and sometimes months at a time. Their posts had that "in spite of how much this sucks, I'm pretending to be happy about it" vibe that made social media so terrible. They wrote things like "I wish this little donkey at the Dinmont Farm was ours to keep" and "It's so much fun staying by the lake to look after this raggedy old cat that needs to be force-fed pills every hour."

For the past two years, they'd posted multiple times about staying on someone's boat. In one instance, Fields put up a selfie of her in a bikini, lounging on the deck of said boat. "I could get used to this. Boat-sitting is the best sitting!"

Big D pulled up the photo and enlarged it. The Nanaimo Harbour was clearly visible in the background, and so was the name of the boat: *A Slice of the Pie.* He called Helen and the rest of them over to take a look.

"That's her," he said. "Fields."

He loved how interested they were. How good a job he was doing. This was even better than being good at drawing pigs.

"Where is that?" asked Gavin.

"Looks like they were moored right between Saysutshun and the float plane terminal," said Nigel. "The island right behind us."

It turned out that the boat itself had an Instagram account. The owners had gone through a phase where they posted about it constantly. They also had an account for their cats and another one for the food truck they used to own. They were, according to their personal account, currently on a wine-tasting tour. The last post on the boat account mentioned that *A Slice of the Pie* was for sale, and they included a link to the listing. This was almost too easy.

"Could they all be on the boat?" asked Tom, sounding excited and impressed, which Big Dough enjoyed. "David and his father and those kidnapper women?"

"What do you think?" Helen asked.

"I doubt it," said Wayne. "Especially if they're moored near anyone else. People on boats don't have much privacy unless they're way the fuck out on the water or the boat is truly massive. I don't think they'd just be cruising around with two kidnap victims held below. If they got stopped, they'd be screwed."

"The video sent to Helen shows them somewhere dark, but it didn't look like the cabin of a boat," said Gavin.

"They were in lawn chairs," said Helen. "Chained in lawn chairs."

At this detail, they all went silent for a minute.

"We should ask the boat broker where it is," said Helen, finally. "Maybe Fields and Nelly are there and they're holding David and his father nearby."

Big D sent a message to the boat broker through the website.

The response was almost immediate. "Happy to show it to you. There are boat-sitters onboard right now so I just need to coordinate with them. Are you free tomorrow?"

Boat-sitters. Big D would bet both his parents that that meant Nelly and Fields.

"We got them," he said. The expressions on everyone's faces. They were so impressed. It felt good.

He'd thought he had no feelings, but it turned out, he did. It had just taken a kidnapping to figure them out.

MADISON CROFT

While the internet troll who she was never ever going to call Big Dough, no matter how many times he asked, researched the kidnappers on the internet, Madison decided to go for a walk. Not because she wanted another walk. She'd had enough walking to last her a lifetime. But she'd snuck her phone out of the pile when Helen, the butler, was giving the kid his devices so he could do research.

Being without her phone had made her feel incomplete. She had no plans to go online and tell anyone what was happening on the island. Well, probably not, anyway. Madison was shallow, but she didn't share much on social media other than heavily edited selfies that were basically just the same picture taken in different locations. Sometimes in the same location. What she wanted to do was shop. It didn't matter for what. She had been burning to buy something online since the juice-throwing incident. The Vipa-whatever technique Helen had done with her had given her some relief. Online shopping would give her more. Shopping was living, as far as Madison was concerned.

And she was a little wound up about her growing interest in the truck guy. Wayne. What was happening there? She didn't know. She liked it, but the uncertainty, especially in the middle of so much drama, was freaking her out. What she needed was some calming online retail therapy.

She would just hit the buy button on a few little things and then slip her phone back in with the others, which were in a basket on the counter. The reception near the lodge wasn't great, but it was better farther down the beach toward the far end of the island.

She slipped out of Poolside Cottage, muttering about having to get something from her cabin. As soon as she was out of sight of the lodge, she turned on her phone, feeling her heart rate quicken. God, it felt good to get connected.

Close Encounters was billed as "Five Days That Will Change Your World," but her passion for buying things was as strong as ever. Though maybe she had slightly less shame about it? Strangely, she felt slightly less shame about everything. Maybe it was from the body scan Helen had shown her how to do when she was so upset after the fight with Tom? Or maybe it was because she was dressing like Helen and there was something about an all-navy outfit that made a person feel like they had their shit together.

Madison left the road just past the last cabin and climbed over a line of driftwood logs onto the crushed shell beach. She held up her phone to see how many bars she had. Two. Enough to load a few websites. She bet Lululemon had some cute navy clothes for when she was dressing like she did yoga, which she did not.

She was peering at the screen, waiting for women's pants to load, when she heard a voice.

"Hellooooooo!"

Oh god. She was busted.

Madison whipped around to see a woman coming toward her, weaving her way uncertainly along the beach. Not too steady on her feet, whoever she was.

As the woman got closer, Madison noticed her distressed denim jacket with black leggings. Her white sneakers. Nike Airs, Madison thought. She was lugging a large tote bag. Her hair was tucked under a white ball cap and a black surgical mask covered the bottom half of her face. She also had on huge, round sunglasses, even though the day was overcast. She looked like a celebrity.

"Oh my god, hi," said the woman. "Am I ever glad to see you. Where *am* I?"

Madison frowned. "You're on Side Island?"

The woman dragged a finger across the small strip of skin visible between her hat and her glasses. "Ha ha," she said. "So crazy, right?" She bent over and felt her own legs, as though to make sure they were still there. "I'm soaked!"

Her voice was slurred, and at first, Madison couldn't tell whether she was drunk or she just sounded that way because of the mask. Maybe she'd hit her head and had a concussion? When the woman stepped closer, the smell reached Madison's nose. Definitely booze. She smelled like red wine was coming out of her pores. She smelled like she'd travelled over to the island in a barrel of the stuff.

"Sorry about the mask," said the woman. "So stupid, but my husband insisted. I have covid, but it's not a bad case."

Madison took a quick step back.

CONTEMPLATION OF A CRIME

"Oh my god, it's not a big deal. I'm wearing a stupid mask, so you can calm down."

Madison wasn't sure what to say. She didn't ask the woman if she needed help because her time in customer service had taught her that the best thing to do with intoxicated people was to make them someone else's problem. Unfortunately, there was no security she could call.

"Do you mind if I wait here for my husband? We sort of had a fight. He didn't want to go to the pub, just because of my covid. And then he got all upset because I messed up the navigat— Well, never mind," said the woman. "I said to him, I said fine! If you're going to be a wuss just because I made a totally normal mistake that anyone could make, I'll just go to shore! I jumped out of the boat and waded over here. The water was only up to my waist."

Madison looked at the water and realized that the tide was very low.

"It wasn't my fault we got stuck on that sandbar! I never said I'd be a good, like, co-captain or navigator or whatever. If he hadn't had so many drinks at lunch, he would have seen the buoys and he should have looked at the tide tables and all that stuff. Maybe we both had too much to drink at lunch, but that's boat life, right? It's all about the cocktails." She gave a wet gurgling laugh behind her mask, and Madison tried not to think about the fumes and virus leaking around the loose edges. "My AA sponsor is going to be *verrrry* disappointed."

This was getting sadder and sadder, thought Madison.

"I think I ruined my purse." The woman swayed as she lifted her large tote bag and tipped it to the side. Water poured out.

"Yes. Do you need help getting back on your boat?" asked Madison, coming around to the idea that she was going to have to assist this woman, even though the group was in the middle of a crisis. Clearly, she wasn't very important to the effort since she was over here online shopping on the beach while the others researched and prepared for the rescue effort.

"Have you been to the bar over there?" The masked woman waved a finger over her shoulder. "The Dingy Bar or whatever it's called. It's really . . . a lot of . . . fun."

Madison nodded. The *Dinghy* Dock Pub *was* fun.

"I guess I should try to go back. Our boat is right around the corner."

"Do you want to go wave at him?" asked Madison.

"Maybe. The tide is coming up and he should be able to get the boat off the sandbar soon."

"I'll go with you," said Madison.

Given the circumstances, she didn't feel totally comfortable being out on the beach with a stranger. The sooner this woman got back on her boat with her husband, the better. What if they couldn't get her off the island at all? She'd throw a major wrench in their plans for the evening. Maybe Madison would be forced to stay back and babysit her? The idea wasn't entirely unwelcome. Madison was not enthusiastic about the scheme.

"Come on," she said. "Let's go find your boat."

FIELDS ENTWISTLE

Fields left Nelly behind on *A Slice of the Pie* and told her to watch the bank account. It was time to get serious with these people.

Yes, it was reckless to actually go onto Side Island, but she'd overheard the participants talking about how much time Helen Thorpe, who they called "Hetty," spent on the beach, "staring out to sea." From what the recordings had picked up, Helen had spent most of the day on the beach near the lodge, doing just that.

It was a risk worth taking.

She would grab Helen, take her to the tent, and watch her while she made the transfer. If it didn't work, Fields would start doling out consequences. She had a feeling that Benedict Levine was playing games. That would end when she cut a finger or two off his butler. She didn't want to hurt him or his son too much. The consequences for hurting powerful people were much more serious than for hurting regular people. According to what she'd learned about Benedict Levine, he was very into the well-being of his employees, and he and his wife were particularly devoted to their butler.

Maybe, once they had the money, Fields would hire her own butler. God knows, she deserved one, after all this.

You would think that someone who was objectively stunning and brilliant would be rewarded accordingly. But no. Doors kept closing in her face. Her parents had cut her off after the issues in her restaurant, which were totally not her fault. No one appreciated her innovations in audio. Yes, that was partly because she didn't really want to work for a company or for anyone else, really.

Fields was an angry woman, but she felt she had reason to be. Once she had the ten million, she was sure her luck would turn around.

What was that saying? Fortune favours the bold? Well, Fields had always been bold. She'd fought for what she believed in. And what she believed in was herself and only herself.

As she followed the butler along the beach, her nose wrinkled at the smell of the wine she'd poured onto her clothes to create the impression of a drunk woman who'd made her way to the island by accident. She'd expected to find someone more impressive. Helen Thorpe was a disappointment. She looked and acted no different from the kind of woman you'd see walking a dog on a suburban street. The kind of woman who checked out your groceries or who went for drinks at a chain restaurant on Friday nights. Nothing about her seemed exceptional. Not like Fields, who felt she was in a different category. She should really be in Los Angeles right now. Or Silicon Valley. She should be the subject of profiles in *Wired* magazine and *Vogue*.

The most attention she'd ever gotten was the media she'd received during the unsanctioned openings of her restaurant. The camera had loved her, even if the comments sections hadn't.

Whatever. Maybe this butler had hidden depths. Nelly had said the butler was a former nun? Something like that? Fields couldn't imagine the mouse in front of her being some spiritual guru. She bet Helen Thorpe didn't even know Brené Brown. Fields had read two of her books and considered herself an expert in contemporary spirituality.

They had walked around the corner. No one had seen them and there were no buildings visible from the beach. The guests were probably getting ready for dinner or walking or something.

Fields's gambit had paid off. She was glad she hadn't had to kidnap the butler from her cabin or take her when she was close to other people. But she would have done it, if necessary. Because: Fortune. Boldness. All that.

The butler turned around. She wore a lot of makeup. Fields would have assumed a butler would be more au naturel so as not to compete with her betters. Maybe not. She'd find out when she interviewed her own butlers.

The butler was staring out at the water, where there were no boats stuck on sandbars. She must be fairly dumb if she'd fallen for that story.

Most people were dumb, in Fields's experience. Like Nelly, they'd believe anything. If you were good-looking enough, people would believe almost anything you said because they wanted to.

"I don't see your boat," said the butler.

"Oh, jeez," said Fields. "Maybe the tide came up enough that he already

CONTEMPLATION OF A CRIME

got the boat off the sandbar. Maybe he went the other way around the island, looking for me."

Now the butler looked nervous, like she wasn't sure what to do with Fields. Fields smiled behind her mask.

"Well," said the butler. "Do you want to call and arrange to meet him? We will just need to figure out how you can get from the shore out to the boat without swimming."

Fields, secure in her disguise, took a step toward the butler. She pulled the handgun out of her bag. Nelly would have a fit if she knew Fields had it. Predictably, conventionally, she was rabidly anti-gun. Oh well. What she didn't know wouldn't upset her.

The butler didn't speak. Her mouth hung open.

"Oh," she said.

"Come on," said Fields. "Walk."

She directed the woman to the Zodiac, which she'd dragged up on the beach behind a pile of logs and some bushes, soaking her brand-new Nike Airs in the process.

Once the butler was in the boat, Fields handed her a mask and ball cap. "Put these on and sit there like you're enjoying yourself. Make a wrong move and I'll shoot you in the back. When we get to the other side, you'll have to wear a hood. But the mask and hat will have to do for the crossing."

She was impressed that the butler didn't cry but did as she was told.

PART IV

IF YOU MEET THE BUDDHA ON THE ROAD, KILL HIM. OR AT LEAST BEAT HIM UP AND TAKE HIS MONEY.

DAVID LEWISTON

When the tent flaps opened to admit the kidnappers, David wasn't surprised. Once again the transfer hadn't shown up, and it made sense that this time they wouldn't wait for hours before they started asking questions. What did surprise him was that there was just one kidnapper and she had someone with her. Someone with a hood over their head. Someone who wore navy slacks and a lightweight navy jacket.

He glanced at his father, who looked suddenly stricken.

"We didn't get our money," said Clint Eastwood's voice. "We've heard that you care a lot about your employees. Especially your butler."

A pause for typing.

"The two of you need to transfer this money. I'll watch. When we have it, I'll let you go."

And with that, the kidnapper, who was not dressed in genderless combat fatigues this time, but like a woman on a shopping trip, in leggings and runners, flung the hood off the head of the new arrival.

There was a long silence as everyone stared at each other.

The newest captive was a little wobbly on her feet. Her face was drawn with fear.

"You and your butler need to get us our money," said Clint Eastwood's voice after a bit of furious typing. "Now."

"That," said his father, "is not my butler."

HELEN THORPE

The plan wasn't one of those that was brilliant in its simplicity. It was complicated to the point of being nonsensical. But it might just work.

Before they could begin, they had to go back to the lodge for dinner and pretend that there was nothing wrong in spite of the fact that absolutely everything was wrong. Helen felt strongly that she didn't want the cook, Bobbi-Lyn, to get any inkling that there was a crisis unfolding because she wouldn't have been a bit surprised to discover that Bobbi-Lyn was somehow involved. It was the concert T-shirts. Helen had found an area of deep prejudice in herself and it was heavy metal concert Ts. She had taken a strong disliking to them. She'd investigate that personal failing later.

The key was to act normally around Bobbi-Lyn before the rescue mission began.

Before they trooped from Poolside back to the lodge, Tom pointed out that Madison hadn't returned from her walk.

"She's probably having a nap," said the participant formerly known as Pain. Helen was having trouble making the switch to calling him Big Dough. She liked the name about as much as she liked heavy metal concert T-shirts.

"I can knock on her cabin door," said Nigel. "The dogs need a walk. Especially since we're facing possible death this evening and they may end up being orphans. At least, orphans from me."

"That's not how orphans works," said Wayne. "Your dogs will be homeless, but not orphans." He patted the broad forehead of Potato, who seemed to sense that some adventure was afoot that might involve her getting left alone. She refused to move more than a few inches from Wayne's legs. When he sat down, she climbed into his lap. From there she manoeuvred her fat body so she could put her paws around his neck and lean her head against his shoulder.

"Separation anxiety," he said when anyone looked askance at what was nearly making-out behaviour.

CONTEMPLATION OF A CRIME

"Sure, buddy," said Tom.

"Me and Potato will come with you," said Wayne to Nigel. "Maybe that'll help her chill out."

The two of them headed for Madison's cabin and everyone else went into the lodge. Murray and Gavin were already inside, preparing the dining room and serving table.

Ten minutes later, the guests, watched by the butlers, were moving down the table, helping themselves to roasted cabbage salad, green salad, and creamy pumpkin pasta covered in a layer of bubbling cheese and toasted breadcrumbs and another pasta with sundried tomatoes and spinach. Helen was impressed with the dishes. They looked hearty, simple, and satisfying.

In general, Bobbi-Lyn, whom they were all avoiding so assiduously, seemed to be very good at her job, even if she wasn't a particularly warm or gracious presence.

Things were going smoothly until Nigel, followed by Wayne, rushed into the foyer and gestured at Helen from the doorway. They looked so frantic that she was glad the cook wasn't there to see them.

She followed the two men outside to the expanse of sandstone that rose in front of the front door and then sloped down to the ocean.

"She's not in her cabin," said Wayne.

Nigel nodded. "We knocked a bunch of times. Then we went inside and checked." His round face was red from exertion and his eyes were worried.

There was no way Madison had gone off for a long walk and lost track of time, but she might have gone off to be on her phone.

"We need to check the beach. She might be looking for a spot where she can get cellphone reception," said Wayne. "She keeps talking about how much she misses her phone. We talked about it."

The concern in his voice was evident.

"I'll do it," said Gavin, who'd come to join them.

"Perhaps you can split up? Go in opposite directions. Check the beaches. I'll check the games room downstairs and have Murray look upstairs," said Helen.

"Do you think she's okay?" Wayne sounded worried.

"Maybe she decided to leave. This is not what she signed up for. Particularly tonight's activities," said Helen.

251

SUSAN JUBY

"How would she get off the island?" asked Nigel.

"She didn't take her luggage. Her giant suitcase is still in her room."

Before Helen could answer, her phone buzzed.

They all went silent.

Helen swallowed and then opened Signal.

—The transfer has not arrived. Consequences begin in one hour.

Below was a photo. It showed Madison kneeling between Mr. Levine and David, who were seated in their lawn chairs. The lighting was poor, but something about the image caught Helen's attention, beyond the fact that they'd taken Madison for some unknown reason. She opened the photo, enlarged it, and had to stop herself from crying out. Mr. Levine's eye was swollen. His lip was cut and swollen. Her gentle, enthusiastic employer had been beaten up.

She felt her hands begin to shake. Helen showed the message to Gavin and watched his face grow grim when he enlarged the photo.

"I think," he said, slowly, "we need to find them or get the kidnappers their money before something very bad happens."

DAVID LEWISTON

The tall kidnapper paced back and forth in the confines of the tent while waiting for Helen to reply to the message.

She'd chained Madison between David and his father. The chain went around Madison's waist and was looped to the other waist chains. There wasn't enough chain left to attach her by her feet.

David's father graciously offered Madison his lawn chair, and there was a lot of awkward shuffling around and clinking of metal to move it over so she could get into it.

"Are you sure you don't mind?" she said.

"I must insist," said David's father, who spoke as though they were at a garden party.

David kept looking at the kidnapper. It worried him that she was alone. Where was Nelly? He was almost certain this was Fields, Nelly's fiancée. He'd only met her once, briefly, but he remembered a tall, slender woman with remarkable eyes. The light in the tent was so dim he hadn't noticed the eyes until now. It was still hard to see what colour they were, but there was something in her mostly covered face that he didn't like.

The kidnapper's phone pinged. She read the message, then typed in her voice answer: "Your butler says she will give us the money. Her money."

"That's not acceptable," said David's father.

"Why not? And how would a butler have that much cash?"

"She has a little over three million dollars," said David's father. "From an inheritance. I know because I helped her invest it."

"I need all of the money. Ten million."

Then the kidnapper stepped outside.

David looked at his father. "Dad, we need to give them the money. I think that one is about to . . ." He shook his head. He didn't want to say what he was afraid of in case that made his fear come true.

His father looked pensive. "Well, I can't transfer them the funds without alerting my bankers. But I can give them bitcoin. I'll have to buy some first. And figure out a way to do so without alerting anyone. And they'll have to set up a wallet to receive it."

"It's time to suggest that," said David.

"I agree."

David's father looked at the silent young woman beside him. Madison hadn't said much. David wasn't sure how she was doing, but she wasn't panicking. That much seemed clear.

"Are you holding up okay?" he asked her. "We'll do what we need to do to get you home safely."

"I'm fine," said Madison. "But she is definitely going to hurt someone if she doesn't get her money."

"Why do you think that?" he whispered, even though he felt the same.

"I have worked retail since I was sixteen years old. You get a sense about people."

His father sighed. "Let's not get ahead of ourselves. We'll be fine. I'm not allowing Helen to send her own money. I'll send them the funds in bitcoin."

"There's one more thing?" said Madison.

They waited.

"I can get out of these chains. If that's helpful?"

David felt his eyes widen.

"When she put them around my waist, I stuck out my belly. I can add like a lot of inches to my midsection. If I suck in my stomach, these things will be on the floor." Madison touched her hands to the chains. "Not bragging. As long as I can get them over my hips, I'll be loose."

"That is very useful, my dear," said David's father. "Let's not make any sudden moves for now."

Before they could say any more, the kidnapper pushed back into the tent.

"If the transfer isn't working, I'll get you bitcoin," said Mr. Levine. "But it will take some time. And I'm going to need a tablet."

TOM AUCIELO

Tom had just started to eat when Helen asked everyone to come outside.

"I'm sorry," said Helen, when they were all gathered around. Tom was the only one who brought his plate with him. He wasn't going to miss a meal if he could help it. Maybe he'd been starved in another life. Or he had a tapeworm. Either way, he was always, always hungry and felt like he had been that way forever.

"We need to go now." Helen stood there, tall and steady, a butler on either side of her.

The scene reminded Tom of the men in the Compound getting ready for what they called "actions." Only he felt reassured by Helen and the butlers, as opposed to terrified.

"Everyone ready?" asked Helen.

"Uh, no?" said Big Dough.

"You can stay behind," said Helen. "No one will blame you." She wasn't being a bitch about it. Her voice was kind.

"Big D don't quit," said the kid.

"But he sure does bitch a lot," said Wayne, grinning at the younger man.

"What's going on?" asked a voice from the front door.

It was Bobbi-Lyn, the chef.

Tom tried to sidle behind one of the butlers. God, that woman freaked him out.

"Something wrong with my food?" she demanded.

"Absolutely not," said Murray, the Irish butler. "It's fantastic."

"I was askin' them," said Bobbi-Lyn. She glared at Tom, who shrunk farther away.

"We have an activity. Unfortunately, it's time-sensitive and it's going to interfere with dinner. It's all part of the program," said Nigel, the butler with all the dogs. He was broad enough to give decent cover and Tom inched closer to him.

255

SUSAN JUBY

"Can you set our plates aside and cover them?" said Gavin. "For when we get back?"

"Not him," said Bobbi-Lyn and she pointed at Tom, who felt himself flush. "He's not doing any time-sensitive evening activities."

Tom gaped at Bobbi-Lyn and she glared back. The sun was sinking behind a stand of trees. The hunter's moon would be up soon. Tom liked knowing the names and phases of the moon. He liked the moon. The thought of it gave him courage. "I won't?" he asked the skinny, hard-faced cook. "Why not?"

"Because it's too dangerous for you to be outside at night. I'm guessing this activity is going to be outside?"

"I'm sorry," said Helen. "Can you please explain yourself?"

"I don't want anything to happen to him. And from what I can tell, you people have a disappearing problem on this island. It's like a goddamn Agatha Christie novel around here."

"Who are—" asked Tom.

"Babs sent me," said Bobbi-Lyn.

"Babs?" Tom looked mystified. "Who's that?"

Bobbi-Lyn sighed. "Your fairy godmother."

"I have no idea what you're talking about," said Tom, thinking that if he had a fairy godmother, she was painfully incompetent.

"Remember a girl from the Compound? Red hair? You drove her to meet the paramedics after she got pneumonia?"

"Yes," said Tom, startled at the memory. "Margaret."

"Babs is Margaret's mother. She hired me to get Margaret out of that place. That's what I do. I go undercover to help people leave cults and dangerous situations. Last time you saw me, I was doing dishes at the Compound."

The various frightening people from the Compound had merged into one blob in Tom's mind. But he remembered a few of them. He didn't remember the cook, but he did recall Margaret. She was a quiet woman in her thirties. She had poor posture and seemed to suffer from some nervous condition. He remembered that she almost never made eye contact but stared fixedly at the floor.

"Oh," said Tom. Margaret had been with one of the worst men at the Compound. A couple of times Tom had distracted the guy when he was about to slap her around in front of everyone to show how tough he was. Tom had

CONTEMPLATION OF A CRIME

directed the guy's anger onto him while Margaret had faded back into the kitchen.

God, the Compound really was the worst.

"I looked different then," said Bobbi-Lyn. "Had curly brown hair. Wore a dress with some padding in the front."

He vaguely remembered a woman who fit that description coming over to him and saying that Margaret was sick. That she was having trouble breathing, that maybe it was asthma. The woman had asked Tom to ask Warren Wiggins if they could take Margaret to the doctor. Tom was terrified by the assignment, but he'd done it and Warren Wiggins had agreed to let her get medical help, but he didn't want his men getting too far away from the Compound and he wouldn't allow any paramedics on the property. So he'd agreed to let Tom take Margaret to meet the ambulance at a gas station just out of town.

"I don't want some snatch dying here," Warren had said.

Such a charmer.

Bobbi-Lyn brought Tom's attention back to the present. "She wasn't really sick. I talked her into leaving."

"I'm sorry I didn't remember you," said Tom. The Compound had been so grim and threatening that he hadn't really gotten close to anyone. He'd tried to block his time there out of his memory.

"Like I said, I looked different then. We never spoke. But I made sure she got out of there when she was ready to leave him."

"So Margaret's doing all right?" he said.

"She's got some healing to do, but she'll recover. Her mother was real grateful for your help. Thinks you're quite the hero. Plus, she wants you available to testify if Margaret ever wants to press charges over what happened to her in that place."

Tom felt an urge to look behind him. He'd felt nothing but shame about his time in the militia where he'd been treated like a dog no one wanted. He was no hero just because he hadn't acted like an abusive asshole.

"The cops mentioned to Babs that the CFRP had a contract on you. She called me and asked if I could help you out. I heard you were coming here to hide. I wasn't sure how I was going to get onto the island during the program, but then they put out a request for a cook and boom. My way in. I used to cook in my old special ops unit. I'm not bad in the kitchen. I like food. Anyway, Babs is prepared to help you once you get out of here. She's even thinking about sending Margaret to take this course. I'm going to have to tell her that would be a terrible idea, from a security perspective."

"Is *anybody* at this workshop who they say they are?" said Big D.

"Well, turns out your name is really Big D," said Yana.

"Babs said she'll give me a bonus if you make it through this course without getting snatched or killed," said Bobbi-Lyn. She pronounced it "kilt." "So I'ma make sure you don't. In conclusion, folks," continued Bobbi-Lyn, "Tom here is under my protection. He's not taking any part in your exercise, as you so suspiciously call it. And maybe you all should tell me where everyone else has got to?"

Helen, who'd been quietly taking everything in, seemed to come to some sort of decision.

"Bobbi-Lyn," she said. "I think we might be able to use your skills. And I would be happy to match and go beyond your boss's bonus."

"I'm listening," said Bobbi-Lyn, in her flat American accent.

WAYNE KRUPKE

While the cook, who was actually some kind of anti-cult spy, discussed the situation with the butlers, Wayne went into the foyer. The last rays of light were streaming through the stained glass windows on either side of the door, creating a solemn, churchy effect.

The lodge was classy and Wayne was going to miss it when the course was over. If he ended up dying tonight, he figured he was going to miss a lot of things and quite a few people. He wondered who was going to miss him? His mom. His sister. Potato, for sure. He wondered if Madison would miss him? He thought she probably would.

He led Potato over to his cabin, feeling like a traitor. He couldn't take her with him. When he closed the door on her, he heard claws scrabbling against it. He hoped the lodge had good insurance because she was going to tear the place up. That done, he hurried over to the dock-less ferry landing just in time to see a small vessel coming straight at him. The boat, which was actually an old bathtub converted into a boat, had a powerful engine on the back that made a high-pitched buzzing noise.

Fucking Andrew. The guy had entered the bathtub races every year since he was seventeen and his boats and the engines he put on his tubs got crazier every year. They'd met in a marine engine repair course they'd both taken right after high school.

When Wayne had called his old friend earlier in the afternoon and told him what he needed, Andrew hadn't hesitated. Now here he was, piloting one of his old bathtubs over to Side Island on a few hours' notice. Now, that was a friend. Coming through for you when it mattered. It made Wayne feel guilty about the political arguments they'd had.

The tide was high enough that when Andrew cut the engine and lifted it, the bathtub made it all the way to the beach.

"Hey, man," said Wayne.

"Hi," said Andrew, who wore small, round glasses and had short, neat hair. He looked like a professor but sounded like a surfer. He sometimes wore kilts. He was part owner of the local fancy cheese store.

"Thanks for doing this."

"No problem. You okay?"

"Can't really get into it now. But maybe we could go for a beer later? I'll tell you all about it."

Andrew nodded. His glasses had so much salt spray on them Wayne wondered if he could see through them. "Absolutely. We'll catch up. It's been too long."

Andrew didn't demand to know why Wayne needed a bathtub boat at night on no notice. That was part of what made him a cool guy.

"I'll take care of the tub," said Wayne.

"It's totally thrashed but I had fun in it. You can throw me some money for the engine if you sink it," said Andrew. He turned to look behind him. "There's Jen."

They watched Andrew's wife approaching in their runabout.

"You got a good life jacket?" Andrew asked.

"Yeah," said Wayne, though he didn't.

Andrew looked at him for a long moment and then took off his own PFD and handed it over. "Here," he said. "We have an extra."

Wayne took it. "Thanks."

Jen nosed the runabout closer, expertly lifting the motor so as not to tear up the propellers. She waved and Wayne waved back. He wondered what she thought of him and the way he'd stopped speaking to them after a couple of heated conversations.

It takes two, he thought. But he still felt bad.

"We better get back. Don't have proper running lights," said Andrew. "Don't want to get caught in the channel in the dark."

"I'll be in touch," said Wayne.

"You better."

The two of them bumped fists.

Andrew handed Wayne the rope for the Mad Max–looking bathtub, climbed into the runabout, and put on another life jacket. Then he and Jen waved. She backed them up and they were gone.

Wayne hadn't been in a bathtub boat for years. He figured it was probably like getting on a bike. Only faster and bumpier.

HELEN THORPE

t took six of them to lift the old dragon boat off the rack in the boathouse and onto the wheeled cart, which they used to bump it along to the water.

"Why do they have this?" asked Yana.

"There are photos downstairs of a Side Island dragon-boating team," said Nigel, who was puffing as he helped to pull the long boat to the water's edge.

A pile of dusty paddles and faded, skinny life jackets waited for them on the shore.

"Anybody here know how to paddle?" asked Big Dough. "Because I don't and I'm not planning to learn."

"Are you sure you don't want to stay behind?" snapped Yana. "And yes, I know how to paddle. Sort of. I went dragon boating a few times."

"So can you direct us?" asked Gavin. "I'm afraid I didn't take rowing at university. Although I *was* the captain of the table tennis team."

"That's hot," said Murray.

"The times I went out, I was put near the back of the boat and I never quite got the hang of the strokes. Someone shouted out instructions, but I can't remember what they said. And I can't remember if the captain or driver or whatever sat at the front or back." Yana shook her head.

"We'll figure it out," said Bobbi-Lyn, who had agreed to help them rescue the hostages. Helen had promised her ten thousand dollars to come along on the rescue mission and another twenty thousand if they got the hostages back in one piece. Bobbi-Lyn had cheerfully agreed. Her loyalty to her employer only went so far.

"Can you even paddle this thing with only eight people?" asked Tom.

The dragon boat had space for twenty rowers.

"I suspect we'll just be a bit slower than we would with a full crew," said Gavin.

"I have the strength of half a man," said Nigel.

"Same," said Tom.

"Don't forget that we have Yana," Big Dough pointed out. "She's stronger than the rest of us put together."

They put on the old life jackets and picked up their paddles. When they were ready, Gavin and Murray held the long, narrow boat steady and the others waded out into the water, griping about the cold, and got awkwardly in.

"Ready?" said Gavin, after he'd given Murray a hand.

"Wait!" called Tom. "Isn't that Wayne's dog?"

So it was. Potato had somehow broken out of Wayne's cabin and was hurtling toward them as fast as an animal shaped like a loaf of bread could run.

"Wayne's already left."

"She'll be fine onshore," said Gavin. "We'll leave her here."

He pushed the boat farther into the water, and Helen used her paddle to steady it.

"Potato's coming in," said Tom.

"We can't leave her," said Yana. Despite her oft-mentioned disapproval of pets, she seemed to have grown fond of the pit bull.

Helen saw that the small, fat dog was high-stepping her way into the water, then backing up and trying again, until she was up to her belly.

"She's going to follow us," said Nigel. "Such a good and loyal girl."

"Okay, fine," said Gavin. He pulled the boat back toward the shore. "Come on, you little root vegetable," he said.

Potato paddled toward him with a horrified but determined look on her face. When she was close enough, he heaved her into the boat, where she shook violently and nearly capsized them.

The sight of the fat dog in the middle of the boat cheered Helen immensely. It was as though their captain had arrived.

Gavin pushed them deeper and jumped into the boat. He carefully made his way over to Helen, grabbed his paddle, and they were off in a flurry of unharmonious strokes and irritated cries to stop splashing.

WAYNE KRUPKE

I n the fading light, Wayne rowed the boat the butlers had rented to get to Side Island over to Saysutshun. He had his cellphone and a headlamp, and he was towing Andrew's bathtub-race boat behind him. It was slow going, but at least the wind had settled down and the water wasn't rough.

If the Nanaimo Harbour Authority stopped him and asked what he was doing out, he planned to say he was bringing his laundry from Protection Island to a laundromat in Nanaimo. People did stranger things. He would explain the bathtub boat by saying that its engine had died and he was bringing it over to his buddy to get it fixed. This was a strange time of year to be doing anything with bathtub boats, but what the hell. Tubbers were crazy. Everyone knew that, including the Harbour Authority.

The moon had risen in the east and it hung over the water like a special effect.

It felt good to be on his own, using his arms to push the boat through the waves. The rowboat was a bit of a pig but that was okay. He was getting where he needed to go.

The harbour was quiet. The float planes had stopped flying and most of the pleasure craft and fishing boats were in for the night. Soon he was at Mark Bay, where boaters could tie up at the dock or rent one of the concrete mooring buoys.

He and the others had talked it over and decided that if *A Slice of the Pie* was nearby and the kidnappers were on it, it would be at one of the buoys rather than tied up at the dock. The kidnappers probably didn't want to be too close to anyone else while they did their dirty deeds.

He listened to the waves slapping against the hull and water dripping off the oars as they rose and fell.

When he was inside Mark Bay, he lifted the oars from the water and looked. Only a few boats were tied up using the buoys. That was good. Fewer boats to check without raising suspicions.

Saysutshun was a dark mass rising to his right. The heavily treed island was a marine park and far bigger than Side Island. During the spring and summer months, it was a destination for tourists and locals alike. Most people got to the island via the dedicated little ferry that travelled back and forth every half hour from April to September, loaded with walkers, sunbathers, and campers. In the off-season, as far as Wayne knew, the island was mostly left to the deer and the racoons. That meant there was probably no one on Saysutshun to report a strange rowboat approaching moored boats in Mark Bay. He just had to watch out for any people on board.

He took a deep breath, and when he got closer to the nearest boat, he turned his headlamp on to illuminate the side of the vessel. He didn't even have to read the name to know it wasn't *A Slice of the Pie*, which was a white Campion.

This was a large red sailboat.

Wayne rowed to the next vessel. It was white. No mast.

There it was. *A Slice of the Pie* written in script down the side.

There were no lights on inside. In fact, there were no lights on in any of the boats, even though it wasn't yet seven at night.

He tried to row quietly up to the Campion. When he reached it, he called out in a soft voice. When there was no answer, he climbed aboard.

"Hello?" he tried again.

Still no answer. He went below and found the door locked. He knocked. Nothing. He couldn't see inside the berth, but he felt sure it was empty.

He got back in the rowboat and pushed off. Then he sent a message to Yana.

—Go

Her text took less than a minute to come back.

—Okay

He waited, rowing to keep the boat in the right place, checking the time. When eight minutes had passed, he moved farther away from the Campion and then manoeuvred the sleeping bag stuffed with clothes and newspaper and topped with a hat so it looked like either a giant slug or, in the dark, an over-dressed human sitting up in the boat. He paddled to keep the rowboat from drifting toward the Campion.

Yana's next text read:

—Go

CONTEMPLATION OF A CRIME

Wayne pulled the bathtub boat close, then jumped out of the rowboat and into the bathtub. He held the rowboat close and reached over with his long barbecue lighter, which he used to light a long row of toilet paper rolls stuffed with cotton swabs that had been covered in Vaseline. They lit, but burned slowly as they went into the stuffed bag. When he was sure the tubes had caught fire, he shoved the bathtub boat away from the rowboat.

Damn it. The rowboat floated back toward him. He had visions of the engine of the bathtub boat catching fire. Of himself dying in a small fireball.

Flames flickered in the bottom of the rowboat, all the way into the sleeping bag. He reached back and the bathtub boat engine sputtered into life.

It growled and then roared, and he turned the little vessel so he was heading back out of the harbour, away from the burning boat that already looked, in the dark, like a human being on fire. Flames licked at the lumpy figure posed upright.

Sirens sounded from the Nanaimo side of the harbour.

Per the plan, Yana had used Bobbi-Lyn's untraceable burner phone to call the police and the news media to report her plan to commit suicide, specifically to self-immolate to bring attention to the climate crisis. It was what the fruitcake contact in her climate grief group had suggested. Wayne couldn't believe Yana had ever considered actually going through with it. Jesus.

He knew that by the time the emergency personnel reached the rowboat, the fire would have consumed the dummy. It wouldn't take them long to realize the only thing that had burned up was a sleeping bag stuffed full of clothes.

But, if all went according to plan, the cops and harbour police would be swarming the area around *A Slice of the Pie* for a while, at least, which meant that no one would be getting on or off the boat in the next few hours or escaping in it with three kidnapping victims.

It had been a long shot, but so far it was working out.

The tiny racing bathtub with the powerful engine hammered through the waves, jarring his entire body every time it rose and fell. Wayne, wet and freezing but stoked, felt even more outlaw than he had in Ottawa.

HELEN THORPE

The modest team of paddlers squabbled halfway to Guide Island, which had been used for Girl Guide retreats until the mine shafts underneath began to collapse. Now the island was in limbo as what should be done with it was being decided.

A skilled dragon-boating crew might have made the trip between the islands in fifteen minutes. It took Helen and the gang closer to forty. They kept splashing each other and banging their paddles together and hitting each other in the back. Soon, everyone was soaked.

When they were halfway across, Gavin leaned over and suggested that perhaps they should space out farther. "Maybe we should move everyone so there's distance between them?" he suggested.

"I'm worried that someone will fall out. Or we'll tip the boat."

"Ah, yes. Good thinking." Gavin was so wet from the Big D's flailing stroke that he looked as though he'd been swimming.

"Want me to call time?" asked Yana from her seat at the back of the boat.

"Let's keep our voices down," said Helen. "Watch the paddlers in front and try to follow their rhythm." She had no more idea how to paddle a dragon boat than they did, but it made sense that the people in front should set the pace. She remembered a talk by an excellent dhamma teacher from Hawaii about how the ancient Hawaiians were gifted ocean navigators who paddled their canoes using the stars and the feel of the currents beneath them. This group was not going to be mistaken for brilliant navigators anytime soon.

"My hands are wet and I think I'm getting blisters," complained Big D.

"Just paddle. The island is right there," said Tom.

Bobbi-Lyn, who sat behind Tom, was silent and watchful.

The only one who seemed at ease was Potato, who had her paws up on the side of the boat and was watching their approach like the gleeful skipper of a pirate ship. Every time Helen looked at her, the pit bull's grin seemed to get bigger.

CONTEMPLATION OF A CRIME

The glories of the full moon eventually seduced everyone on board and their strokes fell into a tempo and they stopped complaining as they paddled into the glittering wake of the moonlight hitting the water.

Helen took a moment to appreciate the sound of the creaking boat and the paddles dipping in and out of the water. She listened to the rhythmic breathing of the crew and some of the tension left her body.

When they were close to Guide Island, Gavin switched his headlamp on to help them decide where to put in.

"Let's go right to shore." Helen imagined them all trying to disembark into deep water. One or more of them would probably drown, even with their life jackets on.

She hoped they wouldn't hit any sharp rocks on their way in. The last thing they needed was to get stranded on Guide Island.

"Do you see any other boats?" she asked. In spite of the brilliance of the moon, it was hard to see very far at night and the trees on the island seemed to cast a line of extra-thick shadow over the shoreline.

"No," he said. "But they could be anywhere. Guide Island is easier to approach than Side Island. Not so many cliffs and hazards around it."

The long wooden boat swept into shore going surprisingly fast, even though they'd tried to slow it down. Helen held up her paddle to indicate everyone should stop paddling and they did. When they hit the sand at the water's edge, Gavin jumped out and began to pull the boat in. Helen followed him. Soon the others were disembarking like ducklings jumping from a log.

A minute later, the four butlers, three guests, and one random spy stood dripping at the waterline.

"Stick together? Or spread out and search?" asked Gavin.

Helen thought about the collapsing mine shafts and decided they should search together.

"I think we can do it without headlights," said Murray. "The moon is giving off enough light."

They found a well-defined path at the edge of the beach.

They began to walk in single file. Almost immediately, the path veered into the forest toward the middle of the island.

"We're going to need our headlamps," said Gavin. "We'll have to hope they don't draw too much attention."

267

They decided that every second person would turn on their headlamp, which would be pointed down at the path so that the person behind them could see where they were stepping.

Few words were exchanged, and in spite of the frightening nature of the situation, Helen marvelled at how well they were all working together. Close Encounters really *did* work.

She stayed at the rear. When everyone stopped, she waited to hear what was going on. How far across the island had they made it?

Whispers came back to reach her ears.

"Something ahead," said Yana.

"A tent."

"Gavin says for everyone to back up."

"Headlamps off," came the whispered instruction. When the last headlight clicked off, the group was plunged into total darkness, as though they'd all fallen down a well.

It took some time for Helen's eyes to adjust.

"There's a tent ahead. Around the corner. It's one of those big canvas ones. And I can see light inside," said Gavin.

"Hooooly shit," whispered Tom. "Maybe we found them."

"We can't just go barging in there," said Murray. "The kidnappers might have weapons."

"I bet they have guns," said Tom.

"They're not the only ones," said Bobbi-Lyn.

Helen turned to her. "You brought a weapon?"

"Obviously. You thought I'd head out on an assignment like this unarmed?"

Helen wondered where Bobbi-Lyn was keeping her weapon. She didn't carry a purse. Her jeans, jean jacket, and awful T-shirt were quite snug. Was the gun in her boot? If so, did she worry about shooting herself in the foot?

"Here's how we'll do it," said Bobbi-Lyn. "Since you people have no idea what you're doing. We'll announce ourselves but stay well back in case someone shoots through the door."

"*Shoots through the door?* Are you serious?" said Big D, whose taste for danger seemed to have been exhausted by the trip over. "I'm not getting near any tent doors that might have bullets ripping through them."

"If they answer, we'll tell them we're not the cops and that we'll stand aside while they get away as long as they don't hurt the prisoners. If they don't answer, and the prisoners are in there, we'll cut them loose and bring 'em back to Side Island. Let the cops deal with the kidnappers. Simple."

Helen thought Bobbi-Lyn's plan sounded reasonable. And at least she hadn't suggested hand-to-hand combat. Helen had head-butted someone once and that was enough violence to last her a lifetime.

"You and me." Bobbi-Lyn gestured at Gavin. "We'll go first."

"I'm coming," said Murray. "I've seen at least a hundred episodes of *Law & Order* so I know how to run into warehouses and industrial spaces in search of suspects."

Yana snorted, but not in a mean way.

No, thought Helen. *I'm supposed to be in charge. I can't let the guests or my friends face danger so that I don't have to.*

"You will all stay back," she said. She turned to Bobbi-Lyn. "No guns. I don't want anyone getting shot."

"That's the kind of smart thinking that gets people shot," said Bobbi-Lyn.

"No guns," repeated Helen.

Helen's body was flashing hot and cold, but she felt she was doing the right thing.

"I'm coming with you," said Gavin.

"And me," said Murray.

"Me too, even though I'm scared I might pass out," said Nigel.

"Ah, shit. I guess we're all coming," said Big D.

"Oh god," said Tom. "Fine."

And so, with Helen in the lead, Potato at her heels, the line of rescuers headed around the corner toward the cabin-sized tent.

DAVID LEWISTON

When the tall kidnapper came back with the short one, neither of them were using their voice changers anymore and David knew they were in trouble. At least they hadn't taken off their masks. There was still a chance that they would be freed after this was over and the kidnappers had what they wanted.

"Move," said Nelly Bean from under her black mask. She had a long stick she was using to push them along, like cattle. Fortunately it was just a stick, not a cattle prod or a Taser. Small mercies.

Fields, the tall kidnapper, told David's father to shut up several times when his dad tried to make small talk during the walk to the boat.

David wondered if either of the kidnappers had a weapon other than the stick.

The kidnappers wore headlamps but they kept looking around, which plunged the trail ahead into darkness, so David, Madison, and his father kept stumbling over tree roots and depressions they couldn't see.

When they broke out of the trees, they were on a beach that was clearly illuminated by bright moonlight. He could see the dark shape of land masses in the distance. There were a few lights visible across from them. Was that Side Island? If so, it was close. Directly across the channel. Shouting distance, practically. Could they make a break for it? Swim across? Probably not. There were likely to be currents. Even a strong swimmer would probably be swept away in the dark water.

"Get in," said Nelly Bean in her high, raspy voice.

Was it worth trying to talk to her? Let her know that he knew who she was? Try to connect with her as a friend? Because they *had* been friends before she decided she wanted what she thought he had. No. He would keep up the pretense that he didn't know who the kidnappers were. He would let them think they could get away.

CONTEMPLATION OF A CRIME

"Ah, I see you have a Zodiac," said his father. "I hear great things about these boats."

"Just get in," said the taller kidnapper. To David's dismay, she took off her respirator mask. It was Fields. And she was done hiding.

Nelly seemed to recoil when Fields took off the mask. She probably knew what that meant as well as he did.

For a while, the five of them stood in the moonlight while a new silent reckoning took place. It ended when Madison, who'd been silent and uncomplaining during the forced march between David and Mr. Levine, suddenly wriggled her body like someone trying to get into or out of too-tight pants. Only in this case, she was getting free of loose chains that she still wore.

In an instant, the chains fell around her feet and she started to sprint. Not back into the dark forest, as David would have predicted, but instead she went straight for Nelly Bean.

Madison, the least opinionated, least confrontational, most checked-out guest at Close Encounters, rushed the kidnapper and knocked her to the ground, where the two women grappled.

"Get off her!" yelled Fields, who fell on the wrestling pair. Fields managed to pull Madison off. Madison crouched on her hands and knees in the dark, panting.

David and his father exchanged glances, then headed into the fray, as ill-prepared for combat as any two men had ever been. It all happened so fast that David had no time to consider his complete and utter lack of experience in such matters.

But the combatants stopped short when, one by one, they saw that Fields had a gun and she was pointing it from person to person.

Nelly, dazed and still sitting on the ground, shook her head at the sight of the weapon. "Where did you *get* that? What are you *doing*?"

Fields, who was still on her knees, waved it at her fiancée, then at the two men.

"Never mind. You guys," she said, looking at David and his father. "Go to the boat."

She looked at Madison, who was still on the ground. "You too."

But Madison didn't get in. She rolled over twice, like she was auditioning for a remake of *The Matrix*, got to her feet, and took off running, zigzagging her way into the woods and somehow not crashing down when she ran into an obstacle.

271

Fields raised the pistol to shoot, but Nelly kicked out at her leg and the shot went wild.

"We don't shoot people," yelled Nelly. "We *do not* do that."

Fields's face was a furious mask. "I do," she said and turned the gun on her fiancée and shot her.

"Oh my god," said David, shock making his legs sag. His father grabbed his hand to steady him.

Blood, black as tar sands oil in the moonlight, spread across Nelly's torso. David couldn't look away. But Fields didn't hesitate. She turned to them. "I said get in the boat."

She stood and followed them as they waded into ankle-deep water and David's father got into the Zodiac.

"Not you," said Fields to David.

HELEN THORPE

The canvas tent looked like a small cabin. It had four vertical walls and a peaked roof set atop of a concrete pad. Light from inside leaked out underneath where the sides didn't quite meet the ground.

Helen found herself reciting lines from the metta chant under her breath as she drew closer.

Step.

May all beings in this world be well and happy always.

Step.

May all beings in the infinite universe be well and happy always.

Step.

May all thieves, robbers and liars be well and happy always.

She had reached the entrance and could feel the others behind her.

"Hello," she said. Her voice was quiet because she didn't want to startle the kidnappers. If she did, they might do something even less wise than kidnapping three people.

"Hello? It's Helen," she said. Then she felt foolish, but no one in the procession behind her laughed.

She looked at the dark canvas in front of her, barely illuminated in the clearing. It didn't make sense to try and knock on the soft walls.

"I'm coming in," she said.

She pushed through the canvas doors.

The tent was empty.

There were two old-fashioned lawn chairs with aluminum frames at the end of the structure and a pile of lightweight chains near them. Two blankets were crumpled beside the chains. A battery-powered lantern set on the floor at the back of the tent barely illuminated the bleak space. There was food in packages. Bottles of water. Two buckets with plastic lids.

No obvious signs of violence.

Gavin stood on one side of her and Murray on the other side. Murray put a hand on Helen's shoulder. "They're probably not far," said Murray.

"Let's go," said Gavin to the others, who had made their way inside around the doorway.

They all turned their headlamps back on as they stood outside the empty tent.

"Where did they go?" asked Tom.

Helen had no idea.

"I've walked around the tent. There's a trail leading away from here," said Bobbi-Lyn. "Not the one we took to get here."

"It's worth a try," said Helen.

She hoped they hadn't missed David and Mr. Levine and Madison.

The searchers walked partway around the tent, Helen in the lead this time. They were heading into the dark woods when they heard footsteps running toward them on the trail.

"Lights off!" said Helen in a loud whisper.

Someone else said, "Shhhh," and the headlamps all blinked out at once.

The group huddled just off the trail at the edge of the clearing, waiting to see who would emerge.

A person burst out of the trail and headed straight for the tent.

Murray put a hand to Helen's arm, but removed it when Helen stepped forward.

"Hello," said Helen. "Who's there?"

The black silhouette stopped abruptly and pivoted.

"Helen?"

It was Madison.

Relief flooded Helen's body, but it was short-lived as Madison walked toward her, arms spread as though she was trying to keep her balance.

"They've got David and his father. They have a gun. And I think they're going to use it. I mean, they already have. One of them shot at . . . They have a boat. You have to stop them."

At that, the whole group moved toward Madison and brought her back to them.

FIELDS ENTWISTLE

Fields was sorry about Nelly. She was even more sorry that one of the hostages had gotten away. But there was no going back now.

Would she get in more trouble for the kidnapping or for the murder? Maybe it would be attempted murder? Or manslaughter? She'd shot Nelly in the heat of the moment. Nothing premeditated about it, which meant she was barely even responsible.

Fields held the idling boat's steering stick with one hand. The gun was in her other hand. She watched Benedict Levine working on the tablet. He was, he said, buying bitcoin. Setting up a wallet and preparing to transfer the funds over to her. A thrill of rage ran through her at the thought that they could have done this when they first took Levine and his son if Nelly hadn't been so hung up on her identity as an anti-crypto activist. She hoped the transfer wouldn't set off alarms at his bank, but at this point it didn't really matter. She was already a fugitive.

When Fields had returned to *A Slice of the Pie* after the botched kidnapping, Nelly had been in a state. She wouldn't stop asking questions. Did you hurt anyone? Can we just let them go? It's not too late.

Fields thought her fiancée was going to have a stroke when she found out that Fields had accidentally kidnapped a guest, instead of the butler.

"What have you done?" Nelly asked, over and over.

That last one really burned Fields. *What have you done?* The nerve.

Nelly hadn't wanted Fields to take the butler. She'd wanted to set David and his father free. Call the whole thing off.

Fields knew then that if they were caught, Nelly would blame the whole thing on her. They'd be broke and in prison.

No thanks. Fields couldn't remember why she'd ever liked her fiancée. She was not made of tough stuff.

There was a splash beside the boat, like she'd caught a huge tuna or maybe a halibut.

That was amusing and she very nearly smiled.

"It's okay, son," said Benedict Levine, who had finally lost his confident nonchalance about the situation. He'd lost his cool almost as soon as Fields got him in the boat, tied him up, and then started the boat, towing his son, still in the water, into the channel behind them.

"You're going to drown him," Levine had cried. But the son, David, never said a word. She could see him surface sometimes, clutching the chain that bound him to his father, who looked for a minute like he was going to jump out of the Zodiac to join him.

"If you don't get that bitcoin to me soon, I'll speed the boat up and he'll be dead for sure," said Fields. "Once I have my money, I'll bring you both back to shore and this will all be over."

It wouldn't. She would shoot Mr. Levine and let him and his son drown together in the dark water under the false hope of the full moon. She liked that she was having poetic thoughts in such moments.

Her plan after that was fuzzy. She would probably drive the Zodiac back to *A Slice of the Pie*. Take the bigger boat to Washington? Or Mexico? Fields wasn't sure but she'd figure it out. She was very good at figuring things out. Not that she ever got any credit for that.

"David, keep your hands on the line," said Mr. Levine, trying to sound calm as he typed into his tablet. "Don't let go. I'm so sorry, son. I should have . . ."

David didn't answer. The guy was fit, which Fields admired, but skinny. She thought he probably wouldn't last long in these waters. She bet after a few more minutes, he'd have hypothermia and then he'd have to let go. Maybe if she sped up the boat, the drag of his body would yank his dad out of the boat and she wouldn't have to shoot him.

There was a lot of noise and lights in the Nanaimo harbour. She could just barely see it from their position in the channel. Maybe someone was having a party on one of the boats. That would get shut down soon enough. People in the expensive condos on the Nanaimo waterfront wouldn't put up with it.

"Okay," said Levine. "You should have it."

Fields lifted her phone up so she could see the screen more clearly. She punched in the numbers. Waited, heart thudding in anticipation.

And there it was. 288.17 BTC.

CONTEMPLATION OF A CRIME

Pleasure flooded her body.

Ten million dollars. And if she wasn't mistaken, those would be American dollars. She was rich. Not rich like the man in front of her. But rich enough for now.

She took a deep breath and stowed her phone away in the chest pocket of her vest.

Time to get rid of these people. Then she would put in somewhere unobtrusive until things died down in the harbour so she could get back to *A Slice of the Pie.*

"Please let my son up now," said Benedict Levine. His overly satisfied face had gone very pale. He seemed to be hauling on the chain with all his strength, as though he could pull his six-foot-tall son out of the water. He'd tried to do it twice already, and both times she'd threatened to shoot him.

She looked at Levine and felt nothing. And she didn't even bother looking at the man in the water. Time to turn up the throttle. The Zodiac could really move when she let it out.

Before she could speed them up, the Zodiac lurched sideways, slammed by something that seemed to have come out of nowhere. In the split second when she was falling out of her seat and into the bottom of the boat, she had time to wonder if they'd been hit by an orca. Weren't they going after yachts now?

A buzzing sound grew louder, which distracted her. What the hell was that noise?

Before she could get up from the bottom of the Zodiac, something landed on her and something tore into her arm and she screamed.

BIG D WAINSCOTT III

Big D, or just D, had never seen anything like it. Yes, paddling the dragon boat had sucked because nobody knew what they were doing, especially at first. But when they ran back along the trail to get the boat and started paddling around Guide Island to intercept the kidnappers, well, that had been dope as hell. No one said anything. They just drove those paddles up and down like pistons. He even tried to do his part in spite of his severe aversion to physical effort.

When they came around the bend, they could see the Zodiac. It was right in the path of the moon's brightest rays. (Did the moon have rays? Or reflection?) Anyway, they could all see the boat clearly, and the person in the water beside the boat.

Big D had seen enough adventure movies to know it was a "boat driver with a gun" scenario.

The crazy thing? He wasn't even scared for himself. Normally, he'd avoid paddling straight into an armed nutjob, but it was a different era now. The Big D era!

The person in the Zodiac didn't hear them, maybe because she was revving the engine on the Zodiac. They paddled faster. Faster.

When the dragon boat slammed into the side of the Zodiac, a little yellow boat buzzed up to them and around the other side. Wayne jumped out of the bathroom boat or whatever it was called and into the water. Gavin and Murray and Yana jumped into the Zodiac, but Potato got there first and latched onto the woman with the gun like a lamprey.

Big D didn't join the fray. Not his style, even with his new name. But he watched. He and Tom held the dragon boat close to the Zodiac. They saw Helen in the Zodiac, helping her boss, the rich guy.

"Helen, Helen, where's my David?" the guy kept repeating while he pulled on something.

CONTEMPLATION OF A CRIME

A chain. Holy Christ. The guy in the boat was chained up to . . .

He was chained to his son, who was still in the water.

It was enough to make Big D also want to bite the woman who was responsible. That was some awful shit.

"I'm here, Dad."

And he was. Wet, shaking, but okay enough to be hanging on to the side of the Zodiac, with Wayne beside him, an arm around him to make sure he didn't slip back into the water. Yana, with her older lady super-strength, helped pull David and Wayne up into the Zodiac, which was getting pretty crowded with rescuers and kidnappers and pit bulls.

"Bring the dragon boat around," said someone. Big D wasn't sure who.

But before they could do it, there was a bang and another bang, and oh my god, the gun was going off. While Big D had been distracted, the people in the boat had started struggling over a gun.

"She shot the boat," said someone.

"Anyone injured?" said someone else.

"We're going down!" said someone else.

Somehow the idiot kidnapper had shot her own boat. Twice. Quite the criminal genius.

In the melee, Potato, who was probably in charge of a group of Vikings in a previous life, fastened herself onto the kidnapper's leg, which resulted in more screaming.

For someone who was into kidnapping and shooting and trying to drown other people, the kidnapper sure couldn't take it when the pit bull was on the other foot, so to speak.

The Zodiac started to sink.

"Hold on to each other," called Helen. "Don't let go."

And they did.

As the Zodiac collapsed into the water, the butlers, the spy, the environmental lady, the convoy guy, and the kidnapping victims held on to each other and people swam from the sinking Zodiac toward the dragon boat. Potato held on to the kidnapper, who'd dropped her gun somewhere along the line.

Only Yana and Murray made it into the dragon boat before the Zodiac sunk.

"We need to get them into the boat," said Nigel, who was still sitting in the boat with Big D and Tom.

SUSAN JUBY

"They're not going to be able to get in without us tipping over," said Tom.

"Shore," said Big D. "Tow them to shore. We're close."

"Hang on, everyone," said Nigel. "We'll get you out in a minute. Don't let go."

So Big D, Nigel, and Tom, world's worst paddlers, towed the rest of them the short distance to the shore of Guide Island. They were followed by Potato, who finally let go of the kidnapper. In spite of her injuries, the woman swam along behind them. She tried to run away when she got to the beach. Gavin caught her in that smooth-operator way of his and subdued her before she made it to the treeline. Gavin was assisted by Potato, who was not a fan of kidnappers and seemed ready to take another chomp out of her.

From there, everything got very butler-y, which is the term Big D had started to use when super-efficient people jumped into action.

Someone got blankets from the tent for everyone who was feeling hypothermic, which was everyone. Big D also felt a bit shivery from excitement but he didn't ask for a blanket, which he thought was noble. Only his feet were wet, but still. It had been quite a stressful experience.

Of the people who'd been in the water, David was the best off, probably because he did that cold dipping thing all the time and was used to spending time in water no normal person would want to be in.

Madison and Nigel rubbed people's feet and hands. Wayne helped to guard the prisoner. Murray checked on the lady kidnapper who'd been shot. She was alive, but not speaking, presumably because of how she'd been shot and it probably hurt like a bastard.

Bobbi-Lyn, the spy, called the cops, who came pretty fast because they were already in the harbour because they thought Yana had given herself a Viking funeral out there.

All in all, it was one of the best evenings of Big D's life.

EPILOGUE
NEAR AND FAR ENEMIES

HELEN THORPE

Helen was pleased when everyone wanted to go back to Side Island to finish the course after they'd been extensively interviewed by the police. Even Bobbi-Lyn went back in her capacity as chef.

The group debrief took place the day they arrived back on the island. Mr. Levine had hired a large pleasure cruiser to take them to Side Island from Nanaimo, where they'd been staying at the Dorchester Hotel. They couldn't get to shore from the cruiser because the dock was still out for repair, but the boat had crew to row them over, two at a time. It was very comfortable. Very dry.

What wasn't comfortable was Mr. Levine's guilt. He and Helen had walked back to the lodge together behind the rest of the group.

"I don't think I'm going to get over this," he said.

She didn't answer.

"David nearly died because I refused to pay. I treated it like a game."

Helen would not argue with anyone, much less her beloved employer.

"Do you think they would have let you and David go if you had paid right away?" she asked.

He sighed and put his hands in the pockets of his floor-length parka. The chill of the water seemed to have settled into his bones and he'd privately told her he wondered if he'd ever get warm again.

"I think maybe," he said. "I could see that in them. At least, I thought I could. They weren't killers. At least, not at first."

"But you couldn't hear their voices or see their faces," said Helen.

"That's true. But at a certain point, the tall one—the one who used Clint Eastwood's voice? Fields, was it? Most unpleasant. Something in her shifted. I pushed her too far."

"I don't think you are responsible," said Helen. "It was not your idea for them to kidnap you and set everything else into action."

"David says he forgives me," said Mr. Levine. They'd reached Poolside

283

Cottage and they stopped. "I'm not sure he should. I should have been more careful. Life is not a game. Sometimes, Helen, it seems that way. Because of how we live. We are too insulated from the harder parts of life."

"I have reached out to Jasper Rushesky. He comes highly recommended as the best trauma therapist in the country. You and David have appointments with him when you return to Vancouver. Should you decide you want them."

"I hate this feeling," said Mr. Levine. "The guilt is so unpleasant. The realization that I made a mistake."

Helen didn't touch her boss. To do so would be highly inappropriate, but she closed her eyes for a fraction of a second and sent him all the metta her heart could conjure. It was a lot of metta.

Mr. Levine seemed to sense it. Take it in.

"Let's go in. I have some things to tell the group," he said.

DAVID LEWISTON

D avid had left something behind in the water. He had left something else behind in the tent.

Fear of the future. Anxiety about the past.

He had been kidnapped and nearly died from being dragged behind a boat. But he hadn't died. He'd kept his head above water. His finely tuned athlete's body had helped him survive. He was, he realized, incredibly strong.

And all of it was luck. Circumstance. What his parents might call karma.

The only things he could control were his actions and the intentions behind those actions. That was enough.

David Lewiston was fine.

Not even his father's apology could shake that sense.

The guests were gathered in a circle in the lodge. The fire crackled in the enormous fireplace. Everyone had a mug of something warm in their hands. It was extremely pleasant, especially compared to being dead.

"I am Praxis," his father said.

No one reacted except for Helen, who looked quickly at David and then went back to listening impassively, waiting for opportunities to help.

"Praxis is one of the charities our foundation supports. It operates a number of innovative social enterprise programs. We made an offer to take over Close Encounters for Global Healing and expand it."

David tried to understand what that meant. "You bought the program?"

"In a sense, yes," said his father. "You loved it so much, and your mother and I could see how much good it did for you. We wanted to support it. Anonymously."

"What about Nelly?" asked David. "She founded the program. She seemed to think she was going to be left behind when Praxis took over. She told me that Close Encounters never made any real money. It operates using grants."

"Ah, well," said his father. "We don't usually discuss terms until we've finished our investigations. Then, if we think the right personnel are in place, we offer them a fair compensation package and outline their expanded or, in some cases, reduced roles. Or no roles."

"What was your plan for Nelly?" asked David. He didn't know who to feel worse for. His father or Nelly or everyone who'd just gone through the ordeal caused by corporate secrecy. He knew that Nelly wouldn't have done what she did if she hadn't thought she was going to get cut out of her organization and left with a pittance or given a small role.

"My people liked what they saw with her. The report I read on her leadership suggested she would need some training and probably the help of a COO or a CFO to help with the business aspects of expanding the program. But when this course was over, depending on your report, we were prepared to offer her a very handsome compensation package."

"Define *handsome*," said Wayne.

"Three hundred thousand dollars a year to start."

Tom whistled.

"Don't people hate it when so much of a charity's profits go to management?" asked Yana. David knew that what she meant was that *she* hated it when she heard about huge payments to people who run charities.

"The funds don't come from the charity, which is fully funded by a trust we have set up. We have enough money to reward people who do good works in the charity sector. We also planned to give her a signing bonus of five hundred thousand dollars for the brand and goodwill and to compensate her for what she'd done already."

Another low whistle from Tom.

"So you're saying that she was going to be financially set if she and her fiancée had just not kidnapped you?"

"Yes," said David's father.

Everyone took that in for a moment. They were all glad that they weren't Nelly Bean, who was recovering from a gunshot wound. She'd already been charged with kidnapping and attempted murder.

David felt sorry for her. But also didn't.

"I guess the lesson is to not kidnap anyone before the miracle happens?" said Big D.

"Something like that," said David's father.

Wayne softly punched him in the shoulder. He was sitting next to Madison.

CONTEMPLATION OF A CRIME

They kept looking at each other. David thought there might be something going on there, and he was pleased for them both.

They spent an hour talking about what they'd gone through together. Then they ate a hearty lunch of Spanish tortilla pie, lemony red lentil soup, and roasted cauliflower salad. When that was done, they talked for another hour. Had naps. Then David began to deliver the rest of the course to the most cohesive group of people who'd ever come through Close Encounters.

That night, when David and his father were sitting alone together in his father's cabin, his father asked if he wanted to take over Close Encounters. David didn't hesitate. "Yes," he said. "I would."

HELEN THORPE

The butlers all wore cowboy hats on the trip to Comox. Helen's was white, Murray's was pink. Nigel and Gavin wore black hats.

Helen drove the new Tundra with the Paddock Stables logo on the sides. They were pulling Helen's horse, Honey, in the brand-new four-horse trailer. Mr. Levine had insisted on paying for everyone's entire holiday and, to Helen's chagrin, had given her a "bravery and holiday loss bonus" of two hundred thousand dollars. When Dr. Levine got home from her retreat in Montenegro and found out what had transpired, she had him add another hundred thousand dollars. Now Helen had even more money that she needed to figure out how to spend wisely.

The butlers ate small, thoughtful snacks and drank from travel cups as they drove. They sang cowboy songs.

And they talked about what was next.

"I'm meeting Cartier in Ibiza," said Nigel.

"As a butler?" asked Murray.

"I don't know," he said.

"Do not tell anyone at the Butler Academy that you're involved with your client or they'll rescind your degree," said Murray.

"Did you hear that Mr. Levine hired Big D to do security analysis for his companies?" Helen asked.

"Perfect," said Murray. "Just so long as he's not in charge of HR or team building."

"And Wayne and Madison are together," said Nigel. "I saw him give her a flag for her car."

"Lucky girl," said Murray. They all laughed.

"I think they're going to be just fine."

"Tom says he's thinking about going to school to take broadcasting. He's also talking about making a podcast about his time in the Compound. A heartwarming story about escaping white nationalism," said Nigel.

CONTEMPLATION OF A CRIME

"I'd listen to that," said Gavin.

"And Yana is working for the foundation assessing environmental impacts of their initiatives."

"She should also work on getting a Guinness World Record. Strongest woman in her age category. That kind of thing."

Helen felt the deep satisfaction that each of the participants had come out of the trauma of their close encounter better off than they'd gone into it. It was a good thing.

"And you two? Now that you're done at Yatra?" Helen asked Gavin and Murray.

Gavin spoke up from the back seat. "We've decided we want to do a bit more training and move into the security space."

"We're going to take police training," said Murray.

"Combat classes," added Gavin. "So I have something to add to my devastating table tennis skills."

"We'll combine our butlering with personal protection skills."

Nigel turned to look at them in the back seat.

"You know what that means, right?"

"What?" asked Murray.

Helen could see the smiles on the faces of her friends in the rear-view mirror.

"You're going to be calling Helen every month to help you solve some crime. I mean, she's just a regular butler and look at how many crimes she's had to deal with. I think you guys are asking for trouble."

"I am retired from being involved in crimes," said Helen. "From now on, I'm strictly focused on taking care of my clients, being present for life, and learning to ride my horse."

Nigel laughed. "Number one horse mom!" he said.

The truck had the wide highway almost to itself, and Helen hoped Honey was comfortable in the trailer, which was the horse trailer equivalent of a suite at the Ritz. Blue mountains rose to their left, and somewhere on the right was the ocean. So far the weather hadn't turned on them. Orange and yellow leaves hung stubbornly on to the trees. They were on the edge of winter and it was glorious.

Nigel leaned over and turned on a country song and they all started to sing.

ACKNOWLEDGEMENTS

I am grateful to all the usual suspects, especially Hilary McMahon at Westwood Creative Artists and my editor, Iris Tupholme, and the rest of the team at HarperCollins Canada, including Canaan Chu, Catherine Dorton, Shayla Leung, Lisa Rundle, Allison Hargraves, Alison Thompson, and everyone else who helped to bring this book into the world.

My test readers once again came through in top form: Susin Nielsen, Andrew Gray, and Bill Juby. I appreciate you all. Particular shout-out to Ken Swain, who gave me advice about navigating the waters around Saysutshun and Protection Island and the Nanaimo Harbour.

As I've noted in the previous books, the character of Helen was inspired by the teachings and example of many spiritual teachers and mentors. I continue to learn about the dhamma from Mia Tremblay, who leads our Nanaimo sangha; my original teachers, Jesse Maceo Vega-Fry and Michele McDonald from Vipassana Hawaii; as well as Tempel Smith, Adrianne Ross, Kristina Baré, and many others. Deepest thanks also to Sandra Thompson, who is still my first best example of living her spiritual principles.

I wrote a bit of this book at Yellow Point Lodge and some elements of the lodge and its stunning landscape have made their way onto the entirely fictional Side Island described in these pages. Guide Island is also made up. What can I say? Fiction writers lie! What's entirely true is that Richard Hill and the Hill family have created in Yellow Point Lodge a refuge for people and nature. Generations of people return every year and find sanctuary there. YPL is one of most beloved places on Vancouver Island for good reason and I appreciate every moment I get to spend there.

As always, thanks to my family: my brothers and mother and my husband, James, and our rapscallion dogs, Ralph and Ranger, who, in their dedication to snacks, naps, and playtime, show us how to live.

I will close this by noting that we live in troubled times. The social contract

ACKNOWLEDGEMENTS

is fraying and sometimes it feels like our political divides are growing too wide to cross. Concern about that feeling is what inspired this book. If Helen and the crew at Side Island can find a way forward, perhaps the rest of us can too.

With metta to all.

Susan